PRAISE FOR CRAIG R P9-CEZ-564

'I can't recommend this book highly enough'
MARTINA COLE

'Robertson's work is marked by crisp prose, smart storylines and an **INVENTIVENESS** most authors would envy' **EVA DOLAN**

'Fantastic characterisation, great plotting, page-turning and **GRIPPING**. The best kind of **INTELLIGENT** and moving crime fiction writing'
LUCA VESTE

'Really enjoyed *Murderabilia* – disturbing, inventive, and powerfully and **STYLISHLY WRITTEN**. Recommended' **STEVE MOSBY**

'The writing is stellar, the characters **VIVID AND MEMORABLE** and the plot strong and **FULL OF SURPRISES**. *The Last Refuge* should certainly enhance Craig Robertson's reputation as one of Scotland's leading crime writers'
RAGNAR JÓNASSON

'**MASTERFUL!** Craig Robertson certainly knows how to hook a reader'
KATI HIEKKEPELTO

'It's a **GREAT** murder mystery'
JAMES OSWALD

'**A TENSE TORCH-LIT TREK** through a hidden city you never knew existed'
CHRISTOPHER BROOKMYRE

'Doing for Glasgow, what Rankin did for Edinburgh'
MIRROR

'A revenge **THRILLER** with a twist' *SUN*

'**CRACKING DIALOGUE**, a captivating plot and that wonderful sense of place'
THE AUSTRALIAN

During his 20-year career in Glasgow with a Scottish Sunday newspaper, Craig Robertson interviewed three recent Prime Ministers, and attended major stories including 9/11, Dunblane, the Omagh bombing and the disappearance of Madeleine McCann. He was pilloried on breakfast television, beat Oprah Winfrey to a major scoop, spent time on Death Row in the USA and dispensed polio drops in the backstreets of India. His debut novel, *Random*, was shortlisted for the CWA New Blood Dagger and was a *Sunday Times* bestseller.

Also by Craig Robertson:

Murderabilia
In Place of Death
The Last Refuge
Witness the Dead
Cold Grave
Snapshot
Random

THE PHOTOGRAPHER
CRAIG ROBERTSON

**SIMON &
SCHUSTER**

London · New York · Sydney · Toronto · New Delhi

A CBS COMPANY

First published in Great Britain by Simon & Schuster UK Ltd, 2018
A CBS COMPANY

Copyright © Craig Robertson, 2018

This book is copyright under the Berne Convention.
No reproduction without permission.
® and © 1997 Simon & Schuster, Inc. All rights reserved.

The right of Craig Robertson to be identified as author of this work
has been asserted in accordance with sections 77 and 78
of the Copyright, Designs and Patents Act, 1988.

1 3 5 7 9 10 8 6 4 2

Simon & Schuster UK Ltd
1st Floor
222 Gray's Inn Road
London WC1X 8HB

www.simonandschuster.co.uk

Simon & Schuster Australia, Sydney
Simon & Schuster India, New Delhi

A CIP catalogue record for this book
is available from the British Library

Paperback ISBN: 978-1-4711-6532-0
eBook ISBN: 978-1-4711-6534-4
Audio ISBN: 978-1-4711-7088-1

This book is a work of fiction. Names, characters, places
and incidents are either a product of the author's imagination or
are used fictitiously. Any resemblance to actual people living
or dead, events or locales is entirely coincidental.

Typeset in Sabon by M Rules
Printed and bound by CPI Group (UK) Ltd, Croydon, CR0 4YY

Simon & Schuster UK Ltd are committed to sourcing paper
that is made from wood grown in sustainable forests and support the Forest
Stewardship Council, the leading international forest certification organisation.
Our books displaying the FSC logo are printed on FSC certified paper.

To Ellis, Khloe, Leo and Riley

PROLOGUE

Lainey Henderson drew down hard on her cigarette with one eye on the clock, her free hand working continually to waft the smoke out of the window. Less than thirty seconds to go, her cheeks sucking the life out of the death stick.

The nerves were to blame but she thought of them as a good thing. What kind of person would she be if she wasn't nervous on behalf of the woman who was about to walk through that door? The woman expecting Lainey to make everything all right when nothing could possibly do that.

It was an ISS, an Initial Support Session. They were the worst and the best.

The worst because you got it all in the raw. The open wound of a victim talking, often for the first time, about their worst nightmare. They might be calm or hysterical, might talk or might not, might lash out at you because there was no one else there or they might

1

cling on for dear life. They might just break down and cry in a way that ripped at your emotions and left you feeling worthless. That happened a lot. An ISS could break your heart.

But it could be the best too, because if you managed to take away even an inch of their pain then it would all be worth it.

The knock at the door was quiet, almost apologetic.

'Just a minute.' Lainey encouraged the final swirls of smoke out the window and pinged the butt out after it. She leaned far enough out that she could see a couple of dozen pieces of evidence of previous guilt and swore under her breath, making a mental note to clear them up before she got fired. The cigarette packet went in her pocket – she liked to have it at hand even when she couldn't smoke. 'Come in.'

The door slid open barely enough to let the girl slip through the gap. Lainey knew she was supposed to say, and think, *woman* rather than *girl*, but the ghost of a teenager who was gliding over the carpet made Lainey want to sweep her up in her arms and mother her. But she wouldn't. Or she'd try not to.

An ISS had rules. The idea was to make the client feel welcome, to assess them and find out what they wanted from the service. The case worker wasn't to ask a lot of questions or offer advice. Lainey had never been one for rules though.

The girl was a shade over five feet tall, dressed in baggy black from top to toe, pale as the moon with dark auburn hair that had been brushed with her eyes closed. She glanced nervously round the room, looking for the monsters that Lainey had seen others search for.

'Jennifer? I'm Lainey. Do you want to take a seat? Coffee, tea, water?'

'No. No thanks. Well yes, water would be good. Thank you.'

Lainey poured her a glass from the bottle, taking the chance to gently touch the back of the girl's hand as she passed it to her. Jennifer flinched, but only slightly. It was a good sign.

Their chairs were just a few feet apart, facing each other. Lainey would rather have moved them till they were touching but she knew better or, more accurately, had been told better. She sat back and gave Jennifer the chance to speak first but soon realised it would be a long wait. The girl studied the walls even though there was precious little to see, just a couple of cheap, bland prints and a shelf studded with leaflets. When she finally returned her gaze to Lainey, Jennifer's eyes were wet with pleading. *Please talk. Ask me something. Say something.* So she did.

'The first time I came here, I had no idea what to expect. No idea what to say. Or even what to think. I might have sat here all day with my mouth shut and a million ideas running riot in my head if someone hadn't finally saved me from it. She told me that it was always scarier in your head than it was when said out loud. It's tempting to think if we don't say it then it's not real, it didn't really happen. That doesn't work though. If we leave them inside, they just get bigger and bigger. Let them out and they get small.'

Jennifer bobbed her head, although still not entirely convinced. 'Have you ... Do you know what I'm going through?' There was a second question in there, unasked but unmissable.

'I do. Maybe not exactly because cases are different. But yes, I know.'

A little noise escaped from the girl. Relief of sorts. She swallowed and nodded and readied herself.

'I was raped. A man broke into my flat and raped me.'

Lainey just nodded to let her know she'd heard and understood. The words were unnecessary but important for Jennifer to say. The evidence of it was all over her, it was why they were here. The stomach-churning damage to her face was proof, too, that the rape had been accompanied with a fearful beating.

'Was it someone you knew?'

'No. I don't think so. He wore a mask. A balaclava.'

Anger twisted in Lainey's gut, something more too, and she had to wear a mask of her own to hide it. It wasn't going to do either of them any good if she had a meltdown. Her cigarette packet found its way into her hand and she began tapping on the top of it the way she always did when she was in desperate need of a fag.

'We're here to help in any way we can, Jennifer. Whatever you want from us.' The words sounded trite, meaningless, and they were. She wanted to be able to say she'd hunt the bastard down and cut his balls off with rusty shears.

'He kept calling me a slag. Like he knew me and it was my fault. He called me a slag every time he punched me in the face.'

Lainey felt like she'd been punched too. Sudden and hard. She looked at Jennifer, unable to say anything. Transfixed by her words and suddenly, though she'd tried not to be, by her face.

'He just kept thumping me. Pounding his fist into my nose and my cheek. Slag. Slag. Slag. Punch. Punch. Punch. I couldn't see. Just heard the noise. Heard my nose breaking. My cheek being smashed.'

Lainey's heart had stopped, her throat closed over.

'He had me pinned down. His knees on my chest and arms. I tried to fight but I couldn't move. He hit me till I passed out. Then he ... he ...'

Lainey managed to nod to save Jennifer from saying the rest. There was no need. She knew.

The girl's nose was almost at forty-five degrees to her pretty face, like a rugby player's or a boxer's. Both eyes were blackened and one was barely open at all. Her ashen skin was a canvas for violent patches of purple and red. Her lips were twice the size they should be.

Lainey had to resist the temptation to put her hand to her own face, mimic the places, feel where her own wounds used to be. There was a burning she wanted to cool with her touch.

Jennifer talked on, about waking to find herself naked, a searing pain between her legs, the bed sheets bloodied, her flat empty again. She saw herself in the mirror and screamed at the sight. She called a friend who called an ambulance.

Lainey knew the rules and the reasons for them. Jennifer had been raped, any semblance of control wrenched from her. It was Lainey's role to empower her as a survivor, not to reinforce the trauma by offering unwanted touching. If she sensed that the touch, the consoling hug that burst to be released from within her, was wanted then she had to ask permission to do so. Rapists never asked permission so counsellors had to.

Her gut told her Jennifer wanted and needed it. She could see it in the girl's eyes. Lainey teetered on the edge of asking and hugging and holding. And couldn't do it.

The words came out of her mouth by rote.

'What happens now is I need to ask if you want to proceed, then we put you on the waiting list and when you get to the top, your new worker will give you a call to arrange your first session.'

'New worker? It won't be you?'

'It might be me,' Lainey blurted out. 'But not necessarily.' It wouldn't be her.

'Oh. Okay.'

They said goodbye and Jennifer slipped out the door as quietly as she'd come in. Lainey waited as long as she dared to make sure the girl had gone then rushed to the corner of the desk, picked up the waste-paper basket and vomited into it.

*

It wasn't that the police sergeant wasn't sympathetic. It was more that he couldn't rather than wouldn't do anything. He would if he could, he reassured her. He had a daughter of his own. She nearly called him on that, being bothered about rape because he had a daughter, but she let it go. The sergeant, McCluskey, called in a female detective, a tired-looking blonde woman named Parks, and they dutifully listened to everything Lainey told them.

'And you're sure, Ms Henderson,' Parks repeated, 'it was the same man that raped you?'

'As sure as I can be. Without either of us seeing his face, I can't be certain, but I know. I *know*. He called me a slag every time he hit me in the face. And he did that a lot. Pinned me down and punched me into unconsciousness then raped me. He broke in while I was sleeping, beat me, raped me and then left while I was still out. The same with the girl.'

'The girl whose name you can't tell us.' It sounded like an accusation.

'I'm not making this shit up! I told you why I can't give her name. Client confidentiality. But it was the same guy. No doubt about it. The same guy.'

'I appreciate that, Lainey.' Parks was trying to be all sisters-under-the-skin. 'But if we don't know who she is, we don't have a case to work. And you told us she didn't go to the police.'

'She didn't. I wish she had but she didn't. That had to be her choice. Look, the man that attacked and raped me is still out there. Still doing this. Surely you see that?'

McCluskey shrugged resignedly but Parks nodded. 'I believe you, Ms Henderson, but I'd be lying if I said we're likely to be able to do much about it. I'm sorry. Your case is obviously still open and I'll add—'

'My case is four years old. *Four!*' She was shouting now. 'And in that time, you've managed to do nothing, find nothing. He's been out there all that time and he still is. Who else has he done this to?'

She left the police station in search of hard alcohol and cigarettes. Drowned her sorrows in vodka and nicotine before ordering a cab, demanding the firm send a woman driver. That added an extra forty-five minutes to her wait and she filled it with shots of Jägermeister until the barman refused to serve her any more. She flicked him the Vs and stormed outside to wait.

When she got home, the taxi driver helping her inside, she double locked all doors, set the alarm and went to bed, where she cried herself to sleep.

Lainey kept a close eye on the waiting list, urging Jennifer to the top and cutting a couple of corners to get her there quicker. It still took an age and every day that passed made Lainey's broken nose throb and cheeks ache, made her that bit more anxious and angry. When the name finally got to the front of the queue, Lainey said she'd call Jennifer herself. There was no answer.

When she didn't get any response on the second attempt, she left a message. When there was no reply to that or the third call, she texted. On the fourth call, the line was dead.

Lainey went out to the address they had, a block of flats on Paisley Road West, but the people there had never heard of a Jennifer Buchanan. *Maybe in one of the other flats?* No.

She searched the phone book, went to the library and pored over electoral rolls. Nothing. She even hired a private investigator. He came back after two weeks and gave her her money back. Jennifer Buchanan, the girl who'd suffered the exact same rape and beating that Lainey had, wasn't missing. She'd never existed.

CHAPTER 1

Detective Inspector Rachel Narey looked at the clock for the fifth time that hour and saw that the hands had barely budged. It was a little before 2.30 in the morning and Stewart Street station was quiet enough that she could hear the rattle of rain on the window on the far end of the squad room. The only other person present, a new DC named Tom O'Halloran, had his head stuck in paperwork.

Two and a half miles away across Glasgow, on Belhaven Terrace, her husband and daughter were asleep. She wanted to be with them. Or at least, they were supposed to be asleep. If the baby was awake, then Tony would be too. She was strongly tempted to text to find out but managed to resist. He was due to start at the *Standard* at eight and wasn't going to thank her if he got any less sleep than he needed to.

Their new life was only nine months old but already she could barely remember what the old one felt like.

CRAIG ROBERTSON

Alanna had changed everything. Sleep patterns. Work patterns. What and when they ate, what they talked about, what she felt and what scared her. Life had been him and her and them and now it was her.

She got up and walked to the window, watching the rain form neon-dappled puddles in the car park. *Two and a half miles away.* It seemed further in the dark, the gloom putting extra distance between her and the ones she loved. She wouldn't mind so much if she was doing something to make the separation feel worthwhile, but the city was as quiet as the grave. It was Tuesday-night slow, for which she knew she ought to be grateful, but it just left her pacing the room and pining for her child.

Something moved in the car park. A figure splashing across the tarmac towards the front door, hood up against the rain. She didn't get her hopes up for a break in the tedium, knowing that the kind of emergencies that required the services of a DI usually started with a call to 999 rather than a sprint through puddles.

She'd been back on the job for four months, part-time to begin with, reduced hours to suit her and Alanna, fitting in with Tony's hours as a photo-journalist at the newspaper. Now she mixed these horrible graveyard shifts with more humane hours, managing a family life as best they could.

Oh, stuff it. She reached for her phone and sent a single line of text. If he was sleeping, he wouldn't hear it. Hopefully. If he was awake then she'd soon find out.

Seconds later, her phone rang.

'Yes, we're awake. What else would we be

doing at this time of the morning except playing pick-up-throw-down?'

Alanna's favourite game. Up, down, up, down, end-lessly, tirelessly. Tireless for her at least.

'Tell me she's not wide awake.'

'Wide as the Clyde. Want to speak to her?'

'You know I do. I hate being stuck here when you're both there.'

'I know. We hate it too, but you can't be so hard on yourself. I go out to work too, remember, and I feel just as bad. But we do miss you.' His voiced changed. 'We miss momma, don't we? Alanna, do you want to speak to momma? Speak to momma.'

There was silence. She imagined the little blonde head shaking violently from side to side, lip pouting. Not speaking to bad momma.

'Alanna, speak to momma. She misses you.'

Nothing.

'Sorry. She's too busy practising for the 2036 Olympics pick-up-throw-down gold medal.' He was doing his best to take the knife out her heart.

'She's punishing me. Which is fine, because I deserve it. Am I the worst mother in the world?'

'Of course not. You're probably not even in the top ten.'

'Thanks.'

'Rach, you know you just make it worse for yourself by phoning. We've talked about this.'

She hated him for being right. 'I know that. I knew it before I called and I know it right now. I just miss her.

There's too much time to think on these night shifts. I need to be busier.'

'Careful what you wish for,'

'Yeah okay, Confucius. Listen, you better get her down and get some sleep.'

'I'll be fine. Sleep's overrated anyway. And ...' he lowered his voice to a near whisper, 'she's gone. Time for us to go, Detective Inspector. We'll see you in the morning.'

It was only once she'd said her goodbyes that she heard the voices floating up from downstairs, weaving like spirits through the silent building. Someone was shouting, but there was no way Narey could make out what was being said. Chances were the late-night, early morning visitor was drunk or high on something. It was Glasgow, after all.

She considered sending O'Halloran down to see what the fuss was but all that was likely to achieve was putting the desk sergeant's nose out of joint. Gordy Masterson captained his own ship in the midnight hours and didn't need telling how to sail it. She out-ranked him but knew enough to keep on his good side if she wanted the pick of whatever cases came in.

Pickings had been slim since she came back. There was a big ugly blot on her record that no one mentioned but everyone knew about. It was a stain that was taking a lot of scrubbing to remove. A reputation can take years to earn and seconds to wreck. She'd made a fine job of it on both counts, hence having to put up with the unsociable hours.

The squad room door swung open and Masterson poked his head inside.

'DI Narey. One for you.'

'The shouting downstairs?'

He nodded. 'I think you'll want to talk to her.'

She picked up something in Masterson's expression, canned any further questions and followed him downstairs.

'She says her name is Leah Watt and is demanding to speak to a detective. She won't tell me what it's about but she's very agitated. Not drunk, not on drugs, perfectly rational, but very anxious and upset. Only a detective will do, apparently. I'd have chased her if I thought she was a timewaster but I don't think she is.'

Cops like Masterson knew when people were genuine and when they weren't. Desk sergeants were on the front line. It was their job to read people, to take their temperatures and keep the crazies from bothering those too busy to get tangled up with them. If he said she'd want to talk to this woman then he'd be right.

The visitor had been placed in an interview room. Narey opened the door and slipped inside, seeing her on the other side of the desk, head down and pulling at her chestnut brown hair. On hearing the door open, the woman jumped to her feet, eyes wide and slightly manic.

'Are you a detective? I need to speak to a detective.'

'I'm Detective Inspector Rachel Narey. How can I help you? Please, sit down.'

She was still intent on standing, that was obvious,

but Narey took a seat and waited until the woman had little choice but to follow suit.

The woman was perhaps in her mid-thirties, brown eyes, nervous and agitated, as Masterson had said. There was something off about her look. She was pretty but wore too much make up, particularly around her eyes and cheeks, as if she was hiding behind it. Something else too; Narey just couldn't figure what it was.

'It's Leah, is that right?'

'Yes, Leah Watt. I need someone to help me. To listen to me. I've been here before but things have changed. What I mean is, my case is still open but there's ... I mean, I know something I didn't know before. Shit, I'm not making sense. What I ...'

The words tripped over each other in her rush to get them out.

'Slow down Leah, please. Look, let me get us both a tea or coffee. I'm happy to take as long as you need but this will work better if we relax. Okay?'

'Okay, okay. Thanks. Coffee, please. Thanks.'

Narey left the interview room and headed for the front desk.

'Gordy, can you get someone to rustle up two coffees? One black and sugar, one with milk and no sugar. And she's talking about her case, saying it's open. Can you get me the crime report and see what's there?'

Masterson handed over the papers. 'Just done it.'

Narey cast her eyes over the headline points and her heart sank. 'Shit.'

*

They had to wait nearly forty-five minutes until a SOLO could get to the station, a specialist Sexual Offences Liaison Officer whose job was to take the statement and work a victim through the reporting process. Louise Crichton was dark-haired and intense, content to listen as Leah Watt told her story to Narey.

'It was three months ago. I'd been out with friends, had a few drinks then home to my flat in Partick West. I'd watched a bit of TV but I was tired and starting to nod off so I went to bed. I fell asleep pretty much right away. It was the sound of breaking glass that woke me.

'I knew what I'd heard even though I'd been dead to the world. My heart was thumping like crazy and I was scared but a bit of me was also wondering if I'd just dreamed it. Then I heard footsteps inside the flat. I froze.

'I just didn't know what to do. I was terrified. I was thinking that I had an alarm, one of those personal alarms that go in your bag and sound a siren if you're attacked. But my bag was in the other room and so were the footsteps. I still hadn't moved when the door flew open and he was standing there. In the frame of the door, tall and all dressed in black. A balaclava over his head.

'He moved so quickly. Just rushed across the room and punched me in the face. It hurt like hell but it was more the shock. I'd never been punched before. He punched me again and again. I could taste blood, feel my teeth coming loose. My nose made this horrible noise as he hit it and I nearly passed out but he

17

kept hitting me, I don't know how many times, until I blacked out.

'I came round, briefly, a while later, God knows how long. The light was on in the room. He was above me. Naked. He was dripping in sweat. And I saw his face. He didn't see me at first but when he did he swung his fist at me, at my eye. He called me a slag like he was mad at me for waking up. *Slag. Slag. Slag.* He battered at my face until I disappeared.

'The next thing I knew, it was daylight. My body was in agony and I could only see through one eye. There was blood everywhere, the sheets were soaked in it and so was I. Everything hurt. My head, my eyes, my lips. *Inside* me. I knew I'd been raped. I couldn't move, could barely breathe. My head hurt so much. My phone was next to the bed but it'd been smashed. I screamed. It was all I could do, but a neighbour heard and called the police.

'They had to break the door down, found me unconscious – I'd passed out again. Called an ambulance and got me to hospital. I didn't know anything about it until I woke up there three days later, wired up to machines. They'd put me in an induced coma to prevent my body from collapsing in shock.

'They said I'd been raped several times. There was no semen, no skin under my fingernails, no DNA that was any use, no fingerprints in the house that weren't mine or family and friends.

'My eye socket was smashed and had to be repaired. It still isn't right, still tender to the touch. My cheek was broken and it's still a bit flatter on that side than the other. Two teeth were pushed back into my palate, my lip was burst. I had two broken ribs. Lost a lot of blood.

'They think he left me for dead. I very nearly was.

'When I could, I gave them a description of him. Tall, maybe six feet two or three, but slim. Wiry. He had these very pale blue eyes. Like ice. He had thick, dark hair, not long but not short either. His face was lean, like he was a runner or something. I remembered a smell too, like musk or sweat. It was all I could tell them and it wasn't much use.

'Nothing happened. Nothing.

'I'm sure they did all they could but they got nowhere. They were nice and kind but they couldn't find him. Couldn't catch him.

'When I was fitter, I moved back home, with my mum and dad. I just couldn't go back to the flat. Couldn't face it. The Family Protection Unit came round to see me, kept me up to date with what was happening. Which wasn't much. I got counselling and that helped but I still didn't sleep much, didn't go out. I was scared all the time, scared he'd come back and find me. That he'd do it again.'

Narey sat in silence through most of it. She felt useless, able to offer nothing more than a sympathetic ear. She had to fight back tears, something she wasn't used to. Murder investigations called for a cool head, leaving your emotions at home. This was different and something that, unlike the SOLO, she simply wasn't trained for. Leah's story shifted her compass.

She wasn't in her mid-thirties as Narey had thought – she was just twenty-seven. The heavy use of make-up was explained, so too the raised eye socket that she couldn't quite pick up on at first. The nervousness was obvious and completely understandable. The agitation was new, though. Something had caused that and brought her running through the night and the rain. Narey braced herself to hear what it was.

'I'd been in my room reading a few hours ago. I stay up late now because I struggle to get to sleep, so when I went downstairs my mum and dad had gone to bed. The newspaper was there, the *Daily Record*, and I picked it up to flick through it. And I saw him.

'It was definitely him. I maybe couldn't have described his face but I knew it when I saw it.

'It was a story about his company, how he'd made all this money before and sold the business for a fortune. A chatroom site. He had some new venture and there were photographs. A photograph of him.

'His name's William Broome. It's him. I *know* it's him.'

CHAPTER 2

'I screamed into a pillow so my mum and dad wouldn't hear me. I was nearly sick. Seeing him made it all real. I know that probably doesn't make any sense but until I saw that photograph, it was like the bogey man had broken into my house and did that to me. Like it was just some horrible, never-ending nightmare. But he's *real*. He's living a life. He's still out there.

'That fucking bastard beat me and raped me and now he's getting his picture in the paper like he's a star.'

Leah's hands were knotted into nervous bunches and her voice was cracking. Narey felt the urge to sweep her up and hug her.

'I didn't know what to do. I was crying in my room for maybe an hour. Part of me didn't want to do anything. Just curl up and forget I'd seen it. A big part of me still does. But I'm here because I'm scared and because I want someone to do something about him.'

With that she looked Narey straight in the eyes,

leaving no doubt as to who that someone was. Narey could feel the SOLO fidget beside her, and knew she was looking at her but ignored it.

'Leah, I'm here to help you and I really will do anything I can, but I'm not a specialist in this field. I can't pretend that I am. That's Louise's job. It might be better if we let her—'

'No! Please. I want you to—'

They were interrupted by a rap on the interview room door.

'Yes?'

Gordy Masterson opened the door and stuck his head round. 'Do you have a minute, DI Narey?'

She gave him half a smile. 'I'm busy right now, Sergeant. Can it wait?'

'It can, ma'am. Fresh coffees?'

'That would be great. Thanks.'

The door closed behind him and Leah looked at Narey curiously. 'What was that about?'

'He was checking if I needed an excuse to get out of here, but I don't.'

'An excuse in case I was some kind of crazy?'

'Something like that, yes. Gordy is old school. He knows that officers can get trapped in interviews when members of the public want them to go on longer than maybe they need to. So, if he's in a good mood, then he'll come into rescue them after a while.'

'But you don't need rescuing?' It was as much a plea as a question.

'No. You've got us for as long as it takes.'

Leah started crying, snuffling and wiping at her eyes. 'Thank you.'

'Don't thank me yet. Let's see what we can do. Tell us more about this newspaper article.'

She sat up, as if startled by remembering something, and reached into her bag to produce a doubled-over piece of newspaper. With nervous fingers, she unfolded and laid it out in front of Narey.

An advert took up the lower half of the page but the rest was devoted to a story headlined: REALITY CHEQUE: GLASGOW TECH FIRM WINS MULTI-NATIONAL INVESTMENT

The photograph grabbed her attention. A stripped-back office, spiked by floor-to-ceiling pillars, peopled with casually dressed twenty-something employees and a slightly older man, mid to late thirties, taking centre stage in a brown leather armchair. She didn't need the caption to tell her this was William Broome.

He looked confident, bordering on arrogant. Not smiling at the camera, content to let it smile on him instead. He wore jeans and a dress shirt not tucked in at the waist, barefoot as his long legs dangled over the edge of the chair. Narey had no problem in taking a dislike to someone based solely on how they looked.

She knew she was probably projecting, seeing the man through Leah's detailing of what he'd done to her, but there was a coldness to his eyes that unsettled her. She'd seen it before in others and it rarely meant anything good.

Broome's name was vaguely familiar but his face

wasn't. 'Reclusive', the article called him in one line. 'Camera-shy' in another. He was described as a technology entrepreneur, the founder of a social media platform called ChitChat which he'd sold for a fortune to a bigger company.

His new company was called HardWire, and they were working on the next big thing. Of course. The story was shouting about investment from Germany and Japan that would let them continue their work on virtual reality software. It seemed a leap from social media, but then again, maybe not.

HardWire was based in the Templeton building at Glasgow Green, a huge, ornate Victorian building originally built as a carpet factory, which seemed an even greater leap from whatever technological advances they were planning.

'Had you ever heard of this man, Leah?'

'I don't think so. Why?'

'I'm wondering if you'd ever come across him, maybe had mutual acquaintances. Some reason that he'd know you. What do you do for a living?'

'I'm a hairdresser. Was. I haven't worked since it happened. I gave my job up because I couldn't be around people I didn't know.'

'Could this man have been a customer in the past?'

'No. Well, not one I'd ever seen.'

'And do you know anyone that works in technology or computing or even works for this company?'

'No!'

Louise Crichton fired a warning glance at Narey.

The DI read it but already knew she'd been pushing too hard and cursed herself. She had to dial this back quickly before she lost Leah to the other side of the edge she was swaying on.

'Okay Leah, here's what I'm going to do. I'm here all the way for you but you need to answer some questions from Louise. We need a full statement. Is that okay?'

It was. Leah was there for another two hours, Crichton gently leading the questioning. Sometimes the words came fluidly and sometimes not, sometimes she was certain and others she was hesitant, eyes all over the room, suddenly less sure of herself. It was completely understandable, but made Narey worry what her reaction would be if they got as far as a court and she had to make the same statement in front of judge, jury and the accused.

There were more tears and unspoken pleas for reassurance, and promises of support. Somewhere in the middle of a wet October night, they all found something to cling on to.

William Michael Broome was born on 23 March 1979 in Glasgow. His parents were Michael and Elspeth Broome, the father a banker, the mother a bookkeeper. The father left home when Broome was just three, and he was brought up by his mother from that point.

He went to school at Merrylee Primary and Hillpark Secondary before going on to the University of Glasgow to study computing science. He lasted just two years before a mutual parting of the ways, something not explained in his records but apparently not an academic issue. He managed to get another chance at Glasgow Caledonian, where he graduated with a BSc (Hons) in Computing.

He got jobs with a few start-ups, never staying anywhere too long before forming his own company, ChitChat, in 2005. It never quite rivalled Facebook or Twitter but it caught enough of the market to encourage a buyout by one of the major American companies in 2007. No figures were officially quoted, but words like *millions* and *fortune* were regularly used in the press. Even allowing for journalistic exaggeration, he seemed to have done well from the venture, and used the money to launch HardWire.

He wasn't really a public figure though, generally only attracting the interest of the trade press and tech blogs. He shunned interviews, was rarely photographed and earned himself the tag 'King of Unsocial Media'.

Both the Criminal History System and the UK-wide Police National Computer declared him clean, nothing so much as a parking ticket. The only mention was on a command and control system which flagged up a public row between him and a girlfriend in 2003, which didn't lead to any police action.

Now, though, he stood accused of a savage beating and a violent rape. The only evidence Narey had was the word of the victim who, by her own admission, was barely conscious at the time she saw him.

She needed more. Much more.

CHAPTER 3

It had taken five phone calls to identify someone who both could and would talk to her about the end of Broome's time at the University of Glasgow. It began with a call to a friend who worked in the library there, seeking a handle on the disciplinary procedure and someone who could point her in the right direction.

Lesley had directed her to a lecturer she knew who'd previously served on the Senate as one of the Assessors for Student Conduct. He had laid out some of the issues that might have caused a student to be thrown off a course but had no knowledge of Broome.

Serious matters, he told her, would be sent up to the Senate Student Conduct Committee and maybe she should be looking there, providing her with another name to try. The administrator she was put in touch with hadn't been there long enough but suggested another. It was this person who paused when Narey mentioned Broome's name and said she remembered the case but that it was 'complicated'.

She said that she wasn't sure anyone would talk about the incident, that *she* certainly wouldn't unless forced to, but if anyone would it would be Maurice Fenton.

Professor Fenton had said that yes, he certainly did remember the Broome case but wouldn't talk about it over the phone. So it was that Narey was in Gilmorehill in the West End, where the university's principal campus was situated, climbing a winding set of stairs in search of Fenton's office.

She rapped on the door at the end of the second-floor corridor and was called inside. A tall, slender man with long, silver-grey hair was at his desk, reading a sheaf of papers. He was perhaps in his mid fifties, and wore a pair of black spectacles on the end of his nose.

'Professor Fenton?'

'It's Maurice. DI Narey, I presume.'

'Yes, thanks for agreeing to see me.'

'Take a seat. As I said on the phone, I'm happy to talk to you but I'd rather it was all off the record. At least until such time as you're conducting an official investigation. Which you say you're not.'

She settled into a chair opposite the desk. 'I'm not. I'm more carrying out background checks, seeing where something might lead. You dealt with this situation involving William Broome in 1999, is that right?'

'Whether anyone actually dealt with it is open to debate but yes, I was involved. I was on the Senate Student Conduct Committee at the time. A student made a complaint that Broome tried to assault her in her room.'

Narey had to make excuses to herself for the excitement that rippled through her.

'She said that nothing actually happened, but only because she'd hit him on the head with a lamp. Broome, of course, made a counter complaint that she'd struck him. We don't have the power to investigate sexual assault but as it had stopped short of that, we interviewed both parties.

'Her story was that she'd been chatting with him in the corridor of her student halls. Or she'd been chatted to, was probably more accurate. She made to leave, opened her door and he followed her inside, trying to grope her and push her onto the bed. She warned him off but he only got more insistent so she picked up the lamp from the bedside table, hit him with it and he ran out.

'His version was that they were getting on great, she gave him all the signals and led him into the room then changed her mind and lashed out at him.

'It basically came down to her word against his. I believed her, didn't think she had any reason to lie and wasn't convinced by Broome at all. He was angry at even having to talk to us, didn't understand why we weren't throwing her off her course.'

'So, what happened?'

'Not everyone took the same position I did. Some, understandably I guess, thought there just wasn't enough evidence to make a clear decision. There certainly was unlikely to have been enough for the police to have been able to take action, but my stance was that the university should expect a higher standard of behaviour from students than just not being a criminal.

'At my insistence, we strongly suggested to him that it would be in everyone's interest if he left his course. We wouldn't, and in truth couldn't, put anything on his record, so he'd be free to continue his career elsewhere. He took it very badly, shouted and ranted at us, saying he didn't want to stay somewhere that took the word of a liar over an innocent man.'

'So, he left the course?'

'Yes. It was unsatisfactory all round. Some thought he'd been hard done by, the female student thought he'd got off lightly. His mother wrote a scathing letter to the Principal. I was left just feeling uneasy about the whole thing.' He paused, weighing everything. 'I'm still uneasy. He's done something else, hasn't he?'

'He might have,' Narey conceded. 'As I said, just background checks for now.'

Fenton nodded. 'My gut feeling, unscientific as it is, is that he's trouble. Put it this way – I wouldn't want my daughter left in a room with him.'

She thanked him for his time and was just about to leave when another thought occurred to her.

'One more thing, I don't suppose you remember an art student named Karen Muir around 2003?'

Fenton looked at her oddly. 'Are you on a fishing trip? The student who made the complaint against Broome wasn't named Karen Muir.'

'No, that's not it. It's a separate matter. Honestly.'

Karen Muir was named on the command and

control system as the girlfriend that Broome argued with in public, leading to the police being called.

'Okay, I believe you. But if she studied Fine Art it was at the Art School, not here. Let me make a call.'

Fenton made two calls. The first unsuccessful but the second producing a series of nods to let Narey know he had something.

'That was a colleague and occasional drinking partner. He does remember Karen. In fact, he still sees her around occasionally. She has a small gallery of her own. She's a landscape painter, apparently very good, but pays the rent by doing scenes for Christmas card companies, postcards for tourist boards and the like. It lets her spend time doing her own thing and she sells the landscapes on top of that.'

'Where can we find her?'

'She has a little gallery on Hidden Lane.'

Hidden Lane was in Finnieston, just off Argyle Street, an old cobbled entranceway leading into another world.

Narey and DC Kerri Wells went through and were greeted by a warren of old buildings that had once been merchant's quarters and old stables and now housed nearly a hundred creative businesses. They were painted in a drunken rainbow of colours, lurid yellows and warm oranges, pale blues and rousing purples. It was very West End, very Finnieston.

There were furniture makers, jewellery designers, a fashion studio, recording studios, artists and designers, picture framers and yoga classes. The brick front of

KM Designs was painted in blood red, with a distressed white door in the middle. Through the glass panes, they could see a woman with her back to them, perched on a wooden stool and working on a broad white canvas.

Narey pushed her way inside, a bell signalling their entrance but seemingly not loud enough to encourage the woman to turn around.

'Hi. We're looking for Karen Muir.'

'Why? Is she lost?' The reply came without a missed brushstroke or the slightest turn towards them.

'I hope not. We'd like to speak to her. We're the police.'

This time, the brush stopped mid-stroke and the blonde head swivelled. The woman pushed a pair of glasses back off her face with the heel of her hand and studied them.

'Seriously?'

'I'm DI Rachel Narey, this is DC Kerri Wells. Can we have a word?'

Muir stood up and turned to face them. She wore a ponytail and her jeans and sweatshirt were daubed with paint. Looking from one cop to the other, her face screwed up in confusion. 'What's it about?'

'It's in connection to an incident that police were called to in Sauchiehall Street Lane a number of years ago, involving your ex-boyfriend, William Broome.'

'*What?* That wanker? That was over ten years ago and he was *not* my boyfriend.'

'The incident report stated that you were together. Is that incorrect?'

'I was *with* him on that night. It was a first date and there was never going to be a second one, even before he hit me.'

Narey was aware of Wells turning to look at her, but didn't share the glance.

'Could you talk us through what happened?'

Muir sighed heavily. 'I'm not really sure I want to. It was a long time ago and I'd rather just forget about it.'

'Please. It's important.'

'Fucksake. Okay, okay.'

Muir strode past them and closed the front door, turning over a sign to show the gallery to be closed. She sat back on her stool and wiped her hands with a rag.

'Okay, find a seat where you can. What do you want to know? And why the hell do you want to know it *now*?'

Narey parked herself on a swivel chair so she was at eye level with the artist, leaving Wells standing at her shoulder.

'I just want to know what took place that night. I can't tell you why or why now, not yet at least. What happened between you and him?'

Muir closed her eyes, maybe remembering, maybe dreading the recollection or the telling. She sighed again and began.

'It was a date, that was all. I was talked into it by a friend who knew a friend of his. They thought we'd get on and they were completely wrong. I think I knew within five minutes that it would be a first date and a last date. He had no chat, no interest in me or what I did. He was far too up himself and I just didn't like or fancy him. There was a coldness to him.

'We had drinks in The Social at Royal Exchange Square but I insisted on going to the bar when it was my round so that I was able to buy myself a soft drink. I wanted to stay sober. Maybe I had a feeling that I needed to, I don't really know.

'I got out as early as I could politely manage it but he insisted on walking me a bit of the way home. I think he thought it had gone a lot better than it had. He was talking about another date and I was ignoring it as best I could.'

Her voice caught and Narey knew they were cutting to the chase.

'We were walking past Sauchiehall Street Lane and he grabbed my wrist and pulled me into it. I didn't like it but wasn't too worried, not right away. It wasn't violent, didn't feel particularly aggressive. More like he was going to try his luck. And he did, he tried to kiss me. I turned my head away so he couldn't but he didn't get the message and tried again. This time I pushed him away.

'He punched me in the face.

'I was stunned. I'd never been punched before. I screamed. I kept screaming and he pulled his arm back to swing at me again but two guys came running into the alley.

'Broome made out it was just an argument, nothing to do with them, but one of them called the cops and they stopped him from leaving till the police got there.

They took statements from us both. I'm not sure what he said but they seemed to believe it, saying it would be difficult to get a conviction as it was his word against mine and I'd started it by shoving him. I think he'd told them he'd shoved me back and I fell. They said it was still up to me if I wanted to press charges.

'He was staring at me as the cop spoke to me. The look in his eyes was terrifying, threatening. I said I'd leave it, not press charges, if they'd just get me home safe. They drove me home and that was the end of it. He never contacted me again.'

CHAPTER 4

November

Narey was trying to make a guess at how many times she'd sat waiting to make the knock and lead the charge through the door. Dozens for sure. Over a hundred? Probably. It didn't get old and it didn't get easier.

This one churned her guts more than most. In the penthouse suite of the luxury block of flats in front of her was the man who'd occupied much of her waking hours and some of the sleeping ones too.

That was what she resented. He deserved every minute of her working life but there shouldn't have been any room left in her head for him to creep in outside of that, yet he'd managed it effortlessly. She'd be changing the baby, her beautiful little sleep-stealer, and he'd barge in. She'd be feeding the wee one at three in the morning and he'd be standing in the shadows. Her head would be full of Tony or her dad, or of Leah Watt. And sure enough, he'd appear. She'd be washing, drying, driving, pacing, shushing, nappy changing, cooking, cleaning, and he'd be there. Lingering like a bad smell.

Now, finally, she'd be able to put an end to it all. William Michael Broome. Rapist. Those were the words she was ready to see printed on Crown Office stationery. He wasn't going to be the first person she'd put away since she returned to the job but he was going to feel like it.

The digital clock on the car dashboard turned over to 2.00, shining a lurid blue in the darkness. With one last fleeting thought to the nine-month-old who was hopefully keeping her father awake, she turned to the three cops in the car beside and behind her. 'Okay, let's do this.'

The four of them, her and a DC plus two uniformed officers, slid quietly out of the car and pressed the doors closed. This was costing overtime and she'd had to twist arms and make assurances to get the constables along. It was going to be worth it though. William Michael Broome was going to be worth it.

It was the wrong time but the images from Leah's case file flooded her mind. Face swollen in angry purples and reds, blackened skin bulging around her shattered eye socket, the other eye sealed shut, nose misshapen, cheekbone collapsed, teeth broken. A human punch bag. Leah was why she was here and not with her baby.

There was no light showing in the top flat, front or back, and there hadn't been for more than an hour. Broome was asleep or at least in bed. The warrant that allowed her to wake him rudely was smouldering in her coat pocket, burning a hole and pleading to be used.

They woke the residents of one of the lower apartments, showing a warrant card through the video entry system, and stole quietly inside and climbed the stairs to the penthouse.

She rapped loudly on the door while speaking. 'William Michael Broome, this is Detective Inspector Rachel Narey of Police Scotland. I have a warrant for your arrest and to search your property. Please open the door now.'

She paused for a heartbeat. 'Okay, that's long enough. Open it.'

The lead uniform, his head encased in helmet and visor, wielded the metal battering ram and the wood groaned as it splintered. He swung a second time and the door flew open as the lock gave way. The enforcer was dropped inside and the uniforms poured through with the detectives at their heels. They'd studied the layout of the house and were sure Broome was in one of two bedrooms either side of the bathroom. The larger of the two was on the left and that's where they were heading.

The first cop crashed through the bedroom door, baton in hand and saw him immediately. 'Boss! He's in here.'

Narey walked into the room, her nose wrinkling at the stale stench of sleep and man and musk. Enough moonlight sneaked through the window for her to see him cowering in the corner, the bedclothes thrown back where he'd leapt from under them. He was crouched, naked, feet planted, his eyes wide and wild, his back pressed tightly to the wall as if trying to force his way through it.

She threw the light switch and stood in front of him, making a show of shaking her head at the pathetic image he presented. He was unshaven, with dark, tousled hair that went where it pleased. A sheen of sweat made his forehead shine and his mouth hung slack with shock. He was shaking with fear.

One of the uniforms, McCartney, moved in front of her and cuffed the man's hands in front of him then stepped back to let her resume. She was savouring it, making him wait. Weeks of donkey work, of knocking on doors and pressing her face up against computer screens till her eyes bled. Weeks with Leah, comforting, cajoling and persuading. All to get to this. She wasn't going to rush the moment. She wanted to see his face when she said Leah's name.

'William Michael Broome,' even saying that felt good. 'You are being detained under Section 14 of the Criminal Procedure (Scotland) Act 1995. I have a warrant to inspect these premises in relation to the assault to severe injury of Leah Watt and to the rape of Leah Watt on 17 July, 2017.'

There it was. Nothing. At the mention of rape, yes, but nothing at her name. He didn't know who she was. The rape engendered no surprise and the name nothing at all. She wanted to slap him. Slap him and throw him to the ground and kick him till he couldn't piss for a month.

'You are not obliged to say anything but anything you do say will be noted and may be used in evidence. Do you understand?

The man nodded his head sullenly, his eyes searching for a friendly face but not finding one. She knew he was a bit over six feet tall but he seemed a lot smaller, skinny too, with his knees pulled to his chest and his chalky skin shaking under the harsh glare of exposure.

She half turned towards the others. 'Bryan, you and Atkinson search this place top to bottom. McCartney, you—'

She hadn't finished before Broome launched himself at her. Springing up and away from the wall, arms outstretched, fingers clawing despite the cuffs, he was in her face, spittle peppering her cheek. His breath filled her nostrils and his crazed blue eyes filled her vision. Cops moved and grabbed, holding him back and leaving him snapping like a dog on the end of a leash.

They hauled him away but he didn't struggle, just grinned maniacally through his pain as he spoke for the first time.

'Get out of my house, you fucking slag.'

It had been her own fault. She should have had McCartney cuff his hands behind him rather than in front but she'd been content to savour him trembling in the corner like the cornered animal he was. She'd enjoyed the fleeting power of standing over him, letting him know she was unafraid and that he was a pitiful piece of shit in the presence of any woman able to fight back.

So it was that she had his spit staining her cheek. She'd been stupid and paid the price. All she could think was that she held that cheek against her baby's own powder-soft one. It was one of their bonding things, skin to skin, heat to heat, mother to daughter. And he'd ruined it.

He was back in the corner, silent once more, his hands handcuffed behind him now and a blanket round him. McCartney stood guard, waiting for the chance to bring him down if he tried anything else.

The others moved around from room to room, assiduously searching for anything to help build the case against Broome. Anything that meant it wouldn't all come down to Leah's testimony. Narey prayed for something concrete that would avoid putting the woman in the witness box and forcing her to endure the humiliation of describing what the bastard did to her.

It was partly why she'd called for the early morning crash through the door. She wanted Broome to feel some of what he'd put Leah through. The fear as his house was invaded in the middle of the night. The trauma of quivering in the dark. Not knowing who was coming to your bedroom or why. It would never be enough but it was something.

The penthouse was flooded with light now, showing off a sterile, minimalist apartment, all whitewashed walls and modern furniture. She wondered if he'd just bought the showhouse and left it as it was.

41

She turned into another room, a second bedroom, and threw the light switch. The walls were studded with photo frames, all in black ash and holding black and white prints, set out in neat rows. It shook her, immediately making her think of Tony's photo collection that had hung on the wall of his flat, his haul of crime-scene images that he'd acquired over the years.

She went closer, familiar visions of Glasgow coming into focus. The Kelvin Hall, the Duke of Wellington statue with obligatory traffic cone on his head, a summer scene across George Square to the City Chambers, the uplifted arms of La Pasionara by the Clyde, the Heilanman's Umbrella and the Provand's Lordship.

The photographs were good, sharp and evocative, capturing something of the spirit of the city, most with people in shot in front of the landmarks. These weren't standard tourism photographs and she imagined Broome had taken them himself.

'Boss!' The voice belonged to Bryan Dawson, her DC for the night. It was urgent, anxious almost, but there was good news in it, she heard that much. 'You need to come see this.'

Narey nodded at McCartney to bring Broome along and the constable pulled the man to his feet.

Dawson was in the hallway, a rolled back rug at his feet and two missing floorboards at the side.

'We lifted these and found just an empty cavity. We were about to put the floorboards back when we realised there was a false bottom.

She turned to see Broome's reaction and saw he was far from happy.

'You've no right. You can't do this!'

Narey wafted the warrant in his direction. 'This says I have and I can. What are we going to find, Mr Broome?'

He tried to kick out at her but McCartney was ready and hauled him back till his legs fell away from under him and he crashed onto his backside.

Make sure one of you is recording this,' Narey instructed. 'I don't want him claiming anything that isn't true.'

Atkinson nodded and tapped at his chest to indicate his Body Worn Video was switched on as Dawson reached down into the hole and lifted out a shoebox tied with a red ribbon in a single bow. He freed the box from its incongruous leash and took off the lid. With a gloved hand, he eased out the contents one by one and placed them on the wooden floor.

'Shit . . .' Narey's voice betrayed her. She didn't know what she'd expected but this wasn't it. She nodded at Atkinson and gestured towards Broome. Film his reaction too. The man's face was contorted in a silent rage, his eyes blazing crazily.

Dawson reached down into the hole again and groped around until he produced another shoebox, tied in a red ribbon like the other. He slid the lid off and they could see immediately that the contents were similar to the first. A third box followed and finally, after he thrust his arm in as far as it could go, he found a fourth.

He took some items from each box and spread them around the floor so they could all see. Dozens upon dozens of them. Narey's guess was that there were a few hundred in all. Photographs.

Many of them were in crowd scenes, some just sitting on a park bench or walking a dog or waiting for a bus or working in shops. They seemed to have no idea they were being photographed.

All women. All attractive. All between their late teens and early thirties.

Hundreds of them.

CHAPTER 5

Narey was glad not to have to explain her feelings at seeing the photographs and their subjects. She knew most people wouldn't understand or sympathise with the emotions that were writhing inside her, coiling round each other like snakes. Other cops would get it. Probably journalists too. Tony would understand for sure.

Coping with conflicting reactions was part and parcel of what they did. If you couldn't cope with that then get out and work in a bank or a bar or an office. She'd learned it was okay to feel the way she did; more than that, it was the only way to survive.

First up, she was shocked at the sheer scale of it. Maybe 400 photographs, most with background details that, just like the prints on Broome's wall, she immediately recognised as being in Glasgow. The Donald Dewar statue at the top of Buchanan Street behind one young woman's head. The net of lights over Royal Exchange Square above another. Byres Road. Ingram Street. Ashton Lane. It was a grubby A to Z of the city's busiest spots, every woman prospective prey for this prying lens.

She was disgusted too. This was a gross invasion of privacy. Being in public didn't mean you were public property. Certainly not the property of this creep and his camera. They were simply walking, talking, sitting with friends or catching the sun, minding their own business and not inviting any scrutiny. She'd sat at most of these places, walked past all of them. It made her skin crawl.

But above and beyond all that – all of which she could freely admit to in the most unforgiving of company – she was excited. It was a squalid sort of excitement, the dirty secret you don't admit to. This was potentially, perhaps probably, something big. But for it to be what she instinctively felt that it was, something bad would have to have happened to some of the women in these photographs. Someone's god forgive her, but it didn't stop her feeling the way she did. Her only saving grace was that she knew it was wrong.

'Who are these women?'

Broome didn't lift his head but stared fiercely at the floor, his eyes not straying to either Narey or the photographs. Anything the man said would most likely be inadmissible in court but she'd ask anyway. She repeated the question but he didn't budge.

'Did you take these? Are they your photographs?'

She saw the skin around his mouth tighten as he

grimaced harder but he wouldn't look at her or reply. She turned to Dawson and the uniforms. 'Do any of these look familiar? Anyone at all that you might have seen before?'

The men just shrugged. 'I'll need to take a longer look,' Dawson offered.

'We all will. And Mr Broome is going to help us. Aren't you?'

She got the response she expected. 'Constable McCartney, you stay with him. If he moves, please be gentle. Bryan, get SOCO in and have these bagged, dusted and catalogued, then you and Atkinson keep tossing this place. See what else you can find. And look for the camera that took these.'

She couldn't take her eyes off the photographs. The women, some of them just girls, were oblivious to the camera and the man behind it. She picked up one of the boxes and took it into the large, barely furnished, sitting room, laying as many of the prints out as she could on a glass table. Some of them had an older feel than others, the quality not so good and the fashions dating them. Others were pin sharp and felt just days old.

Wait. She'd seen this girl's face before, in one of the other prints. Blonde hair cut into a bob and a broad smile. Where? She scanned through the others until she found it. Different clothing, different location, but the same girl. Early twenties, button nose and pretty. There she was, walking on what Narey was sure was Argyle Street, dressed in skinny jeans and trainers with a long lacy sweater that came to her knees. There she was again with what had to be Hillhead subway station behind her, a black trench coat buttoned to her neck. Same girl, different days.

Shit. There she was again. Narey didn't recognise the street but the trees in the background looked like the West End. A pink umbrella raised above her blonde hair, the photo taken from across the road and closed in beyond reasonable focus.

Another woman appeared twice. Tall with long dark hair, possibly Asian or mixed race, strikingly attractive. First stepping down a short flight of concrete stairs from an office, wearing a dark, tailored business suit, her hand sweeping through her hair. Then in another, sitting on a park bench with another woman who was only half in the frame, this time dressed casually and hair worn up.

Narey took her phone from her pocket and quickly photographed as many of the prints as she could before going back to the hallway where the other photographs were still laid out on the floor. Broome watched her work. There was the businesswoman, looking in a shop window in Princes Square, different outfit, different day. A pencil-slim redhead appeared at least twice. *No, wait, three times.* She was in a group of friends in two of the shots, one walking along Cresswell Lane and the other through the window of University Café, but the other women were cut out either partly or completely. The photographer only had eyes for her.

When Narey looked up, she saw Broome had a smirk on his face that she immediately itched to wipe off.

'These aren't all random, are they? You have your favourites. You do know that stalking is an offence and each of these multiple cases would represent a separate offence, each liable to imprisonment for up to five years?'

Broome smiled at her and said nothing.

She kept flipping through them. Woman after woman. Familiar backgrounds. Disgust and a mounting fear crawling over her.

She felt the next print before she saw it. It lay underneath the one she was looking at, a pretty Asian woman with raven-dark hair who was going down an escalator in Princes Square. Her fingers sent a message to her brain, alerting her to something different, urging her to leave the photo in front of her.

She could feel ragged edges, her forefinger slipping across and almost through the print. Was it torn?

She slipped out the rogue print and placed it on top. And stared.

There was just one woman in the frame, standing in front of an unidentified shop window. Could have been anywhere. She was slim, wearing black ankle boots and tight black jeans. A grey, fleece-lined hoodie billowed in the wind over a dark green top.

And that was it. No more to be seen.

There was a hole in the print where her head should have been.

Someone had taken a pair of scissors and cut out a rough section of the print, completely removing the woman's head and hair.

CHAPTER 6

It was around four thirty when she sneaked back into her own bed, the cold of her flesh wakening Tony immediately. She'd already slipped into Alanna's room and risked everything to pick her up and cuddle her. Her baby had stirred briefly but didn't open her eyes, just alternately grumbled and purred like a cat.

'Shit, your feet are freezing! You didn't wake her, did you?'

'No.'

'You didn't pick her up, right?'

'No. Of course not.'

'Liar. How was it out there?'

She slipped an arm over him and pulled herself against his back, causing him to flinch again before he settled and let her steal some of his heat. 'It was okay. We got the guy but ... oh, I don't know. It's not a world I want our daughter to grow up in.'

'Want to talk about it?'

'Nope.'

'Off the record.'

She bit playfully at his neck. 'Nope. You're never off the record. Seriously, it's bad stuff. Weird shit. Saying it out loud will just make it real. Just lie there and make me warm. It would be nice if you're still here when I wake up too.'

'Can't. But I will feed Alanna before you wake up, then I'll drop her in beside you.'

'Mmmm. Perfect. I'd rather have her than you anyway.'

'I know. Last chance to talk about it or I'm going back to sleep.'

'Thanks, but no. I need to think this one over by myself. It could be ... Shit, it could be anything. Go to sleep. It's nearly—'

'Don't tell me. Let me believe I've got another six hours before I have to get up. Don't tell me it's twenty minutes.'

'Not saying a word.'

She snuggled her head into the middle of his back and shielded herself from the world. Why couldn't it all be like this?

It seemed like hours before she fell asleep but it was probably minutes. She lay there, clinging on to Tony and the bed and the world, in that state where she was either awake or simply dreaming that she was. Behind her eyes, she could see the prints, all those women, all those faces. Yet as she drifted somewhere between reality and nightmares, one by one the women filed past her, their heads carelessly removed, leaving just raggedy holes in raggedy photographs.

CHAPTER 7

Leah Watt was twenty-seven going on fifty-five. Her premature ageing wasn't her fault.

Narey often found herself wishing she'd known Leah before Broome had wrecked her life, her confidence and her future. Everyone said she was the heart and soul, a party girl with a big laugh and eyes that lit up the room. A personality stolen.

It wasn't lost forever though, Narey kept telling them both that. In the couple of months that she'd known her, she'd seen a change. An unfurling, a re-emergence, however slight, into the world. Her voice was that little bit louder, a touch bolder too. Rather than wrap herself in her own arms, she now occasionally had the courage to throw them wide as she spoke. It was a sign of the thing Narey was thrilled to finally see in Leah – anger. Where there had been meek acceptance and quiet self-loathing, there was now the slow burn of righteous rage.

She was still battered and bruised inside but a partial recovery had started. Which made Narey feel all the worse for giving her news that made her turn back in on herself.

'Two weeks? I'm not ready. I'm not ready for court. Rachel, I can't! Why so soon?'

'Leah, it will be fine. Trust me. I wouldn't be putting you through this if I didn't think you could cope. Please, sit down. It's going to be okay.'

Broome had appeared in court the day after they'd found the photographs in his home and he'd been remanded in custody. Now it was down to the Procurator Fiscal to decide what happened next. They had 140 days to get him to trial but Narey knew it would have to be sooner, while Leah still had the nerve to do it. No one knew how long her will to face him would last and they needed her.

Narey burned with some shame as she watched Leah's ravaged face crumple into reluctant agreement. Most of the discolouring had gone, the remainder hidden under make-up. Her eye socket remained tender but no longer swollen. Her right cheek was still strangely flat and probably always would but you'd only likely see it if you knew to look. Anyway, Narey knew it was what couldn't be seen that hurt most.

They were in Leah's parents' house in Knightswood, a bit over four miles from her old flat in North Kelvinside, the one Broome had violated. She didn't have anywhere near the nerve to go back there or to live alone so had moved back into the bedroom she'd occupied as a teenager, with posters of Justin Timberlake and the cast of *Friends* on her wall. Mum and Dad, Heather and Charlie, had gone out to give them space.

Narey watched Leah sitting in a chair that was too big for her, a little girl lost, worn down with the world-weary jaundice of the middle-aged. She needed to be tucked in and cuddled but she also needed to be given the strength to stand on her own two feet.

In her hand was Oliver, a toy owl that she'd had since she was a kid. It had seen better days and was ripped at one ear but Leah wouldn't be parted from it. She hugged it now as if it was magic.

'Leah, this may sound a strange question, but were you ever aware of someone hanging around, perhaps taking photographs of you?'

Her eyes narrowed in confusion. 'What? Where's this come from? Why are you asking me this now?'

Her confidence was as fragile as a bird. Anything unexpected and she'd fly.

'I'll explain in a minute. Trust me. But I have to ask you before I tell you what it's about. Do you remember ever seeing anyone hanging about with a camera?'

The young woman pulled her legs up and tucked them under her, withdrawing as deep into the brown leather armchair as she could. She took a deep breath and held on to it while twirling the ends of her copper-coloured hair. It was a mechanism Narey had seen dozens of times.

'Okay. Ask me again.'

'Maybe when you were out shopping or with friends, somewhere public. The person with the camera might have been on the other side of the street, might not have looked like it was you he was photographing. Can you think of anything like that at all?'

She took her time. Pulling a cushion over her face as she thought. Little gurgling noises coming from behind it.

Narey found herself crossing her fingers and saying a silent prayer to whatever god might be listening. *Please. Let it be.*

When Leah re-emerged, she was damp eyed and apologetic. Tears began to stream the way they always did when she felt she was letting Narey down.

'I'm sorry. Rachel, I'm really sorry but I can't. This is important, isn't it? I'm sorry. I wish I did but I don't remember anything like that. I just …'

'It's okay. Shhh.' Narey was out of her seat and perched on the arm of the chair, wrapping her arms around the girl. 'Leah, you can't remember it if it didn't happen. It's okay. It's just something I needed to ask.'

Leah's head broke loose from her grasp. 'Why? Tell me now. What is that all about? *Photographs?*'

So Narey told her. About Broome and his grotesque collection that Leah wasn't in. About how she wondered, no more than that, if he'd stalked and photographed potential victims. How it could help them in court. How it would go to character. How they could now run his DNA against what they had from the night of the attack. The rape.

All it did was confuse her. Narey was guessing at many of the thoughts she could see twisting their way across Leah's face. *Why me? Why not me? Did I miss him watching me? Why me?*

'That will go against him at the trial, right? I mean, it's got to.'

No lies, that was Narey's rule. Just hopeful truths. 'We think so and we hope so. It can only be bad for him.'

The girl looked sad and weary.

'Are you still having the same nightmares?'

Leah breathed out hard as she nodded. 'Most nights. Always the same. I can't move. I freeze. Just like I did when he broke in. I can smell him in the room, feel his weight on me but I do nothing. I just lie there and let him hit me. Let him put—'

'Leah . . .'

There was the flash of anger. 'I *know*.' She talked as if spooling back what she'd been taught. 'It was *him*. I didn't have to fight to make it wrong but I should still have fought him. I *wish* I'd fought him. I'd feel fucking better about myself if I had. And I know all the arguments about that, I've heard them all. This time, Rachel, this time I'll fight. I promise.'

She wiped a last defiant tear from her face with a violent swipe of her sleeve. 'I'm doing this for you though. So you can get him. You'll be beside me, won't you?'

'All the way. But, Leah? Don't do it for me. Do it for you.'

Leah managed half a smile and half a nod.

CHAPTER 8

Narey fretted in the quiet of the incident room while she waited for the team to join her, pacing back and forth talking the facts through, just loud enough that they didn't go past the door. It was pre-match nerves, she knew that. Trying to get herself together enough that it would come across as if at least one officer in the room knew what they were talking about. Even if that officer was damaged goods.

The Anti-Corruption Unit's investigation had been thorough to say the least, rummaging through every cupboard in search of a skeleton. The press had been all over it too, sensing at least a story if not a scandal. She'd told the truth and thankfully the truth had been enough. There had been no charges to answer but that didn't mean there wasn't an asterisk against her name. She knew damn well there was.

There had been cases since her return. A kidnap, an attempted murder and one that was eventually knocked down to culpable homicide even though they had little doubt there was intent to kill. This one promised to be different. *Bigger. Harder.* There were other descriptions fighting to be heard and she gave in to them. *More meaningful.* She wanted this, needed this, badly.

She did a final check of the PowerPoint, ran through the facts in her head one last time and reminded herself that she was good at this. Nothing had changed.

They began to file in one by one, forcing her to put her game face on. It was a small team and would stay that way for now until they proved they had something that demanded more bodies, more time and more money.

Rico was in first, as always. They'd come through the ranks together and became detective sergeants on the same day, staying peers until Narey got promoted. *Promoted for being a woman* was the canteen gossip, but Rico Giannandrea never joined in. He was as smart as they came and if he ever resented her promotion then he hadn't once even hinted at it.

The three DCs came in together, deep in conversation. Bryan Dawson had been there the night before and was no doubt bringing Kerri Wells and Steph Harkness up to speed. The group was completed by the two constables who'd been there to arrest Broome – Connor McCartney and Andy Atkinson. With a bit of luck, she'd have the uniforms for the duration to do whatever donkey work was needed.

Narey walked to the front of the room, took a deep breath, and was about to begin when the door opened again. DCI Derek Addison. A long, lanky streak of foul-mouthed outrage, who was a friend but also her boss, and no less a pain in the arse for that. She really didn't need him being there.

Holding an apologetic hand up to the waiting troops, she went back to speak to him. He grinned irritatingly, seeing her displeasure.

'Did you get lost, wander in here by mistake?'

'*Funny.* I heard what you found and I'm interested. It's your show, though.'

'Yes, I know it is. I don't need babysitting.'

'Just as well that's not what I'm fucking doing then, isn't it? From what I'm hearing, this could be big. Big enough that I need to know about it.'

'You're a terrible liar, Addy. For someone with so much practice, you really should be better at it, *sir*. Have I got this case only because you promised you'd keep an eye on me, make sure I didn't kill anyone?'

He huffed. 'You should be a detective. Your card's still marked, you know that. So yes, I'm on the ticket but I'd just as rather not be doing any work and leaving it all to you. That way everybody wins. Go, tell your troops what you have and just pretend I'm not here.'

'You'll just be the elephant in the room?'

'Give me peace. And Rachel?' he dropped his voice to a whisper. 'Before you went off, it would never have occurred to you that someone thought you needed babysitting. Because you didn't. And you still don't. Remember that.'

She screwed her face up in mock confusion. 'Are you ... are you being *nice*?'

'No, I'm fucking not. Now get your arse up there and get this thing started.'

'William Broome,' she began. 'IT entrepreneur and businessman. He is charged with rape and assault to severe injury and will be up in court tomorrow. All stops have been pulled to bring things forward. However . . .'

She let the pause hang there, as much to get the tone right as for dramatic effect. She didn't want this to come across as being *more* than what happened to Leah. She couldn't diminish that for a second. But . . .

'. . . there's more. On a search of his house last night, DC Dawson, along with constables McCartney and Atkinson, found a little treasure trove. Over five hundred photographs of women, all seemingly taken on the streets of Glasgow without their knowledge or permission. If this had been done by anyone else, it would seem highly suspicious and worrying. Done by Broome, I'm not sure I really want to start speculating just what it might mean. But we *need* to find out.'

She watched their faces, looking for reactions. Some had already known, some had just been told. All were professional, all hard-set and outraged as they should have been, but the two women – she was sure she wasn't just projecting it – they felt something more. The same thing she'd done. It was subtle, almost unexplainable, but she saw it for what it was.

'This is the kind of photograph we've found in boxes under Broome's floorboards,' she kicked the

PowerPoint into action and an unknown young woman filled the screen. 'There are hundreds of them. Some appear just once while some' – she moved the images on – 'appear in multiple photographs and on different days. We simply do not know who they are. *Yet*. That is our principal task.

'Today, I want to explore just what the significance of this find is. We cannot ignore the fact that the man we believe to have taken them, and who was certainly in ownership of them, is a violent rapist. He isn't talking, so we're having to guess at his motivation for having photographed these women. All my guesses leave us with something pretty bad, so if you have anything else, let's hear it.'

There was a noisy silence. The kind filled with thought and internal debate. No one could think of a good reason for anyone to have done what Broome had. They could all think of plenty of reasons that they didn't like much.

Giannandrea broke the hush of deliberation. 'If, as you say, these had been taken by anyone else, someone without a rape charge against them, then I'd think it was just someone we hadn't caught yet. This isn't right. Nothing could make *this* right. But taken by someone like Broome? I'd want to know that these women were safe. And I'd be gratefully surprised if they all were.'

'I'm completely creeped out by this, I don't mind admitting it.' Steph Harkness opened up. 'This has stalking and rape and God knows what written all over it. I'm creeped out and I'm angry and I'm available

61

for however many hours you need. No way this guy is taking photos for some travel guide to Glasgow. This is sinister as fuck and there's no other way to paint it.'

Kerri Wells sat next to her, nodding grimly, her jaw clenched, fists bunched.

'Okay,' Narey took control of it again. 'So, we need to know who they are and we need to know where and how they are. Some, hopefully all, might remain unaware of Broome and his camera and whatever the fuck his next move was. But we need to find out. Rico, organise a gallery of every woman missing, murdered, raped, assaulted, verbally assaulted, whatever, that is on file for the last, I don't know, ten or fifteen years. We need to establish if they're victims.'

'They're already victims,' Wells blurted out. 'He's photographed them. They're victims of that.'

Narey took it on board and nodded, acknowledging Wells was right. She hesitated before making herself push on. 'Then, there's this.'

She moved the presentation forward and the rogue print appeared on screen. All but Bryan Dawson moved back in their seats, eyes screwed up in confusion or disgust.

It had a power that even the others didn't. Having no face was more disturbing than the endless array of innocent faces. The untidy edges of the cut paper suggested violence, harm, frenzy. Nothing that could be good.

'What the fuck is that about?' Kerri Wells got straight to the point. She was a little tough nut who'd started – or finished – more than her share of arguments among the squad. She was only five feet three but never took a backwards step, combative because of rather than in spite of her height. Kerri was the one that would never let the guys away with anything remotely resembling a sexist remark, always calling them on it and shoving it back down their throat. Given how often such remarks were made, it kept her busy.

'It's a good question. Let's hear some suggestions. Why is this one different from all the rest?'

'Is it his mother?' Connor McCartney qualified his question before anyone could have a go at him. 'I'm not trying to be funny. Is he keeping her secret because she means something different to him than the others? I don't necessarily mean his mother but a girlfriend, a sister, a neighbour, *something*.'

'Is it Leah Watt?' Giannandrea wondered.

'No. Well, most probably not,' Narey answered. 'It was the first thing I thought but the body shape, it's just not her. It's possible it was taken when Leah was a lot slimmer but it just doesn't look like her. I'm saying no.'

They all studied the photograph. All staring into the abyss.

'Is it because she's recognisable?' Harkness wondered. 'Famous in some way?'

'But why would he need to remove her face to keep her hidden when she's already in a shoebox under the floorboards?' Giannandrea wasn't convinced.

No one knew the answer. Or any answer.

'I'm sure McCartney is right that this woman is

different from the others, perhaps because she means something to him, perhaps because of what happened to her, perhaps because of who she is. But I don't want to guess why, I want to know why. Bryan, find a psychologist, try Lennie Dakers if he's available. Ask him the question. Steph, get me a photographic expert, find if there's any way we can date these.'

Both DCs took notes, bobbing their heads in agreement. Narey let the room have a moment, letting it breathe.

'We might have a serial rapist on our hands here. Possibly on a scale we haven't seen before. Broome is vicious. He's violent. The attack on Leah Watt was, in my opinion if not that of the Procurator Fiscal, attempted murder. We don't know how much further he might have gone.'

She turned and faced the screen, flicking through face after face to make her point.

'Look at them. Study them. Remember every face. Every item of clothing. We're going to have to look at a lot of missing women aged between twenty and forty and I don't want anyone slipping through unnoticed because these faces aren't ingrained on your brains. Remember them.'

There were nods, some quiet, some fierce.

'And another thing. This stays within the investigation. It's not going to do any good for this to become public knowledge, not until we need it to be. So, we keep it out of the media. It's only going to cause a panic and that's not going to help.'

'Better make sure your husband doesn't know about it then,' chipped in a voice from the ranks.

There was an uneasy ceasefire until Narey herself was the first to laugh. Bryan Dawson had the fortunate ability to say something like that with a straight face, saved by the schoolboy twinkle in his eyes that must have enabled him to get away with murder as he grew up. The joke broke a spell in the room, just as it was intended to.

'Yeah, and you better make sure that reporter on the *Sun* that you're so friendly with doesn't hear about it either, you cheeky fucker.'

'My relationship with her is strictly professional,' Dawson protested, his chubby cheeks puffing up with mischief before he broke into an operatic guffaw.

'You can't even spell professional without using your fingers. Okay, calm down. We know what we've got to do here, right?' They all nodded. She looked to the back of the room. 'DCI Addison, is there anything you want to add?'

'Not really.' He pushed himself from the wall and addressed them. 'DI Narey has told you everything you need to know. She's in charge of this and you come back to her with everything you find. And what you need to find are these women. Just one thing though. That –' he pointed at the missing-head photograph on the screen – 'is key. Find out who she is and why that sick fucker has cut away her face and you'll be half-way there.'

CHAPTER 9

Leah and Narey were standing on a flight of concrete steps, being buffeted by wind and the occasional sheet of rain as November howled at them from all sides. Leah worked nervously at a cigarette, her ragged breath struggling to keep it alight amid the bluster. Narey was there as a barrier to it all.

Their shadows reflected dully on the hulking brown marble wall that declared the building behind it to be the Sheriff Court of Glasgow and Strathkelvin. It was reckoned to be the busiest court in Europe and Narey wasn't likely to argue with that. Half her life seemed to be spent there or at the high court just a couple of minutes' walk away. It was the sheriff court that saw the traffic though – thousands of lost souls trudging in and out of twenty-two separate courtrooms either in search of justice or hell-bent on escaping it.

The Clyde was just a few yards away, black as night, but rushing noisily as it cut through the city. Narey caught Leah staring at it through a gap in the trees, watching the river run. It had been a battle to get this far, a few minutes away from Broome's preliminary hearing, and Narey didn't want to lose her now.

'You doing okay?'

Leah kept her eyes on the Clyde, intently following the surge and swell. She nodded tightly, hugging her cigarette closer. 'I'm okay.'

'It's going to be okay in there. With a bit of luck, we'll be back out in an hour.'

The younger woman dipped a hand into her bag and produced her toy owl, waggling the head back and forth just above the rim of her bag. 'Yeah, Oliver says no problem. We'll be lucky. Bound to be.'

Narey smiled at the dog-eared toy peeping out at her from the bag. What could go wrong with a lucky owl on your side?

'You know how this is going to go, right? Broome's going to be asked to enter a plea for all charges. Guilty or not guilty. If he pleads guilty, then he'll be sentenced and this ends today. If not, the court wants to know that we've agreed on all contentious evidence. That's where it might get interesting.'

Leah chewed on her cigarette and glared at the river.

'He can't get to you, Leah. You're safe.'

'You can guarantee that, can you? I used to always think I was safe. Didn't really imagine any other way to be. Then, once your world's been invaded, turned upside down, you never feel safe again. You know nothing's guaranteed. Nothing.'

'You're right, I can't guarantee it. But I guarantee I'll do my best to make sure of it. He won't get near you.

You don't even have to look at him in there. Listen, maybe it's best you just skip court today. I'll let you know how it goes.'

'No!' There was panic in her voice. 'If the first time I see him is at the trial proper then ... I don't know how I'll be. I know I might freak out. I need to do it this way. We've been *through* this.'

This had been the bone of contention for weeks. It was highly unusual for a victim in Leah's case to attend a first diet but she'd insisted on it. Then she'd fled from the notion and come rushing back to it again, twisting on the wind, spinning on her fears. They'd finally relented despite the warnings from the rape task force and the SOLOs, and despite their own worries.

'Okay, okay. Calm down. You're right and it's your choice.' Narey glanced at her watch. 'It's time to go in.'

As they wound their way along a corridor, searching for their designated courtroom, Narey saw a woman ahead with her eyes fixed on them. She looked to be in her late fifties but as they got nearer it became obvious she was prematurely grey and not much more than forty, overweight and puffy around the eyes. She had a cigarette pack in her hands and was tapping nervously on the top of it. She got agitated at the sight of Narey and Leah and began to pull herself up in readiness for them. She was standing outside Court Fourteen, clearly waiting for them.

Shit. We don't need this, Narey thought. She had no idea who the woman was or what she wanted but she doubted it was going to be anything that would help

Leah's state of mind. She manoeuvred herself to Leah's right to keep herself between her and the stranger.

'DI Narey? Can I have a word. I'm—'

'No, I'm sorry. This is not a good time.'

'But this is—'

'Excuse us.' Narey had Leah by the arm and turned her own shoulder to the woman as she firmly led them past her. She walked them both to seats just a few rows from the front, close enough to see everything yet far enough away from where the accused would soon be. She put her hand on Leah's, reassuring her, then stepped to the side to tell a WPC that if the woman with the grey hair and black raincoat tried to sit near them she should be removed.

Within a few minutes, Leah was struggling. Her left leg tapped out an unsteady rhythm despite the hand that rested on it trying to keep it still. The other hand wandered through her hair, pawing at her eyes and wiping at her mouth. She kept turning her head to the door, drawn to it every time it opened or closed, her ragged breathing signalling hope or disappointment.

It was just a first diet, held two weeks before the intended trial to make sure it was going to proceed, but the courtroom held the power to intimidate. The trappings of the law were designed to instil fear and command obedience, all oak panelling and cut-out portcullis designs, heraldic lions and the glower of stern men in suits. Leah was wilting under its gaze.

She shook visibly when Broome entered the room. He walked to the front of the court without a glance to where his victim sat, dressed sharply but not flashily in a plain grey suit. His hair was neatly brushed and he gave off a calm, unthreatening demeanour. Leah's eyes followed him, Narey's too.

It was hard to reconcile this figure with the one that launched himself at her from the corner of his bedroom. That was animal. She'd seen something primal in his eyes in that moment and heard the guttural snarl of the wolf as he attacked. She'd had a glimpse of what he really was. Now, she saw he wasn't calm. Rather he was cold. The cold, unthreatened, uncaring air of the predator at rest.

He shifted in his seat, his head swinging round lazily till he was looking at the two women, his face expressionless. He made eye contact with each in turn but still showed no reaction, barely recognition. He lifted a hand to his face as he looked at Leah and traced a finger across his nose and cheeks, a gesture so innocent it could easily have been passed off as nothing. Then he let two fingers drum gently at the side of his face and Narey felt his spittle on her cheek.

Leah's dancing foot had graduated from a slow beat to a quickstep. It juddered manically and her breath followed suit, hammering in and out, pumping her heart rate ever higher. She couldn't stop looking at Broome, backing as far into her chair as it would let her. She was terrified and the scale of her fear frightened Narey in turn.

Broome towered over his solicitor, a small, slight man named Arthur Constance whom Narey had the misfortune to have crossed several times in the past. Constance looked like a bird but was nicknamed the Velociraptor for the delight he took in taking chunks out of cops and lawyers for the Crown.

Broome had made a smart choice in hiring Constance. Not only was he very good at what he did, he was a small, physically unintimidating man, softly spoken, and wouldn't be seen as bullying Leah in the same way as someone bigger or more aggressive. But in his own quiet way, Constance was perfectly capable of ripping Leah to shreds and not shedding a single tear as he stood over her carcass. His presence was not a comforting factor.

Narey looked round to see that the courtroom was largely empty, as would be expected for a hearing of this nature. There were a number of cops and court staff, lawyers collecting their fees and just a handful of members of the public. An older woman, seventies maybe, sat on the other end of the same row as her and Leah. She dabbed at her eyes with a white hand-kerchief and was comforted by what seemed to be a much younger relative. Narey was fairly sure it was Broome's mother.

Further back was the woman who'd tried to accost them outside court. She looked at Narey resentfully, her mouth fixed in a scowl. Whoever she was, she wasn't happy.

The sound of chairs scraping made Narey turn and she saw that the judge had entered the court. The play was about to begin. She reached for Leah's hand and squeezed.

Judge Erskine called the proceedings to order, the charges were read out and Broome was asked how he pled. Narey felt Leah's hand twitch.

'Not guilty.'

Leah gasped despite knowing it was coming. From the corner of her eye, Narey could see a tear begin to make its way down the young woman's cheek.

Grant Whittle, the procurator fiscal depute who was prosecuting the case, read out his list of witnesses, Narey and the other cops who arrested Broome in his home among them. Constance did the same for the defence.

However, as Whittle began his pronouncements of uncontested evidence, Constance stood and interrupted him. 'Your honour, I'd like at this time to broach the matter of a piece of evidence which is very much in contest and which I believe can be dealt with summarily. May we approach the bench?'

Whittle protested immediately, saying that Constance knew very well the order of such things.

'My learned friend is, of course correct within the letter of the law but not, I suggest, within the spirit of these proceedings. I believe that if the evidence in question is even mentioned in court then my client's ability to be afforded the fair trial to which he is entitled will be placed in extreme jeopardy. For that reason, I ask to be heard now.'

Whittle groaned theatrically but his breath would have been better spent making legal argument. The judge called them both forward and switched off his microphone.

'What's happening?' Leah's voice wavered.

'I don't know. Broome's lawyer is the kind who is always trying something. We need to just let them deal with it.' She tried to sound more confident than she felt.

From behind, all Narey could see was much arm waving from both sides while the judge remained impassive, taking notes without speaking. As Whittle turned side on, she saw his face was heated, the blood rising in his cheeks. He was jabbing a finger in Constance's direction then turning to wave an arm towards Broome. Constance remained calm, as if explaining something very simple.

After ten minutes that seemed so much longer, the judge raised the palm of his hands to both men, urging them to desist. He shooed them back to their seats and announced the court would be adjourned until he made a ruling on the evidence in question. Whittle fell back into his seat with his face the colour of a sky full of thunder.

'What's going on?' Leah demanded. 'This isn't good, is it? Rachel, I don't like this.'

'It's okay. Just stay here. I'm going to talk to him.'

She made her way to the front row where Whittle was just about to get out of his seat. She squatted beside him with an arm firmly on his.

'Grant, what the hell's going on?'

He exhaled noisily. 'That prick Constance is insisting that the photographs you found in Broome's flat are thrown out.'

'*What?*'

'Sorry, but I think he might succeed too. He's argued that no crime has been committed. That—'

'That's ridiculous.'

'It's not. His argument is that the photographs of the women were taken in a public place and that the European Court of Human Rights says anything done in public has no legitimate expectation of privacy. Further that there has been no complaint of harassment from any of the women pictured in the photographs and therefore no crime.'

'Because they don't know they've been taken!'

'Yes, *I know*, but still no complaint. Further, our victim, Ms Watt, is not among the photographs, therefore, in the gospel according to Constance, the photographs bear no relevance to this case. They do not go to motive or character or suggest previous behaviour. He wants them excluded and Erskine is making a decision right now.'

'*Shit!* And you think that's what will happen?'

Whittle heaved his shoulders. 'I've argued that the case for the inclusion of the photographs is self-evident. That they are clearly Broome's, he has clearly taken them and they demonstrate behavioural patterns consistent with psychological profiling of violent rapists. That to not allow them to be presented would be a miscarriage of justice. That each of these photographs potentially represents a crime as serious as the one before this court. And on and on. Erskine will make his own mind up. But if he throws out the photographs then we might well be fucked. We'll only have your ...'

Whittle stopped, realising that Leah was standing beside them, her eyes wide and face flushed, tears streaming down her face.

'All you'll have left is me? Is that what you're saying?'

'Leah, let's not panic ...'

'It will all be down to me? Well that's not going to happen because I'm not doing it. It's too much of a risk. You said it would all be okay, that we had him. Well it's not and we don't!'

Her voice was getting higher and louder. 'If there's no photographs then I'm not testifying. I mean it. I won't do it.'

'We can talk about this. Let's just—'

'No!' She was shouting now. 'I won't testify. I can't. I don't recognise that man. I've never seen him before. I made a big mistake. It's not him.'

The whole court was listening now. Arthur Constance most definitely was.

Ten minutes later, Judge Erskine called both sides into his chamber and told them he was throwing out the photographs. If that wasn't enough, he ruled that they were Broome's property and had to be returned to him. He ordered Police Scotland to hand over the originals along with any and all copies both digital or in print. No mention of the photographs could be made in court or elsewhere.

By the time they returned to the courtroom, Leah

Watt had disappeared and so had their case. Whittle managed to argue for a continuation to allow Leah to be spoken to and confirm her evidence. And everyone knew she wouldn't. It was over.

Narey wanted to throw up. For herself, for Leah, for every woman that was in every one of Broome's photographs and every woman that might have been. *Shit.* Her bosses were going to go through the roof.

She was walking from Court Fourteen in a daze, her head trying to make sense of how they'd messed up so badly and desperately trying to think of a way to change things. As she stepped into the corridor, she almost walked straight into someone standing there waiting. Her peripheral vision took in grey hair and a black raincoat. The woman from earlier. This was all she needed.

'DI Narey. Can I speak with you, please?'

The woman was wide-eyed and anxious, so not what Narey needed to deal with. There was something manic about her. Narey had enough anger and agitation of her own without having to share someone else's.

She pushed on past her. 'No, I'm sorry. This really, really isn't a good time.'

The woman kept on at her frantically from behind. 'I have information that can help you. I know things about William Broome.'

Narey kept walking.

The stranger's voice went up an octave. 'He's done this before!'

Narey slowed, then spun on the spot. 'I'm listening.'

The woman took a deep breath, composing herself.

'My name is Lainey Henderson. I'm a rape counsellor. And I *know* he's done this before.'

CHAPTER 10

They sat either side of a table deep in the corner of the Victoria Bar in Bridgegate, two coffees cooling slowly between them. Narey had used the short walk across Victoria Bridge to try to call Leah but had got no reply. She left a message more in hope than expectation.

There was a young couple sitting just a few tables away and a small group of women chatting animatedly over a bottle of prosecco to the other side of the bistro. It was enough to make both Lainey and Narey keep their voices low.

'He got to her,' Lainey warned. 'Broome got to her while you were talking to the lawyer. I saw him.'

'What? He spoke to her?'

'Yes, but I don't know what he said. When you left her alone, Broome turned and said something. I couldn't hear it but I saw her reaction and she was terrified. I tried to go over but a lady cop stopped me. Whatever it was, it was a threat, simple as that. She got up and left the court. I didn't blame her because I knew exactly how she felt.'

Narey let that statement swim in the air for a while. Lainey Henderson had a story to tell and it would be better to let her tell it in her own time than drag it out of her. She'd been trying to get a read on the woman opposite her but was struggling. Narey thought she was probably anxious rather than nervous, angry rather than worried, but wasn't sure. She looked like she didn't sleep much or care that it was obvious. The dark rings under her eyes weren't covered by make-up but worn like badges of honour.

'I still resent the smoking ban,' Lainey announced. 'What's it been, ten years? Still doesn't feel right. I remember coming in here when it smelled like a proper pub. Not like this.'

'And when your clothes stank of it whether you smoked or not. And you got second-hand smoke whether you liked it or not. I prefer a bit of progress over nostalgia and lung cancer.'

'Each to their own. I could do with a fag, I know that much.'

She'd smoked one on the walk across the Clyde, puffing furiously while Narey was on the phone. They hadn't said much, little chance that they had, both trying to process what had happened in court. Lainey had a thick blue plastic folder wedged under her arm, clinging onto it like it was solid gold. It now lay next to her on the table and Narey's eyes kept getting drawn to it.

Lainey saw the look but ignored it, looking for answers in her coffee instead. Her hands were continually on the move, picking things up, putting them down, pulling at her hair and her clothes, constantly fidgeting, tap tap tapping on the top of the cigarette packet she couldn't open.

'I've known about him for thirteen years. I've been ... following him.'

Narey's coffee mug stopped halfway to her mouth. 'Following him?'

Lainey shrugged unapologetically. 'Not physically. I didn't know his name, not till very recently anyway. I didn't know who he was but I knew he existed, knew what he did. I've been keeping a file on him.'

Narey looked at the folder again but knew she'd be made to wait. Lainey told her story.

'In 2004, a man broke into my house, beat me and raped me. He left no evidence, no fingerprints, no useable DNA. No one saw him enter or leave. I could tell the police nothing other than an estimate of his height and build and what he did. They did nothing, could do nothing. I was told to get on with my life.'

She drank some coffee to buy some time, composing herself as best she could.

'I gave up my job, just couldn't handle being round people, round men. I couldn't concentrate, couldn't stand the thought of being touched or being in a relationship. I was a mess. A friend suggested counselling and that helped a lot. Helped enough that I retrained and actually became a counsellor myself. I'm not sure

I was ever the best counsellor in the world because I became angry too easily, too emotional. But I sure as hell knew what they'd gone through and I used that as best I could. I was still a mess in my own life – I got fat, I didn't trust anyone, I drank, I smoked too much, pissed off my friends and family, all the good stuff – but I was able to help others.'

She lowered her voice still further and Narey could see she was struggling to hold herself together.

'Then a woman, a girl, came for her first session. Her name was Jennifer Buchanan. She turned up black and blue, her eye cracked, her nose flattened. Just seeing her set off all my old anxieties. Then she sat down and told me what had happened to her. How a man had broken into her flat and beat her to a pulp then raped her. How he called her "slag" every time he punched her in the face.'

Lainey watched for Narey's reaction to that and saw what she'd hoped for.

'She was telling me all this and my head was scream-ing inside. She was describing what had happened to me. It was like she'd stood in the room and saw what the guy had done to me. Except he'd done it to her too. She told me her story and when she left, I threw up. I had to leave and go home.'

When Lainey paused, Narey found she'd nothing to say. She wanted to reach out, to console, to hug, but she already knew enough to know that wouldn't be welcomed. She could only sit and wait, smothered in the distant chatter and the silence at its heart.

'The way the support sessions work, when your name gets to the top of the waiting list you get a phone call to come in and begin counselling. I called Jennifer myself and there was no answer. We went to the address she gave us and there was no one there by that name. I hired a private investigator to look for her and she couldn't be found. This woman, who'd spelled out my own nightmare, had given a false name or disappeared or gone into hiding or something worse. All I knew was that if what she'd told me was true then the person who raped me had raped her and had probably raped others too.'

'Did you take this to the police?'

Lainey laughed in her face. 'Oh, brilliant idea. Why didn't I think of that? I *took* it to the police. *Twice*. And twice they weren't interested. Or not interested enough. Inspector, I tried to get your lot involved but they didn't want to know. So, I did it myself.'

Narey felt duly chastised. 'What did you do?'

'I knew he was out there, somewhere. I didn't know his name but I knew what he did so I began looking for signs of him anywhere I could. News articles, case reports, talking to other counsellors, to people I knew at Glasgow Archway. Looking for attacks that fitted the profile. I volunteered for more shifts, figuring the more hours I did, the more chance I'd hear something.'

'And did you?'

Lainey reached out and laid her hand on the folder in front of her, tapping it with her fingers. 'More than I wanted. And less. You know what I mean?'

Narey did.

'Some of these might not be him. I can't be sure. But I *know* that a lot of it is. None of it has ever been proven. Nothing has ever come to court. Until today. I never even had a clue to his name until now.

'Listen, Inspector. I know I look crazy. Plenty of people seem to think I *am* crazy. And you know what, maybe I am but I'm not making this stuff up. Everything in the file is real. This is nearly ten years' worth of work.

'I know the precise moment I began searching for him. Not from the time he raped me. Not even from the moment Jennifer Buchanan told me what happened to her, although that was what really started it all. I was still scared then, shocked to a standstill. It was when I found out Jennifer disappeared, or hadn't existed, or whatever her story was. That's when I knew I couldn't be prey any longer. Prey always ends up dead.'

She pushed the folder across the table towards Narey but then slapped a hand on it as the DI reached out to pick it up.

'I'm not just giving this away. I need to know you'll do something.'

'Then keep it,' Narey edged the file back towards Lainey. 'I can't give any guarantees. Not after today. Today, William Broome effectively walked free. I might well not even have a case against him that I'm working any more. I can't make any more promises that I can't keep.'

Lainey's eyes widened and she leaned forward in

disbelief. 'You're not seriously telling me the police are turning me away for a third time?'

'No, I'm not. I want to look at it. I want to know what you've got. Believe me, I do. But I'm telling you that I come with no guarantees, with no promises. Except one. I'll do whatever I can because I want that bastard put away as much as you do. I just don't know what I'm going to be allowed to do – today has changed everything.'

Lainey stared back at her for an age, her eyes locked on Narey's, looking for something she could trust. Finally, she lifted her hand from the folder, hesitated, then pushed it forward.

'I'm trusting you. With a lot.'

Please don't, Narey thought. *Please don't.*

CHAPTER 11

It was two hours after getting home before Narey could get close to looking at Lainey Henderson's file. The preceding time had been filled with Alanna.

There was a prolonged period of 'hey I'm home' time, which as ever was a mix of Alanna's relief and Narey's guilt, resulting in much hugging and kissing and discussion of how their days had been despite the lack of verbal communications skills.

There was play time and bath time, all classified as precious time. Someone must have switched the speed setting on those to overdrive compared to the long office hours without her. They flew by.

She never failed to be amazed at how her daughter was capable of pushing her close to laughter or tears or edging her heart close to bursting just by a smile or a giggle or doing something that probably wasn't that remarkable but seemed extraordinary in the moment. She was the mother she never thought she'd become.

Their little green-eyed ball of fun was now fast asleep and her attention could turn to the file. She poured herself half a glass of wine then, with a glance at the folder and thoughts of what lay inside, she topped the shiraz up to the brim.

With a final sigh, she flipped the folder open and began to work her way through it. Within seconds she was glad of the wine as inoculation against the horrors inside.

Lainey had been nothing if not thorough. Obsessive was closer to the mark but it sounded more critical than Narey meant it to be. This was missionary work and Lainey was a zealot.

She'd labelled her attacker, the man she thought responsible for Jennifer Buchanan's rape and the others, as The Beast. His name, his presence, was everywhere.

On newspaper clippings and typed-out A4 sheets, the word Beast was scrawled in highlighter pen or scribbled in the margins, sometimes with question marks, sometimes underlined twice, very occasionally in capital letters.

A woman named only as 'Cathy', the quote marks making it clear it wasn't her real name, had been spoken to. Interviewed would have been overstating it.

'Cathy' very nervous. No surprise. Didn't want to talk. Tried to slam door in my face. Terrified. Only spoke because I'm not police. Wouldn't talk about attack but agreed to answer one question, yes or no. Confirmed attacker called her slag while punching her. THE BEAST!!

It had been all she'd got from the victim but the rest was filled in with a brief client report that seemed to have been copied from files, most likely without anyone else knowing. Lainey had been taking risks.

Client CMcD. Age 28. Victim of home intrusion, violent beating and rape. Client has not reported crime. Says she will not go to the police. Refuses any persuasion to do so. Agreed to counsel without further reference to Police Scotland.

Lainey wasn't working entirely alone though. There was also a note suggesting help from an uni-dentified female police officer. Whoever she was, Narey approved.

WPC Goodcop says she attended Cathy in hospital after call from paramedics. Cathy wouldn't talk but was in very bad shape. Broken nose and cheekbone, fractured skull. Paramedics said someone had obvi-ously broken in and bedroom was like a war zone. Cathy wouldn't press charges.

Then finally:

Tried to talk to Cathy again. She'd moved. Neighbours no idea where she's gone. Said she didn't speak. Hope she hasn't taken same route as Jennifer B.

There was a cutting from the *Daily Record* from 2009. Court reporting on the trial of a man found not guilty of rape and assault on a twenty-nine-year-old Glasgow woman. Douglas McPhee walked free from court after a trial lasting eight days.

The jury had heard gruesome details of the woman's ordeal after a man, later identified as McPhee, broke into her house, beat and raped her. She had suffered a broken arm and ribs, suffered severe damage to her face and neck, as well as being raped.

McPhee was six feet tall and slim built. He certainly fit the physical profile of the descriptions that Lainey had collated. He had a previous history of nuisance calls – heavy breathers – and a caution for an attempted rape charge that never made it all the way to trial. However, he also had an alibi that stood up to the prosecution's attempts to demolish it. Five people said he was at Shawfield, the greyhound stadium, at the time of the attack. He even, conveniently, had ticket stubs of two losing bets.

The victim's right to anonymity was sacrosanct and correct, however much Broome protested, but right now it wasn't helping Narey's cause. She had advantages that weren't available to Lainey Henderson, though. She could, and would, call in every bit of intel that might help get a line on the woman who was attacked.

As she waded on through the file, more than anything she found case histories that had never got near newspapers or the police. Women whose courage had got them as far as a rape crisis centre and no further, although God knows the strength it took to do even that.

If there was any crossover at all with the profile of The Beast then Lainey was all over it. Some of it looked like a stretch to Narey's more dispassionate eyes but three of them were a much closer fit.

Anna C was attacked in her own home. She woke to the sound of breaking glass and didn't get as far as the telephone before her bedroom door burst open and a man rushed her. She couldn't be sure if he was masked or not, the room was too dark to tell. She thought he was probably tall but could only really remember his smell, an aftershave that reminded her of wood or bark or campfires. He hit her hard. He hit her often. He was speaking but she couldn't make out a word. She spent three weeks in hospital and had to have surgery to save an eye.

KD was a student at Glasgow University. She woke to find someone on top of her, a hand clamped to her mouth, the other alternately pinning her down and punching her. She slipped into unconsciousness quickly enough that she believed she'd been drugged with chloroform or the like. She woke to find she'd been beaten and raped.

D was also a student. She was studying late into the night, working towards a history degree at Glasgow Caledonian when she heard a noise in the bedroom of her ground-floor flat in Partick. She had a cat, a year-old tabby named Ed, who was wandering somewhere in the flat so thought nothing of it. When she heard another noise, catlike but wrong, she went to investigate.

She was grabbed as soon as she was through the bedroom door, her head bashed against the wall making her brain crash against her skull and the room judder and spin. As she hit the floor, she saw Ed, skull broken, lying a couple of feet away. Hands grabbed her again and threw her on the bed.

'Hayley' seemed to be one of Lainey's own counselling clients. Both the levels of detail and secrecy were higher. The notes suggested Lainey had spoken to her directly but they were sparse, only half a sheet of A4.

Hayley endured a classic Beast attack. Woke to the sound of glass, intruder burst into her room and punched her repeatedly until she was unconscious. She was raped several times.

Hayley ended up in a coma and had to endure protracted surgery. The little description she was able to give to the police matched the height and body shape of The Beast.

Then, seemingly later and in a different pen, were updates.

Hayley is feeling stronger physically, if not yet emotionally.

Have convinced her to report the attack. Incredibly brave decision on her part to do so. The Beast damaged her but hasn't broken her.

Every case, every report, had Narey horrified. Sure, she was professional, she'd done her job long enough to know how to safeguard her emotions from the worst of it, but it tore at her. It was a catalogue of wickedness.

Lainey's dossier also held cases that Narey really struggled to link to Broome or The Beast, assuming they were one and the same. But they were no easier to read for that. Latest figures showed three sex crimes reported in Greater Glasgow every day – that added up to a thousand a year.

Miss SM had been drinking with friends in Bath Street, leaving them to walk home alone to her Merchant City flat. She was walking by the entrance to St Vincent Lane, one of the many narrow, dimly lit lanes that criss-cross the city centre, when her arm was caught and pulled, a hand clamped over her mouth to silence her. She was hit repeatedly, punched into submission, before being raped and left unconscious. An hour later, she was found wandering dazed and bleeding by a young couple walking home. She remembered her attacker calling her a fucking slag as she was hit.

Miss TN was a runner, in training for a summer 10k. Her regular route took her through Bellahouston Park. Her mother and her fiancé had warned her often enough, asked her to run somewhere else, but she was fearless and headstrong, why shouldn't she run where she wanted? She was skirting past trees not far from the Palace of Art when the masked figure stepped out and knocked her to the ground. She took a kick to the guts and one to the head before she was dragged out of sight. She remembered him as being around six feet tall and slim, his balaclava was black. She never ran again.

The file was like wading through a sewer. The stink of it was dripping from Narey and sending her into despair.

She thought about her own wee girl, wrapped up in Peppa Pig pyjamas. She thought about William Michael Broome. And she went back to read the file through from the beginning again.

CHAPTER 12

Leah's anonymous statement was made through her lawyer. Delivered by him to the Crown Office and leaked to the press. Narey's hurt was that she only got the news with the rest of the world. Her anger was at the damage the statement would cause.

It was short, simple and straight to the point.

I am the person identified as Miss W in the court case brought against William Michael Broome.

It was only when in court that I realised, beyond any doubt, that Mr Broome was not the person who attacked me. I made a grave error. I categorically state that I made a mistake in identification and that I alerted the police to the wrong person.

I apologise fully and sincerely to Mr Broome. I deeply regret any damage done to his reputation and hope that he can forgive me.

This case should never have come to court. I shouldn't have made the mistake but also, the police and Crown Office should never have let it happen. I was wrong and they should have known that.

The shit and the fan were on a direct collision course.

CHAPTER 13

The bitter taste of disappointment was still curdling her stomach when word came through that Broome and his lawyer were to make a statement on the steps of the court. Cops and the Fiscal's Office swore loudly and journalists rushed to Carlton Place.

When they got there, they found Arthur Constance in his element. A free opportunity to grandstand and no one to tell him to play nice. He positioned himself and Broome at the top of the steps with the court in the background and the assembled press below. They could have held their press conference anywhere but Constance wanted it to look like they'd just walked free and vindicated from the arms of injustice.

'My client has committed no crime, broken no law and yet his name has been dragged through the courts and the mud for all to see. This public humiliation has been incredibly trying for him and he has borne unspeakable stains on his good character without the opportunity to defend himself. Even now, he has been deprived of his day in court where he could and undoubtedly *would* have proven his innocence in this matter beyond any doubt whether reasonable or otherwise.'

Constance was building himself up into a crescendo of righteous indignation.

'And yet, while he has been forced to endure an iniquitous and very public slur, his accuser has been allowed to hide under the veil of anonymity. This is a travesty which goes against the very fibre of natural justice and the inevitable consequence is that women like this are given free rein to make spurious and unsubstantiated allegations, to cry rape, against decent men like my client. It is a poor interpretation of the law that cannot offer the same protection to men from outrageous accusations as it does to those who lie for their own gain.'

There was a collective murmur among the press, the noise that signalled they knew they had a story. The sound had no regard for whether what they heard was accurate or right, only that it would make a headline. Tony Winter recognised it for what it was, an easy page lead that would come with the scaffolding of inevitable outrage. It didn't prevent him from wanting to tighten Arthur Constance's tie till he squeaked.

Constance was nodding gravely at the press, sure that they all understood the obvious truth of his statement. With that, he retreated two steps and let Broome take the stage.

He was dressed in a navy-blue suit, red tie neatly in place, hair brushed perfectly, his face a picture of hurt.

He stood looking at the ground, seemingly composing himself, milking the moment for all it was worth.
Finally, he lifted his head and began with a tremble in
his voice and a shake in the hand that held two sheets
of A4 paper.

'The law, such as it is, prevents me from being able
to challenge, far less name my accuser. She has the
freedom to say what she wants, claim what she wants,
with no consequences for her but incredibly traumatic
and quite undeserved consequences for me. However,
the law does allow me to name, and indeed shame,
those who colluded with her to bring this sham case
to trial.'

Winter looked up from his notebook, pulse quicken-
ing, dread souring his mouth.

'And I am going to take that opportunity today.
Detective Inspector Rachel Narey of Police Scotland
saw fit to bring to court a case with no evidence,
with no motive and with no chance of prosecution.
She took the side and the word of a woman who
lied, who concocted a fake story for reasons known
only to herself. My accuser may be mentally ill and if
that is the case then I can have *some* sympathy with
her. However, I can have no sympathy for the officer
who blindly believed her despite all indications to the
contrary, who took up her cause with the ferocity
of a suffragette, who enabled this woman in her lies
and madness.

'It is my personal view that Detective Inspector
Narey could not see beyond the possibility of the

CRAIG ROBERTSON

woman being right and the man being wrong. She has been conditioned to always believe the woman, to always condemn the man. Truth and justice are easy victims when it comes to blind hatred of men. There was a time, I'm sure, when women did not have equality in society but that has gone so far the other way that men are increasingly the victims of miscarriages of justice and of blatant prejudice. I am living proof of that.'

Winter could barely wield his pen because of gripping it so tightly, strangling it in anger. Broome was getting a taste for his lies and wasn't finished yet.

'Detective Inspector Narey is the epitome of what is wrong with the law and society today and I intend to bring a civil case against her for defamation. I *will* have my day in court and she will have to answer to that. This woman lied when she came forward to hurt me. The event never happened. It was a total fabrication. I can't sue the liar but I can sue the woman that chose to bring the lies into court.'

Some of the other reporters shot sideways glances at Winter. Their notebooks were full, as were their front pages and news bulletins, but they all knew he was married to Narey and all twitched at the prospect of a response. One look at his face left them sure they'd only be told to fuck off. He was raging.

When Constance announced his client would answer a few questions, it was Winter who was at the head of the charge. The anger in his voice was controlled but obvious.

'Mr Broome, you say DI Narey couldn't see beyond a woman being right and a man being wrong. Is that not in itself defamation of someone who was only trying to do her job? How can you seriously believe that men are so prejudiced against? Surely a rape victim has the right to—'

'*Right?*' Broome worked himself up to a fury. 'Why should she have *rights* and I have none? She can just say what she wants, you think *that's* right? And as for Narey only doing her job, that slag—'

Constance stepped forward in front of Broome and Winter felt two arms grip him by the elbow and side and hold him firm. *Don't say anything. Leave it, Tony. Don't rise to it.* Sympathetic voices restrained him.

'I think we've taken that line far enough, ladies and gentlemen. Any other questions?' Constance narrowed his eyes at Winter, seeming to recognise him but not being sure. He continued to look while other questions came to his client, less demanding lines, ones not designed to wreck the story but to support it, sensationalise it.

When Broome was done with it, pontification over, he and Constance left and the journalists switched off their recorders and closed over notebooks. They formed an instinctive huddle to discuss what had happened and Winter strode into the middle of it. He didn't know them all but recognised most. Not that it mattered. He was going to say his piece regardless.

'Listen, I asked those questions as a reporter, same

as you. But I'm not part of this story. If anyone quotes me by name then I will cut your fucking nuts off and feed them to squirrels. Do you understand me?'

They did.

CHAPTER 14

'He won't sue. He can't and he won't. It's just noise. He can't take the chance of suing me for fear of what might come out in court. But he'll say it often enough and loud enough that people will believe him.'

'People that want to.'

'Exactly.'

Winter and Narey sat with a clutch of newspapers in front of them, the *Standard* included, pages open at the coverage of Broome on the steps of the court. Her name was plastered all over them.

Broome's claims were shouting from headline after headline. His accusations, his promises of legal action. All meat and drink to the press. Fuel too for pressure groups, men's groups, who suddenly saw Broome as some kind of oppressed Messiah. There were quotes from them, screaming how Broome was right, how unfairly men were treated, and how the courts and the police were all against them. Her name was brought up again and again.

The main group quoted, Men for Equality, said

Narey should be sacked and called for Police Scotland to do it right away. They looked forward to her being sued and imprisoned. In the meantime, they would not let up until 'justice' was served.

The online attacks had already started.

The Police Scotland Twitter feed had been inundated with offensive tweets and #SackNarey was trending for a while. Someone had also discovered her police email and it had found its way onto one of Men for Equality's online forums. From there, her mailbox was flooded with abuse until she got the tech guys to shut it down. She didn't read any after the first few but it was obvious the trolls were all men, mostly young, all embittered.

Some of them had found her Facebook page and even though all her settings were at private, meaning they couldn't see anything, they had invaded the Message Request folder and dropped their poison there. She deleted them without reading but it still felt like someone had broken into their house.

He continued to read the newspapers while she went to the desk to see what the news sites were making of it. Just because she knew it was a masochistic torture didn't mean she could resist.

'They'll haul me off what little is left of this case,' she called to him. 'It's the same as a journalist, when a cop becomes the story then it's time to change the story.'

'If that happens, then these fuckers win. They can't decide the narrative. They can't get to choose who investigates what. Some angry teenager sitting wanking in his bedroom doesn't get to decide who runs the world, he doesn't get to have someone sacked just because a girl laughed at him or got the job he wanted.'

'They're keyboard warriors, that's all. Impotent, angry little boys. Best ignored.'

'Yeah maybe. Or kicked in the stones.'

She went silent for several minutes and he sat reading and shaking his head at the madness of it all. When he heard her sigh heavily, he looked up to see her staring at the laptop. When she spoke her voiced was laced with despair.

'Well there's certainly plenty of angry wee boys.'

'What now?'

'You don't want to know.'

'Yes, I fucking do. Let me see.'

She leaned back and he walked over to look at the screen from behind her. He was immediately confused by what he saw.

'I don't understand. You don't have a Twitter account.'

'Well, I do now.'

'I'm not sure I ...'

'Someone has set one up for me. Kind of them, huh?'

Her photograph was there. DI Rachel Narey as her handle. The clues were under the profile pic.

Detective Inspector for Police Scotland. Bitch. Slag. Liar. Manhater.

Joined December 2017.

'What the hell is this?'

'Someone has set up a fake account. Got my

photograph from somewhere. And look, I've got over a thousand followers already. All men.'

'Christ.'

'No, he's not one of them. Quite the opposite. I've made a few tweets. *I'm sorry for trying to ruin William Broome's life. I'm a liar and I hate men. I knew that bitch was lying but I didn't care.* That sort of thing. But most of the traffic is in the form of replies. Mainly threats.'

He tried to keep his voice calm. 'What kind of threats?'

'The actionable ones aren't from real people. The ones saying I should die. Or should be raped. Or that I'd be raped and I'd like it. Or that I should have my tits cut off. Those ones are anonymous – just vile, macho bullshit nicknames they've dreamed up for themselves. They could possibly be traced but it would take a long time and a lot of work for not much return. The real ones, the ones that just call me a bitch – and oh, a lot of them call me a bitch – they're not going to get prosecuted, maybe a warning at best but probably not even that.'

Winter didn't want to but he read the tweets he could see on the screen, all directed @DIRachelNarey.

> You should have your tongue cut
> out BITCH

> I'm going to rape the fuck out of you!

Dont close ur eyes cos am wait to
kill u

Hater! U should get sacked bitch

Hope u die slow and painful u
fucking slag

You will get raped for real and no one
will listen you LIAR

'The standard of grammar among these fuckwits is appalling,' she said matter-of-factly. 'I blame the schools.'

'Don't joke about this, Rach. I'm not finding it funny.'

'You think I am? Click on the banner photograph.'

He reached past her and did so. The picture expanded from a slightly blurred light-brown to full size. It was her. Except it wasn't. 'She' was naked, legs wide apart, staring at the camera and smiling. Her head photoshopped onto some porn star's body.

'I'm going to kill someone.'

'Not yet,' she told him 'There's also this …'

She moved the mouse down, scrolling past tweet after tweet until she found the one she was looking for.

I'm going to rape and kill your baby

He said nothing but she heard his breathing stop. The lack of shouting scared her, betraying the true depth of his rage.

He put both hands on her shoulders and squeezed gently, massaging her silently for a full minute. Then he let go and she could hear him turn and walk away.

'Where are you going?'

'To hug my daughter.'

CHAPTER 15

Three of them sat in a silent office, waiting for the chair behind the desk to be filled. Three overgrown school-kids anxious to discover which of them was in most trouble. They might as well have hung a sign reading *Headmaster's Study* on the door.

Narey. Addison. Detective Superintendent Helen Connarty, head of the National Rape Task Force. All awaiting the imminent arrival of Deputy Chief Constable James McInally at his office in headquarters at Tulliallan.

Addison was fiddling with his mobile, unconcerned with his fate or pretending to be. The two women were more obviously apprehensive. Narey was expecting the worst.

She'd messed up. The case had gone to court and was going to be shown not to have been fit for pur-pose. That would all come down on her. Leah didn't testify. That had been her job and she couldn't finish it. McInally was unlikely to be happy.

She knew that Helen Connarty was likely to be there

107

hoping to take what was left of the Broome case over to the NRTF. Connarty came with a big reputation and was said to be a formidable operator. Narey had wanted to meet her for a good while but this wasn't the way she'd envisaged it.

The door opened and McInally was halfway to his desk before they'd fully realised he was there. His opening sentence seemed to have begun on the other side of the door and all pleasantries were finished with by the time he sank into his chair.

'. . . late but there are too many fires needing to be put out for me to be anywhere on time today. Okay let's get on with this and try to clear this shit up so we can all get some real work done.'

Most officers that got anywhere near McInally's rank were politicians, but he'd worked his way up from the beat without ever forgetting its language or where he came from. He was one of three deputy chiefs and he oversaw crime and operational support. He'd not only call a spade a fucking shovel but he'd happily hit you over the head with it too. With his shaved head and lean features, he was an intimidating prospect.

'The Fiscal's Office is thoroughly pissed off with us. Your Mr Whittle has been complaining about our prep. The press think we're idiots. And there are people in offices above mine who might just agree with them. Can someone tell me they're wrong?'

Narey began to speak but McInally cut across her.

'Not you, Inspector. Not yet anyway. I want to hear what your colleagues think first.'

She bit her tongue, nodded and waited for judgement to be pronounced. Addison stepped into the breach first.

'We could have done better. No one's arguing otherwise. But everything was done in good faith and professionally. Broome wriggled and his snake of a lawyer got him off the hook. It's not what we'd hoped for but we regroup and figure out another way to get Broome. The will is certainly there in the Major Investigation Team to put him away.

'Sir, the bottom line for me is that if DI Narey couldn't get Watt to testify, then I don't think anyone could. And I'd still like her to be leading any investigation going forward.'

Narey thanked Addison internally but saw McInally looking back at the DCI blankly, not convinced and wanting more. He was a hard man to please.

'Helen?'

The task force chief cleared her throat. 'First of all, we'd like to have been more involved in this from the start, not just now when things have fallen apart. We have specific knowledge and experience that could have been put to good use here.'

Narey might have argued but for knowing Connarty was right.

'I don't know Detective Inspector Narey personally but I'm very much aware of her and I've heard nothing but praise for her work. Clearly the court case was a disappointment and we had been hoping to see some action on the photographs that were discovered. We still are. They have a lot of potential for us.'

'*Had*.' McInally bared his teeth. 'Those photographs are off the table and there's no real prospect of them returning.'

'Sir—' Addison and Connarty started together.

'No. The judge was clear. Whether we like it or not, Broome has got the photos back and we better make damn sure every copy is disposed of. The chief has made it clear he's embarrassed and angry about this. He won't be bitten by it twice.'

'Sir,' Addison persisted. 'Broome may have been responsible for—'

'Derek, we don't know that he was responsible for anything. He took photographs. That's all we know. And as we no longer have those, the matter is concluded anyway.'

'Then what's the point of this meeting? Sir.'

Narey willed her boss to shut it. There was no point in him being a white knight only for the deputy chief to ram his lance up his arse.

'The point, *Chief Inspector*,' McInally leaned forward and stepped on Addison's rank like it was a bug, 'is to establish whether anything can be salvaged from this clusterfuck and what disciplinary action, if any, is required. Is that okay with you?'

'Yes, sir. Although I don't think there's any need for disciplinary—'

'Fucksake Derek, any chance you can stop digging a hole for yourself? That's my job.'

'Sir.'

McInally shook his head at Addison before swinging

it round towards Narey. He studied her just long enough to give her the fear.

'Inspector, this whole mess has become an arse kicking contest and you're at the end of the line. I've been briefed on the threats you've received – and I'm genuinely sorry and angry about those – but I have to regard it entirely separately from the issues with the Broome case. You'll have to take your lumps on that.'

'Understood, sir.'

'Good, because you fucked up. As Helen rightly says, your case record is excellent and that's what's saving your arse now. But you cannot go back into court with everything hanging on the testimony of someone who you're not certain will actually turn up and go through with it.'

'Leah Watt had to—'

McInally held up a hand. 'I'm not saying I've got the first clue what she went through or what it took for her even to get as far as she did but I am saying none of that matters. *All* that matters is whether we are *sure* she will deliver when it comes to it. And we got that wrong.'

'Yes, sir. And I'm sorry for the mess it caused.'

He waved the apology away. 'Just get it right next time. Make sure you learn from it. What we need to sort is what, if anything, we can do now. I'm aware that you all came in here ready to argue your case for going on with Broome but I'm not sure any of you will be winning that argument.'

'We're giving up on Broome?' Narey blurted it out.

McInally sighed loudly. 'We're not giving up on him,

Inspector. But we need to have something else to work with. Those photographs, whatever they were, are off the table. If you want to build a case against Broome then you have to go back to square one. You can't use the photographs and you can't use Leah Watt. And in that scenario, I suggest you need to show you have something concrete to justify spending time on him at all. God knows we have enough to deal with without chasing causes we can't win.

'Sir, there is a potentially massive case here. Each of the women photographed could represent—'

'Inspector, as I suggested to DCI Addison, the key word there is potential. Right now, we have nothing. We don't know that Broome has done anything other than take photographs. Yes, we could show that he's followed these women and yes, that could constitute stalking but that's not enough for me to allocate the hours it would need. And we *don't* have the photographs, anything obtained through them will be thrown out by a judge, so we have nothing to work with. He's already embarrassed the force once with no little help from us and I'm in no hurry to see him do it again. Any case that is initiated against him will need to come with a cast-iron guarantee of conviction. Frankly, I do not see where that is coming from.'

Narey was ready to pitch in again but Addison silenced her with one look. McInally saw it and approved.

'Okay, I'm going to leave you three here to discuss it for a while as I've got more shit I need to deal with.

If you can find a way we can all live with then let me know what you've decided. The leash on this is a very short one if there's no prospect of a result. And remember, this is my office, don't steal anything and don't make a mess.'

When McInally left, Connarty had seniority and she assumed it immediately.

'Okay, let me be honest here. Not very much of this makes me happy. Far from it. I came in here wanting the Broome case but, to be honest, after what McInally said ...'

She shook her head and sighed, falling back in her chair. 'Now it suits me more to let you have it, Rachel. Politically, this could create problems for me that I really don't need. We've been warned off from this and while my instinct is to tell them to shove it and throw everything at Broome, I just can't.

'I've got the whole task force to think of, not just this case. I need the sympathy of courts and sheriffs and judges in ways that you don't. I simply can't afford to piss them off. *You* can stick two fingers up to them because if you come into court with enough evidence then it won't matter a damn if they're on your side or not. Evidence is only half the battle for us. We need them to believe it too.

'So, you run with it. McInally isn't going to let you run far or long unless you produce so you better make it happen quickly. If you need anything, then ask. If I'm at arms' length, then I'm protected and the task force is protected. Keep me in the loop and I'll give what I can.'

CRAIG ROBERTSON

'Okay, that suits me. I want it.'

'Wanting it is all very well,' Addison chipped in. 'But it's not enough. Without the photographs your biggest lead is in the bin. Before we leave this room, we need a plan. And we're going to have to get creative.'

114

CHAPTER 16

Narey's phone rang as she sat at her desk in Stewart Street, Giannandrea's name showing up on her screen.

'Yes, Rico?'

'Boss, you need to take a look on Twitter. It's not good news.'

'Oh Christ, what are they saying now?'

'It's not you, not this time. All due respect, it's worse. Leah Watt's been publicly named as Broome's accuser.'

'Shit! I'll call you back.'

She scrambled to bring up Twitter on her laptop, about to type Leah's name into the search function when she saw that she didn't have to. #LeahWatt was trending.

She felt sick to her stomach.

> Lying bitch who made up story about
> William Broome is #LeahWatt
>
> Cry wolf, cry rape. Broome liar is

called #LeahWatt. Let her know she's
a #liar

Send Leah Watt to jail for lying in
court #LeahWatt #bitch #liar

Leah Watt is the Broome case liar.
Bound to get raped for real now

Narey picked up her phone and called Leah. As it rang,
her eyes couldn't help but follow more tweets.

See they've named the bitch that took
Broome to court. Leah Watt. Lying
Twat more like

Anyone know this lying cow Leah
Watt? She needs to feel the burn #liar
#LeahWatt

The call rang and rang.

The Glasgow rape liar is called Leah
Watt. Spread the word

No one will believe #LeahWatt
when she gets raped. That's called
karma bitch

It went to voicemail.

'Leah, it's Rachel. Give me a call back when you can. Don't shut me out, please. I'm here for you.'

They'd named her. The bastards had actually named her.

It was a gross violation of the law and her right to anonymity. If it had been done by a newspaper or a TV channel then someone would already have been charged with contempt of court and an editor or reporter heading for jail. Instead it had been done by some malevolent shit who she knew might not be traced.

She called Giannandrea back.

'I want whoever did this, Rico. Are we on it?'

'I've already spoken to Grant Whittle at the Fiscal's Office, telling him we want this shut down and to get on to Twitter with everything he's got. He's as angry about this as we are.'

'Oh, I seriously fucking doubt that.'

'I've been on to the techs. They're able to separate out tweets and are working their way back to find the first offender. The problem is that it's already spread fast and it's spread far and wide. It's growing as quickly as they can cut its legs away.'

'Rico, every person in Scotland that retweets that or posts a tweet with Leah's name in it is breaking the law. And that's even before we get to the threats.'

'Yes, boss, but with all respect, you know we're not going to get anyone into court for retweeting it. The best we can hope for is to identify the initial culprit and hammer them. *If* they're real and *if* we can find them.'

As he was speaking, she'd refreshed the #LeahWatt feed. Three tweets down, there was a post that took her breath away.

Giannandrea heard the noise she made.

'What's up?'

'Someone's tweeted a photograph of Leah. I think they might have ripped it from her Facebook page.'

'Jesus.'

'Those shitty little bastards. Get back on to Whittle. Now. I want these taken down. I want every tweet deleted. No excuses. And I don't care what time it is in America if that's where the HQ is. Wake up whoever needs to be wakened and get this done.'

She heard the unspoken irritation in Rico's pause before he answered.

'I'll make sure everything that can be done, is done. But it's already elsewhere on the internet, on places we won't be able to shut down. If they're outside Scotland, they're not breaking any laws and we can do next to nothing about it.'

She sighed heavily. 'I know, Rico. I know.'

She phoned Leah again and the call was terminated immediately. She tried again a few minutes later and the result was the same. She sent her a text. *Call me. Please.*

Five minutes later, her phone beeped. A text from Leah. Just one line.

Leave me alone.

CHAPTER 17

Winter was driving home from the *Standard* office, crawling along Great Western Road in nose-to-tail traffic. He'd have been quicker walking but had a boot full of camera gear plus a couple of large packs of nappies that would have taken a lot of juggling.

He was in a bad mood to start with and the congestion wasn't helping. He wasn't usually quick to bang on the steering wheel but when a car three ahead blocked up the junction, he snapped and hammered on the horn. All it succeeded in doing, of course, was rousing a retaliatory chorus from those who thought he was beeping at them. It made everyone feel a little better for a handful of seconds.

Turning on the radio to drown out the impatience all around him, he found himself half-listening to talk radio, some shock jock blasting out from his pulpit. It flowed over him far faster than the traffic, only really jolting into his consciousness when he picked up on keywords.

Men haters. Rights. Rape. Fake news.

The other voice, the guest, wasn't familiar but it took him just moments to work out who it was.

'I was put on trial, shamed in front of the world, for something I hadn't done. They had no case, no evidence, the court saw that in a matter of minutes and threw it out. But you've got to ask how it got that far. How the hell did this farce ever get as far as court? Because the police officer in charge of the case was a woman. Simple as that. She'd made her mind up, as soon as she heard her sister's sob story, that the man had to be guilty.'

William Michael Broome.

Winter's hands tightened on the wheel and he blasted his horn again for no reason that the cars around him could possibly understand.

'There's no way a male police officer would have made the same decision. He'd have been detached and professional and seen that there was *no* evidence. But no, this DI Narey just ignored the facts and wasted time, public money and my reputation. Quite honestly Phil, it's disgraceful. This woman is a … a …'

'I've heard people use the word feminazi,' the host offered. 'Is that maybe what you're thinking of?'

'Yes! That's exactly what she is. And she should lose her job for it. She clearly isn't capable of doing her job properly. But the Crown Office is just as bad, letting this get as far as it did. Someone there should get sacked too.'

'Well, I have to agree with you William. But do you think it might be a problem that the head of the Crown Office and the Procurator Fiscal Service is the Solicitor

General, and the Solicitor General is a woman? I wouldn't want to suggest she was anything other than impartial, of course.'

Broome's voice got louder. 'Of course she's not impartial. It's a political appointment and that makes everything about it political. She's a woman trying to keep women happy by perpetuating the myth about the number of rapes that they say take place.'

'You don't think the figure is as high as they say?'

'Of course it's not. I've read that it's less than ten per cent of what the feminazis claim it is. The mainstream figures are just fake news. It's practically impossible for it to be that high. They are taking every false claim, counting them as real and multiplying by ten. I should know, it's exactly what happened to me. This Leah Watt woman—'

'Whoa, I've got to stop you there, William.' Phil the shock jock didn't seem too fussed at all, but was having to go through the motions. 'Right or wrong, that young lady's identity is protected and we're not allowed to name her.'

'Well it's wrong!' Broome protested. 'It's very wrong. Leah Watt made false allegations against me and the law doesn't protect my name, doesn't keep my name secret. She is . . .'

Phil let out a small laugh, like he was dealing with a cute but misbehaving infant. 'William, William. I know you're angry but we really have to obey the law on this one. Sometimes the law is an ass but you still have to give it carrots, you know what I mean?'

Winter couldn't take any more and slammed his hand against the radio button. It was only when the speaking stopped that he became aware of the cars raging all around, horns blaring directly at him.

A green traffic light was staring him in the face, perhaps four car lengths in front. He'd missed the cars moving, being so wrapped up in the bile seeping from his radio. As a gesture of apology, he blasted his horn before stamping on the accelerator and lurching forward.

CHAPTER 18

'Tea or coffee, Rachel? I could do with something stronger but for some reason they're against me bringing gin in.'

Helen Connarty's otherwise sparse office was dotted with family photographs. Small family groups, her and what was presumably her husband plus two children at various ages. The boy and girl smiled out of frames on the desk and on shelves next to bound books, from toddlers to teens. Narey had little doubt it was an attempt to anchor some sense of normality amid the swamp Connarty had to wade through. She declined the offer of a hot drink.

Connarty fell into the chair behind her desk with a heavy sigh. Her face was lined and the dark circles suggested a distinct lack of sleep.

'Christ, I'm done in. I didn't get into this to be a bloody politician but it feels like that sometimes. I've been explaining strategy to a Holyrood committee and it was like describing Brexit to four-year-olds. Except the four-year-olds would have pretended to listen before throwing a tantrum.'

The Detective Superintendent kicked her shoes off and pushed back into her chair. 'Heading up the task force is so different from anything else I've done. It's like being constantly knackered and yet energised at the same time. You know what I mean? Being drained by it but ready to go again.'

'I do ma'am. It's the same on the Major Investigation Team. A case gets a hold of you that you work till you're ready to drop but you just keep going.'

Connarty nodded. 'Exactly. Except don't bother with the ma'am stuff. The door's closed. Call me Helen. You ever thought of a move, Rachel? Away from the murder squad?'

It took Narey by surprise. She'd never thought of a switch, what she did was in her blood. At least until Alanna was born.

'I'm happy doing what I'm doing. Never say never though, I guess.'

'How's your daughter doing?'

The timing of the question meant Connarty either read her mind or had thought this out beforehand. Either possibility was a bit unsettling.

'She's great ma'am ... Helen. Developing her own personality and not slow to let you know how she's feeling.'

'Yes, I remember that stage. Wonderful, isn't it? Mine are both in their teens and they certainly let me know how they're feeling. I'm guessing it would be good to always get home before she goes to sleep and be there when she wakes in the morning, right? We're not exactly nine to five in the task force but we're more regular than you're used to. We could really do with someone like you on the team.'

'Someone like me?'

'Dedicated. Determined. Smart. Caring. Professional. A woman.'

'Thanks Helen but I'm not ...'

'Do you know how many sex crimes are reported in Scotland? It's now over ten thousand a year. The highest it's been in forty-five years. Other crime is at its *lowest* since the same time but rape and sexual assault have gone up.'

'I know the statistics but—'

'Do you? Do you know how many rape victims in Scotland are asleep when they're attacked? One in five. Twenty per cent of them. Sure, they're not all like Leah Watt, their homes might not be broken into, but still, one in five are sleeping when some guy decides to help himself. I'm not having that, Rachel. Not on my watch.'

There was a crackling intensity to Connarty. Words and numbers spat out of her.

'And the fact that reported rapes have gone up five per cent? That's the only bit of good news. It's not rape that's risen; it's reporting. If we're making women more confident that they can come forward, that they'll be taken seriously and that the rapist will be put away, then we're doing our job.

'You've not been with us but you've been around long enough to know how much things have changed. We've made huge strides, Rachel. The way we work is night and day from what it used to be. And thank Christ it is. We failed them before, the victims. We let them down time and time again. Historically, it was a disgrace. Not just in Scotland but the rest of the UK too and probably most of the world.

'I've worked damned hard to make sure every cop in every cop shop in Scotland knows they can't be the way they were. They know they have to treat victims with dignity and respect. They have to be thorough no matter who's involved, no matter where it's happened. Our focus is the victim, no matter whether it was a husband, a boyfriend or a stranger who attacked them. The old boys' way of doing things is finished.'

Narey knew it was true. Processes had been over-hauled, focuses had been shifted. Maybe it still wasn't all it could be but it was unrecognisable from how it was.

'Do you remember the John Worboys case?' Connarty was in full crusading mode now. 'Multiple rapist who drove black cabs in London.'

Narey did, although not much of the detail. What she did remember was that two of Worboys' victims had successfully sued the police for not properly investigating their complaints.

'I remember two victims came forward, the police did next to nothing and the women later sued the Met.'

Connarty's face twisted. 'Of course that's what you remember. It took getting sued before the force sat up and took any bloody notice. What you *should* remember is that John Worboys raped and sexually assaulted over a hundred women in a five-year period. You *should* remember that if the Met had done their job, taken the first woman seriously, then another seventy-four women would have been spared what they went through. If they'd done their job properly when the second victim came to them in 2008, when they actually arrested the bastard and let him go again, then another twenty-nine women wouldn't have been attacked. All we have to do, is do our fucking job.'

It stung and it was probably meant to.

'Are you saying I didn't do my job and that's why Broome is back on the street?'

Connarty didn't blink. 'I wasn't flattering you when I listed your qualities. That's what I hear from everyone I talk to. First-class cop. Would make a first-class asset to the task force. Most likely with a promotion thrown in. But we have a problem and that problem is William Michael Broome. I'll tell you this right now, Rachel, he's not going to be my John Worboys. I won't let him be. He gets put away or he gets forgotten about, no middle ground.'

'Him being put away is exactly what I want. You said I had a reputation for being determined and I am. I don't give up on something lightly. Something like Broome I don't give up on at all. Give me the chance and give me time and I'll bring him in. And this time—'

Connarty interrupted her with a raised hand.

'It's not as simple as that. Everything we do is as much about perception as it is reality. You can go into a courtroom and it doesn't matter if a judge or even a

127

jury likes you or hates you. As I said to you before, if you've got enough evidence, you can get your conviction. I need more than that. I need them onside, need them believing me.

'Do you know why the reported rapes are up? Because women are beginning to trust that we'll treat them with respect, that we'll take every report seriously, that we'll act on it and justice will be done. It's all about giving them the confidence to come forward. Every case that goes wrong dents that confidence and sets the reporting rates back further. You understand?'

'Yes, ma'am.'

She understood all right. This wasn't all about girl power, no sisters under the skin, no call me Helen, no job offer. This was about making sure Narey knew she couldn't afford to mess up. There was far too much at stake for everyone.

CHAPTER 19

The house on Belhaven Terrace was asleep, or at least its inhabitants were. A building of that age never fully slept. It slumbered at best, groaning and creaking as it breathed in and out. The same noises were there during the day but passed unnoticed as the world talked and walked and wondered. In the dead of night, they reverberated. Whether the squeak of a loose floorboard or the rumbling rumour of wind in the attic, an old house was never truly silent.

That was maybe why neither Winter nor Narey paid any attention to the phone on its first ring. It was another mid-night sound to add to those they'd learned to ignore. Winter stirred on the second ring as it seeped into his dream and pulled him out.

He sat up, shaking the sleep from his head as he tried to gather thoughts. The clock next to the bed read 2.14. There was never good news at that time of the night. His mind did calculations, worst case scenarios forming. He stretched a hand out to his left and was relieved to feel her lying next to him.

He heard the third ring echo on the extension in the hall, next to the baby's room. Damn. Alanna would be awake in no time.

He lifted the receiver, head fog slowly clearing.

'Hello?'

The sleepiness meant he wasn't sure if the line went dead as soon as he'd answered or whether there was a gap. The click woke him though. He was trying to process if it was good news or bad that the call had ended, thinking maybe someone had changed their mind about how important it was when he hadn't answered immediately, when he heard Alanna start to cry.

'Whassit?'

Rachel was more asleep than awake, barely able to form a sentence, looking at him through half-shut eyes.

'It's Alanna,' he half-lied. 'I'll get her. Go back to sleep.'

She mumbled something that might have been 'thanks' and rolled back over, leaving him to head to the baby's room. Alanna was standing in her cot, holding onto the side and emptying her lungs.

'Come here, darling. It's okay, it's okay.'

He lifted her up and cradled her to him, her head at his shoulder so he could whisper in her ear. 'Did the bad phone wake you up and give you a fright? Yeah, it scared daddy too. But it's okay now. Probably.'

He excused himself on the basis that she didn't know what the words meant. Probably.

The crying stopped but there was no way she was going back to sleep. He tried to put her back down but she complained immediately, forcing him to scoop her up in his arms again and walk round the room talking to her.

The phone call plagued him. Did the caller hang up just as he answered or after he'd spoken? He wandered into the hall, shifting Allana's weight to his left shoulder so he could pick up the phone, dialling 1471 to see who'd called. The automated voice informed him that the caller had withheld their number.

He paced the bedroom, his daughter chuntering away in her own language, enjoying having daddy to herself while the world slept. Or some of it.

The phone rang again, cutting through the night like a chainsaw.

He strode out of the bedroom towards the hall, conscious of not scaring Alanna but desperate to get to the phone before her mother did. It rang three times, four, and he thought he was making it but when he was two yards away, it stopped.

Rachel's voice was faint from the other room then rose. '*Hello? Hello?*' He heard the chink of the phone going back into its holder.

When he got into their bedroom, she was sitting up, clearly irritated but still only half-awake.

'Was there anyone there?'

'No. Went off just before I answered it.' She gestured towards Alanna. 'Is she awake?'

'Only just.'

'Just bring her in. Come here, baby girl.'

The three of them snuggled. Rachel and Alanna

asleep within minutes, Winter staring into the dark, listening. Sometime in the next half hour, he drifted into that half-world between sleep and dreaming. That's how he was when the phone rang again.

He caught it on the second ring, awake enough to hear the disconnect click just as he picked up. He checked for the number but, of course, there wasn't one to be had.

'What the hell is going on?' Rachel demanded. 'If this happens again I'm going to rip that phone off the wall.'

'Probably kids.'

'Yeah. Maybe. Maybe big kids. One more and I'm phoning it in.'

'Why don't you go sleep in the spare room? Take Alanna with you. I'll deal with the phone.'

She didn't argue, just lifted her sleeping child from the bed and left, only stopping in the hall to bend down and pull that phone from its socket.

Winter wasn't going to sleep this time. He switched on the bedside lamp and sat up, watching the digital numbers turn on the alarm. As they slowly moved over, glowing red in the half-light, he watched them edge to 3.29 and felt a buzz of expectancy.

His hand hovered over the phone, waiting. At 3.30, on the dot, it rang.

He had it to his ear immediately. When he heard the line was live, he knew he'd beaten the caller to the punch.

'Who is this?'

There was just silence, maybe a surprise at getting caught out, but there was breathing. There was definitely someone on the line.

'Who's there?'

There was laughter. High-pitched, slightly manic giggling. It was out of control, coming from booze or drugs or madness.

'*Who the fuck is this?*' he kept his voice low but the anger was unmistakeable.

There was silence again, other than the sound of the person breathing. It was broken just enough to say one thing before the line clicked dead.

'Bitch is gonna die.'

CHAPTER 20

Winter's desk in the *Standard* office faced the door. His news editor, Archie Cameron, figured that was appropriate, as his photo-journalist lived in constant danger of being asked to leave through it. Except he put it more colourfully, suggesting that one more fuck up and Winter's arse wouldn't stop till it bounced onto Waterloo Street.

It suited Tony though, giving him first view of anyone coming in while having his own back to the wall and avoiding anyone seeing his screen over his shoulder. Not that he particularly had much to hide but it was still better not to have everyone know you're on Facebook or football forums half the day. The other half he was looking at photographs of his daughter.

The first couple of weeks, he took maybe a hundred pics a day of Alanna. Mainly of her sleeping because that's what she tended to do. Except when they didn't want her to. He slowed down when he came to realise that although she was indeed a miracle and the most beautiful child ever seen, not every second of her life had to be chronicled on film.

Lately however, he'd started up again in earnest as she began to do things which were actually interesting. Like laugh and play and crawl and look cute. She was especially good at looking cute. His plans for her later life included being prime minister, a total ban on dating men until she was over the age of sixty or her father was dead, whichever came first, and being the first astronaut to land on Mars.

Nothing that he'd ever dreamed for her included threats on her life or her mother's.

His first reaction to the caller's message had been to assume it was referring to Rachel. *Bitch is gonna die.* Then he wondered, fretted, if it meant Alanna. The troll's Twitter message haunted him. *I'm going to rape and kill your baby.*

First thing that morning, Rachel had rung the station and reported the calls, ordering traces on the numbers more in hope than expectation. Winter had hesitated about telling her the wording of the last message, thinking that one of them freaking out was enough. It wasn't a time to hold anything back though.

She'd just nodded, grimly professional, sizing it up for whatever it might be, kissed them both then gone to work. In a sense, he envied her. She could do her job and protect their family. He had to do his and it was nothing more than a distraction.

He used his time to go through the fake Twitter feed, partly to torture himself, partly to find something, anything, that might give him a clue as to what was going on. He half hoped to read one of the little bastards boasting about the phone calls, give him somewhere to start. There was nothing.

He'd do something to protect them though. He simply had to.

The email that popped up on the screen interrupted his flow. The sender's 'name' was just a string of letters and numbers. R568dh389sl8w@hotmail.com. The subject field had been left blank.

Who the hell was this and what the fuck were they sending him? The file was huge. Had they never heard of a zip file?

He hesitated before opening the email at all. Common sense said he shouldn't. Spam. A virus. Porn that could get him sacked. There was no shortage of reasons to be cautious but if he only opened it and didn't follow any links then he'd be fine. Probably.

He glanced over to Archie Cameron's office, where the news ed had his face buried in his own screen, a hand rummaging through what was left of his hair. Archie was occupied enough that he wasn't going to see anything and while Winter knew that wasn't quite enough to keep out a hack attack, it would do for now. He opened the email.

There was one folder inside. File name BROOME.

Christ, what now?

Winter leaned back in his chair and considered it. There were still plenty of reasons to be cautious. The aresholes online, the ones sending the filth through

Twitter and on the men's group website, they were more than likely capable of sending something that would do some major harm.

Why would it come to him though? Surely they'd launch that kind of attack against Rachel instead. His finger poised over the button, ready to open it.

Someone knew their home phone number though. A number that was under his name. Anyone that could figure that out must have known their relationship and could easily have got hold of his work's email address.

Fuck it. There was only one way to find out.

He clicked and opened and was assaulted by the appearance of photographs. Hundreds of them. All women.

There was no virus, no trojan horse. Just jpegs of unidentified young women. Late teens to early thirties, he thought. None of them aware they were being photographed. Familiar backgrounds in many of them. Glasgow.

They were Rachel's photographs, obviously. Broome's photographs.

All she'd told him, and all he knew, was that incriminating photographs had been found in Broome's house, that they'd formed a vital part of the case against him but had been thrown out. He'd asked what it was but she wouldn't tell him. Maybe now he knew.

He looked at the sender field again. Almost certainly made up for the sole purpose of delivering this one email and no way of tracking who sent it. It was a gift horse with its mouth wide open. All he had to do was avoid looking in.

He got up from his desk, slipped out of the front door and downstairs onto the street. It teemed with traffic and people rushing from one place to another. Suits and overcoats, briefcases and umbrellas, the central business district reflected in glass-fronted buildings.

Shit, he should have put a coat on. He'd been fooled by the winter sun and the rush of receiving the photographs. The gale blowing up Waterloo Street towards Central Station soon reminded him it was December.

He had his phone in his hand, her number on the screen and conflicts running though his mind.

If this was the evidence that could convict Broome, then he had to play it for all it was worth. A rapist, certain to be guilty from everything that Rachel told him, and a huge collection of secretly taken photographs of random women on the streets of Glasgow. It read like an entire city of potential targets.

He'd only been a journalist for two years, even though it seemed so much longer. But in that short time, if he'd learned anything it was to know a story when he saw one. This one looked like a story, smelled like a story and quacked like a story. Big time.

But it wasn't just as simple as that. It was Rachel's case, it had been *her* evidence. Now it was his and that had all sorts of potential implications, only some of them good.

He could find out the back story to the photographs without asking her, there were enough people who would give him that information. The bigger problem was telling her about it.

His finger wavered over the call button, dithering and debating. Damn it.

It rang for a while before she picked up, reluctantly so by her tone.

'Tony, sorry but I'm up to my ears in it. What do you want?'

He could hear a hubbub of voices in the background, a squad room full of cops probably. He started and stopped and chickened out.

'I'm just making sure you're okay.'

She sighed. 'I'm okay. I'm at work, doing what I do and I'm okay. I'm a big girl and I'm busy.'

'Rachel, I love you and you're the mother of our child. After last night, I think I'm entitled to worry a bit, don't you?'

He heard a soft laugh. When she spoke again, her voice was muffled and he knew she'd put her hand over her mouth so the squad didn't hear.

'Okay. You can worry about me. Just occasionally though. I really am okay and I love you too. This is the best place for me, at least I'm doing something. Is that really why you called?'

She knew him too well. 'Yes, just being a doting husband and father.'

The pause was laden with doubt. 'Okay, go away. I'll see you at home.'

He ended the call, screwing his eyes shut and swearing at himself for not telling her. Sure, it was easier this way for now but he knew it was simply storing trouble up for later. The wind howled at him again, forcing him back into the building. He took the stairs two at a time, running back to his desk and the hoard of photographs that demanded his attention.

He was still running when he charged through the office doors and nearly ran full pelt into Archie Cameron, who was standing just a few feet inside the door, squeezing the life out of a mug of coffee. Cameron had to step back and a couple of dollops of his brew splashed onto his shoes.'

'For fucksake, ya bam. Want to watch where you're going? I should rip your heid aff for that.'

To say Archie's bark was worse than his bite would have been a wild understatement. He talked the talk but couldn't batter a fish supper. Winter knew to let him be, though.

'Sorry, Archie. Sorry. Just in a bit of a rush.'

'Jesus Christ. Don't tell me you've actually got a story. Wait till I take a seat, the shock might be too much for me at my age.'

'Piss off, Archie. Aye, I've got a story. Well, the start of one.'

Archie liked to play the old-school arsehole but he also knew his stuff. He smelled the story in Winter's words. His eyes narrowed and nose wrinkled like an alcoholic at a sniff of Buckfast.

'Something good?'

'I think it could be. Could be very good. I need to check it out.'

'Too right you do. Go get it. Once you know what you've got, come talk to me. And stop running about like a teenager trying to get his first shag. Just makes you look daft.'

'This could be worth it though, Archie. Could be worth every bit of it.'

CHAPTER 21

Narey had spent much of the day on a fruitless trawl into what they had on Broome that might sustain a fresh investigation. She urgently needed something that would enjoy enough confidence from the top brass that they'd allow her to go after him again.

Lainey Henderson's file promised more than their own casework but it was still strewn with ifs and buts, wishful thinking and leaps of imagination that McInally wouldn't give the time of day.

It had been the day after the night before. A perfect hangover of frustration following the phone calls and the threat. *Bitch gonna die.*

She'd come home, got on the outside of a glass of shiraz, and pretty much collapsed. Tony had a couple of phone calls to make but that was it, any further work talk was banned. She'd kissed her sleeping daughter, hugged her fretting husband then locked the world outside. Their front door was their portcullis on the madness and it was slammed shut. There was no way in other than through the phone line.

She was lying on the sofa, her head in his lap, a TV show playing that neither of them could have answered two questions on if quizzed there and then. It fluttered by them in shades of mediocrity, a time-filling, conversation replacement service.

The doorbell rang and they both jumped.

Unannounced visitors were rare. Those calling at just after ten at night were unheard of and unwelcome. Coming after the night of phones calls, the bell sounded like an alarm.

They looked at each other, sharing mutual shrugs and creased brows.

'Stay here,' he told her. 'I'll go.'

'I don't need looking after,' she reminded him.

'Just do me a favour and let me go. You're the tough nut but I need the practice. Pick up something heavy just in case.'

'Don't joke, you dick. I don't like someone being at the door at this time of night.'

He didn't answer but strode across the room and headed for the front door. She was irritated and called after him but he ignored her.

She heard voices in the hall, one raised, the other quieter, arguing. The louder, more urgent voice was Tony's. The other was familiar but her nerves were jangled and that fact didn't reassure her any. Both voices were coming closer.

She took a few steps to the fireplace and grabbed the heavy metal poker that formed part of an ornamental set. If she needed to, she'd use it.

The door to the living room swung open and Tony walked through it. Someone was behind him and she squeezed the handle of the poker, feeling its heft in her hand. The other figure took two more steps and came into view. The poker became slack in her hand.

'Uncle Danny? What the hell are you doing here?'

The man grinned and held open his arms. 'Aye, nice to see you too, pet.'

Danny Nielson was Tony's uncle, an ex-cop and a father figure for both of them.

'Sorry. We're both just a bit ... I mean, it's great to see you!'

They hugged, her hanging on for a bit longer than she would normally. It didn't go unnoticed.

'So, how are you? How's my goddaughter?'

'She's great. She even sleeps sometimes. Go through and see her.'

'I will, I will. Can't wait to see her. But first things first. How are *you*?' His face screwed up in concern. 'I know about all these threats, the online stuff and the phone calls. Are you doing okay?'

She looked towards the door, seeing the two large holdalls that Danny had brought in with him. They sat there, begging questions.

'No, I'm not doing okay at all. What's this all about? What are you doing here, Dan?'

'Can't I come visit my—'

'Why are you here? One of you, tell me now or I'll skin both of you.'

'Danny is moving in. Until this all blows over. I'm not arguing about it. It's happening.'

She rolled her eyes theatrically. 'Oh, did you two white knights dream that up all by yourself to save the poor damsel in distress here? It's okay that you never thought to discuss it with me first because my opinion doesn't really matter that much, does it? What were you thinking?'

Tony wasn't budging.

'Are you finished? I told you, this is happening. I was going to discuss it with you tomorrow but Danny obviously decided not to wait. And maybe that's for the best because you would've just argued. So he's here, bags and all. He's staying. It makes sense and it might be the only thing that does right now. You're working. I'm working. I don't want to leave this place empty for long. They know our phone number so they know our address. And yes, I know, most of these nutters will never leave their bedrooms but I'm not taking any chances. It's not just you, Rach. It's Alanna too. I'm not happy with just the sitter being here. We need Danny.'

'And I'm happy to be here . . .'

'Shut it, Dan. I'm talking to him. Sorry, sorry, I didn't mean to say it like that. This is all just so hard. Look' – she wiped at her face – 'I know you're worried. I'm worried. We're all worried. But these guys will do nothing. They are just keyboard freaks. Trolls, nothing else.'

'Can you be certain of that, Rach?'

She hesitated for an age. 'No.'

'Then Danny's staying.'

She exhaled. Beaten. 'Okay. Okay. Jesus, Danny, come here.'

The two of them hugged again, neither in a hurry to let go.

'So,' Danny looked at them both. 'Can I say something now? Rachel's right. They are wee boys who wouldn't say boo to a goose in the real world. Tony's right. We can't be sure. If you can put up with me leaving half-filled cups of coffee around and using up the last of the milk then we'll all get along fine.'

'And not putting your dishes in the dishwasher,' she reminded him.

'Aye okay, that too. Look, can I go see Alanna now that we're all sorted?'

'Yes, go. For God's sake, try not to wake her up though. And Dan? Thanks. I'm a moany cow but I'm grateful. After the day I've had, you're just what I need.'

'Rachel, I love you guys and you know I'll do anything that's needed. Just keep some beers in the fridge and don't call me a nanny and I'll be a happy man.'

Danny went through to the nursery, leaving them alone. They held onto each other, saying nothing.

'It's just a precaution,' he whispered eventually. 'Just to be safe. Those creeps won't do anything.'

'No. Of course they won't.'

They'd all been in bed for a couple of hours when the phone rang. Winter answered it but the whole house woke.

The line was silent but it was still live, still someone

there. Winter had decided not to say anything, maybe force them into speaking and revealing something.

It didn't work. There was nothing other than a sense of someone breathing, maybe some background noise but too faint to be sure what it was. After ten or fifteen seconds, the line clicked dead.

He shook his head at Rachel, indicating nothing had been said. Her fists were balled and he had to put his hand on hers to suggest she cool it. She was about to argue with him when they heard Alanna's cries.

Danny had beaten them to it. When they got to her room, the big man was walking in a slow circle, her face nuzzled into his shoulder.

'Thanks, Dan.'

'Are you kidding me? I'm not sure anything could make me happier than holding onto this wee one. Actually, the only thing that makes me happier is that she lets me.'

'You're lucky. She won't usually go to anyone else. She knows you love her.'

'Oh that I do, pet. That I surely do. So, tell me about the call.'

'The usual,' Winter told him. 'Saying nothing then hanging up. They've only spoken that one time.'

'I'll sort it,' he assured them. 'I can get the numbers traced quicker than the force can. I'll put in a call to a friend at BT. They'll be either phone boxes or pay-as-you-go mobiles. These cowards aren't brave enough or quite stupid enough to use their own phones unless they're burners.

'I'm also going to get you a call blocker. I'll have it by lunchtime. Basically, every time you get a call you don't want, you press the button and they're permanently blocked. It won't help us catch them but it means you'll get some sleep. They'll run out of phone boxes or burners very quickly.

'After that, I'm going on Twitter. These ...' he glanced at Alanna and chose a different word, 'idiots are more stupid than they know. They'll leave clues. And I'll find them.'

'Better that you find them, Dan.' Winter could barely stand still. 'Because if I do then I'm likely to kill them.'

There was another call just ten minutes later, then another half an hour after that. The final call, silent and lingering, came a bit after three.

The next day proved Danny to be right – the calls came from three different numbers. Two phone boxes a half mile apart in Battlefield on the south side and a pay-as-you-go that would be near impossible to trace.

The cops kept an eye on those phone boxes the following night but saw nothing that tied in with the four silent calls that woke them in the wee small hours. Winter pressed the block button and shut them out. There were just two the night after that. Then only one the next.

For three days, they had peace, but then it started again. Three or four of them a night and once they were traced they turned out to be much further afield. First Edinburgh and Dundee, then the north of England, then the south. The callers spiralled out as the viral hate grew in bigger and bigger circles.

In the end, they had no choice but to change the number, giving a new contact out only to those that needed it. It meant giving in to them, but it meant getting peace.

Before then, though, the first set of trolls had new ideas.

CHAPTER 22

It was too late to change Leah's mind, Narey knew that full well, but she still had to speak to her. To say sorry, to say don't worry, to say she understood. To say she'd still get him. Or at least that she'd do her damnedest to.

It had been her job to get Leah into court, to fill her with the confidence to do it and hold her hand every inch of the way if necessary. But it was more than her job. She'd made a contract with Leah, a deal beyond cop and victim. She'd made it personal. She'd invested in Leah and she'd promised she'd do it for *her*. As a friend. And she'd meant it.

She'd heard cops round the station sniping about Leah's change of heart, bitching about the statement claiming she'd been wrong about Broome all along. They hadn't been where she had though, they hadn't suffered what she had. They were wrong to think Leah had let them down. It was entirely the other way round.

Narey made the journey once again to the Watt family home in Knightswood, in the far west of the city. A nice semi-detached on Archerhill Gardens, a decent place to grow up. Narey wasn't sure Heather and Charlie would be all that pleased to see her but she'd no choice. She had to speak to their daughter.

She parked on the street and saw the curtains twitch as she got out of the car. The front door opened before she got to it, throwing light onto the darkness of the path. Heather Watt standing there, arms folded across her chest, her face like a kettle ready to boil. The body language wasn't exactly welcoming.

'Don't you think you've done enough damage, Inspector?' The woman's voice was just loud enough for Narey to hear, trying to keep it from the prying ears of nosey neighbours.

'I just want to talk to her, Heather. I just need to let her know I understand.'

The woman's eyes narrowed, suddenly confused. '*Talk* to her? You're a bit late for that. Haven't you heard? I thought that was why you were here.'

A surge of panic rose in Narey's stomach. 'Heard what? What's happened?'

Leah's mother looked left and right, seeing who was listening. 'Come inside. Now.'

Narey followed her inside and found the door firmly closed behind her. Leah's dad Charlie was walking down the stairs to join them, looking like a man bereft. Narey's heart sank further.

'She's gone,' Charlie told her. 'Leah's gone.'

The mother's hand rose to her face, covering her mouth and her grief. Her husband, a thin, balding man in his early sixties, his face in a daze, took her in his arms and hugged her.

'Charlie, what do you mean she's gone? Where is she?'

'You tell us. You made this happen. You told her she should go to court when she didn't want to. When none of us wanted her to.'

'Where *is* she?' Narey repeated.

'Gone. Just gone,' he told her. 'We phoned your lot an hour ago. Isn't that why you're here? Come to finish the job off.'

'When did you last see her?'

The Watts looked at each other. Heather answered. 'Late this morning. She went into town, said she'd just be half an hour, but never came back. We told her to stay in. We'd have got anything she needed. We've called her phone a dozen times and there's no answer. She's gone.'

Narey pulled her own phone out of her pocket and called Leah's number. *The number you have called is currently unavailable.* Dead battery? Phone switched off? Neither seemed a positive option.

'What did Leah take with her? Did she take a bag, anything of any size?'

Heather shook her head. 'Just a handbag. A large one but nothing other than that.'

Stay calm, Narey told herself. *It might still be nothing.*

'What was she wearing?'

Charlie looked lost. 'I don't ... Damn, I don't know.'

152

'Jeans and a chunky, dark-green polo neck,' Heather told her. 'And a heavy black waterproof with a hood.'

Narey made a note of it. 'Have you tried her flat? In case she's gone back there.'

'She wouldn't.'

'*Have* you?' She cursed herself for biting at the parents but couldn't help herself.

'I went down there,' Charlie barked back. 'I knocked on the door and rang the buzzer but there was no one in. My wife's right. She wouldn't go there. I just wanted to check to make sure. She's gone. Somewhere.'

Narey hated to think just how far away Leah might actually have gone.

'I'll check the flat myself. Just in case. But I need to look in her room first.' She saw the look of resistance on the mother's face. 'Heather, this is important. I need to look.'

Mrs Watt said nothing but nodded her head in the direction of the stairs. Narey didn't need to be invited twice.

The bedroom looked as it had done. Kitted out for late-teens Leah rather than the woman she'd become. Narey rooted through drawers and the wardrobe, all packed with clothes, no sense of a planned evacuation.

On her bed, half-hidden under a pillow, she found Oliver, Leah's owl. The soft toy she loved, kept for luck and wouldn't be parted from, her guilty childhood pleasure that she clung to. Now more than ever.

Wherever Leah had gone, she hadn't intended to go there.

*

Leah's ground-floor flat in North Kelvinside was empty. A young woman from the letting agents' opened it up for Narey and Kerri Wells. They searched the place but had barely crossed the threshold before knowing they were the first to spend any time there in months.

The flat was cold, heating running no more than intermittently to guard against frozen pipes. There was dust on the surfaces, not something Leah would have let slide. Junk mail was piled up on a table, placed there by staff from the agency who checked once a month and forwarded anything that looked genuine to her parents' address. The kettle was stone cold, the fridge was empty, the bed hadn't been slept in. It failed every test.

Narey stared out of the window onto Garriochmill Road, cars wedged into the few available parking spaces. The area was called North Kelvinside or sometimes Kelvinbridge, probably depending on whether you were trying to buy a house or sell one. Either way it worked for the likes of Leah, who wanted to be in the West End but couldn't afford the genuine article.

Leah hadn't been here, hadn't run for a bolthole as obvious as this one.

Had she run further? Had she run at all?

She ordered up checks on Leah's bank accounts, wanting to know if she'd used an ATM or bought a rail ticket or a flight. Hoping she had, fearing she hadn't. She'd got a list of friends and was having each of them called, reaching out in optimism. She made sure the hospitals had been called too. And the morgue.

Her mind had long since spun to Lainey Henderson's story of the client who mirrored her own rape trauma. Jennifer Buchanan. The woman who wasn't who she said she was. The woman who'd disappeared and was never seen again.

The potential witness to William Broome who'd disappeared off the face of the earth.

CHAPTER 23

Winter had a new office. Of sorts.

He'd needed somewhere he could work on Broome's photographs, somewhere with wall space and privacy. Home was out and so was the *Standard*, given the need to keep them away from both Rachel and other reporters. So, he'd rented just about the cheapest bit of property he could find, a room above a pub in Partick.

It had been a flat but knocked into three separate small office spaces off a central hallway. He'd taken out such a short lease that the landlord must have thought he was using it as a knocking shop or a drug den but still took his cash. It was beyond basic but would do a job.

Below him, on Dumbarton Road and opposite the bottom of Byres Road, was the Three Judges. It promised to be a place of refuge if the photographs proved too much.

He fixed both a whiteboard and a corkboard to one wall, brought in a set of file folders and cleared a space for his laptop and a printer. All he needed was the answer to the question that bothered him most.

Where the hell was he going to start?

There were hundreds of photographs on the desk in front of him. He'd made a print of every photo that had been sent to him and looking at them now was over-whelming. Unknown face after unknown face, each of them a story, each of them possibly the key to whatever Broome had done.

It's like eating an elephant, he tried to tell himself, *just take it one bite at a time.*

There was just so much of it though. So many of them.

He needed to glean anything and everything he could from the photographs, even though there seemed to be precious little to go on at first sight.

Those who had been photographed most frequently seemed likely to offer the best chance of that. He intended to identify those, place them on the wall and make them the focus of his search.

He'd file them into broad groups to begin with. Start with hair colour, separate the blondes from the bru-nettes from the redheads. Then he'd divide the blondes by age or shape until he got down to those that appeared most often. It would work, with one exception.

He lifted one of the prints from the stack, holding it up to the light. It was the photograph where the wom-an's face had been cut out. Except, being just a printed copy of the digital image, it showed a solid white where the face had been.

Winter took a pair of scissors from a drawer and began cutting along the lines of the marks on the print. He knew this one had to go up on the white-board, whether the woman appeared again or not. She was key.

He made his last cut and stuck the photo on the wall, its centre raggedly cut away like the original.

Okay, let's get going.

The woman with no face looked down on him as he worked.

He already knew there were 524 photographs. In the time he'd had to look through them, he thought that maybe somewhere around twenty women had appeared multiple times.

Sifting through them, quickly separating the blondes from the pack, he tried to make it a cold, calculated operation, but the faces defied being ignored, challenged him to see them as more than hair colour, more than objects to be sorted. *People. We're people.*

He couldn't help but think of war photographs. It was like looking at innocent bystanders or boy soldiers in uniform, you knew what was coming and they didn't. He thought of images by Robert Capa or Alexander Gardner, the Scot who photographed the American Civil War. They had the same sense of care-free foreboding, with a dark cloud hanging over them that they couldn't see.

These women were – hopefully – all alive and well, yet there was still a clear and obvious feeling of dread. The fear all belonged to him though, not the subjects of the photographs. It was *for* them not felt by them.

Like this young woman who was in his hand now. One of the blondes. She was sitting on the steps in front of the Royal Concert Hall at the top of Buchanan Street, lunchtime sunning on a warm day. Her head was tilted back to catch the rays, her eyes closed and a smile spread across her face. She was very pretty, obviously happy and content in the moment. And oblivious to the man who was photographing her.

Who was she? Had Broome followed her there or had he just chanced upon on her and liked what he saw? Did she ever see him, meet or talk to him? Maybe they worked together or had mutual friends, maybe he never saw her again. She couldn't have been any more than twenty-five, probably a year or two younger. Doing nothing more than enjoying some rare Glasgow sun. And she became prey.

She was someone's daughter. Probably a sister, girl-friend or wife, work colleague, friend, maybe a mother. Broome had reclassified her with one click of a button. He'd made her prey. He'd objectified her. Made her a target. And then what?

Damn. This was going to take a long time if he focused on every woman as he was doing this one. The only judgement he had to make for now was if she was blonde, and she clearly was. He needed to wear blinkers and push on past this.

She was just sitting there, minding her own business. Looked like a nice person, nice smile. She deserved better. They all did.

It struck a chord and he realised he'd seen her

already. He rummaged through the pile of blondes until he produced another print. It was her. Different day though, different clothes, different weather for sure. Same smile. Different haircut.

The background looked like the West End. A corner of a shop sign peeped into view and looked very familiar. He thought it was Cresswell Lane, near the arcade. It was a start.

He placed the two photos together at the edge of the blonde pile and continued.

It turned out there were 197 photographs of blondes of varying shades. Twenty-six of them appeared more than once. Of those, twenty-one featured just twice. The remaining five were found in no less than sixty-two photographs.

Each time one of them appeared, his heart sank a little further. They represented weeks of photography, day after day of obsession in multiple locations.

He pinned one photograph of each onto the whiteboard. These five were where he was going to start.

There were seven photographs in all of the smiling woman in front of the concert hall. He'd christened her Smiley Susan, thinking he'd need to call her something. In five of them, she seemed dressed for work, business-like but not overly formal, perhaps suggesting working in an office or a school. She was alone in some shots, with friends in others. Seven photographs taken on six different days.

In just one of them did she face the camera. A full-on, posed head shot. It very obviously had not been taken by the same photographer or at least not in the same way. He was sure it had been lifted from her Facebook page.

The same thing had been done with Blonde-bob Barbara and Little Lisa. Their personal Facebook pages had been invaded and their photographs stolen, no doubt along with whatever information Broome could garner from their pages.

Winter hoped it was a strange kind of good news, reasoning that if Broome could trace them through Facebook then so could he.

Blonde-bob Barbara looked like her new name suggested. Dyed-blonde hair cut close to her face. She smoked, enjoyed a cigarette and a chat standing outside The Counting House on St Vincent Place and in the beer garden in front of Sloans, off Argyle Street. She was also smoking as she strode down Hope Street under an umbrella, the shops in the background flagging where she was. Barbara was in her early twenties, a girl about town, switching between business suit and skinny jeans. Day to night, a camera following her.

There were fourteen prints of Barbara. Fourteen different occasions.

She was about five feet five, seeming taller in her heels, slim, always well dressed, fashion conscious. She could have been any one of a thousand young women in Glasgow. And yet she wasn't. She was the one that he'd taken more photographs of than anyone else. She was target number one.

He spotted a badge on her lapel in a few of the prints

and had it blown up till he could see what it was. A circle with three lines dissecting it. The peace symbol and logo for CND. Another fragment of knowledge about her, another chance to find out who she was.

He reckoned that Little Lisa Picasso was no more than five feet tall. A bundle of obvious energy even in a still photograph. She wore electric shades of red, orange and green, loud in-your-face fashions that screamed her personality. She was small with bigness bursting out of her. She might have been a student but seemed slightly too old to make that likely. He thought she was something artistic. Designer or painter or an office girl with a poet's soul.

Lisa Picasso wore her blonde hair up, wore it down, wore it in pigtails. In each of the eleven photographs of her, she had a different look entirely. Enough that he had to inspect them all carefully to make sure it was her and to guarantee he hadn't missed any. She was pictured in the city centre, on Bath Street and coming out of Princes Square. There she was outside GoMA, and inside too. She was in a bar he didn't recognise but was sure he could find, all wood and low-beamed ceilings, shouting hipster makeover. And there she was on her Facebook page, smiling at the world.

The two other blondes were quite different. Both were elegant, expensively dressed types who never stepped out of character. In their early thirties, the way they looked was clearly important to them and probably to their jobs. Heels, tailored skirts or business suits, hair and make-up perfect. They could have been sisters even though they'd most likely never met.

Sister Sara was mostly seen in the West End. Sister Mary shopped and drank and walked around Merchant City and the thoroughfares off Buchanan Street. Sister Sara was taller and curvier, Mary was as slim and straight as her stiletto heels.

Were they company executives, art gallery directors, restaurant managers, bankers or jewellers? Always on show. Not just for their customers or employees but for whoever was watching as they sipped coffee or walked to subway stations.

Winter suddenly realised he'd had enough.

He was doing what Broome was doing. Labelling them, dehumanising them. Blonde this, brunette that. Big, small, slim. Like they weren't real people. It felt like he'd been dragged into Broome's world and was playing by his rules, thinking how he thought.

It was different though, he had to remind himself of that. *He* was different. He might have to think like Broome to work out what he'd done and what he might do next but that didn't mean he was like him. This guy wasn't wired the way other people were.

He couldn't afford to get caught up in the process or be bothered by it. Only the end result mattered.

He had to wade through shit to get out of the sewer.

CHAPTER 24

'Dan, I need your help with something.'

'Name it, Rachel.'

'That trick you pulled to get the numbers of the calls in the middle of the night? Your contact who can trace things. I need him to get me something. Fast. I don't have time to fanny around doing things by the book and waiting for warrants and phone companies.'

'It's a her but it won't be a problem. Just make sure you cover yourself by also getting it done through channels.'

'Christ, it's not my first week. I do know what I'm doing, Danny.'

She closed her eyes and took a breath. 'Sorry. Again. Look, Leah Watt has gone missing and I'm terrified that either she's done something stupid or Broome has got to her. I need to know where she was yesterday, not just calls she's made but where she was. And I need to cut corners. Your contact, she can triangulate from masts or whatever it is and give me some locations, right?'

'If it can be done, she can do it. Just give me the girl's

number and leave it with me. But listen to me, this isn't your fault. Go find her but don't do it out of guilt.'

'You don't know that, Dan. Even I don't know that. Right now, it sure as hell feels like my fault.'

While waiting for technology to do its stuff, Narey did what she knew best. Old school. Feet on the pavement and knock on doors. Sure, her phone was burning hot with the calls in and out but if Leah was out there then there would be someone who'd know where she was.

The 'if' hung over her, a dark cloud waiting to tip down in buckets. If it fell, she'd drown.

Leah had been a hairdresser until the rape, working out of a shop on the south side. She'd tried to go back part-time a few months later but it was just too public – too many knowing looks between the customers, too much tea and sympathy from the staff.

She'd packed it in and did temp office work when she could get it. It suited her not to be in the one place for too long, before word got round.

Her best friend still worked out of the same hair-dressers, though, and Narey wanted to pay her a visit. Cover Girl sat next to the Rum Shack on Pollokshaws Road. Across from another bar, along from another hairdresser's, near another bar, near another bookies.

Narey saw Shazia Karim through the window and said a silent thanks for the first bit of good news in a while. She'd met Shaz once before and remembered her ferocious protectiveness of Leah, a bond forged through secondary school and on through college to

the world of boyfriends, broken engagements and prosecco pick-me-ups.

A bell sounded as Narey entered the shop, causing
Shaz to look up from the blonde hair that was loop-
ing through her left hand. Recognition became alarm
became anger. The woman in the chair yelped as her
hair was tugged. Shaz held up a finger, signalling Narey
to wait. In a flurry of snips she was done, the poor
customer left as half cut as anyone in Heraghty's pub
across the way.

'Through the back,' Shaz snapped. She was a beautiful girl with large, haunting eyes and long hair so dark
it almost had a hue of blue under the lights. Beautiful
but fierce.

She closed a door firmly behind them, a violent tug
on a light pull revealing a small kitchen with a formica
table and three odd chairs. A kettle was brewing huff-
ily on a worktop and Shaz stared at it as if deciding
whether politeness overruled anger. It clearly didn't, as
no offer of tea or coffee was made.

'So, where is she?'

'Shaz, I'm hoping you can tell me. Have you heard
from her, anything at all?'

The chestnut eyes flared and for an instant, Narey
thought one of the mugs on the worktop was going to
be flying in her direction. Shaz settled for holding on
to it, just in case.

'I wouldn't even be in today except we're short and I
couldn't get the time off. I was going to tell the old cow
to ram her job but then I realised I didn't know what

I'd do anyway. Go knocking on doors, go to the places we'd go? I didn't know where to start.

'All I know is she's not answering her phone. It goes straight to voicemail without ringing. It's switched off or the battery's dead. You're the bloody police! Where *is* she? What the fuck has happened to her?'

'When did you last speak to her, Shaz?'

The younger woman was nearly strangling the mug to death by its handle. Her other hand was squeezing the life out of the worktop edge.

'Two nights ago. The night before she ... when she was last seen. We spoke on the phone.'

'How did she seem?'

'Down. Angry. Pissed off at you. Scared too, I'd say. She never said as much but I heard it in her voice. But she wasn't ... I didn't hear anything that made me think she'd run off.'

'Do you think that's what she's done? Run off?'

'I'm fucking *hoping* that's what she's done! I'm terrified to think it's something else. If that bastard has hurt her again ...'

The handle snapped in her hand, ceramic splinters crashing onto the work surface and one slicing into her palm. 'Shit!' She ripped off sheets of kitchen roll and wrapped her hand in a makeshift bandage.

Narey strode over and despite some resistance, took Shaz's hand in hers, applying pressure to the cut.

'Think back to what she said, Shaz. Please. Any little thing might be useful. If she has run off, where do you think she might have gone?'

'I don't know. And I'm not sure I care, as long as she's all right. I'm just pissed off she didn't take me with her.'

Narey pressed slightly tighter on the cut to gain Shaz's attention. 'Think, please.'

There was a heavy sigh. 'Grasmere, maybe? You know, in the Lake District. She'd been a couple of times and loved it there. She talked about it a lot. I'm not saying she's gone there. Just maybe.'

'Thanks, that helps. We'll check it out. Anyone that she might have run to? Another close friend?'

Shaz seemed to take it as an insult, her lips pursing.

'I'm her best friend.' She sniffed. 'There is her rape counsellor but I don't know where she is, just that she's in Broomhill somewhere.'

It was little information but a little more than Narey knew and the fact stung. All Leah had told her was that she was getting counselling and that progress was slow but worthwhile and she was feeling better about herself because of it. Any more than that was declared off limits. It seemed Shaz shared her frustration at being shut out.

'Tell me what Leah said when she last spoke to you, Shaz. I need to know.'

'Yes, but are you sure you *want* to know?'

The tone of her voice made Narey doubt very much that she did. But she had to.

'Tell me.'

'She said you let her down. That she should never have listened to you. You'd told her everything would be okay and it wasn't. It definitely wasn't. She said you'd pretended to be her friend but in the end you did nothing.'

It hurt. The truth often did. This wasn't about her, though.

'What else did she say? Did she talk about Broome, about her mum and dad, about any plans? Did she mention anything at all she was going to do yesterday? Or make plans to meet you?'

The rage on Shaz's face was starting to give way to distress. Narey had seen it so many times. Scaffolding collapsing because the weight was too much to bear.

'She said her mum and dad were doing her head in. She felt guilty about that but couldn't listen to them worrying much longer. She said she couldn't live with the look in her dad's eyes. Disappointment. She didn't mention Broome. She never did by name. Just by what he did to her. She talked about moving to Spain or Italy and getting a job where no one knew her but she can't speak the language. She didn't mean it. I'd have known if she did. *I* wasn't pretending to be her pal, Inspector. I really was.'

Narey wasn't going to rise to it. It would do no one any good.

'How did the call finish? Were you going to call each other yesterday, or text maybe? Did you arrange to meet up?'

'She was going to come over to mine last night and I was going to cook and open a bottle. I texted her in the afternoon to make sure she was still on but didn't get an answer. I called her later and just got the voicemail.

When she didn't show up, I called her mum and dad and they told me.'

'Shaz, what was the last thing she said to you?'

'*What?* Are you fucking *trying* to make me greet?'

'No. I'm trying to find out what happened to her.'

The brown eyes grew damp, dousing some of the fire, and her voice softened into a plea. 'Don't say *happened*. Please. Don't say that. Don't let it be that.'

Shaz closed her eyes, part thinking, part hiding. Finally. 'She said she wasn't taking this shit any more. Those was her exact words. Not taking this shit. I asked her what she meant but she just said she'd see me tomorrow. She said she loved me and hung up.'

Narey had more questions than Shaz could answer. Mainly they boiled down to the same one that Shaz had asked Leah herself. What had she meant? *I'm not taking this shit any more.*

Before the rape, Leah used to work out a lot. She'd told Narey that she hit the gym three or four times a week, usually straight after work. Spin classes, body pump and something called velocity were her favourites, along with circuits of the various machines. It kept her in shape and looking good.

Then Broome came along, turned everything upside down and inside out. She couldn't face people, didn't care if she was fit or fat. Self-respect was swapped for self-loathing and the gym was abandoned to a past she longed for.

She drank. She didn't hide the fact, which was a good

170

sign, but neither did she apologise for it. Narey had seen empty wine bottles stacked ready for recycling and when Leah saw her looking she just shrugged unashamedly. People with less reason than her drank at least as much; who was to say she shouldn't.

It wasn't all home drinking though. Sometimes Shaz would venture over the river and they'd knock back vodka or Belgian beer in Brel on Ashton Lane, not caring if anyone saw them crying. Leah would never go alone.

According to Shaz, her solo excursions were confined to making her weekly visits to Broomhill for counselling. There was a café nearby that she told Shaz she'd grown fond of, named Kothel. Shaz said Leah would often pop in before or after her therapy sessions. Surely it was worth a try. Narey could make some calls, grab a late lunch and maybe, hopefully, someone in the café would know something that could help.

She parked on Crow Road, just a few yards from the café but far enough that a sudden cloudburst had her scurrying from her car and through the door. She was assaulted by the sudden heat and the aroma of coffee and cakes. There was a strong hipster vibe to the place with heavy wooden tables and hanging hams, exposed piping and bare bulbs. She liked it, though, and could see why Leah did.

She took a seat at a high wooden bench, eyeing up the array of vintage bottles and books when a waitress breezed up bearing a smile and a menu. She was about Leah's age with a sweep of dark hair tied back and large brown eyes.

'Hi, I'm Georgina. How are you today?'

It was the question that people didn't really want an answer to. Depressed, devastated, desperate and angry. That would have been the truth, but Narey settled for the default setting.

'Not bad, thanks. Can I get a coffee and ...' she looked at the array of cakes on display by the counter '... and one of those, but don't tell anyone.'

'Our secret,' the waitress laughed. 'They're great.'

There was a newspaper lying on a tabletop and despite knowing she probably shouldn't, Narey began flicking through the pages. The face that looked out at her from the top of page five confirmed her initial resistance was well founded.

Broome stared at her above an opinion piece. WHEN WILL MEN GET AN EVEN BREAK? It was a bitter whinge about what he saw as a new inequality; the female-dominated society where poor men were continually left holding the shitty end of the stick. She got through six or seven paragraphs of his garbage and threw it aside.

She made calls but none of them reaped anything that made her happy. There had been no activity on Leah's bank account since a little after noon the day before. She'd bought a bottle of still water and a tuna crunch baguette from the Greggs on Buchanan Street, near Queen Street station. And that was it. No train ticket, no flight, no large cash withdrawal, nothing.

Her other friends, none of them as close as Shaz Karim, all said they hadn't heard from her in days.

There was nothing from the hospitals and, thank God, nothing from the morgue.

She called Tony's mobile, just wanting to hear his voice, but it went straight to voicemail. She tried Danny but his did the same. For a brief moment, she struggled in the quicksand of self-pity before remembering that was the surest way to drown.

The waitress came back with the coffee and a million calories disguised as a cake.

'Georgina, before you go, can I ask you something?'

'Of course.'

'I was wondering if you knew a friend of mine. She's a regular customer in here.'

'Oh, I might do. What's her name?'

'Leah. Leah Watt.'

Georgina lifted her shoulders apologetically. 'Sorry, doesn't ring a bell.'

Narey brought a photograph from her bag. 'This is her.'

There was instant recognition. 'Oh yes, I know her. She comes in once a week. Always has a hazelnut latte. And a chocolate brownie. Is she okay?'

'Why do you ask?'

'It's just that' – she wasn't sure whether to go on, worrying about betraying a confidence – 'she often seems quite sad.'

'In what way?'

'Well, maybe I shouldn't be saying but sometimes I've been sure she'd been crying. She covers it up but you can still tell. I always felt sorry for her but I knew she wasn't the kind who wanted me to ask about it. So, we all just sort of ignored it.'

Even in her place of refuge, Leah couldn't escape her nightmares.

'When was she last in?'

'Oh, three days ago. Always a Tuesday. *Is* she okay?'

A sigh escaped like a prisoner. 'I hope so, Georgina. I really hope so.'

When she got back into the car, she checked her phone. Two missed calls, one each from Tony and Danny. Tony had left a voicemail, just checking she was okay and saying that he'd call later.

'Hey, Dan.'

'Hey love, you doing okay?'

'Yeah, I'm fine. Sorry for snapping at you this morning.'

'Stop apologising. I do know what it's like, remember.'

'I know, I know. So, did your contact get anything?'

'Yeah, she came through. It's probably going to cost me a case of gin so I hope it's worth it. She's got a tail on your girl for yesterday.'

Her pulse accelerated.

'First up, Leah made no phone calls yesterday morning. That's the bad news. The last call she made was the night before. My contact checked it out and the number's registered to a Shazia Karim. Call made at 19.28, lasted a bit over fifteen minutes. However, she did use her phone yesterday and we've got a trace on where she was.

'It was used three times in the morning, between nine and eleven. Probably texts but they don't leave a fingerprint of where they went except on the hardware of the phone itself. Not that my girl can pick up anyway. You'll need GCHQ or the like for that. But she can tell that they were made from Leah's home, either in or very near to the house. It's later that it gets interesting.'

'Don't tease, Danny. Spill it.'

'You said she left home late morning. About eleven thirty, right? She was on her phone half an hour later in the city centre, again no call but probably using the internet. She was on Milton Street.'

Danny waited to hear the sound of the penny dropping.

'Milton Street? That's where the passport office is.'

'Yes. Maybe just coincidence.'

'There's not much else there. The *Sunday Post* used to have its offices across the street but they've been demolished. It's just car showrooms plus the work and pensions office.' She paused, thinking. 'And it's a five-minute walk to Stewart Street.'

'Yeah, I thought that too. But you'd have known if she'd turned up at the station asking for you. Anyway, she couldn't have been there long. The next signal was from just below St Vincent Street at Hope Street. Corner of Boswell Lane. From there, happily for us, it kept signalling. She was on the internet, on the move.'

'Using Google Maps?'

'That's what we think. Trying to find her way to somewhere specific.'

The itch at Narey's wrists and the prickling of the hairs on her neck were a sign of something bad on its way. Not a prophecy, more a consciousness borne out of experience. Cop sense, not magic.

'Where did she go?'

'She went south on Hope Street and turned onto Gordon Street. Then Union Street to Argyle Street and from there onto the Trongate, past the Barrowlands Ballroom then on along London Road.'

Narey's mind was in overdrive, a flag somewhere just out of reach.

'She walked for about twenty-five minutes, using the internet the whole way.'

Narey's cop sense was screaming at her. She wanted to say the place before he did but didn't want it to be true. Except, a small part of her did. The cop part.

'She got as far as Binnie Place. It beeped out from there for a while then it went dead.'

Danny's words battered her head. If he knew the significance of Binnie Place then there was nothing in his voice to give it away.

It was where William Broome's company had their offices.

CHAPTER 25

She ran back to her car and pulled out into traffic with a U-turn that caused three cars to stand on their brakes. Horns beeped and drivers screamed at her but she didn't care. The Templeton building at Binnie Place was six miles across town, and she wanted to get there as quickly as she could. The trail was already a day old and she didn't want to let it get any colder.

What the hell had Leah been doing?

Her last words to her pal Shaz came back to Narey. *I'm not taking this shit any more.*

Successive lights kept her stuck on red for an age and she could feel the tension rising like a kettle on the boil. *Come on, change.*

A light turned on her again but she pushed on through, attracting the loud censure of the hypocrites who'd have done the same if they had the chance. She floored it, through Finnieston, south across the river, through Laurieston and the Gorbals and back across the Clyde again at Glasgow Green.

She threw the car into a space at Binnie Place, seeing

the vast frontage of the old Templeton's building loom large in front of her. It was an incongruous but beautiful blot on the city landscape.

At one time, it was the largest carpet factory in the world, all housed in a massive and flamboyant glazed-brick, red-brick and terracotta building that was modelled on the Doge's Palace in Venice. Now, in the Glasgow way of things, it was a brewery and a bar.

It had housing now too, new additions to the sides in terracotta and glass-fronted extensions, plus office space on the upper floors. One of those was the site of Broome's lair, the home for his HardWire company. Leah had come here the afternoon before but, if her phone signal was to be believed, had gone no further.

Narey walked across the lawn to the front of the building, the feeling of dread deepening. The ridiculous, striking facade leaned towards her, all turrets, spirals and mosaics, mocking her in its grandeur and its secrets. It was a medieval castle, a palace of dungeons and hidden rooms, somewhere to be imprisoned or lost.

It was four o'clock and almost dark, the light fading even faster under thick, leaden skies that threatened snow. Lights were on in the belly of the beast, the WEST bar lit up like Christmas. Up above, dotted offices shone white through the palace's windows.

She stared up where she thought HardWire's offices were but saw nothing other than glass staring back down at her. Standing on the grass, she tried to picture Leah. Angry, desperate, irrational. Taking no more shit. Here for what?

Leah would have stood where Narey was now, the easiest way to view Broome's offices. Had she hoped to see him or to be seen? Was it a gesture of defiance, a last box she had to tick before disappearing? And what had it cost her?

Narey followed the wall down the slope of the lawn and around the corner, her hand tracing its way round the red brick. She'd walked just a few feet, Broome's offices still high above, when she saw it. It was a dull scrawl against the red and she had to use the torch on her phone to be able to make sure what it said.

RAPIST

Three feet high in thick, black spray-painted letters. RAPIST.

She started at it for an age, wishing it away, wishing it something else, before taking her phone out and photographing it. She checked the image then called Rico Giannandrea. The DS answered immediately.

'Rico, I need you to get some bodies together for me. I'm at the Templeton Building on Glasgow Green. Possible crime scene.'

'Sure thing, boss. Are you okay?'

'I'm fine.'

He knew she wasn't. 'What do you need?'

'Whatever and whoever you can get at short notice.

I'll take whoever's available because I want this done now. Get a hold of Baxter and have him get a forensic team down here. A couple of constables and however many detectives you can sneak out without anyone noticing. You too if you're free.'

'I'll be there. Someone you don't want knowing about this, boss?'

'The chief, the deputy, Addison. Anyone, basically.'

'Is this about Broome?' Giannandrea never missed much. 'Hang on, his offices are in the Templeton. Are you sure you should be—'

'Just get them over here, Rico. Let me worry about the rest of it.'

'Yes, ma'am. On their way.'

'Oh, and Rico? Get a hold of whatever CCTV covers the building and find me Leah Watt arriving at the building yesterday. And please find me some tape of her leaving safely not long after that.'

Campbell 'Two Soups' Baxter, the crime scene manager, led the funereal charge of the white-suited forensic brigade. His heavily jowled face, magnified by bushy grey whiskers, was set in its habitual mode of grumpy old git. For a man who loved his job, he seemed to take little pleasure from it.

He made a show of looking round before turning to face her, arms wide, palms upturned in mock confusion.

'Inspector, I was led to believe there was some urgency to this call. I abandoned a very late and much-needed lunch to rush over here and I don't see a body or signs of a break-in. Are you sure this is actually a crime scene?'

Narey could see he hadn't abandoned his meal entirely. Flecks of food clung defiantly to his beard like gannets to a rock face.

'It is, Mr Baxter. And it is because I say it is. Have the area cordoned off – I want an inch by inch search.'

He harrumphed loudly. 'Can you at least tell me what I'm looking for?'

'Any signs of a woman named Leah Watt having been here and any indication of what might have happened to her.'

Baxter's face lost some of its glower. 'Your rape case victim? I heard she'd gone missing.'

He was a curmudgeonly old sod but not completely bereft of compassion.

'This is the place she was last known to be. And the offices up to our left belong to one William Broome. You'll want to start with the graffiti she left just round that corner.'

'I'm on it.'

Narey got on the phone to Addison. She knew full well that the DCI would much rather she'd made the call before bringing in forensics but this would count as better late than never. Hopefully.

'You're *where*?'

She had to move the phone from her ear as he bellowed down the other end. Not surprisingly, he hadn't taken the news too well.

'What the hell are you playing at?'

'Just following the evidence, sir. Leah Watt's phone was last used at this position. It would be negligent of me not to have the site picked over.'

'Don't take the piss, Rachel. You're still talking to me, not preparing for a disciplinary panel. And how do you know that's where she last used her phone? Or do I not want to know?'

'Not want, I'd say.'

'Great. Fucking great. Rachel, you do *not* go to speak to Broome. You do *not* bring him in for questioning. You hear me?'

She was expecting it. 'I can justify questioning people in all the neighbouring offices on the grounds of them being potential witnesses.'

'No chance! Rachel, you can't go anywhere near him. You know what McInally said. You go to Broome and you'd be as well diving head first into a giant vat of shit because that's how deep in it you're going to be. And you know this or else you'd have already gone to see him rather than phoning me first.'

'But we know she was here. Outside his place.'

'Not legally we don't. You've pulled some fast one without authorisation and we sure as hell aren't going to be explaining that to McInally. We cannot go after Broome with what we've got. And *you* definitely can't. He'll crucify you.'

The thought of her crucifixion made her look up again at the office windows above her. The figure was framed by the light against the darkening building. William Broome stood there watching her impassively.

She'd made sure she'd put on enough of a show for it not to be missed. White-suited forensics, police tape, uniformed officers. Word of that spreads quickly through an office.

There was a calmness about him that bothered her. He just stared, face expressionless.

'Rachel? Are you listening to me?'

'Yes, sir. I'm just wondering if you think it's a coincidence her being at Templeton's. That maybe you think it's got nothing to do with Broome?'

'Oh, give me fucking peace. Why are you booting my balls over this? Of course it's not a shitting coincidence. I know how bad this looks and how you're feeling but that's not the point and you know it. It's what we do about it and what I'm telling you is we do not go charging in there half-arsed. I don't want Broome on the phone to McInally screaming about harassment.'

She stifled a sigh on seeing Broome take his phone from his pocket and making an obvious display of bringing it to his mouth. Right on cue.

'None of us want that, sir. I won't speak to him. Maybe he won't notice we're here.'

She heard footsteps squishing across the grass and turned to see Giannandrea striding towards her. In the moment it took for her to look over her shoulder then back, Broome had gone.

The sergeant stood next to her, following her gaze to the old carpet factory.

'Some building.'

'It's something all right,' she agreed. 'I've looked at it

a hundred times during the day but not sure I've seen it up close at night. It's giving me a very different feeling.'

'Certain dank gardens cry aloud for a murder. Certain old houses demand to be haunted.'

'Who said that?'

'Robert Louis Stevenson, I think.'

'You got anything for me, Rico?'

'I just had a call to say they've got Leah on CCTV. Having the precise time meant we could go right to it. She came down London Road, onto Binnie Place and then she's seen going to the front of the building. She walks on the grass, around the corner, then she's not seen again. They've only just started looking, though, so they can still find her leaving.'

'*If* she left.'

'You don't think she did?'

She stared at the window where Broome had been, daring him to come back, willing Leah to appear. *Surprise. Fooled you.*

'I've got to hope she left, Rico. I've got all these things telling me one thing. Instinct, fear, experience, lack of evidence to the contrary, what we know of Broome. They're all telling me she didn't walk away from here. Hope is the only thing telling me she did.'

They looked across the dank garden to the old house and made silent prayers that Stevenson didn't know what he was talking about.

Baxter waddled over to them ten minutes later, his hangdog expression low enough to gather dew from the lawn.

'We're done, Inspector. There's a couple of things you might want to see. First of all, there are indentations, footprints, immediately in front of where that message was sprayed. They have been partly trampled over by another set which I am assuming are yours and we'll need to take prints to exclude them. It is unfortunate, as they are the only useful set we have – the ground's firm, so has only been marked where the person has stood in one place for long enough to write the word on the wall.'

Two Soups was scolding her, but by his standards it was a toothless mauling and she was grateful to enjoy one of his rare lapses into humanity.

He led her and Giannandrea in a wide arc around the area where the message was painted and to a spot a couple of yards beyond it. Shining a powerful torch onto the wall, he highlighted two areas about eighteen inches apart, about four feet up from the grass.

'There is also this. You said Miss Watt was wearing a dark-green sweater when she was last seen.'

Narey nodded and Baxter waved a hand to one of the SOCOs, who handed him a camera.

'I don't want you going any closer, so this will let you see what's up there.'

The picture in the frame was well-lit and pin-sharp. Two tufts of dark green wool snared on the rough-hewn surface.

'It is not my practice to speculate,' Baxter offered reluctantly, 'but given that Miss Watt was said to be wearing a coat, something she's unlikely to have removed, given the weather, then I'd suggest this would indicate her making contact with the wall face first. If indeed this is from her sweater.'

Narey nodded, mouth tight, only just resisting the urge to go back and look for Broome at his office window.

'Can we get some analysis on it? See if it's hers?'

Baxter sighed. 'That, I'm afraid, is a very imprecise science and unless Miss Watt has bought two of that sweater and we can find the other one in her wardrobe then it's of little use. But,' he relented, 'we will try.'

As the SOCOs finished their work, bagging the wool fibres and removing the crime scene tape, Narey and Giannandrea walked back to the front of the building, skirting the area where the graffiti was and heading for their cars.

She glanced up as they crossed the green, seeing lights still burning in Broome's offices, stark against what was now a pitch-black sky. She got as far as half-way to her car, Addison's warning ringing in her ears, when she stopped in her tracks and turned.

'Fuck it.'

'Boss? *Boss!*'

'Stay here, Rico. There's no point in both of us getting into trouble.'

'Boss!'

She was gone, marching across the lawn and heading for the entrance to Templeton on the Green, where she could access the upper floors of the Doges. Anger took her through the lobby and into a tiny lift without any thought of consequence. It opened on the top floor and she pushed through a set of glass doors and past an enquiring secretary at a desk inside.

The room was vast and open plan, propped up on a series of slim white pillars in two rows of eight, left over from its carpet factory days. The office was high on tech and low on personnel, just a handful of occupied desks but banks of computer screens, yards of cabling snaking from one station to the next.

The little wall space between the windows looking down on the green and out onto London Road were adorned with printed messages of intended inspiration. All greatness is precarious. Win or learn, never lose. The creative adult is the child who survived. Only dead fish go with the flow.

Heads lifted at her approach, alarm on the faces of one or two who recognised her. The largest desk in the room was at the far end and that was where she was headed. She could see he had his head down but the clack of her heels on the uncarpeted floor raised the alarm.

Broome was on his feet instantly, outraged at her unheralded arrival. His eyes darkened and mouth twisted. He looked around accusingly, an unspoken demand to know why no one had stopped her walking in. A young, dark-haired woman was the nearest to him and she took the brunt of the blast. Narey didn't miss the woman's obvious anxiety at Broome's anger.

'If this is more harassment then I think you might

find yourself handing out parking tickets or looking for a new job altogether, Inspector. You better have a warrant to be in here.'

She wasn't going to be cowed though. No chance.

'A warrant? You need to get yourself better acquainted with the law, Mr Broome. I don't need a warrant when all I'm doing is seeking witnesses in a missing persons investigation. The person I'm looking for was last seen at this location and I'm looking for anyone who might help us with our enquiries.'

She turned and addressed the slim, raven-haired woman directly. 'How about you, Miss? You must have been aware of the activity outside. We're seeking information on the last-known whereabouts of a woman named Leah Watt. Have you seen her?'

The woman's eyes shifted nervously between Narey and Broome.

'No, I haven't.'

'How do you know? I haven't shown you what she looks like yet.'

'Claudia has already given you an answer,' Broome interrupted. 'We've all been working and we haven't seen anyone outside of this office all afternoon.'

Narey's phone was ringing in her coat pocket but she ignored it. 'It wasn't this afternoon I was referring to. Leah was here yesterday. Did you see her, Mr Broome?'

'Your superiors have warned you against harassing me, Inspector. Haven't you suffered enough embarrassment over your incompetence?'

The phone was insistent, demanding to be answered.

She knew who it would be. She needed a read on Broome though, needed to see it in his eyes.

'Did you see Leah Watt yesterday, Mr Broome?'

He said nothing. Just stared back. Her mobile kept ringing. She snatched it from her pocket, saw Addison's name and hit 'answer' without speaking.

'Are you in his office? Rachel, I fucking told you not to go anywhere near him. Get out of there now.'

'I am.'

'In or getting the fuck out?

'In.'

'Then get out! That shite called his lawyer who called McInally who called me. Get the fuck out of his office.'

She forced a wide smile. 'That's great, sir. Thanks for letting me know. Oh, I'm sure Mr Broome will be completely cooperative.'

'What? Don't piss me about, Rachel.'

'Absolutely, sir. I'll wait for the warrant to search the premises. I'm leaving now. Thanks again.'

'Rachel!'

She hung up on him. The phrase 'search the premises' had annoyed Broome, but had it worried him? Although if all it did was piss him off then it had been worthwhile.

'It's nearly closing time, so I'm leaving it for the day. If any of you' – she turned her head to take in the whole staff – 'remember anything, then please call your local station. Anything at all. Your call will be treated with the strictest confidence.'

Still nothing from Broome other than controlled

anger. She began walking out but slowed at the desk of the woman Broome had called Claudia. She was shaking.

'You should look for another job.'

CHAPTER 26

The phone had rung, the line had been silent and the click had echoed through the room. The clock showed 1.04.

It hadn't woken them, as neither had been able to sleep. They were staring into separate darknesses, consumed with interlocking fears and worries. They knew the other was awake, the way that people used to each other do. Different breathing, more movement or a lack of it.

'Do you want to talk to about Leah?'

'Thanks, but no. I don't have the energy to talk about it. Or the inclination. And it goes without saying I don't want to read about it in your newspaper.'

'That's not why I'm asking and you know it.'

'I don't know what I know any more. No, that's not true. I'm terrified for her, I know that.'

'You think Broome's hurt her?'

'Which bit of I don't want to discuss it didn't you understand? I don't know and I don't want to

191

guess. All I want to do is try to sleep and tackle it in the morning.'

'Okay but before you do . . .'

'Uh huh . . .'

'We need to talk.'

She dropped her head onto his shoulder and groaned. 'The four words no one wants to hear. Do you know just how shitty a day I've had?'

'Yes, and I'm not trying to make it any worse. But there is something I've got to tell you.'

'Is it something I want to know?'

'No.'

'Great. Then don't tell me.'

'That's not an option.'

She pinched the top of her nose, exhaling hard then opening her eyes. 'Are you having an affair?'

'No.'

'Pity. Okay, is it better or worse than that?'

He thought then shrugged. 'It could go either way.'

'Go on.'

'It's about Broome's photographs. I've got them.'

She sighed heavily. 'I can't know about this.'

'They were emailed to me anonymously.'

'I can't know anything about it.'

'Fine. I won't mention that I'm trying to track down the women in the photographs.'

'Good. Thanks for not telling me.'

'You're welcome.'

'Seriously, I don't want to know what's going on. I *can't*. I need to be removed from it and be able to deny any knowledge if the shit ever hits the fan. And it probably will. So, this is the last conversation we have about it. But,' she exhaled long and slowly, 'there's someone I think you should meet. Her name is Lainey Henderson.'

CHAPTER 27

Alanna was first up, as was regularly the case. She wasn't much for crying but she was quick to let you know when she was hungry. If she was up, everybody was up.

So it was that Winter, then Narey and finally Uncle Danny were sitting round the breakfast table watching Alanna stuff Cheerios down her throat and follow it by drinking the milk from her bowl.

They were all a bit biased but each of them was convinced it was more entertaining than anything on television. Alanna loved the attention and the fact that she had a bigger audience than normal. She grinned at them all as if she'd just invented it.

Narey hadn't slept well, her dreams filled with chases through the maze of the old carpet factory, Leah always just out of reach. The dread still sat in the pit of her stomach, gnawing at her. Only her daughter was getting her through it.

'I'm convinced she's a genius,' Winter told them, obviously trying to lighten the mood. 'I'm thinking of putting her name down for Oxford or Cambridge. Or Mensa or something.'

Narey was leaning forwards, rubbing her nose against her daughter's and making her giggle.

'A genius, are you? Well, maybe Daddy's right. You're certainly bright as any button. But maybe we should wait until you work out how to stop getting half the Cheerios on the floor before we get you an application for *University Challenge*.'

'That's just being artistic. An untidy table and floor is a sign of a creative mind. She's a genius, I'm telling you.'

'Aye well, is Daddy going to clean up the genius's Cheerios off the floor before he goes to work or is he expecting her to do it herself?'

Winter looked at his watch. 'I don't want her to think I'm curbing her creativity. Stamping on artistic dreams at such a young age can be shattering.'

They all looked at Alanna, who was busy pouring milk over her head.

'Yeah, she certainly looks like her dreams have been shattered. Go, get to work. I'll clean them up then head in myself.'

Winter kissed her, whispered in her ear that it would all work out, grabbed a coat and shouted goodbye to his uncle. 'Don't you be watching Jeremy Kyle all day, Danny. You've got housework to do.'

'You're not too big for a slap round the lugs, son. Do what your wife tells you and get to work.'

Danny followed Tony to the front door, out of earshot of the rest of the household.

'I've made some headway with some of those wee dicks on Twitter. They think I'm one of them and are drip-feeding me little bits of info that might add up to something before long. I'm keeping files on each of them. I'm not there yet but getting closer.'

'Cheers, Dan. I don't really care if they get nicked or not, I just want it to stop. She doesn't need any more hassle than she's getting. She's going out of her mind with this Leah Watt stuff. But thanks. And thanks for being here.'

'Shut up and get out. You don't need to be thanking me. You know I want to do it.'

Winter opened the front door and swung it back before stepping out. 'I'm grateful all the same though, Danny. It's a big help that you're staying.'

He moved towards the doorstep but stopped mid-stride. 'What the . . .'

Danny was at his side in an instant, straining to see what the problem was. A shoebox sat outside the door.

'Don't touch it,' Danny cautioned him, 'Let me. You might want to photograph it though. And close the front door.'

Danny fished in his pocket till he pulled out a Swiss Army knife. He flicked a blade out and eased the lid from the shoebox. There was already a smell that didn't bode well. Winter had taken his camera from the bag slung over his shoulder and had fired off a couple of shots.

Slowly, Danny eased the lid higher as he bent to see what was inside. When the lid was raised three or four inches at one side, he'd seen enough and let it drop. 'Fuck.'

'What's in there, Danny?'

The older man expelled a blast of breath before taking the knife to the edge of the lid again. With a single flick of the wrist, he sent the cardboard spinning, revealing a large dead rat, its body bloodied.

'Jesus Christ!'

'Do your stuff as if this was a crime scene. Photograph every angle, get a scale, whatever you do. Then get it the fuck out of here. You got gloves?'

'In the car. Danny, I am going to break someone's neck when I find out who's doing this.'

'That doesn't matter right now. Just get this away before Rachel sees it and get it to the cop shop at Stewart Street. She'll find out about it eventually but the later the better.'

Winter took just a couple of photographs of the rat where it lay. Its eyes were blank and its pink, fleshy tongue poked out of its half-open mouth across sharp teeth. Its earthy brown flank was scarred with rusty blood and a ragged hole where it had escaped from.

Without another word, he rescued a pair of gloves from the car, put the lid back on the box and sat it in the passenger-side footwell. As he turned back to Danny, he saw Rachel looking out of the window, Alanna in her arms and a slightly confused look on her face.

He smiled and waved. All fine here, nothing to see. Move along quietly.

She turned away and he walked to the door where Danny stood, worry etched on the grizzled lines of his forehead.

'We need to put an end to this, Danny. I'm not having it. Whoever this is, we find them and we sort them. Not in my house. *Not* in my house!'

Danny nodded, resting an arm on Winter's shoulder.

'Let me deal with it, son. It's why I'm here. Get yourself to work.'

'Dan ...'

'Just go, Tony. I'll sort it.'

CHAPTER 28

Winter was back in the office on Dumbarton Road. He had a line on one of the blondes, the one he'd christened Little Lisa Picasso, and wanted to spend an hour chasing her down and then getting in to the *Standard* before Archie Cameron sent out a search party or sacked him.

He didn't hear the knock on the door. He was so caught up in the search that he didn't hear the door open, didn't hear it close. She stood there unnoticed for a couple of minutes, breathing it all in, overwhelmed by the images on the whiteboards and fighting the urge to turn and flee.

She'd gone there determined to be strong, steeling herself against what she might find, but her resolve had deserted her. By the time she spoke, there were silent tears making their way towards her chin.

'How many of them are there?'

Winter looked up, startled at her sudden appearance, seeing her staring wild-eyed at the photographs pinned to his board.

'Three hundred and fifteen individuals,' he told her. 'Who are you?'

'Women,' she corrected him, her eyes never wavering from the wall. 'They're not individuals, they're all women. In case you hadn't noticed.'

'I'd noticed. You still haven't told me who you are.'

She had her back to him now, standing directly in front of the photographs, staring at the photo of the faceless, nameless woman whose head had been cut away from the print. She reached out towards it, tracing the shape of the ragged edges in the air.

'Why has he done this?' she demanded. 'Is this the only photo that's been cut away like this?'

'As far as I know.' Winter moved next to her. 'Assuming I have all the photographs then yes, this is the only one where the face has been removed. And no, I don't why. You're Lainey Henderson, aren't you?'

The woman was still transfixed by the photographs and Winter had to repeat her name twice more before it broke the spell. She turned, her mouth in a tight O as she breathed out hard.

'Is it okay if I smoke? I need one.'

'Not supposed to,' he told her. 'But I won't tell if you won't. Let me open a window, the landlord would go nuts if he found out.'

She lit up, hands shaking, and drew down on the cigarette in short, sharp pulls. Once she had enough in her lungs to anaesthetise her nerves, she began to explain.

'The bastard that took these.' She jabbed her

cigarette towards the photos. 'I've been tracking him for years. You have the pictures of his victims. I've got their stories. Or some of them.'

She slipped the bag off her shoulder and reached inside, pulling out a blue plastic folder that had clearly seen a lot of use. She dropped it onto the table beside her with a clatter.

'There's a file in there with nine years' work in it. It's a copy. Every case I could find that fits his profile, victims that even the police don't know about. Some of them will, almost certainly, match the women in those photographs. Some have got names, some haven't. Some might speak to you, some definitely won't. Most times, I don't know which is which. If it helps, then it's yours. But I want something in return.'

'It'll definitely help,' Winter smiled at her. 'It's gold dust. What do you want in return?'

The tears returned to Lainey's eyes and she bit down on what was left of her cigarette. 'I want to see the photographs. All of them.'

Winter fetched her a coffee, the only comfy chair in the place and the boxes with the photographs in.

She breathed deep and dived in, sifting through one by one, labouring over each image, studying the faces of Broome's collection. After a minute, she stopped and flicked back through the ones she'd already looked at and then skimmed ahead.

'These women are all blonde. Every one of them.'

'I've sorted them into an order,' he explained

CRAIG ROBERTSON

awkwardly. 'It made it easier for me to work my way through them'

'By hair colour?' Her disapproval was obvious. 'You don't think you were maybe dehumanising them just a bit?'

He groaned inside but didn't try to explain that he'd already had this debate with himself and lost.

'I don't want the blondes,' she was shaking her head in a mild panic. 'No blondes. Not now anyway. I need brunettes. I need to see them first.'

The statement confused him, worried him too. It didn't seem as rational as he'd have liked.

'I'm looking for two women,' she told him. 'Two brunettes. One of them's me.'

When she didn't offer an explanation, Winter didn't seek one. If she wanted to tell, she'd do so when she was ready.

'The other is a woman called Jennifer Buchanan. Or at least she told me that was her name. I don't think it's real and the address she gave me definitely wasn't. But I do know what she looks like.'

She told him Jennifer's story. The break-in, the rape, the beating. The failure to come back for counselling, the false address, the disappearance.

He listened in silence, hearing another truth in Lainey's voice. There was no need to ask why she was also looking for her own image among the pile of photographs in her hand.

She placed them neatly one on top of the other, occasionally stopping to look a second time or third or to

202

wipe away a tear. At one point, she stood up abruptly and walked over to the open window to fire up another cigarette, pacing back and forth as she drained it.

'Can I ask you something? Why are you doing this? What's in it for you?'

Winter shrugged. It was a question he'd never stopped to ask himself, not properly. He was chasing a story but there was much more to it than that.

'I'm a husband. I'm a father. I'm a human being. That seems reason enough.'

As she searched through the prints, he worked too, reading Lainey's file and beginning to compare the information in there with what he knew. He struggled to concentrate, his eyes constantly drifting over to her, unable to stop himself from monitoring her reactions, looking up as he became aware of her showing interest in one photo or another.

She was scouring her way through the brunettes and also a group of darker blondes that he'd pulled from the other pile. He heard her breathe hard, sometimes muttering or swearing, another cigarette on the go. Her head would fall into her hands and he could only guess at how hard the going was.

'I don't know whether I actually want to find her,' she announced. 'I don't know if I want her to be in this fucking pile of shite or not. That's what's driving me crazy. I've been trying to find her for nine years but I don't want to find her in this bastard's private wank collection. And ...' she struggled to spit the words out, 'I really don't know if I want to find myself in it. I don't know if it's better or worse if I find he'd been following me.'

Winter didn't have words. He just let her search.

Five minutes later, she sat straight back in the chair, a print dropping from her fingers. He watched her pick it up again and study it, holding his breath. She got up and walked round the room, circling the chair, the table and the photograph.

When she had enough in her, she sat down again, picking the print up using just the tips of her fingers. She lifted her head to look at him, nodding slowly.

'It's her.'

CHAPTER 29

It had been fifteen minutes since Lainey had identified the petite woman with dark auburn hair as her missing Jennifer. Since then, she'd sat and stared at the three photographs he'd grouped together, working her way through a succession of cigarettes. There were tears and largely incomprehensible swearing, her hand repeatedly slapping the table at one point.

'I only met her once,' she announced, more to herself than Winter. 'Just once. And I've spent nine years looking for her. Now I don't know what to do.'

She turned to face him, eyes red. 'I didn't want to find her in here. Didn't want him to have photographed her.'

Winter crouched down so he was at eye level with her.

'I'm going to try to find her. The photographs on the board are my priorities, the ones I've been putting most time and effort into because I think they're my best chance of getting Broome. If it's okay with you, I'll put Jennifer's photograph up there with them.'

Lainey nodded, the back of her hand wiping at her nose.

'Oh, it's okay with me. Thanks. But I don't know how you're going to find her. And if you do . . .' she had to catch her breath, 'she might not want to talk to you. And if she doesn't then that's her choice, right? Because I know you're trying to find women who will go to court. Testify against him. And I want that too. Want that bastard put away. But only if they want to. If they can.'

'Right. I know that,' he assured her. 'And I'll respect it.'

She sniffled and nodded her appreciation.

'What address did Jennifer give you?' he asked.

'I told you, it was false. I talked to the people who lived there and they'd never heard of her. I described her in case she'd just given a fake name but they didn't know her. I went to the neighbours, went to the block of flats next door, but nothing. It's a dead end.'

'Maybe not. She probably came up with the address for some reason. I doubt she chose it completely at random. There would be something even it was subconscious. Maybe she used to live there, maybe she knew someone that did, maybe she passed it on her way to work. It's worth another look.'

'It was almost ten years ago.'

'Let me try.'

A heavy sigh but a grateful one. 'It was on Paisley Road West. The number's in the file. Above an ice cream parlour and a halal food shop.'

Lainey left Winter's office, taking much of the life of the room with her.

She was why he was doing this, her and Jennifer and the rest, and having that reality shoved directly in his face was sobering. This wasn't a game. He needed to find at least one woman, preferably more, among Broome's compilation who could take him where he wanted to go.

He had leads and half leads and sometimes nothing but hope. He had faces without names, victims without a crime and a criminal but no complainants. He had needles but that didn't make the haystack any smaller.

Above all, he had faces. So many faces.

He was staring now at one that had bothered him from the start. He thought he'd seen her somewhere before all this started but had been seeing all of them in his sleep so couldn't be certain of anything.

The rather sad looking brunette under his finger had only been photographed three times and didn't make the most-wanted list. However, he'd move anyone up who he thought offered a chance of a breakthrough.

She was walking towards the camera in one photo, head slightly down, her expression thoughtful. The composition was bang on, the woman front and centre, suggesting there had been time and privacy to frame it. It also meant Winter couldn't tell where it had been taken because it had closed in on her, just half bodies of other shoppers around her. In another, she was feeding a parking meter with Hope Street sloping away beneath her. In the third, she was just a few feet away from the camera and the photographer, sitting at one of the ad hoc pavement restaurants set up on Sauchiehall Street in the summer months.

Had he seen her before all this kicked off? She might just be someone he'd met in a bar or passed in the street but he didn't think so. She had mileage in her, he was sure of that. Either way, he needed to know who she was before it drove him crazy.

He picked up the print and found a space on the board. So, what was her name?

Mystery Maggie. *No. Maggie May.* She *may* be someone he'd seen. She *may* be a complete red herring. But she wasn't. He felt it.

He stared hard, forehead creased. *Oh Maggie.* He wished he'd never seen her face.

CHAPTER 30

Lainey left Winter's temporary office on Dumbarton Road and made her way towards where she'd parked on Partick Bridge Street. She'd gone just a few yards when a car pulled up alongside her and the passenger door popped open.

The action made Lainey stop in her tracks and she started to edge away from the kerb, ready to flee. A voice emerged from the car, just familiar enough to stop her from running.

'Lainey, get in.'

A head ducked down and towards her. Lainey was both relieved and startled to see Narey looking out at her.

'I said, get in.'

She reluctantly slid into the passenger seat and closed the door behind her, resisting the instinctive move to pull her seatbelt on.

'What is this? I've got my car round the corner. I don't need a lift.'

'I know where your car is, Lainey. I've been

waiting for you to finish your meeting so we can have a little chat.'

Lainey's eyes widened. 'You want me to tell you about what we found out. Me and your husband? Because—'

'No!' Narey interrupted her firmly. 'That's precisely what I don't want to hear. You deal with him. I can't have anything to do with it.'

'Then *what*?'

Narey turned to look at her, held her gaze just long enough to make her uncomfortable, then drove off. 'I think you know, Lainey.'

That provoked an awkward silence that Narey enjoyed as she negotiated the car back onto Dumbarton Road, heading east. A young ned with platinum hair dashed out in front of the car and across the road, causing her to brake and jangling Lainey's nerves even further.

'What do you mean, you think I know. Know what?'

Narey drove on, saying nothing until she ran into a queue of traffic.

'About you and Leah.'

She heard Lainey swallow hard.

'What do you mean, me and Leah?'

Narey laughed. 'I've got a tankful of petrol and a tankful of time. You can keep saying "what do you mean" but I'll still be driving. Why don't you just tell me?'

'Is this a kidnapping?' Lainey was more defiant now. 'Why don't *you* tell *me* what you're getting at?'

Narey took a glance in her rear-view mirror. 'Okay, let's do that.'

She stood on her brakes, throwing Lainey back in her seat, and switched off the engine, switching on her hazard lights and letting them throb. There was an immediate angry blare from the car behind and then others as the traffic ground to a halt.

'What the hell are you doing?'

'Lainey, I'm telling you what I'm getting at. And we're staying right here till I've done it.'

The car horns were an orchestra, blasting their fury. Narey ignored them.

'You and Leah. You haven't been honest with me, have you?'

'I don't know what—'

'Don't bother.' Narey was looking straight ahead, confident enough not to need to look at the expression on Lainey's face. 'You do know what. You know exactly what. I get why you kept it secret and I've got a fair idea of what your excuses will be for not telling me but the game's changed, Lainey. You've got to know that.'

A couple of cars had managed to manoeuvre their way around them, fingers gesturing and faces screaming. Two guys on the pavement outside the Lismore were shouting at them and one had come over to stick his head to the windscreen to see what eejits had decided to just stop in the middle of the road.

Narey turned and looked straight at Lainey, seeing her discomfort as she reeled from the anger around them.

'You're Leah's counsellor, aren't you?'

Lainey's mouth opened and got stuck.

'*Aren't you?*'

A man was slapping his hand against the windscreen, suggesting that maybe they should move.

'*Aren't you?*'

'Yes!' Lainey snapped. 'Yes! Can we move now? Drive, please!'

Narey didn't budge. 'Why didn't you tell me?'

'It's none of your business. It's no one's business. This kind of counselling is extremely personal. It's private.'

She nodded. 'I thought you might say that. But it's not the whole truth, is it Lainey? You made out you didn't even know Leah. You pretended in court you were strangers. Why?'

Another car slid past them, just avoiding a bus coming the other way.

'I didn't want you to know. What Leah tells me is confidential. I didn't want you pressurising me to tell you anything. How did you know, anyway? For Christsake can we drive? Please.'

Narey calmly switched off her hazards and started the engine, driving off slowly and oblivious to the jeers and shouts.

'How did you know? No one is supposed to know.'

'I'm a bit suspicious about coincidences. That's my job. I think I'd suspected for a while but when I put Tony in touch with you, I realised I didn't know where you lived. It took me five minutes to find you lived in Broomhill. Near Kothel. It took me another few seconds to put that together with the victim in your file,

Hayley, that you clearly knew well but had so few notes about. Same story as Leah's just with some details missing. Enough to bolster your case, not enough to make it obvious. Leah, Hayley, almost an anagram.'

Lainey breathed hard and angry, resenting the conclusion.

'So what? She needed a counsellor, I'm a counsellor. That relationship is private and sacrosanct.'

Narey let that simmer for a few seconds, easing to a stop at the next set of lights.

'Like I said, I'm suspicious about coincidences. You just happen to be the counsellor of someone who was the victim of the same rapist as you? I buy that with Jennifer Buchanan, but *twice*? So, I talked to the Rape Crisis Centre and your story doesn't quite stack up. Does it?'

'Yes. *No.* I *am* her counsellor. It wasn't a coincidence though, I sought her out. And I'm not apologising for that. I'd learned about her case, was sure she was a victim of the man I was tracking and knew she needed me. I went looking for her.'

Narey's eyes closed at confirmation of what she'd suspected. She let her head swing side to side at the senselessness of it all.

'Does Leah know this?'

'No. And she doesn't need to. I'm her counsellor and her friend. *That's* all she needs to know.'

Narey took a look in her mirror and slammed on her brakes, bringing the cars behind her to a sudden, angry halt.

'Are we going to have to do this again? That was then but it's all changed, Lainey. I need to know anything and everything that will help me find Leah. I don't have time to waste.'

The look on Lainey's face was different this time. No panic, just determination. The other cars could blast their horns all day.

'Client confidentiality. Trust. That's an unbreakable bond no matter how the counsellor–client relationship starts. I'm telling you nothing and there's nothing I can tell you. *You* broke Leah's trust by telling her everything would be okay when you couldn't promise that, *you* told her you'd see her through court and a trial. *You* let her down, I'm not doing the same. Now it's *you* that has to find her.'

CHAPTER 31

Winter had taken photographs his entire adult life. First as a hobby, then for a living. He found a freedom, a way of expression behind the camera that he'd never experienced elsewhere.

He found some kind of clarity through the lens that he couldn't with the naked eye. He became an observer of the world, a one-click philosopher. The camera allowed you to take one step back from it all and see it for what it was. In his days on scenes of crime, he saw life and death and the transition from one to the other and he was changed by it.

His camera was an extension of himself, his window on society. He didn't always like what he saw but that was part of the contract, taking the good with the bad with the worse.

This though, this was different.

He was on Buchanan Street and on a mission. He wanted to get into Broome's head, however dark a place that was. He wanted to know what the man thought as he trawled the streets in search of prey. How he went about his task without getting caught. He knew it was whacked but Winter believed if he could work out the practicalities of it, somehow understand his mindset, then he'd stand a better chance of *getting* him.

There was a price to be paid, of course, and he was already shelling out. He didn't like it at all.

It felt grubby from the outset. His camera hot in his hands, a compact Canon EOS 70D with a near-silent, powerful zoom. His eyes looking only for the attractive ones, those in their twenties and thirties whom Broome targeted. He found himself scoring and dismissing, swiping left and right, his thinking muddled, his conscience trampled on.

This wasn't how he behaved. Sure, he knew an attractive woman when he saw one. He was married, he was in love with his wife, but he wasn't blind. He didn't do *this* though, eyes actively searching, hunting. He didn't think like this. Like a wolf. Like a predator.

It felt alien and yet somehow primal in a way he was completely uneasy with.

There was a petite brunette who'd just come down the steps from Buchanan Galleries. She was really pretty, with startling eyes, a toned body and great legs. The description came too easily to be comfortable. Like there was something in his DNA that was waiting to go there.

She wore heels and tight jeans, her top clung to her body. She was prime Broome prey. All he had to do was point the camera and click. All he had to do. And he couldn't.

She wandered off, oblivious to his attention, into a crowd and out of sight. He hadn't even managed to lift the camera, never mind aim it in her direction.

He'd been similarly conflicted when he'd gone looking for one of the women in Broome's collection. He'd christened her Maureen because her flaming red hair reminded him of Maureen O'Hara in *The Quiet Man*. The woman had been photographed going into Kelvingrove, the city's massive and magnificent art gallery and museum. There was also another shot, taken on a different day, of her emerging from the Pelican bar and bistro on the other side of Argyle Street, directly opposite the museum.

It hadn't been much of a stretch to think that Kelvingrove was where to start looking. He'd stood across the street, admiring the wide frontage of the red sandstone palace with its towers, turrets and arches. It had reminded him that local legend had it that the building was accidentally built back to front and that the architect threw himself to his death from one of the towers when he realised the mistake. Like all the best stories, it was a load of bollocks.

Winter had wandered in like a tourist, one eye on the museum and one out for Maureen. The foyer had stopped him in his tracks, looking up to see over fifty white, floating heads suspended from the ceiling. All male, each had emotion frozen on their face, most twisted into macabre expressions. Some bore the savage twist of evil, reminding him why he was there.

He passed through the towering central hall with its

golden arched ceiling and immense concert pipe organ on high. On, past a glowering elephant and a question mark of an ostrich, both ducking under the wheels of a World War Two Spitfire.

On the south balcony on the first floor, he'd paused at the museum's signature piece, Salvador Dalí's *Christ of St John of the Cross* and drank it in as best he could. He remembered seeing it as a boy and it scaring him.

There was no fear on his return visit. Instead, as an adult and an atheist, he'd looked at the Christ hung from his cross at a dizzying angle, his flesh golden against a darkened sky, crucified without nails, without blood or a crown of thorns, and felt sorry for him.

His eyes had drifted down from the painting, a fleeting flash of red grabbing his attention. Maureen O'Hara. Mary Kate Danaher from *The Quiet Man*. It was her. It was the Maureen of the collection, he was sure of it, striding past the Dalí. He'd made a respectful nod to the messiah on the cross and made after her.

The height was right, about five feet seven, and the slim figure as it was in Broome's photos. She stopped to talk to a member of staff, allowing him to walk past her and turn as casually as he could to see her face. He'd felt a familiar sense of shock, as if realising for the first time that it was real people, real women, that had been violated in this way.

Something heavy had lurched in his stomach at the prospect of what he had to tell her and he'd backed off, trying not to be any weirder than was necessary. She said goodbye to her colleague and walked past

Moses along a narrow corridor and took up residence at a desk.

As he'd stood in front of her, nervously waiting for her to look up and make backing out impossible, he read her nametag. Suzie O'Brien.

He started off down the hill on Buchanan Street, eyes alert, heart heavy, knowing this had been a bad idea.

After twenty yards, he saw a woman standing outside Gap. She was tall and elegant with long blonde hair. Classy was the word that came to mind. She was perhaps in her early thirties but with a more mature, refined look. She was very attractive and he could see other men turning to look at her. Prey for the masses.

He took up a spot across the pedestrianised street, outside H&M. This time he'd do it. He'd photograph her. She was waiting for someone, which meant he had time to both work out just how to do it and work up the guts. Except it wasn't courage he needed, it was something more. And something less.

She kept disappearing between fleeting figures, the flower hidden by the moving forest, then emerging again into his viewfinder. She was there now though, the long blonde standing still among the public turmoil.

He had his camera at waist level, the lens pointed at her as best he could. He fired off a volley of shots, adjusting the angle as he did so, trying to improve his chances of framing her as he wanted.

He caught a couple of people looking at him oddly but no one went so far as to challenge him. When he

219

brought the camera up to look at what he'd hit, the results were very patchy. Some had caught just her head or a shoulder, or half her body, two had missed completely. Three shots had hit the target though. Bullseyes.

With some practice and enough frames, it would be easy enough to get it right even holding the camera somewhere so far from the eyes. But eventually, you'd get caught, surely?

She was on the move. Winter saw the blonde check her watch and sigh before turning to walk down the hill. He didn't know if he'd made a decision or went on impulse but he was following her. It was instinctive. He was thinking like Broome, acting like Broome. Doing what *he'd* do.

He'd had to follow others, to be sure they were who he thought and so he could, reluctantly, approach them and explain his mission. None of Caitlin Murray, Carolina Zaleski, Hannah Thomson or Meena Chabra had known of Broome other than what they'd read in the newspapers or seen on TV.

Two of them had cried. Carolina had sent him packing with threats to call the police. Caitlin Murray's boyfriend was with her and wanted to hit someone, not particularly caring whom.

It had been a recurring pattern with those he'd managed to identify and find. Anger, resentment, fear and incredulity, a feeling of being violated. And that was from those whom Broome had 'only' photographed but never approached.

He'd gone to an insurance broker's on Bath Street, walking the length of the street to look for a partial office sign after recognising the trademark steps down from its buildings. All in the hope that the slim, fair-haired woman in her late twenties actually worked there rather than just visiting. When he'd found the red and blue sign that he knew to have begun 'Bre', his heart had pounded and he forced himself to go in before his courage deserted him.

It hadn't been easy to get to speak to someone in management, not when his story was so vague and suspicious. Not when the receptionist had reacted to the photograph the way she did. It had been enough though, to know that he'd been right. The office manager looked for answers before finally confirming that yes, the lady in question had been a former member of staff. Her name was Helen Scanlon but she'd left the company. In fact, she'd left the country, emigrating to New Zealand.

Winter had, of course, asked why. The manager hadn't wanted to say, hadn't really known himself. All he knew was that something distressing had happened and Helen had wanted a new start.

The long blonde weaved in and out of human traffic on Buchanan Street, her height and hair making her easy to follow. He kept far enough back, sure not to lose her, sure not to be seen. Is this what it felt like? Being a wolf.

He felt dirty and yet his mouth was dry. Thirty yards behind her as she turned into Nelson Mandela Place.

CRAIG ROBERTSON

Turning with her, dropping further back with fewer people there. She wound her way round to West Nile Street, turning left and continuing down the hill.

Cops. Two uniformed cops in high-vis vests were walking up the hill. Winter's heart leapt in irrational fear. He wasn't doing anything wrong, except he was. He was following a woman, quite literally stalking a stranger. His camera was loaded with photographs of the woman he was trailing.

He knew the law. It wasn't illegal to take photographs of people in a public place. Stalking and harassment were, though. The cops had the right to examine his digital images and if they did, he'd surely be done for breach of the peace.

The blonde and the cops were closer now, passing each other, one of the officers nodding and smiling at her.

They didn't smile at him though. They looked at him suspiciously, staring him down as he tried not to look at them, glancing down at the camera in his hand. They picked up on his unease, their cop sense tingling at whatever vibes he was giving off. In turn, he could feel them turn to look as he passed them. The blonde was ahead, continuing down the street. He felt exposed and guilty.

At the lights, she walked straight on. He took the first left at All Bar One onto St Vincent Street without looking back.

CHAPTER 32

Leah Watt. Walking down Union Street onto Argyle Street, passing KFC and Waterstones. The film was the usual crappy quality but it was definitely her. Jeans, green polo neck and the black hooded waterproof. She had her phone in her hand and was following it.

Narey and Giannandrea watched mostly in silence, occasionally stating the obvious just for the sake of breaking the hush. She was finding it hard, seeing Leah walking to whatever fate awaited her at Templeton's and unable to do anything about it.

'The sooner they invent time travel the better.' Giannandrea's thoughts echoed her own.

The cameras lost her then picked her up again on the pedestrianised precinct, the phone in front of her like a divining rod, and then again on the Trongate, heading east. The techs had spliced the sightings together so that it tracked her journey like a broken dream, a filleted film where the star hopped off stage and on.

There she was passing the Barras, the camera catching her head on. Her expression was unsmiling, even grim. From there, they picked her up twice more on the straight shot along London Road until she reached the Calton Bar and crossed the road into Binnie Place.

'Why would she walk?' Narey asked out loud. 'From the city centre to Templeton's is a couple of miles. Not that far but why wouldn't she take a taxi?'

'Maybe she didn't know how far it was. Maybe she didn't want anyone seeing her who might remember.'

'And maybe she just wasn't thinking at all. Unlike me. I'm overthinking everything.'

It had been daylight when the cameras first saw her on Gordon Street but the light had all but gone as they watched her approach the old carpet factory. She faded in and out of the darkness, a ghost in the gloom on the green.

'She puts the phone away there. That's when the internet connection stopped.'

'That's Broome's offices she's standing looking up at. Surely someone saw her even with the light as it is.'

'What the hell was she trying to achieve?'

The camera saw her go around the corner but didn't see her return. She was back on the front lawn again a few minutes later, head raised as she stared up at the offices as before. The last film of her, she was walking left, past the WEST bar and round to the side of the building that faced London Road.

'There's an entrance just there,' Narey told him. 'It's not the main one but there's a small lift that takes you to the upper floors. Anyone can go in.'

'But can they get out again?'

It was the last they saw of Leah. No clear indication that she went in but real doubt she could have gone anywhere else. A camera on the car park showed plenty of others on the way out. Narey recognised faces at 5.24 – the receptionist and the woman named Claudia, two of the male staff who had peered at her from over their screens. The staff leaving for the night.

'No sign of Broome?'

'Not till 6.17.' Giannandrea fast forwarded the tape. 'Here is he leaving and getting into his car, nearly an hour after his staff.'

It was dark and the film quality poor but Broome was clearly on his own, carrying nothing other than a briefcase. He didn't rush, didn't seem in a hurry or worried about being seen. He got into his car and drove off as if it was any other day.

'They've been though the film on every street surrounding Templeton's for two hours after Leah got there. There is no sighting of her anywhere. Not on London Road, not on Templeton Street, Monteith Row or on Glasgow Green. They've gone a couple of streets back too but found nothing.'

The film spooled a succession of streets, glowing yellow in the dark. Couples and dogs, a car briefly stopping, runners, groups of teenagers. No Leah.

'Let's talk through the timeline. Leah arrives at Templeton at 4.27. Our last sighting of her on camera is at 4.48. She's heading towards the entrance and entering the building.'

'Broome's staff are seen leaving at 5.24. That's thirty-six minutes later.'

'Then, a further, fifty-three minutes later, Broome leaves too. The staff haven't seen her, I think we can be sure of that. So has she hidden until they've gone?'

Rico shrugged. 'There's no shortage of places in there she could have hid. Even if she was seen, no one would have paid much attention. The security is pretty much non-existent.'

'So, say she's hidden herself. Then gone into the HardWire office after the rest have left the building. To challenge Broome or to attack him.'

'And he kills her.'

Her instinctive reply stuck in her throat. 'Okay, let's say he did. What has he done with the body? There's no way he's got it out of there.'

'It's a big place.'

'And we're going to have to find a way to search every inch of it.'

CHAPTER 33

The *Standard* still had a cuttings library. It was proper old-school stuff but Winter remembered Archie Cameron waxing lyrical about it and how all staff should make use of it and not just rely on the interweb. Archie was as old school as Mr Chips or Billy Bunter.

His mantra was that the cuttings had been put together by professionals, done with journalists in mind, whereas search engines just produced what they wanted you to find. Google wasn't for real journalists, he regularly lectured. Google was like a press release or some other shit fed to you by PR firms. Real journalists wanted the story *they* didn't want to give you.

There used to be a librarian but she'd been humanely destroyed during the march of the machines, along with the copytakers, linotype operators, switchboard operators and most of the journalists. Her name had been Eleanor, a legend of the *Standard*, and although she'd been dispensed with a couple of years before

Winter started, the cuttings files were still habitually referred to by her name.

So it was that Winter descended to the floor below editorial to venture in search of Eleanor's Cuttings. His thinking was that if they were all that Archie said they were, there might just be a chance of him finding something. Or someone. Above all, he was hopeful that the cuttings would have one thing often missing from archived news results – photographs.

In the *Standard*'s old offices, Eleanor's Cuttings had hung in rows of purpose-built adjustable shelving that opened and closed at the turn of a wheel, all arranged by topic and alphabet, cross referenced on master files that were kept with a precision the military could only have dreamed of. Now they were dumped in a bunch of boxes.

Archie's face had lit up when Winter told him he was going to search the cuttings. Like a man despairing of the modern world who'd been told that digital watches and computers had been uninvented. Like Santa Claus might have looked if a child's Christmas wish was for an apple, an orange and a hula hoop.

He'd been apologetic about the state of the resources, now packed and stacked like an afterthought in little more than a stationery cupboard, but evangelical about what Winter might find within. 'Missing people?' he'd enthused. 'There's definitely files on that. If you want to find missing people then Eleanor's Cuttings is the place to look.' Winter had to dismiss a mental image of Lord Lucan, Amelia Earhart and Shergar hanging out in the room downstairs.

Archie had been so happy at someone wanting to hunt through the files that he hadn't bothered to ask what Winter was looking for. Which was just as well, as Winter didn't quite know. It was more scattergun than laser-guided missile. His stepping-off point was Jennifer Buchanan and Leah Watt but he'd also considered the possibility of other women in Broome's photographic collection having disappeared.

His heart sank when he saw the boxes though. Piled up against a wall, gathering dust and in no order that a librarian would recognise. More Huey and Louie than Dewey Decimal. He grabbed at the first box and pulled out a few pink file folders to find they'd been rearranged into alphabetical hell. He could only imagine the fabled Eleanor sighing in disappointment.

He nearly turned tail and gave up on it but steeled himself to the task. One by one, he worked his way through dozens of boxes and hundreds of folders, in an ironic search for a file labelled 'Missing'.

There were folders on people and places, on exhibitions and explosions, football and factories, murders and marriages. Curiosity pulled him into some and he found carefully clipped newspaper pages, old-fashioned fonts and hazy black and white photos, packed with type and odd adverts, all yellowing with age.

It took almost an hour before he found the folder labelled 'Missing (1 of 3)', and a further twenty-five minutes before he found its partners. All three were packed with cuttings.

There were names and faces that he recognised,

cases that had made nationwide headlines. A blue-eyed, blond-haired toddler who disappeared from his grandmother's garden. An eighty-eight-year-old woman last seen heading to the shops. A twenty-year-old not seen since being with friends at a farmhouse in Aberdeenshire.

Others had only made local newspapers, fleetingly famous until they were found or else forgotten except by those closest to them. It was the way of the world that the very young, the very old or the very attractive could grab the national consciousness while the rest struggled to take up any ink or airtime.

One cutting suggested ninety people were reported missing in Scotland every day. The vast majority turned up within forty-eight hours but there were over 600 open cases of people termed as long-term missing, which meant they'd been gone for twenty-eight days or more.

He ploughed on. Some of the missing had earned one single article, others had their own catalogues. Often, the real story was between the lines. Among those who'd disappeared were the vulnerable, perhaps with a history of mental illness. Children, left briefly unattended or walking to and from school, who were assumed to have been abducted. Some of the adults, the women in particular, were thought to have been murdered, their bodies buried deep.

It was easy enough to identify the reports where the police were in no doubt there had been foul play, often sure who the killer was but lacking a body and the evidence to prove it. Such stories tended to come back again and again, resurrected from unknown graves to make new headlines and to ask new questions of old suspects.

He got lost in some of them, dragged off track into tangled webs of deceit and gossip, finger pointing and brazen denial. There were often no such things as facts in these cases, just conflicting opinions dressed up as the truth and memories distorted by time and prejudice. There was a whole lot of 'he said, she said' and a whole lot of lies.

After two hours, he had to take a break from it. Mining the catalogue of despair with not a single good-news story in sight was emotionally draining. It was death by a thousand cuttings. He had to stretch his legs and free his mind.

He checked in briefly at his desk, greeted by a happy Archie as if he were a soldier returning from the front. The news editor pinned on him the most valuable of medals – a free pass to the pub for an hour. Winter made a note to use the cuttings library more often.

He walked to the Admiral Bar and oiled the wheels with two pints of Guinness. He studiously avoided eye contact or conversation, wary of the punter who might ask how he was when they really wanted to tell him their own woes. He didn't have room in his head for any of that.

As a shield, he took out his phone and scrolled through the photographs. It had become a spare moment habit, something between mind training and obsession. He'd look at face after face after face. He had them in two folders, one with every photograph in Broome's collection, and one with the regulars, the favourites. Both were well thumbed.

Archie's honour hour had come and gone. With a glare at the clock on the wall, Winter wiped the last drops of Guinness from his lips and put the phone away. It was time to get back to it.

The files hadn't moved and the pile didn't seem to have shrunk. It was a slog. A slow, painful and mechanical trudge through the past.

Every time he came across a photograph, he made mental comparisons between the images in Broome's collection and those fading in ink. He'd tell himself it was unlikely he'd see any of them here but then argue, knowing he'd no real idea what Broome was capable of. He looked at the faces of the lost and tried to match them against those they'd found.

He sat with his back against the wall, folders in his lap, legs cramping up and his mind a mess of misdirection. Was the personal trainer who left home to meet friends but never got there the same person as the woman photographed walking out of Central Station and having a coffee outside the Italian Centre? Was the accountant who was last seen en route to babysit her nephew the same woman pictured on three occasions in the West End?

For another two hours, faces morphed somewhere between memory and hope. He knew he was seeing them where they weren't, realising he was almost willing the women in the collection to be missing and how wrong that was.

That's why he stopped warily when the next face grabbed him. The name was familiar but he hadn't seen the photograph or heard of her in a number of years. *Was it . . .?* It looked like her but his mind had played enough tricks already for him not to trust it.

The woman was missing, thought murdered. The page was from 2009, the cutting still in good condition, the photograph looking out at him pleadingly like a stray in a rescue centre. He was sure. He thought he was sure.

He brought up the folder of photographs in his mobile and worked his way through till he found the three images of the sad-looking brunette. The woman he'd christened Maggie May.

He held one photo against the other, thinking yes, thinking no. So similar and yet the hair was different, the angle not helping. The other cuttings had the same photograph of her. *Shit.*

Did she have her own file? That might be the answer. He scrambled round, trying to remember which of the boxes had most folders listed under P. They were all over the place but some of the people had been thrown in together alphabetically. *In the far corner*, he thought.

It was the third box he looked in but there it was. There she was. A slim folder but it held cuttings not in the Missing file and it had other photographs. Different angles, different ages.

He looked long enough to be sure, to be excited and scared. He said a silent prayer to the Blessed Eleanor of the Cuttings, stuck the folder under his arm and closed the door behind him.

CHAPTER 34

Twitter wasn't Danny's world. He was born at least thirty years too early for it to be a natural playground. He knew the rules though. They were the same as the street.

Most people, the vast majority of them, played nice. Policing them was easy because they wanted to do the right thing, wanted to be liked. They helped each other out, shared good news and consoled bad, introduced friends to other friends. Sure, a lot of what they said was trivial stuff, pointless even, but they meant no harm. Everyone could get along.

There were others, there were always others, who would be different.

It wasn't Twitter that made them like that though. Twitter, Facebook, social media, the entire internet come to that, didn't make people behave badly. It just enabled their bad behaviour. It was nothing new. People had been arseholes since arses were invented. It didn't need digital technology for them to be malicious, they'd managed it fine long before that came along.

It had taken him longer than it probably needed to choose a user name for his new account. He wanted something suitably stupid and macho, something that would fit in with the bullies and the haters. He tried variations on gender-based names but they seemed too forced, so in the end settled for 'BigD @BigDog92'.

He was portraying himself as being twenty-five. A bit of a risk when it came to the lingo but he was hopeful he could pull it off as long as he just copied a lot of what was around him. Text speak covered a multitude of sins and as much as he hated it, he'd picked up enough from his granddaughter, Chloe, that he could bullshit his way through.

Twenty-five again, Dan, he thought. *You remember the moves?* All gallus, knowing everything and knowing nothing. Testosterone sweating out of every pore, horny twenty-four hours a day and able to eat like a horse without a danger of putting on an ounce, drink what he wanted without a hangover, do what he wanted without a conscience. The main thing he had to remember was that he was an idiot.

He needed a profile pic and obviously couldn't use his own. Twenty-five he wasn't. He could have just nicked a photo of any young guy but it didn't have the right feel. What were twenty-five-year-old trolls into? Same as the good guys, he guessed. *The Walking Dead*, *Star Wars*, Marvel's *Avengers*, football and twenty-five-year-old women. He couldn't bring himself to do the zombie thing so settled for a *Star Wars* baddie. Darth Vader was too obvious so he went for

Darth Maul. Blood red and black with horns. Seemed about right.

He knew where his prey was, hiding in plain sight, being all big and brave and cowardly by attacking under cover of aliases. Going straight to them would be fatal though, like an old lion charging after a herd of gazelles and seeing them scamper into the distance at first sight of his mane. Instead, he had to circle them, get cover, then pick them off one by one when they were looking the other way.

So, he didn't follow the worst offenders, not to begin with. He followed their followers and those they followed, infiltrating the pack. He liked and retweeted their outbursts, flattered their fragile egos, buddied up to them and endorsed their views, however hateful.

He made a particular point of liking and retweeting the posts that talked about Broome. It wasn't hard to find them. The bastard had become some kind of twisted martyr for the men's movement, a totem for perceived injustice. The collapse of the case against him had been seen as a validation of every rapist that had ever cried Not Guilty, conveniently ignoring that Broome was as guilty as sin.

Broome himself retweeted some of the dark, hateful remarks that wore his name but he was clearly very careful with his own original words. 'Retweeting is no endorsement' was the get-out clause for the culpable. Danny retweeted Broome retweeting them.

He started to throw his own tweets out there too, looking for hashtags as bandwagons to jump on. A young actress was getting heat for losing a lot of weight and then doing a lingerie photoshoot. The bullies were out in force, all of them paragons of physical perfection somewhere in their own minds.

> You may as well get back on the
> biscuits. Makes me puke just looking
> at you

> U were fat and ugly. Now ur skinny
> and ugly. Well done

> Now I only need to put a bag over
> your head and I could fuck you

It didn't exactly make him feel good but he piled on. His own barb was crafted with all the subtlety of the others.

> Funny how u were a feminist when u
> were fat. A slut now ur skinny

It got likes, then it got retweets and replies. Good 1 dude. U tell da bitch pmsl. These brought followers and more retweets. None of it brought him pleasure but it was getting him nearer where he needed to be.

The online gaming community was a rich seam for increasing his band of disciples. It was predominantly male, teens and early twenties, mostly locked away in their bedrooms and insulated from the boundaries of real human interaction. Any woman who dared to be part of this world, either as gamer or designer, ran the risk of constant abuse. Getting told to get back to the kitchen often came neatly sandwiched between death and rape threats.

He picked up on a barrage of abuse directed at a software designer who was getting all the blame for the latest edition of a popular game not being all that the geeks thought it should be. It had already been confirmed she was only one of dozens who worked on the game but she was the only woman, so she took the hit. Apparently, the *ugly bitch* should *leave it to men, get back to the kitchen,* stop *being a whore just to get a man's job,* and she'd be *stabbed* and *raped* if she ever *dared to work on* the game again.

BigD was a pig about it too.

> If women were meant to design
> games, god would have given them
> balls and a brain. Get back to the
> kitchen u slut

The unwashed lapped it up. Liked, retweeted all day long. Not quite viral but plenty of traction and a few hundred new followers.

There were still no nibbles from the core group of Rachel haters but he had cover and used it to creep closer.

There were four who attacked her more than the others. Four who seemed to have nothing better to do than to continue their assault. Some of the tweets must have been on an automated loop as they hammered away at it all day long.

BigWeegie. Tormentor. ItsaMansWorld. BlueSnake.

Those were his prime suspects for the night calls and the rat. Them and, of course, William Broome. They were *his* prey.

He was sure at least one of them was responsible for the fake Twitter account. Their obsession was so all-consuming that it seemed unlikely they wouldn't be involved. What he needed to know was how much further they'd gone. And how far they might go.

He'd noticed that Tormentor had taken his eye off Rachel just long enough to launch an attack on a pop star who'd had the nerve not to give in to the pressure to be anorexic. Tormentor had taken it upon himself to lead the fat shaming charge.

> *Ur so fat u should just hang urself bitch*

Danny 'liked' it and retweeted it. Then he replied.

> **Need to be a really strong rope**

He sat and looked at it on the screen, waiting for it to make an imprint, reminding himself he was entitled to a proper drink later to wash the taste away.

The likes arrived, retweets too. Lots of lols in reply. Then his notifications went up by a full count in a single jump. Like. Retweet. Reply.

Tormentor.

Nice one bro. Fat bitch would need
a forklift truck to get her up there

Danny responded immediately. Like. Retweet. Reply.

lol she would break the truck

And so it went on. Puerile, unfunny, cruel, and all too easy to do.

He waited for Tormentor to tire of abusing the singer, waited for his Rachel obsession to kick in again. It didn't take long. The troll's attention span was about as short as his penis. He posted yet another call for *the bitch* to resign or be sacked, ending it with the haters' two favourite hashtags, *#SackNarey* and *#lyingcopbitch*.

Danny didn't like or retweet this time, trying not to be any more obvious than he could avoid. Instead, he made a mental apology and posted a tweet of his own. It played well to the crowd, got picked up through #SackNarey and was retweeted dozens of times. Nothing from Tormentor though.

Had the troll even seen it? It was so easy for a tweet to get lost in the blizzard.

He tried again. A little more poisonous this time.

DI Narey. A liar & a slut. Die Narey
#SackNarey

The likes were immediate. Some passed it on with a new hashtag *#DieNareydie*.

In jumped the Tormentor. Like. Retweet. Follow. Direct Message.

> *Cool tag bro. Die die Miss Piggy*
> *die. Keep the heat on that bitch.*
> *Ur one of the good guys*

Danny followed him back and sent a direct message in return.

> She deserves all she gets. Hope she is
> getting loads of grief

> *Oh she is bro. Believe me. Tons*
> *of grief*

> Good. Bitch asked for it

He left it at that. Mark made. Don't push it. Not just yet.

He closed the laptop and headed for the fridge. His mouthwash was chilling inside a brown bottle. As he downed a large gulp of the beer, a quote came to mind. Something he used to have stuck inside his locker back when he was on the force. It was from Frederick Nietzsche.

'He who fights with monsters should look to it that he himself does not become a monster. And if you gaze long into an abyss, the abyss also gazes into you.'

CHAPTER 35

It had taken Addison a full day to get permission from on high to seek an interview with Broome over the disappearance of Leah Watt. Officially, it had gone as far as the Deputy Chief Constable but no one doubted that McInally had covered his own back by going one step higher again. The prevailing mood was for no further hassle on that front, but that the Watt situation could not be ignored.

Narey's unauthorised venture into the HardWire office hadn't helped, but Addison argued that the circumstances had demanded it. She'd added more fuel to her own funeral pyre by strongly suggesting to Leah's parents that they make their feelings known and they'd duly done so. Command didn't enjoy being squeezed but had to be seen to both satisfy justice and follow procedure.

They wouldn't sanction Broome being brought in as a suspect but only that he be approached as a potential witness. The decision on being interviewed was to be his and his lawyer's. As far as Narey was concerned, they'd crawled on their bellies and let Broome walk all over them.

After much hesitation and declarations of persecution, Broome's people agreed, but with a long list of caveats that the Deputy's office agreed to. There was to be no taping of the interview, neither audio or visual. Broome was not to be cautioned and nothing he said would be used in evidence against him. He was helping the police with their enquiries. He was not a suspect.

The rules of engagement had all been settled in Broome's favour but the defining decree as far as Narey was concerned was that his lawyer could simply reject anything he didn't want his client to talk about. She was going into battle with both hands tied behind her back.

It was the best they could do, she was told. Just be grateful you're getting to talk to him at all. Don't blow it. Don't make things worse.

It sickened her. If she could handle the fallout and embarrassment from the case collapsing in court then they should too. They were allowing themselves to be bullied by this man and his little prick of a lawyer.

Addison was to sit in with her, riding shotgun but also to stop her from getting herself or the force into trouble. The very notion bugged the hell out of her. Broome *was* the trouble.

'So, whatever happens, stay cool,' he told her. 'Don't get angry, don't bite no matter what he says. If we piss them off then Connie will haul Broome's arse out of there and we'll be done. He'll be able to say he helped the police with their enquiries etc. etc. and we'll be back where we started.'

She resented his advice as much as the situation. Maybe because she wasn't sure she *could* stay calm. She wore thoughts of Leah like a shroud but this was her job, this was what she was trained to do.

Arthur Constance escorted his client into the interview room in Stewart Street like a courtier advancing in front of royalty. Clearly, money could buy you a man's morals as well as his counsel.

Broome took a seat across the desk from them, shuffling awkwardly into place with all the unease of someone who resented being there. He positioned his shoulders and studied the desk, his face tight and surly. When he raised his head, he looked at Narey for longer than was necessary, a clear and successful attempt at making her feel uncomfortable.

She thought there was a hint of bloodshot to Broome's eyes, a puffiness to them too. Had he been drinking heavily, perhaps a sign of him struggling under the pressure of what he'd done?

Constance made a show of making unnecessary adjustments to the sleeve of a navy pinstriped suit that probably cost a month of Narey's wages. He cleared his throat and demanded attention.

'Before we commence, I would like to place on record that my client is here willingly but reluctantly. He has already suffered harassment and public ignominy at the hands of Police Scotland and would be entirely entitled to feel sufficiently aggrieved at his treatment to deny

CRAIG ROBERTSON

such an unreasonable request for interview. He has, however, agreed to participate under the conditions agreed with your superiors but is doing so while reserving the right to terminate this interview at any time. A right we shall not hesitate to use.'

Narey had Addison's warning to stay cool and calm running on a loop through her head.

'It isn't an unreasonable request, Mr Constance. A young woman has disappeared. Her last known location was adjacent to your client's place of business. We trust that as a responsible citizen, he would like to assist us in any way he can to help find that young woman.'

Constance smiled. 'An admirable attempt at sleight of hand, Inspector. Your interest in Mr Broome goes beyond that of neighbourhood witness and it would serve us all well if you admitted that so we could bring these unnecessary proceedings to a swift conclusion.'

She ignored it. 'Mr Broome, were you aware that Leah Watt was outside your building around four thirty that afternoon?'

He lifted his head and looked at her as if for the first time. 'No, I was not. In fact, I've only got your say so that she was ever there.'

'Oh, she was there. We have indisputable evidence of that.'

Constance let out the smallest of laughs. 'All evidence is disputable, Inspector. You of all people should know that.'

'Your office overlooks the lawn in front of the Templeton Building, does it not, Mr Broome?'

246

'You know it does.'

'The lawn is barely used at all during the winter months. Anyone out there would stand out, wouldn't you say? Easy to spot, hard to miss.'

'Inspector, do you have anything other than statements of the obvious? My client is familiar with the geography. We readily concede that fact.'

'Were you in your office at that time, Mr Broome?'

'I can't recall.'

'I'm sure your office staff will remember. Should we talk to them? I'm sure your diary will confirm or deny it. Should we go to your office and look at it? Perhaps we should check your emails.'

Constance laughed again. 'You're a trier, Inspector. I'll give you that. Such a pity that your unbridled enthusiasm sometimes gets the better of your judgement. As I'm sure you're aware, we have no need or desire for you to pick your way through Mr Broome's offices in search of wild geese. Next question, please.'

She tried a different tack. 'You're interested in photography, aren't you Mr Broome?'

The lawyer's face darkened. 'You know those photographs are off limits. We are not going there.'

It was what she'd expected and it pleased her. 'I'm not talking about *those* photographs. It's you that's brought up *those* photographs. I'm talking about the prints on Mr Broome's wall, the photographs of Glasgow. Tell me about those, Mr Broome.'

The man shifted in his seat, unsure if he was being tricked. His lawyer looked equally uncertain.

'I'm a photographer,' he shrugged. 'It's a hobby. I love Glasgow and I love photographing it. That's it.'

'They're very good,' Narey encouraged him. 'Really captured the city.'

'Thank you.' Broome was flattered but Constance was wary.

'People make a city, don't you think? The landmarks are great but I really like the way you have people in all of them. It brings the photos to life. Do you always like to have people in your pictures? Even if they are unaware you're photographing them?'

Broome was about to answer when his lawyer shut it down.

'No chance, Inspector. Move on or we move out.'

'Okay, I'd like to ask Mr Broome once more if he was in his office at four thirty that day. It was only a few days ago and I think he ought to remember. As I said, it would be easy to confirm.'

Constance swivelled his head to look at Broome. The message was obvious. She can check, just tell her.

'I had a meeting in the West End later that evening so yes, to the best of my recollection, I was in my office at that time.'

'Thank you.' Her voice contained the minimum of gratitude.

'Has anyone in your office reported hearing a disturbance, perhaps a scuffle?'

'No.'

'Did anyone hear a scream or shouting?'

'No.'

'How can you be sure of that? Have you asked them?'

'*Inspector* ...' Constance's voice resonated with warning. 'My client won't be answering that question. It is provocative and he has already answered it.'

'He hasn't answered in terms of his workforce but okay, let's move on. There was graffiti spray-painted on the wall of the building. Were you aware of that, Mr Broome? Either having seen it personally or heard of it from your staff?'

His eyes narrowed. Unhappy with the suggestion.

'No.'

'The word painted on it was 'rapist'. Given recent events, I'd have thought that would have been the talk of the steamie. You sure you didn't hear any talk about it?'

'I'm sure.'

'Really? That's surprising. I'd have been sure someone would have noticed.'

'My client has already told you he heard no such talk. Move on, Inspector.'

'I'm happy to. CCTV footage shows Leah Watt arriving at the Templeton Building. It does not show her leaving. Can you explain that?'

'No. How could I explain it? Why should I?'

'You don't think it's strange? Or worry that she might still be in the building?'

Broome sneered. 'I might be worried about what she's done. Or that she'd infected the place.'

She just let that hang, feeling the contempt from the rest of the room, Constance included. She could hear

Addison's anger, nothing more than a rush of air from his nose but she knew the sign. Like a bull readying to charge.

'We also found fibres of clothing snagged on the lower wall. They are a match to the sweater Leah was known to be wearing when she disappeared.'

'A match?' Constance interrupted. 'A confirmed scientific match to a sweater that you don't have possession of. That sounds unlikely in the extreme.'

Narey ignored it. 'The location of the fibres suggests she was pushed face first against that wall. It paints a worrying picture of violence, don't you agree, Mr Broome?'

'I wouldn't agree that it was worrying, no. And it's got nothing to do with me.'

'Why do you think Leah might have been at the Templeton Building?'

Constance ran interference again. 'My client isn't a mind reader, Inspector Narey. He can hardly be expected to know why a stranger was in the vicinity of his workplace.'

'Why do you think Leah Watt might have been there, Mr Broome?'

She saw anger in his eyes. Nothing else so much as flinched but she saw the response where he couldn't hide it.

'I don't know.'

'Had you arranged to meet her?'

'No, of course not.'

'Do you think it's a coincidence that she was there?'

'I wouldn't know. How am I supposed to know how a woman like that thinks?'

Constance was ready to interrupt but Narey was quicker. 'A woman like that? A woman like what, Mr Broome?

'Inspector, my client—'

'I don't mind answering that. In fact, I'd like to.'

Everyone else in the room shared glances. The one who found the words most uncomfortable, quite clearly, was Constance. He questioned it with nothing more than a raise of his eyebrows, but Broome was determined to have his say.

'I think it's quite clear the woman was mentally ill. Possibly a pathological liar. Certainly a fantasist. If she was outside the building? Well, for one thing I'd consider it harassment and if you do find her then I'm instructing Mr Constance here to bring a case against her. At the very least I want a restraining order against that slag.'

The atmosphere in the room tightened like a noose. Every one of them felt it. It was the last word that did it. Broome's signature insult for women.

'Do you have a problem with women, Mr Broome?' She tried to keep her voice level, determined not to rise to his bait.

'That is hardly within the scope of this interview, Inspector,' Constance cautioned. 'You have a small window of opportunity yet seem determined to slam it shut on yourself.'

'Connie,' Addison's patience, always on the tightest of

wires, had snapped, 'if your client continues to be a complete arsehole then I'm going to lob a half brick through that window of opportunity and I don't give a flying fuck if it smashes or not. He's not coming into my interview room and using terms like slag and talking about victims as if they were shite on his shoe. He can behave himself or he can crawl back into the hole he came from. Now, is that within the scope of this interview?'

Constance's mouth made like a goldfish. Broome exploded.

He was out of his chair, face contorted and spittle flying from his mouth. The first few words were almost unintelligible amid the fury and the rest tripped over themselves in their rush to get out.

'... talk to me like that. Came here of my own free will. Sue you. Sue all of you. Slag. Have your job for this. You really don't want to mess with me. Who the fuck do you think you are?'

Even Constance, not unaccustomed to representing scumbags, was taken aback by the wild ferocity of it. His eyes bulged.

'Mr Broome, sit down please. Do not say anything further! Chief Inspector—'

'I'll call her a slag because she's a fucking slag. This one here too,' he jabbed his finger at Narey. 'All in it together. Think they can run the place. Think they can ruin men's lives.'

Addison leaned back in his chair and smiled. For a moment, Narey thought he was going to put his feet up on the desk and cross his hands behind his head.

'That's enough!' Constance was shaking. 'This apology for an interview is over. Chief Inspector, you know you have not heard the last of this. Mr Broome, we are leaving right now. Accompany me out of the door now please, sir.'

The lawyer had to take his client by the arm, the man looking around as if unaware of what he'd said or where his anger had come from. He knew his mask had slipped and they'd all seen his face. He was led away, still muttering.

When the interview-room door closed, Narey looked at Addison with a shake of her head. 'You know Constance is going straight to McInally with this, don't you?'

Addison shrugged. 'Fuck it. You remember the scene from the end of *Rocky III* where Apollo Creed tells Rocky to be cool then Apollo loses it and starts scrapping with Clubber Lang before the fight?'

'Funnily enough, no.'

'Well he did. Rocky says, "I thought you said be cool?" and Apollo is like, "That *was* cool".'

'So, you're telling me you were cool?'

'Nah. I'm telling you I just couldn't take any more of that bawbag's shite.'

She couldn't keep a smile off her face. 'I think I might need to buy you a drink, sir. You won't be able to afford one once they sack you.'

CHAPTER 36

Winter's Maggie May was actually named Julie Petrie.

It had taken him an age to be sure, because Broome's photographs of her were so different from the ones used in the press. He'd looked online as well and it was her. No question.

Julie Petrie. *Christ*.

She'd made headlines. The story was she left her home in Cambuslang one morning and was never seen again. The presumption was she'd been murdered. The presumption by many was that she'd been murdered by her husband.

Except, Winter now knew she'd been photographed on at least three separate occasions by William Broome.

He felt like a dog who'd been chasing a car and had no idea what to do with it once he caught it. He had to think.

Everything he knew said that Julie Petrie was pushing up daisies so he could hardly ask her to testify against Broome.

He could tell the cops, of course. He could tell Rachel. That wasn't in his game plan though. Not yet.

As he stared at Julie's photograph pinned to the corkboard, her sipping on a glass of wine on the Sauchiehall Street pavement restaurant, an idea began to form in his mind.

It would be risky, but what was life without a little risk?

What if he were to convince Archie Cameron to let him run a piece on Julie Petrie in the *Standard*? Retell the story and interview relatives, hang it on some anniversary or maybe some new information coming to light.

And he'd interview the husband, of course. The prime suspect. Until now.

He'd get the family and the grieving widower to say how they've never given up hope but fear the worst, to make a fresh plea for witnesses, for him to proclaim his innocence.

A smile crept across Winter's face as the plan unfolded in his mind.

He was sure he could write a story that would enrage Broome, provoke him enough that he might lose it and do something stupid.

Except that it wouldn't be the story that would inflame Broome. Not quite.

Winter would, obviously, illustrate the article with a photograph of Julie.

Not any of the photos that had been used in the past, though. He was going to use one of the photographs that Broome had taken. It would drive him crazy.

His smile spread wider.

CHAPTER 37

Danny was on the fake Rachel Narey Twitter page, keeping his enemies close and his new online friends closer still, looking to see which of them was posting abuse.

There were fifty-six new notifications. Direct messages, likes, tweets and retweets, all of them vile. He forced himself to read every one. Every insult, every threat, every puerile sexual remark, every invasion of privacy and violation of decency. Any one of them might hold the clue he was looking for.

He saw that BigWeegie had been on the rampage again, posting a succession of hate-fuelled messages about what he'd do to Rachel, empty boasts of sexual prowess studded with violence. It all read like the bludgeoning menace of a thirty-year-old virgin screaming in frustration, yelling words he'd heard others use.

Tormentor too was trying to live up to his name. Nasty little essays in bad grammar and phonetic spelling. Tormentor hated everyone and everything but right now he was focusing his bile on Rachel. His vocabulary consisted of little more than rape, bitch, cut and die.

BlueSnake kept playing the sacking card. He was tweeting everyone he could find, from the First Minister to MPs to celebrities demanding they sign some petition to have Rachel kicked off the force. When they didn't respond as he wanted, they became the enemy and were accused of endorsing prejudice against men.

There were new haters too, odious cowards who piled on, unable to resist the howl of the pack. For them, victims were there to be victimised. Most had Twitter handles they aspired to, usually chauvinist shit or something anarchic. Little boys playing big boys' games.

It took him a while to notice the profile picture had changed. He'd become inured to the fake Rachel staring back at him and had only ever once looked at the disturbing photoshopped image that he didn't want in his head. He'd worked his way through the notifications and some of Fake Rachel's tweets before he saw that it was different.

Instead of the police-issued portrait photo that had likely been stolen from a news website, there was a more informal head shot, Rachel not quite looking at the camera. Not looking at it because she didn't know it was there.

His fingers moved quickly through the page, searching for other photographs. He found what he didn't want to see.

There were another five photographs of Rachel that

CRAIG ROBERTSON

hadn't been there before. Judging by her clothing, three were taken on one day and three on another. They were taken on the street. Her getting out of her car, walking on what looked like George Square, on her phone in front of some shops, putting Alanna into her car seat.

The photos were recent. No more than a few days old.

It took him five minutes before he could react to the pictures. Five minutes of pacing round the room talking to himself, searching for some calm and finding only more reasons to get angry.

He couldn't lose it though, no matter how tempting. He had to think like them, become the monster in order to fight it. He returned to the laptop, forced his fists to unclench, and began to type.

Every one of the four main bully boys had tweeted the photos. They didn't mention that they were newly taken, they didn't have to. The menace was there, just waiting to be found.

He stared at the Like button under BlueSnake's tweet for an age. *Become the monster.* He hit it, liked it, signalled his approval to the world. He doubled down and retweeted it too, spreading the poison.

For Tormentor, he added a reply.

> New pix of the lying piggy? Nice job
> from someone. Lovin their work!!

The response was almost immediate.

*She gonna shit herself when she
sees these! Bitch gonna be scared
to leave her house bro. Best for
her she stay at home!!!*

Stay in it, Danny told himself. Don't blow it. He sent
the troll a direct message.

These ur pics bud? Okay if I
share them?

*Share away bro. We want the
bitch to see them. Are they mine?
That be telling* ☺

So tell, you nasty little scrote. Spill your guts. Boast.
You know you want to. But he didn't and Danny
couldn't push him, not yet.

Say no more bud. Keep the pressure
up and piggy will squeal. Anything I
can do just let me know

*Will do bro. Need all the good
guys we can get. Bitch needs
taught a lesson. We'll teach it*

I'm up for it. Going for a drink to
celebrate ur pics. Merchant City
for me.

Merchant City? U made of money?

Where u get ur poison then bud?

*I like the Rum Shack innit. Catcha
later bro*

The Rum Shack. It was on Pollokshaws Road. It was
a start.

Maybe he could go there and rip Tormentor's throat
out. See how he managed to drink rum like that.
Christ, those photographs.

Some bastard had followed Rachel. Rachel and
the baby.

CHAPTER 38

Julie Petrie was twenty-eight years old and a teacher at a primary school in the East End. She'd been there three years, popular with staff, pupils and parents. No disciplinary issues, no complaints, no problems.

She'd been married for four years and she and her husband Iain lived in Cambuslang on the south-eastern outskirts of the city, where he was an estate agent. They didn't have children; friends said that they didn't seem to be in a rush, happy to be enjoying their lives.

She was a member of the gym, played squash once a week, ran two after-school clubs, went to the pub quiz at their local and had a good circle of friends. Life had seemed pretty good.

One Tuesday in December 2009, she'd spent much of the school day taking her primary fours through their role in the upcoming Christmas concert. Herding nine-year-olds wasn't easy but Julie loved it. Once they'd been drilled until they knew their cues, their steps and most of their lines, she collapsed into a chair in the staff room for a while before heading home. Everyone said she was happy, healthy and nothing at all seemed out of the ordinary.

She was never seen again.

There were fleeting, unconfirmed reports of her car being seen between the school and home. It was picked up at two points on CCTV and that was it. The car, a blue Ford Ka, was found abandoned two days later.

It had all the ingredients the media needed. Young, attractive, school teacher. A class of cute kids heartbroken before Christmas. A murder mystery.

And it had a villain in waiting.

Julie's husband had been the chief suspect as far as the cops were concerned. *Look close to home and you'll never go far wrong* is the way most detectives think and it doesn't let them down often. It's a thousand times more likely to be a family member or friend or lover than a stranger.

Iain Petrie swore that wasn't the case. Sure they'd argued, sure they'd had their problems like any young couple but that was as far as it went. He'd never laid a hand on her, never would. Hated the idea that anyone could even think it. He'd always wait for her, would never give up hope.

That was what he'd said in newspaper interviews eight years ago. Now, he was remarried. Now, Julie was officially declared dead.

He was still an estate agent. The rise of the internet hadn't yet killed his firm and a quick search showed he was working out of the same premises as he was when Julie disappeared.

Winter had asked around among his cop contacts and the favoured scenario was that Iain Petrie had been having an affair with one of his clients, Julie found out about it and he killed her. Some thought it was an argument that got out of hand, some thought he planned it all out and did away with her to be with the other woman. Either way, he was suspect number one.

There were press comments from Julie's family when Petrie got remarried. Nothing too critical but nothing too complimentary. The space between the lines reeked of suspicion. It was the chatter of Cambuslang too. All fingers were pointed at one man.

Now, however, Winter knew something that no one else did. No one except, probably, William Broome.

Winter telephoned Atheneum, the estate agent's office on Cambuslang's Main Street, and was quickly transferred to Petrie. The voice was firm, friendly and ready to do business.

'Iain Petrie? Hi, I'm sorry to bother you at work. My name is Tony Winter, I'm a reporter with the *Scottish Standard*. I was hoping to have a word with you.'

The ensuing silence spoke volumes before it was broken tersely.

'I'm very busy. What is this about?'

'Mr Petrie, I'd like to speak to you about the disappearance of your wife. Could we meet to discuss it? I'm happy to come to you.'

'No ... I ... That's all in the past. I don't want to talk about it any more.'

'I have some new information, Mr Petrie. I think

263

you'll want to hear it. If you talk to me, I intend to run a story that will stop people from thinking you had anything to do with your wife's disappearance.'

'I didn't!' It was blurted out before he took in the significance of what Winter had said. 'What new information?'

'I'd rather discuss that in person. Do you have time to meet today?'

There was a heavy sigh. 'I'll make time.'

Petrie had aged quickly in the years since the last press photos Winter had seen. Your wife disappearing, probably murdered, would do that to you though. There were hints of grey at his temples despite him being just in his late thirties, and his face was lined, heavier.

The man was a little over six feet tall, sharply dressed in a grey business suit, with dark hair fussily swept back on his head. There was a faded attractiveness about him, like someone who'd once nearly made it big on TV.

He seemed nervous as they shook hands, his eyes barely meeting Winter's. He shuffled and fidgeted, constantly looking around the café to see if anyone recognised him or was likely to listen in. They were in McCallum's, a greasy spoon on Main Street with a bright red sign promising hot and cold filled rolls, all day breakfasts and homemade steak pie. Winter had eaten in it a few times before and really liked it even if his arteries didn't. Petrie didn't seem quite so impressed.

'Just a coffee. Black.'

Winter ordered the coffee and treated himself to a black pudding roll while he was at it, knowing he might regret it in the long run but he would love it in the here and now.

Petrie sniffed at the brew as if expecting it to poison him. He didn't seem a happy man.

'My paper is running a series of features on cold cases, particularly unsolved murders. And I've been looking at your wife's case.'

'Julie isn't a murder case. Not technically, She's a missing person. Or she was.'

'Do you think she was murdered?'

Petrie swept the room again for anyone listening in. 'Yes, I do. I think someone killed her and dumped her body. She wouldn't have just walked out, disappeared. She just wouldn't. Someone murdered her.'

'Who do you think did it?'

Petrie's eyes flashed furiously. 'It wasn't me. That's all I know. It wasn't my job to find out who did it. It was the police's. What's this new information you talked about?'

Winter had taken an instant dislike to the guy. He was full of himself and overly defensive, bordering on flat-out offensive. Victim or not, he was a pain in the arse.

'We have reason to believe Julie was followed by someone over a period of time. She was photographed in public on a number of occasions without her knowing.'

Petrie's jaw slackened and dropped. He tried to speak but his mouth just opened and closed again.

'Photographed her? How? I mean, I don't understand.'

'Did Julie ever talk about being followed, maybe about being worried someone was showing too much interest?'

Petrie stared like he didn't understand the question. Brows furrowed, mouth twitching.

'Maybe. I mean she didn't say it quite like that. Not that I remember. But someone interested, being a pest, yes.'

'You remember who?'

'A name? I don't think she knew. I just knew it was unwanted. She was married. She wasn't like that. Of course it was unwanted.'

'So, she talked about someone that bothered her?'

'Yes. I think so, yes. It was a long time ago now and she didn't make that big a deal of it. I think she wasn't sure herself if it was a problem or not. You think ... you think you know who it was? The person that took these photos you're talking about?'

'Maybe. Mr Petrie, did you tell the police about your wife mentioning someone was bothering her?'

'No. I'd forgotten about it till now. Till you said.'

Winter doubted he'd ever forget something like that. If Rachel said someone was pestering her, he'd have had it ingrained in his memory. Maybe Petrie didn't care as much as he said he did.

'Can you remember the day your wife disappeared?'

'Of course.'

'Like, the details. Where you were when you realised. What you did. How you felt. It's colour like that will make the piece work and get public sympathy.'

Petrie looked interested at the word sympathy. Winter felt he was an arrogant sod who believed people should love him, not hate him for something he didn't do.

'I came home from the office, a bit late, around seven, and she wasn't in. That was unusual, especially without her saying, but I wasn't too worried right away. I called her phone but it just rang out. An hour later, I called again, left a message, asking where the hell she was. When it got to eleven, I was frantic. It just wasn't like her. I called her best friend, who didn't know anything. Then I called the police.'

'What did they say?'

'That they couldn't do anything. That it was too soon. She'd probably be at a friend's and I should call again in the morning if she hadn't shown up. I didn't sleep at all. Kept calling her phone but never got an answer.

'I called the cops back next morning and they still said I had to wait. She was an adult, entitled to come and go as she pleased. But I knew it wasn't like her. She'd never done anything like that. They eventually came out, searched the house, looked at her clothes, took away a photo of her and me together. It became this big investigation. Everything just got crazy. They all turned on me.'

The self-pity was nauseating. He'd forgotten who the real victim was.

'They said all kinds of things. Said I'd buried her body. Kept pushing at me. Trying to get me to admit something I hadn't done. They didn't care about the pain I was in. Didn't care I was suffering.

'Everybody here,' he glanced accusingly round the café, 'thinks I did it. And I didn't.'

He was spoiling Winter's black pudding roll.

'You said the night Julie went missing that you called her best friend. That was Leanne Wilson, right?'

Petrie looked uncomfortable. 'That's right.'

'There was speculation that you and Leanne were involved. Is that true?'

The man flushed angrily. 'I thought you were going to write a piece that would show people I was innocent?'

Winter shrugged slightly. 'I just need to get the full picture.'

'Well I just want to talk about what happened to Julie. Who is this guy you think took her photos?'

'Have you ever heard the name William Broome?'

There was no reaction. 'I don't think so, no. Who is he?'

'He's the man that might mean people stop thinking you're just a heartless bastard.'

CHAPTER 39

Archie Cameron loved Winter's feature on Julie.

The husband's anguish, the mystery, the fruitless search for the body, the hint at new information that could reignite the investigation. He also loved the bits that Iain Petrie wouldn't be so keen on. The remarried husband, the vague hints at infidelity, the unlikability of the man.

Petrie's annoyance would be nothing compared to Broome's though.

The quotes from Petrie about someone pestering his wife, some mystery man she was worried about, the man in Glasgow who was bothering her and followed her. Those would have Broome raging.

As would the headline.

**MYSTERY MAN LINKED TO
JULIE PETRIE MURDER**

As would the subheading.

Husband says wife was being stalked

And the photograph. The never-seen-before photograph taken just before she went missing, presumed murdered. The photograph of Julie Petrie standing at a bus stop on Hope Street. The photograph that Broome took and that the court said should be returned to him, all and any copies, and that was his own copyright. The photograph which was plastered over half a page. The photograph which would, hopefully, and in all likelihood, have him spitting blood.

It was his. They had no right to use it. And it left him with a clear choice.

He could get his lawyer to sue them for breach of copyright, sue the police too for it being leaked out, and in doing so link himself to the disappearance and murder of Julie Petrie. Or he could do nothing but rage and drive himself crazy.

Winter's money was on him going for option two.

CHAPTER 40

Danny's initial reaction at realising Rachel had been photographed on the street had been to deal with it himself. To double his efforts on the Twitter trolls and find a way to choke them till they told him what he wanted to know. If he could sort it while keeping it from Tony and Rachel, he would. Neither of them needed this.

He knew it couldn't, wouldn't work out that way though. They'd see it or be told, the very nature of social media dictated it.

He had no choice but to tell them before they found out from somewhere else.

'Okay, this isn't good,' he warned them both before bringing up the Twitter page. 'Just how bad it is, I'm not sure yet. But I intend to find out.'

'Christ, Dan. Whatever it is just show us. We're grown-ups.'

'Okay, love. As you say.'

As Twitter came on screen, Winter swore. 'Not these wankers again. What shit are they writing now?'

'No, it's worse than that.'

He brought up the photos of Narey and let them sink in one by one.

'That was taken yesterday,' she blurted out. 'I was wearing those clothes yesterday. And *that* was the day before. That was on George Square. And the other was on the south side. And ... oh my God.'

'Alanna.' Winter only managed one word.

'Yeah, I know,' Danny agreed with all that was unsaid. 'But none of it's good. If it's any consolation, looking at all the pictures, it's not Alanna that's being photographed, it's Rachel.'

'I don't know if that's a consolation or not,' Winter fired back. 'But I know I want to kill someone.'

'You need to calm down. And I know that's easy for me to say because I've had time. But if anyone's doing any killing it will be me. A life sentence at my age isn't going to mean very long.'

'Stop it, both of you,' Rachel shouted. 'No one is going to be killing anyone. I'm treating this professionally, not personally. I'll get CCTV on the areas these were taken. I know the times, within a few minutes, and I want to see what the cameras have. If he's there, he's going to be seen. I need evidence.'

'We don't know it's him,' Danny reminded her.

'It's him,' she murmured. 'One way or the other, it's him. But how the hell can someone take photos of me without me knowing? I'm supposed to be aware of this!'

'You're not unaware of it,' Danny told her, 'but you're not looking for it either.'

'I bloody will be now!'

'You're not always going to see them,' Winter snapped. 'It's easier, much easier, than you think. I've already been looking into it. Trying to work out how it's done.'

'To other people maybe,' she insisted. 'But I'm a cop. It's my job to notice things.'

'There are loads of articles showing how to take pics covertly,' he told her, taking his phone from his back pocket. 'Let me google it and show you.'

'I don't care what Google says. I know what my training tells me.'

In response, Winter turned his phone round and showed her the screen. Instead of a search engine page and results, there was a photo of Narey, clearly taken there and then.

She let out a low, slow sigh. 'You fucker. You're trying to prove a point? *Now?*'

'Yes. And I'm not apologising for it. That's how easy it is. I silenced the shutter and disabled the flash so there was no sight or sound to give it away. And you didn't see me doing it. All anyone needs is a phone and to pretend they're using it for something else.'

'You're not making me feel any better.'

'Good, because I'm not trying to. There are apps to make it even easier. Spy camera apps that show a fake background so that no one behind can see the phone's camera screen. If you want to you can easily rig up a USB camera through something like a laptop bag so that it looks like a button on a shirt. You can even hide an iPad in a book with a slot for the camera. If I have headphones on my iPhone, I can use the volume controls as the shutter release. No one's going to notice or care. It's that easy.

'And that's just assuming it's someone that's close enough you can see them. There's a Nikon Coolpix P900 with an optical zoom that's so powerful you can see the moon moving. And the moon is over two hundred thousand miles away. And you can buy that camera for under four hundred pounds.'

'So you're not trying to make me feel better, you're trying to scare me?'

'Maybe. Because I'm scared. Rach, I'm terrified. Someone is taking photographs of you. And of Alanna. And we've obviously got a good idea who that might be. It scares me and I want it to scare you too.'

'Well, you should be happy then, because I am. But I'm half as scared as I am angry. And I'll tell you this, I'm not sitting around waiting for something to happen to me. If the fucker who took these wants me then he's not going to have to look too hard. I don't care if it's Broome or someone Broome has fired up, I'm not prey. Lainey Henderson told me that prey always ends up getting killed. Well, that won't be me.'

CHAPTER 41

Elspeth Broome lived in a semi-detached on Carlaverock Road in Newlands, a grey sandstone set well back from the road and just yards from the park. Winter was sure that a preliminary phone conversation would result in a call to the son and the plug would be pulled on any interview. So, he went in cold.

She pulled back the door with a smile on her face, happy to see the world. Winter wondered how long that would last. She was in her early seventies, hair still long but tied back in a silver-grey ponytail. Her round glasses were perched on the end of her nose and she was wrapped up in a cardigan so thick it could have doubled as a sleeping bag.

'Mrs Broome?'

'Yes. How can I help you?'

'My name's Tony Winter. I'm a reporter with the *Scottish Standard*.'

'Oh.'

'Don't worry, I'm not here to bring bad news. I know you've probably had enough of that.'

'And good news,' she countered defiantly. 'My William was found completely innocent of that terrible lie.'

Well, that's not entirely true. Winter thought it but didn't voice it.

'Yes, that's why I'm here. Your son was found innocent but there are still things being talked about and well, you know how it is, no matter how unfair, mud sticks. I wanted to give you a chance to talk about William, say how proud you are of him, that sort of thing. Let people know the kind of person he really is rather than what they've read in the papers.'

She looked doubtful. 'I don't know. Maybe I should talk to William.'

'That's a good idea,' Winter agreed. 'Although, and you'll know better than me, William doesn't seem the kind to boast about how well's he's done. I've seen it before, people too modest for their own good. It's better to hear it from someone else. I think it takes a mum to really know a son.'

'You're right. If a mother doesn't know her boy then who does? Well, if you're sure it will help him. I guess you better come in.'

'I'm sure.' If there was a hell, he was going to it.

The house smelled a bit musty but the real assault was on his eyes, courtesy of a violently floral carpet that he had to stop staring at. Mrs Broome led him into a room off the right of the hall and urged him to take a seat. He lowered himself into an armchair and sank a foot lower than he expected.

'Tea or coffee?' she offered.

He didn't drink either but some time alone in the room might be useful.

'Tea, please.'

'Milk and sugar?'

'Um. Just milk?'

She looked confused at his uncertainty but nodded and left him. When he heard her footsteps recede, he got up and looked around. Every available space was occupied with an ornament, most of them very odd-looking to his eye. Strange animal figures, pieces of shell, little boys carrying fishing rods, a number of novelty teapots and what seemed to be a collection of insects in amber. There were a few sporting trophies too, little ones that might have been given out for attendance rather than winning.

On the mantelpiece above the Victorian fireplace there were six framed photographs. Winter moved closer and saw, as he'd expected, that all were of William Broome as a boy. They chronicled his growing years, from around five until his early twenties.

First-day-at-school William was a mop of brown hair and freckles, smile shy and lopsided. Butter wouldn't have stood a chance of melting.

Gap-toothed William was next, comically grinning wide to show off his missing incisors. His school tie was neatly fixed, his hair side-parted. There was something forced about the smile, or maybe Winter was just looking for it. He was only a kid.

The shyness was back big time in William at ten

or so. He leaned against a wall, somewhere sunny in summer. No smile for the camera, barely a reluctant removal of the frown. The eyes were sad or uncertain, Winter couldn't read them. Not happy though.

He'd filled out in the next one, freckles fading and chin broadening. He was looking at the camera as if questioning if he really had to do this. Too big a boy to smile for his mummy. If Winter had to pick a word it would have been stubborn. Maybe defiant.

Eighteen or so. Freckles replaced by acne but no less assured for that. William saw the world as his, that much was clear. Confident, smug even. He could have it all. He was a hard kid to like.

The last one was the photograph that got to Winter. The expression was a pose, eyes hard and cold, mouth turned down to the hint of a sneer. Daring you to look back. *You talking to me?* The words that came to mind this time were different. Sociopath. Dangerous. Entitled.

'Sorry it took so long. They say a watched kettle never boils and it seems they're right.'

Mrs Broome lurched back into view, a laden tray in her hands, stopping warily as she saw Winter studying the photographs. Her eyes switched between them and him, her feet lodged in uncertainty.

'Always great to have family photos, isn't it' Winter enthused. 'You must be really proud.'

The old lady's feet found gear again and she placed the tray on a low table in the centre of the room. 'Oh,

I am. My William didn't always like getting his photo taken. I never understood why because he's such a handsome lad. Could have been a film star. Like Cary Grant, I always say.'

Winter coughed some form of agreement and brought the cup of tea to his lips, managing to put it back down without drinking any.

'Is it difficult not having him living at home any more? You must miss him.'

She looked confused. 'Well I don't really think of him as not living here. Yes, he has his house but this is his home. Have you got children, Mr Winter?'

'A girl. She's nine months.'

'Aw, that's lovely. Well, you'll understand when she's older. Your house is always their house. It's a bit different for girls though. They get married and go with their husbands. Boys are always their mammy's though. Nothing ever changes that. You'll be the same with your own mother, I bet.'

'My mother died when I was young.'

'Oh my. I'm so sorry. So sorry. That's terrible and here's me putting my foot in it.'

'It's fine. Don't worry about it.'

'Oh no, but I feel terrible. Every boy should have his mammy. I'm sure she loved you very much. She still will in heaven, trust me. She'll still be looking down on you and looking after you.'

Winter worried that she was going to try to hug him. He had to get this back on track.

'Can we talk about William?'

'Are you sure you're okay?' She affected a soothing, caring voice that grated with him.

'I'm fine. It was a long time ago. What was William like as a child? Did he have many friends?'

'Well,' she considered it. 'He was very popular but he didn't always need to play with other children. He was content to be his own company or to be with me. He'd read a lot or draw. He wasn't a rough boy like so many of them are.'

'It's good that a boy spends time with his mother. And with his dad, too?'

'We don't talk about William's father. There's no need.'

There was nowhere to go with that. The door was shut firmly in his face.

'What kind of things was he interested in when he was younger? I see some trophies on the mantelpiece.'

'Oh yes,' she beamed. 'He liked football and he was very good but the other boys were so rough. I was really quite glad when he decided to stop. He liked comics. American superheroes, you know? And computers. He was always so good with the computer.'

'Did he have many girlfriends?'

'Oh, he didn't have time for girls. He was always studying or working on one project or another. Or on his computer. There's always time for girls later. And anyway, he has his mammy.'

She said the last line as if she was joking but Winter knew she wasn't.

'No girlfriends at all? That's a bit unusual though,

isn't it? Maybe he had and you just didn't know.'

'No,' she was immediately defensive. 'He could have had if he wanted. William could have any girl he wants. He's so handsome. But he didn't and I'd have known. He tells me everything.'

'Mrs Broome, do you think maybe William is gay and that's why he's never had a girlfriend? And, of course, it's perfectly okay if that's the case.'

Her eyes widened and she sat back in her chair. Winter might as well have suggested her son was a penguin from Mars.

'Gay? No. *Gay?* There's nothing wrong with my boy.'

'I didn't say it would be anything wrong. In fact, it's perfectly—'

'*No!* He's quite normal. *Very* normal. He could have the pick of any girl he wanted. But they have to be good enough for him. He's not going to settle for second best. He doesn't have to.'

'So would you say he was his mother's boy then?'

'Oh yes, definitely. And that's a good thing, whatever anyone says. He was a mummy's boy but that just meant he loved me.'

Mummy's boy. Winter was going to use that.

'What did you think of the charges against William? About what they said he'd done?'

Elspeth Broome leaned forward and aggressively stared at him over her glasses.

'I thought it was disgusting. Letting a pack of lies like that get as far as court. That woman should have

been the one put on trial. She should be locked up
for what she said about my William. Locked up! The
things she said. They made me sick. She's perverted,
that's what she is.'

CHAPTER 42

It wasn't what they called a death knock. Not quite. Narey knew it felt like one though.

Taking bad news, often the worst news, to someone's door was the part of the job that everyone hated. That it had to be done was of little consolation. That you could never care as much as they did always left you feeling you'd let them down.

Narey parked in front of the semi-detached on Archerhill Gardens, DC Kerri Wells next to her in the car, and sat for a moment before going to the door, pretending to check email on her phone. They wouldn't be welcome but that was hardly new. She seemed to have spent an entire career going to places she wasn't wanted. No, what bothered her was she couldn't tell them anything definite, could only fill them with dread and leave them with tattered hope.

Get on with it, she told herself. *It's not about you, just do it.*

'Okay, Kerri. Let's do this.'

Charlie Watt opened the door looking like a boxer

who hadn't figured out he was beat, knocked to the canvas three times but still determined to get up and be hit again. He was small and bony and the lines on his forehead stretched back across his bald skull.

He tried for words but had to settle for inviting them in by the movement of his head. Narey knew his wife would be the one with the words.

In the living room, Heather was seated on one end of their floral sofa, her hands working away nervously. She half rose but sank back down just as quickly, neither the time nor the energy for politeness. Charlie stood next to her, an arm round her shoulder, designed to comfort but working equally well as scaffolding.

'Tell us,' Heather started. 'Just tell us. She's dead, isn't she?'

'Wheesht,' her husband told her, rubbing at her arm. 'She's not.'

'Aye she is. Look at her face. She can't bring herself to tell us. Well, just spit it out. We can take it.'

Narey really doubted that was true.

'Charlie, do you want to sit down? I think it'd be best.'

Heather's hand flew to her gaping mouth, covering a silent scream. 'I told you. Oh mammy, no.'

'Charlie, please. Sit next to Heather and let me tell you what I know. I'm not here to tell you she's dead. Please, sit down.'

Husband looked to wife for approval, neither of them fully taking in the reprieve Narey had given them. Heather gave an urgent nod and Charlie slid onto the seat beside her, barely room for a breath of air between them.

Narey took a breath of her own, feeling the weight of their expectation. She had to tread carefully.

'We know where Leah went on the day she went missing. We've been able to track her by her phone and CCTV. But ...' she had to cut off the hope she saw rising on Heather's face, 'this isn't necessarily good news.'

'Can you not just tell us? I can't take this, I swear I can't.'

'We don't know where she is now, let me tell you that. We know she went to Binnie Place in the East End, on the corner of Glasgow Green, where the WEST Brewery is. The old Templeton's carpet factory.'

Heather's face crumpled in confusion. 'Right. I mean, why? Why would she go there? I don't understand this.'

'Templeton is where William Broome has his offices. We believe Leah went there to see him. We don't know why but we're trying to find out.'

The blood drained from Leah's mother's face. 'No, no, no. No. She wouldn't do that. She just wouldn't. She was terrified of that man. She wouldn't go there by choice. Someone must have made her.'

'She went there on her own. We have CCTV shots of her walking from the city centre and approaching the building. Heather, Charlie, I'm still only guessing why she went there and I don't like doing that. But she might have gone to confront him. I think she'd maybe decided she'd just had enough and had to do something about it.'

'That will be your fault then, hen.' Charlie had

had enough too. His face had hardened. 'If my Leah felt she had to do something about it will be because you didnae.'

'Where did she go after the factory, after his office?' Heather's voice was cracking.

'We don't know. There's no CCTV showing her leaving or being anywhere else after being in there.'

'So, she's still in there? Oh, Jesus Christ, why're you here and not in there looking for her? What's he done to her? What's that bastard done to my lassie?'

Charlie grabbed his wife round the shoulders, scrawny fingers digging into her flesh. 'Wheesht, wheesht.'

'We don't know what he's done. We don't know if he's done anything. But I think you should prepare yourselves for the worst. If she's alive, I'll do everything I can to find her.'

'And if she's *not*? You think he's killed her, don't you? *Don't you?*'

Narey was stuck. Wedged between a determination not to lie to them and a need not to scare them any more than she had to. She fudged with a hopeful truth.

'I just don't know.'

'Then find out!' Charlie Watt was on his feet, his face turning purple. 'Find out! Take that bastard in and beat the shit out of him. Or let me. Just let *me*.'

It was getting to it. 'We can't arrest him, Charlie. All he is, is a witness to where Leah was last seen. We're over a barrel on this. They're not going to give me the go ahead to bring him in on circumstantial evidence. I'm sorry but that's the way it is.'

'I don't understand,' Heather was shaking her head forcefully. 'I don't understand. Search that place. Why not just search it?'

'We need a warrant and I can't get one.'

Heather started to stand up but Charlie leaned on her shoulder and pushed her back onto the couch. 'Aye? I'm phoning your boss. I'm going right to the top. Warrant? I'll get you a fucking warrant.'

She dropped Kerri Wells back at the station, leaving the Watts to pile on the pressure, and headed for the south side. Shazia Karim didn't have to be told, not the way the parents did, but Narey felt the obligation.

She'd called ahead, hearing the fear in Shaz's voice but telling her she didn't want to discuss it over the phone. They were going to meet at Shaz's flat on Terregles Avenue.

Narey had played the Watts, she wasn't hiding from that or apologising for it. She needed into the Templeton Building and angry, grieving parents increased her chances of being able to do that. She hadn't suggested they petition her bosses. She'd just led them there.

Rico had arranged for all available CCTV on the building to be stepped up. Favours had been called in, too, to have patrols drive by and be visible. If they couldn't get in, they had to make sure Broome couldn't get anything out. Unless he already had.

Shaz was waiting for her, standing at the second-floor window, the curtain pulled back in her hand, her face grim. She waved anxiously, telling Narey to come up.

CRAIG ROBERTSON

At the front door, she studied Narey's face, looking for signs and somehow sensing or seeing that it wasn't what she feared most. She breathed a cautious sigh of relief and led the detective inside.

They sat down opposite each other, Shaz with her hands trapped between her knees.

'You haven't found her.'

'No, we haven't.'

'And that's the good news, right?'

'Yes.'

'So, what's the bad? Because I know there is some. I can feel it.'

She explained. About tracking Leah's phone. About the CCTV, the Templeton Building and Broome's office.

Shaz sat, nodding fiercely, trying to hold herself together, taking it all in.

'Right, okay. Okay. There's things that could explain it. That she's still maybe okay. Or being held somewhere but not hurt. Or got out when no one was looking and is hiding out somewhere or . . .'

Her voice drifted away and the tears burst loose. She tried speaking through them, snuffling and wiping and trying to convince either of them that it would be okay.

'You sure she went there? Sure she went in?'

'We saw her walking there. Argyle Street, the Trongate, Barrowlands, London Road. She walked all the way. No one following her. And she went into the Templeton.'

'Oh Christ, the Barrowlands.' Shaz choked out a laugh of sorts. 'The nights we had there. So many gigs

288

and so much booze. I need her to be okay, Inspector. She's my best friend and you only get one.'

Narey felt the need to hug her but stopped herself. 'You two did a lot together, didn't you? Talk about her if it helps. Why do you get on so well?'

Shaz shrugged. 'She gets me. I know that's a cliché, but she does. No need to pretend, you know? We've always just been able to tell each other everything.'

'I get that. What bands did you see at the Barrowlands?'

'Everyone. Belle and Sebastian, Saw Doctors, Biffy Clyro, the Manics, Pigeon Detectives. It was about a night out, just me and her. Drinks in town then the ballroom. We even went to see Runrig and we can't fucking stand Runrig.'

She dissolved into laughter and more tears at the same time, her mascara scarring her cheeks.

'Find her. Please. Find her safe.'

Narey could only nod. Half a lie. She was sure she'd find her.

CHAPTER 43

Charlie and Heather Watt hadn't stopped at a phone call to Police Scotland. They'd followed it up with a personal visit and refused to leave until they were interviewed by the most senior officer possible. Shouts of their daughter having been murdered were effective but threats to go to the press even more so.

There were meetings way above Narey's head and although she wasn't privy to the contents, she was quickly apprised of the result. A warrant would be issued for a search of the Templeton Building, including the HardWire offices. Broome wasn't to be considered a suspect or treated as such but his premises could be searched. Not computers, not files or folders, not company documents, just the office itself.

They were to get in and out as quickly as possible and to treat everyone with the respect due. She knew she'd struggle with their assessment of how much respect was owed to Broome but it wouldn't show. She'd done this before.

She led the team in through the front door of the

building, Rico Giannandrea and Bryan Dawson at her heels and the troops following behind. Dawson would take the lower floor and the brewery, Giannandrea the stairwells, lifts and middle floor. The top floor was hers.

She took two DCs, Kerri Wells and Steph Harkness, with her as well as the SOCOs. She wanted Broome to be faced by three women and see how he liked it.

Pushing the door open a bit harder than was necessary, she grabbed the attention of the entire office immediately.

'I am sorry to interrupt, ladies and gentlemen, but we're authorised to conduct a search of the entire building as part of an ongoing investigation into the disappearance of Leah Watt. We will try to minimise the disruption. We will need to take fingerprints from each of you to eliminate you from any prints we find. I also need you to give me a list of anyone else likely to have been in here in the last few days. Your cooperation is greatly appreciated.'

A tall, gawky guy in a stripy long-sleeved T-shirt and jeans shot to his feet. 'You need a warrant for that.'

'Well, lucky that I've got one, isn't it? What's your name, sir? My colleague here would like to ask you some questions.'

Harkness took out her notebook and stared down the geek, who quietly declared himself to be Marty and had clearly lost his enthusiasm for complaining.

Narey strode down the length of the room, heading straight for Broome, who faced her approach, sat behind his desk like it was a throne. The man clearly wasn't surprised at their arrival and she got the distinct feeling he'd been tipped off. Quite possibly by whoever seemed to be on his side at Tulliallan.

Not surprised but no less angry; she saw in his eyes something of what she'd seen that night in his bedroom when he'd been arrested. The cornered animal, resentful and dangerous. He didn't get up as she approached, just glared from his seat, eyes burning.

'This is provocation, unwarranted and actionable. My lawyer agrees.'

'I'm sure he does. Is he on his way?'

'Yes.'

'That's fine, but just make sure he stays out of my way. You might be well advised to give your staff a couple of hours off. I'm not sure they'll be able to concentrate.'

Broome said nothing but his contempt was obvious.

It had been days since Leah had been in the building, not exactly ideal in forensic terms but they'd find what they could. Every surface would be examined; doors, pillars, desks, computer screens, telephones, cupboards, handles. All undoubtedly mired with a myriad of prints, but all they'd need was one.

They'd search the basement, roof spaces, locked cupboards, all the hidey-holes that a building as old and strange as this one would have. The hunt was not only human. The lower floors were being nosed by a cadaver dog who'd work his way up through the building, sniffing out death.

The dog would search the HardWire office too, because although there was nowhere, seemingly, to hide a body, the dog could also tell if someone had been killed there and later removed.

Broome could neither hide his anger or stand that it was so obviously on show. He kicked back his chair and got up to leave.

'I hope you're not going far,' she stopped him in his tracks.

'I'm going for a coffee if that's okay.'

'Of course, it is. DC Wells will accompany you until you're ready to return.'

Broome stormed off, a mischievously grinning Wells in his wake, leaving the lair without its beast. That he would leave her in there made her surer than before they wouldn't find anything in his office. They'd search and dust, making the maximum of minimal disruption.

She studied the printed messages on the brick walls. *Win or learn, never lose.* Was this Broome's personal philosophy as well as the company's? She intended to make sure he both learned and lost.

Her phone rang. Rico. 'You might want to come down the stairwell, boss. Something interesting.'

'On my way.'

One flight down, she saw the huddle. Two SOCOs, one – Paul Burke – hard at work with camera in hand, with Baxter and Giannandrea looking on. The buzz from them was contagious.

'Blood,' Giannandrea told her. 'Easily missed unless you were specifically looking for it.'

It was arterial spray, concentrated on the wall about four feet from the ground in a dull arc, and peppered on the floor. There was no trail away from the spot.

'They're going to do an inch by inch of the area. Paul has skin scrapings, too.'

'Miniscule amounts,' Burke warned.

'We'll take whatever you can get,' she told him.

Christ, Leah. What have you done?

CHAPTER 44

Lainey Henderson's file contained case histories on a number of named women who'd suffered sexual assaults and who seemed to fit her profile of The Beast. Some of them didn't come with addresses and others had moved since they were attacked but they were all relatively easy to trace using electoral rolls and credit checks.

What was much more difficult was approaching them.

Winter knew it was what he'd signed up for but it was the reverse of the way he'd been working and it was making him uneasy. Tracking down the women in the photographs and determining their fate seemed somehow less invasive than searching for known rape victims.

The first was in files dating back to October 2012. The woman woke to find someone in her bedroom, was overpowered, beaten and raped. The police had investigated but got nowhere.

Her name, rightly, hadn't been released to the press

but Lainey had got it through her cop contact. She was Anna Catherine Collins, then living in Inchinnan, now in a flat in Paisley. They had to find her and see if she matched any of the Broome photographs.

They ruled out doing the simplest thing, which was to knock on Anna's door and see what she looked like. That first step would be much easier than the one that would have to follow.

Instead, Winter decided to camp out till he saw the woman, and photograph her. The irony in that act wasn't lost on him but the deception was surely more tolerable than having strangers turn up on her doorstep and ask about something so traumatic.

So there he was, parked up on Wallace Street at eight in the morning, just twenty yards from the flat. The short window offered by the Scottish winter made his task more difficult. Like most people, Anna was likely to leave for work in the dark and return home after daylight had gone.

The street was beginning to come to life, making him more conspicuous, catching sideways glances from passers-by. He huddled as deep into his seat as he could, a hat pulled down low across his forehead, but it couldn't hide his unease. It just felt wrong.

He sat there for half an hour, the entrance to number 12 opening twice but yielding only a teenage boy on his way to school then, five minutes later, an older man going to work. Every minute made his toes colder and his sense of foreboding deepen.

A flash sparked in the corner of his eye and he turned

his head to see the door to number 12 briefly framed in light again. A woman was walking onto the street, wrapped up against the cold, a scarf and hat muffling clear sight of her face. He fired off shot after shot, catching her under the glow of the street lamps until she turned at the corner.

He didn't know what he had, the naked eye being no match for his zoom lens, particularly in this light. Sure that she'd gone, he checked out the results, her face immediately being familiar.

Large, startling eyes, pencil-thin brows, a slim nose and full lips. Strands of blonde hair poked out from under her hat. He *knew* her.

He started up the engine and slowly drove off, parking just a couple of streets away so that he could go through the collection on his phone without being seen.

He flipped through them, memories filtering through, seeing the woman he now knew to be Anna Collins on Buchanan Street. Sunny day, sunglasses pushed through her blonde hair, wearing . . .

A white blouse. The photograph was in front of him now.

There were two others. One by St Enoch subway station the same day and another crossing at traffic lights on what might have been West Nile Street, when she was wearing a black leather jacket.

It was her, he was sure of it.

His dilemma then was what to do about it.

He wasn't keen to approach her, at least not yet and certainly not without Lainey accompanying him. The confirmation that another of Broome's photo subjects had reported a vicious, violent rape, added to the weight of the file he was putting together. Circumstantial in the eyes of a court but damning and disturbing in the view of any decent person.

What would he tell Anna, though, that could make her day any better? That he knew the identity of the man who'd raped her five years earlier but that he couldn't prove it? That didn't quite seem worth the trauma he'd inevitably visit upon her.

He parked it. Adding Anna to the file and moving on.

He knew that D, the former student in Lainey's file, was Donna Irwin. She'd never graduated, dropping out of her course just a few months after being raped. She'd left the flat in Partick and now lived in Saltcoats in Ayrshire.

Home was a small, whitewashed bungalow on Melbourne Terrace, with views across the park to the sea and over to Arran. Parking on Winton Street to give himself a clear view across the park to her house, he settled in and waited. And waited. After an hour, he got out and walked to stretch his legs and minimise suspicion, always keeping the white bungalow in view.

He made a few slow circuits of the park, the wind howling at him off the sea, before giving in to the cold and getting back in the car, hoping not to have been too conspicuous. No one and nothing had stirred in the house and he was well aware he might be wasting his time.

After another hour, he moved the car onto Eglinton

Street and walked again. He was walking by the shore, the wind battering at his back, when he saw the figure emerge from the bungalow and turn right. He picked up his pace to go after her until he saw she was turning into Wilton Street and he would walk right past her. The camera was in the car but would be ridiculously obvious in any case.

His collar was up, hat down, probably an unnecessary disguise given she didn't know him or have reason to suspect him but it still felt like a defence, if only against his own awkwardness. She was fifty yards away now, about five feet seven, slim with short dark hair. He mentally flicked through the folders of files, looking for her.

As they got closer and closer, he discarded most of the possibilities, thinking of a brunette waiting at a bus stop on Hyndland Road. If not her then the young woman photographed through the window of Velvet Elvis when it was still open on Dumbarton Road.

She was just fifteen feet away, ten, and she didn't look familiar. *Closer, they'd get closer. Don't stare.* But how could he avoid it? She was aware of him looking, pointedly looking the other way, but her brows low and furrowed. He was scaring her.

He made a show of looking to his left, away from her, but as she passed, he turned back and saw her face close and clear. Donna Irwin, if that's who she was, had never stood at that bus stop on Hyndland Road or at the window seat in Velvet Elvis. She hadn't been any of the places or in any of the photographs. He'd never seen her before.

His final, frantic stare had freaked her out though. She threw him a frightened, wary look and crossed the street at a trot. She wasn't in Broome's photographs but she had been attacked, had been raped.

Winter took the turn back to where the car was parked, got in and got the hell out of there.

The third and final named victim in Lainey's files was Khalida Dhariwal.

There were only seven Asian women among the huge collection of photographs and Winter had all of them at hand. If he saw her, he'd be able to refer to them immediately.

He'd tracked down her address through a local government contact and found she was living in Claremount Avenue in Giffnock, south west of the city. He prepared himself for another stakeout, far from relishing it after his brief but close encounter with Donna Irwin.

Claremount Avenue was leafy and fairly expensive. A quiet street of Victorian and Edwardian semi-detached houses and bungalows, it was solidly middle-class. The Dhariwal house had a two-car garage off to the side and a large beech tree sheltering it from the street.

Most of the houses had driveways, so very few cars were parked on the narrow street and those that were, were going to be noticed quickly. He parked, driver's side to the kerb, as far from the house as possible while keeping it in view and waited it out.

He'd sat there for no more than half an hour, drawing

quizzical looks from a couple of dog walkers, when he saw someone emerge from the house. It was a woman, tall and slim, with long, dark hair tied back behind her, dressed in all-black running gear. She emerged from the drive and began running straight towards him.

He had his camera ready but didn't have time to get it into any kind of useful position that wasn't going to be very obvious and likely to have her calling the cops. Instead, he pretended to be on his phone but was ready to photograph with it.

Long strides took her towards him quickly, her eyes focusing on the pavement ahead and he praying they'd stay that way. *Oh shit.* he knew her. She was one of his. One of Broome's.

High cheekbones, arching eyebrows, dark-eyed, light-skinned. There were two photographs of her, both in the West End. One walking on Byres Road, her hand going through her hair. The other on Ashton Lane with a friend.

Winter was still staring when Khalida saw him out of the corner of her eye and turned her head to catch him in the act. The look on her face left no doubt she was highly suspicious. She ran on, but in the wing mirror he saw her throw a look over her shoulder.

Time to move. He reached for the keys in the ignition and made to turn them. Just as he did so, he heard a knock on the glass by his ear. He knew even before he looked, but turned his head to see Khalida Dhariwal crouched down and looking in at him.

Shit, shit, shit. Reluctantly, he lowered the window.

She stared him out for a few moments before speaking. 'Is there something I can help you with?'

'No. I'm just waiting for a call.' He held his phone up as if that explained it. 'Didn't want to have to take it while I was driving.'

'Uh huh. I thought you were maybe lost. Or looking for someone. I've got my phone on me too. I could call the police if you're needing help.'

It was direct and confrontational. She didn't think for a moment that he was lost.

'No, I'm okay thanks.'

'Are you now?' She laughed at him, knowing she was in complete control of the situation. 'Well, why don't you tell me just what you're doing here watching me or else I *will* call the cops. I'm a lawyer and I happen to know quite a few of them.'

'Look, there's nothing to tell. I'm just—'

She held her phone up as a warning to cut the bullshit.

'I'm a journalist.'

Her eyebrows raised sharply. 'Possibly the only occupation more hated than mine. Why are you here and what the hell do you want?'

He really didn't want to do this here and now but his head wasn't working quickly enough to come up with something she wouldn't see right through.

'I'm following a story about a man named William Broome.'

He saw the reaction. She knew the name. Knew what he was.

'And what would that have to do with me?'

302

He looked around. Breathed deep. 'William Broome had a collection, a large collection, of photographs of women taken in public without their knowledge. I wasn't certain until I came here today, but I'm now sure you were among the women he photographed.'

She blinked, her mouth bobbing open, and took half a step back as she lost balance, having to put her arm down to steady herself.

'Can I see some identification? See that you are who you say you are.'

He pulled his press card from his jacket pocket and held it up for her to see.

She studied it and him in turn. 'Okay, Tony Winter. There's a café called Bramble on Fenwick Road. I'll meet you there in five minutes.'

By the time Winter drove the half mile to Bramble and found somewhere to park, Khalida had beaten him to it. She sat with her back to the wall, a large glass of orange juice in front of her. The only other people in were a young couple having a late breakfast in the other corner. Winter ordered an orange juice for himself and joined her.

She got straight to the point. 'These photographs, I assume you have copies with you. I'd like to see them.'

He produced his phone, the folder already at the two images from Broome's collection.

She took his mobile and studied them. She breathed out hard.

'Well, it's me all right. I've never seen these before

303

but they must be … eight or nine years old? I haven't lived in the West End since then. How did you know where to find me, Mr Winter? I'm assuming, maybe hoping, these photographs didn't have addresses on the back of them.'

'I've never seen the originals, only digital copies, but I very much doubt there was an address on them. This is a difficult thing to explain. Sensitive.'

'Well that worries me. But just tell me.'

'As I think you know, William Broome faced trial for rape.' He saw her eyes tighten. 'The case collapsed, partly for technical reasons but mainly because the witness refused to testify at the last minute.'

'Go on.' Her voice was dryer, tenser, quieter.

'There was a woman, a rape counsellor who had been following cases like Broome's, rapes that followed a similar pattern. She made a point of collating them.'

'And I was among them.'

'Yes.'

Khalida held the glass of orange juice in front of her face, nibbling on her lower lip, head nodding. 'Tell me about the case that collapsed.'

Winter did so. Trying to spare the gratuitous detail but not miss anything relevant. When he'd finished, she took a large gulp of the juice, buying herself some composure time.

'There are differences. This poor woman wasn't drugged and I'm sure I was. She was beaten into unconsciousness, the bastard that raped me used something like chloroform. I could smell it, smell something.'

She hesitated and refuelled with air. 'But he called me a slag before I was unconscious. A number of times. I think I went out with that word being repeated at me. I was somewhere between passing out and out and I remember being hit in time with the word.'

Winter could only hold her gaze and nod.

'How many of these photographs are there?'

'Five hundred and twenty-four. Three hundred and fifteen individual women.'

She stared at him as the numbers sank in until she couldn't cope with the enormity of it, letting her eyes slide over and both hands come up to cover her face. She blew out hard.

'Okay. So, what the fuck are you doing about it? And why you and not the police?'

'It's complicated for now. We're trying to find the women in the photographs. We're trying to establish just what he's done and to who. We're trying to build a case to prove that he is a dangerous and extremely violent rapist and that he has been over a number of years and on a scale that is frightening.'

'And what do you want from me?'

'Whatever you feel you're able to give.'

'Mr Winter, I've been waiting for this for eight years. I'll give everything I've got. It's not going to be much but I'll give it. My husband knows what happened to me. It was four years before we met but I told him everything. He had to know that if I sometimes acted in a certain way then there might be a reason for it. I have nothing to hide from him. My daughter is only two and, of course, knows nothing but nor will she. Not until I'm ready to explain it to her myself.

'Can I identify the man that attacked and raped me? No, absolutely not. I did not see his face. Can and will I testify that I was attacked and raped and that I am the person in two of Broome's photographs? Yes, absolutely I will.'

CHAPTER 45

Opening mail was rarely a pleasurable experience for a journalist. For a start, complaints outnumbered compliments by about twenty to one. Everyone was a critic and they could all do a better job. If only they could spell, have a rough grasp of where an apostrophe might go and have the first idea of what a story was.

Winter got tired of opening letters a long time ago. They were easily divided into two categories; those with typed addresses and those that were handwritten. The former were usually press releases, which was basically someone trying to buy advertising on the cheap. The vast majority of those went straight in the bin. The handwritten ones? Well that depended on the handwriting.

Neat often meant over sixty and therefore usually polite even when ripping your story to shreds. The interesting ones were in untidy scrawls with speculative spelling and tended to come from drunks or sociopaths or drunken sociopaths. The wilder ones liked to use red or green biro. Those were usually death threats or claims of alien abduction and there were far more of those than you'd think.

The envelope in Winter's hand now didn't quite fit any of those categories. It was typed but it still managed some of the scariness of the scrawlers. The font used was big and chunky, not the usual corporate style at all. His name, the paper's title and the address were all in capitals too. It was a letter determined not to be missed.

He didn't like it much when a letter came addressed directly to him. When he started, he expected them either to contain tips for stories or a pat on the back for some great photographs. He soon learned it just meant the abuse was personal.

Reluctantly, he slid it open and fetched out four sheets of A4 paper. The first three were blank, serving only as additional wrapping for the one inside. It was typed with the same chunky font as the envelope but in a much bigger size.

A series of letters and then numbers stretched across the page.

WMB JP 55.648608, -4.170116

Winter turned each sheet over in turn, checking the other side for something that explained it. He'd become used to his mail making little or no sense but this was a new take on it.

He laid the paper out in front of him on his desk, holding down the curling corners with a combination of books, a mug and his phone. The numbers meant nothing to him. He checked the envelope again. Definitely for him, his name being shouted out in those ugly block capitals, leaving no doubt.

An inner voice told him to take more care. Keep his fingers off the paper and the envelope as much as he could. Sure, it might just have been some nutter, there was certainly no shortage of those, but instinct told him otherwise.

He had ideas, some more fixed than others, but the numbers baffled him. If it was a code then he was the wrong person to crack it. Alanna could solve a sudoku puzzle quicker than he could.

Was it a sum? Did the dash mean take the second number from the first one? He tried but got nothing that made any more sense.

A combination to a safe? Computer programming code? Number plates, DNA strings, passages from the Bible?

In the end, he took the only logical twenty-first century route. He stuck it into Google.

The string WMB JP 55.648608, -4.170116 produced precisely zero results. It didn't completely surprise him. He tried again, this time typing in just the numbers.

The top result was a rectangular image, beige in colour, featuring a few wiggly blue lines that looked like veins. In the middle of it was a green downward arrow. In the bottom, right-hand corner were the words 'Map data 2017 Google'. He clicked on the arrow.

The numbers were coordinates. Latitude and

longitude. The map it produced was nothing more than a bigger beige canvas with blue veins for rivers but no identifying place names. He reduced the scale, bringing words into view. Hareshaw. Rotten Burn. Hall Burn. West Hookhead Farm. Caldermill. He reduced it further till he saw names he vaguely recognised, Darvel and Strathaven. Smaller still and he saw it was South Lanarkshire.

He switched to the satellite view and closed in again, seeing the coordinates sat in the middle of a dark green swathe. Trees. Hundreds upon hundreds of trees, thick together, light barely penetrating and just a few tracks of earth as paths criss-crossed the forest.

Winter switched out again, trying to get his head round where these woods were. North was East Kilbride. Further north still was Glasgow. West was Kilmarnock.

He stared at the map, studied it, followed the roads west, east and north. Finally, he saw it. Or maybe he saw what he wanted to see. About ten miles due north of the thick, dark green area of woods that the coordinates had brought up on his screen, near as dammit straight north as the crow might fly, was Cambuslang.

Home of McCallum's Café. Home of Atheneum estate agents.

JP. Julie Petrie.

And the initials he'd long since guessed at. WMB. William Michael Broome.

CHAPTER 46

Winter's first decision was going to be his biggest. Who to tell.

If he went to Archie Cameron then it would be out of his control. Archie would get excited and probably demand they ran the story as it was, in case anyone else got there first. It was half a story, though, and Winter wanted all of it.

He had to go to the police, but did he go with head or with heart? It had to be either Addison or Rachel. He knew where his loyalty lay but he might be doing her more of a favour by going to Addy instead.

She'd want it but she wouldn't. If he bypassed her and went to Addison, he'd save her from herself and from all the accusations that would come from other cops and other media. As long as she saw it that way.

And, of course, it might be nothing. A prank or a set-up, someone's idea of a joke. It didn't feel like it though. It felt very much like something.

He chose Addison and whatever consequences came his way because of it.

A quick phone call set up a meeting in their usual haunt, the Station Bar on Port Dundas Road not far from Stewart Street station. Addison had asked what it was about but Winter didn't want to talk about it on the phone. That and the prospect of Guinness was enough to get his pal interested.

Their relationship had changed, on the surface at least, since Winter had become a journalist. Addison was a bit more guarded, seeing them on opposite sides, and shied away from work talk when they got together. Neither of them was above using their relationship when it suited, though, and this was one of those times.

Addison had got to the TSB first and was queuing up two pints of the black stuff, the creamy heads settling as Winter walked into the bar.

'All right, wee man?'

'Yeah, I think so. How's things?'

'Things are interesting. A royal pain in the arse but interesting. What's happening at home? Rachel still getting bothered by the wee bawbags online?'

'Danny's on the case, thinks he's getting somewhere so let's hope so. Let's find somewhere quieter to do this.'

Addison raised his eyebrows. 'Like that, is it? Sounds promising. Okay, we'll go through the back.'

The picked up their pints and made their way through to the raised level at the rear of the bar. It might have qualified as a mezzanine but that seemed altogether too wanky a term in a pub like the TSB. There were two guys in their twenties already ensconced there but

Addison sized them up and knew they'd budge. They took him for a cop right away and exchanged glances before getting up and moving through to the main bar.

'Never fails,' Addison lamented. 'Too many people with guilty consciences.'

'Maybe they just think you're an arse.'

'Could be. Anyway, cheers, wee man.'

They raised their glasses towards each other, then supped. Addison's mouthful was considerably longer and larger.

'I could really do with more than one of these. Luring me down here with your gateway drugs and promises of information. What you got, Tony?'

'Well, first of all I've got a reminder that I'm not one of your informants. This is a two-way process. I'm going to want a story back in return.'

'Aye, aye, wee man. Whatever.'

'No. Not whatever. Don't piss me about, Addy. This is serious. For both of us. All of us.'

Addison's brows furrowed, confused by Winter's insistence.

'Okay. You'll get your story if there is one. But you know that. Come on, I get that this is important. So, tell me.'

Winter nodded, satisfied, and reached into the bag he had over his shoulder. He took out two plastic bags with sheaves of paper inside each, placing one on the table and opening the other.

'That is the original, you probably want to get it checked for prints. And this' – he handed it over – 'is a copy. I got the original through the post this morning, addressed directly to me at the *Standard*.'

Addison studied it. Looking from the printed page to Winter and back.

'Give me a clue?'

'You read the piece I ran on Julie Petrie, the woman who disappeared from Cambuslang. Presumed dead.'

'Presumed murdered. Of course I read it. And it was with a photograph I'd never seen before. Want to tell me where you got that?'

'It's not important.'

'Well, maybe I think it is. Anyway, JP is Julie Petrie?'

'I think so, yes.'

Addison took another gulp at his Guinness. 'Okay, you've got my attention. And going by what I know you've been up to, I'm assuming WMB will be our friend William Michael Broome. And these' – he traced a finger across the number sequence – 'are coordinates. So many degrees north by so many west. Do you know where it is?'

Winter nodded. 'Let me show you.'

He took out his phone, opened the Google Earth app and punched in the numbers. The blue globe spun on its axis until it settled on the lonely rock near the top of the world then spiralled in, rushing towards the west of Scotland.

Addison watched the earth spin until it stopped above the dark, dense green of the forest. A low whistle signalling his interest. 'Good place to bury a body.'

'That's what I thought. It's eleven miles almost

due south of Cambuslang, directly west of a hamlet called Caldermill.'

'Due south?'

'If you'd been looking for somewhere secluded and drew a straight line from Cambuslang, this is the place you'd come to.'

'Well, well. And, let me have one final guess for the grand prize. The photograph you used for your piece on the woman, Broome took it. It was from his little collection.'

'Yes.'

'Fuck.'

Addison drank and thought. 'Why didn't you take this to Rachel? Broome is her case.'

'Well, for one thing, that's not what we do. She does her thing, I do mine. Also, I don't want to make any more trouble for her than she's got. I figured that if I took it to you, you'd bring her in on it.'

'I will.'

'Okay, good. So, what are you going to do?'

He finished his pint, letting the last few drops trickle down his throat.

'I'm going to get some shovels.'

A small convoy left Glasgow early the next morning bound for the woods west of Caldermill. It wasn't yet daylight and the drive took them just a bit over forty minutes. Winter and Narey had been picked up separately and travelled down in different cars, each trapped in their own chilled silences.

315

The cars, four of them plus a van pulling a low-loader, parked as near to the woods as they could. Three constables manhandled a jackhammer into the trees while others brought shovels and pickaxes. The last of them steered the ground-penetrating radar equipment as best they could.

All the while, a small team of forensics waited in the relative heat of their car for a call to action that might never come. They all knew it might be a hoax. It would come down on Addison's head if it was. He was the one giving credence to the journalist's tip-off, the one buying some numbers printed on a piece of paper like they were a bag of magic beans.

Winter was there, given permission to photograph but under strict conditions. Nothing evidential, nothing that showed the precise location and absolutely none of his pish taking photos of officers. He'd agreed to it all.

It took him back, though. No more than two years to when he took the police shilling and photographed for forensic science rather than the *Standard*. He felt the same sense of anticipation he always had waiting for the curtain to go up on the main show. The difference this time was that there might not be a show and although Addison would get the blame, the fault would be his.

The radar machine looked like a lawnmower with a screen fitted at the push bar. It had its own inbuilt GPS and they were going to use that to match to the coordinates sent to Winter. The advice was that they could expect the numbers to be five or ten feet out in any direction if they'd been taken from Google Earth. If the person that mapped it had just stuck a pin into the woods then it could be anywhere among the trees. If it was there at all.

Winter and Narey had kept their distance from each other after arriving, a forced attempt at professional detachment, but as the radar went to work, inching over the frozen ground, they too inched closer together.

At last they were just a few feet apart, breaths misting in front of them as they stared at the machine doing its thing.

'Do you think this is genuine?'

'I guess we'll find out soon enough. It felt real when I opened it up. Either way, it couldn't be ignored.'

'Who do you think sent it?'

'I'm trying not to look a gift horse in the mouth by bothering myself with that too much. Obvious answer is the killer, who else would know? And the obvious answer is that it's Broome. As to why? Fuck knows.'

'Hmm, maybe. I'm not a big fan of the obvious, as you know. Thanks for talking to Addison.'

'You being sarcastic?'

'No, I'm not. If this turns out to be someone's idea of a joke then it would look doubly stupid if it had been me who'd acted on something you'd come up with. If it's real . . . then it's what we need and it doesn't matter a damn who got it first.'

'I managed to do something right?'

'Probably more by luck than judgement.'

'Cheers.'

317

'You're welcome. It's times like this I wish I smoked. Be something to do while watching this machine work.'

The guy operating the radar wasn't helping them at all. His face was impassive, deep in concentration, giving nothing away either way. They still watched him though, desperate for the first sign that this was real.

He'd moved on, a few yards away from the spot suggested by the coordinates, widening the search bit by bit. Everyone on the site watched him work and waited, shivering in the chill of fresh daylight.

Winter photographed him. Reluctantly, he did so from behind so as not to show his face. It meant missing out on seeing his expression and not being able to record the quiet determination that was so riveting. He caught the work though, the solemn diligence of it, the breath of life frosting before the operator's mouth as he searched for death in the frozen ground.

The man stopped in his tracks and heads rose around the site. He backed up a few paces and retraced the route he'd just taken. Breaths were held, pulses quickened in anticipation. He held up one arm to signal for attention, as if unaware they'd been watching his every move.

Addison was at his side in moments. The rest of them couldn't hear the discussion but they saw the operator's head nod in answer to Addison's questions. There was something.

The DCI waved the constables towards him, giving them instructions that saw all but one of them ready the digging equipment. The other went to fetch the forensics.

'About three feet down,' Addison told Narey. 'He's pretty sure but caveat is that it could be an animal, could be something else entirely. But he's confident.'

'Well, let's find out.'

They broke the frozen topsoil with the jackhammer, taking the first couple of feet of soil out quickly with shovels. All the while, one of the SOCOs, Paul Burke, did the job that Winter still thought of as being his. A bit of him ached to be recording it, standing over the emerging grave and capturing the uncovering of truth, grain by grain. Instead, he had to stay back and content himself with nothing more than stock shots of men bending their backs as they dug deeper.

The donkey work done, forensics took over, carefully scraping away dirt for fear of damaging evidence. The process slowed and time seemed to slow with it. Everyone on site edged closer and closer, eager for a look, eager to see the white of bones.

The final stretch was done by brush, flicking away soil, inch by agonising inch. Those watching could see they had something but the wait was stretching everyone's patience. Finally, one of the forensics popped his head above ground and waved Burke closer. Winter's jealousy knew no bounds at the approach of the money shot.

Once Burke had photographed the find from all available angles, the remaining mourners were allowed to congregate on the graveside. They formed a solemn circle, heads bowed, staring down at dust and ashes. And bones.

The hole was no more than four feet long and two feet wide. However, it was plenty big enough to hold the concertinaed skeleton that had been eked out of the earth. Winter, his finger itching to pull the trigger on the camera he'd been forced to set aside, could make out the long femurs and the shorter fibulas tucked below. The rib cage was shattered, probably crushed by the weight of earth. But the skull had been broken by something much less natural. An ugly, jagged crack ran across the top and there was an enlarged hole around one eye.

'She'd been in something close to the foetal position, either for protection or forced into it to make her fit the grave,' the SOCO announced. 'I'd say she was five feet six tall. She has a fractured skull, fractured eye socket and a broken arm. And there's this . . .'

Gloved fingers held up a tarnished silver bracelet in an evidence bag. 'It was round her wrist. The lettering isn't easy to make it out but there's a name engraved on it.'

He passed the bagged bracelet to Addison, who held it up to the light. All he needed to say was one word.

'Julie.'

CHAPTER 47

It was one of those stories sold and told by the headline.

JULIE PETRIE'S BODY FOUND
IN SHALLOW GRAVE

The strapline added some explanation for those who didn't recognise the name.

MISSING WIFE'S CORPSE DISCOVERED AFTER 9 YEARS

There wasn't, and couldn't be, any mention of Broome. There was no evidence of his involvement, at least none that could find its way into a newspaper just yet. As much as Winter would have loved to have included the link to Julie being in Broome's collection, that was off limits. For now.

The story didn't need it though. It was a slam dunk of a front-page splash.

Even those who might not have remembered or known about the Petrie case couldn't miss the draw in a murdered woman's body being dug up from a grave in the woods. It screamed out to the ghouls and the rubberneckers, calling to their need for gossip and gore. He'd done his best not to make it lurid or any more sensationalist than he had to but inevitably a few choice adjectives had been added by the subs to spice it up, dripping from the page like blood.

The wood became sinister, the grave became hastily-dug, Julie became tragic and her killer became brutal. The few killers who weren't brutal in the tabloid world were either merciless or evil.

His photographs were used large and there were more inside where the story careered over a further two pages, all bolstered by a bold and underlined EXCLUSIVE. The facts were few so the description and the back story were given full rein.

He'd spoken to Julie's parents and her brother, and of course to the grieving husband. While Tom and Kathleen Fotheringham and their son were stuck somewhere between relief and horror, Iain Petrie could barely contain his glee that he'd soon be off the hook. It was more in the telling than the words but even on the page, he came off as more interested in himself than his murdered wife.

'I was shocked when the police told me they'd found a body and it had been confirmed as Julie's. I always prayed this day would come but it is still a huge personal blow.

'I knew Julie had been murdered, knew she

wouldn't just have disappeared and left me without saying anything. I'd told the police it would be like this but nobody believed me.

'I hope that the police will now be able to finally find the person who killed Julie so that I can have some peace of mind and bring an end to some of the scandalous and frankly evil rumours that have circulated since Julie disappeared. The last nine years have been a nightmare for me, I've been put through hell, and I hope this marks the beginning of the end.'

The take-up on the story was immediate and widespread. The other newspapers scrambled to get it into their online editions, using stock photographs of Julie and stealing what they could from Winter's copy until their reporters were able to get quotes of their own. Julie Petrie's face looked out from every newspaper and every television screen, and it was all over the social media that had been in its infancy when she'd disappeared.

But the *Standard* flew the one photograph that no one else had. Julie, the rather sad brunette, walking towards the camera, head slightly down, her expression thoughtful.

Using it once must have enraged Broome. Using it a second time, particularly in relation to her body being dug up, might just push him dangerously close to the edge. It was a risk Winter was willing to take.

When Archie Cameron asked him if he wanted to put the interview with Broome's mother on hold, Winter hesitated. Part of him wanted to drive the boot home, kick the fucker when he was down and apply as much pressure as possible.

The danger, however, was that the interview with Elspeth Broome would get lost in the fallout from the finding of the body. There were only so many column inches to go around and Winter wanted maximum exposure. He also liked the idea of Broome reeling and fuming from the Petrie story, on his knees and struggling when, *bam*.

He told Archie to hold it. For two days.

CHAPTER 48

Liz was a cleaner. 'Domestic operative' she liked to call it when anyone asked. She did three lots of three hours a day in a regular cycle of houses where people were too lazy or too busy to do it themselves.

She liked it. Sometimes the owners were at home, sometimes not, but even if they were they tended to get out of her way and let her get on with it. The roar of a vacuum cleaner or the stink of furniture polish kept most people at arm's length. She could work at her own pace, get lost in her thoughts, try to work out how to make her youngest do his homework or her man to stop at four cans of Tennent's a night. Sometimes she'd drift off completely – her hands would be wiping off someone else's dust but her head was on a beach in St Lucia with George Clooney rubbing sun cream on her back and whispering filthy stuff in her ear. Fair made the time fly.

It was a bit weird at first, being in another person's house. She felt like a burglar or a peeping Tom, spent too much time thinking, *Really, they thought that colour was a good idea?* or *Christ, look at the state of those curtains.* She'd wonder what their houses said about people, thinking she was seeing their secrets, into rooms where visitors would never go, seeing what they had in their bathroom cabinets. She'd found all sorts. Hair dye, Viagra, incontinence pads. All the things that people needed to be what they wanted when the world wasn't looking.

She quickly got past that, though. People were people and people were strange. That was the beginning and end of it. Wasn't her business to wonder or to judge. The whole thing only worked if they trusted her. If she found women's underwear in the man's drawer then she'd shut it and forget it. If she found porn in the teen-ager's bedroom then she'd leave it undisturbed.

Liz liked what she did. They were nice people for the most part, a couple of stuck-up arses and one or two proper weirdos but she could live with that. She got £27 for a three-hour cleaning shift and most of them rounded it up to thirty. Plus a wee bonus at Christmas, either cash or a bottle. Of course, her man usually helped himself to the bottle, but that was another story.

She was looking forward to her stint on Carlaverock Road that morning. The cold was chilling her bones but old Elspeth always had the heating on full blast and the house was like the Caribbean, even if George Clooney wasn't there.

It was an old, rambling detached sandstone, much bigger inside than it looked from the street. Horrible carpets with floral patterns that made Liz want to throw up but loads of interesting things, knick-knacks on shelves and cabinets and the like. Elspeth wasn't one for throwing anything out. She had all this stuff in its own place and hell to pay if any of it was moved. A right bugger to dust they all were too.

Liz knocked on the door, waited, then knocked twice more. Elspeth was in more often than not but sometimes she was at her son's or he'd have taken her shopping. When she didn't answer on the third knock, Liz used her key. It had taken Elspeth eight months before she'd trusted Liz enough to give her it. She was pretty sure it had been her son that had stopped her from doing it earlier. She and Elspeth had got on fine, would even take ten minutes sometimes and chat over a coffee at the dining table.

She pushed her way inside, dusting the frost from her feet and shouting out just in case. No answer though. A wee bit of her was quite glad, the house to herself and no lecture about moving Elspeth's things about even though she never did. She was even happier that the son didn't seem to be there; he creeped Liz out something terrible.

The heating was on, sure enough. It was on a timer and blasted out like the furnaces of hell for most of the day. Elspeth's laddie had a bit of cash and was always telling her not to skimp on the heating because the cold would be the death of her. Elspeth took him at his word and was a one-woman global-warming machine.

Jeez, this house was musty. Not Liz's fault because she had it as clean as it could be. It was just old and overheated and had the horrible carpets. It smelled.

She'd start in the hall, get the hoover as deep into the carpet as possible, maybe suck up the bloody pattern if she worked it hard enough. She sang a bit as she got into it. Kings of Leon, 'Sex on Fire'. She'd never be able to sing it at home, her man would just go off on one. Empty house, it was fine.

She didn't really know all the words to the song but that didn't matter. She just repeated the first two verses a couple of times, going to the chorus whenever she got stuck. She did the same with 'Hotel California' and then 'Mr Brightside'.

The carpet, the bloody carpet, ran all the way from the hallway up the stairs to the landing where the bedrooms were. A never-ending swirl of wall-to-wall seventies eye-ache. She'd wanted to burn this thing from the first minute she set foot on it.

She pushed the hoover round the landing then stopped, seeing cobwebs in the ceiling corners that were going to need a chair or stepladders to reach. She wondered if she could get away with them till next time, pretend she'd never seen them. *Oh bollocks*, she better do it.

She switched the hoover off and started downstairs to get the stepladder from the alcove. She'd only taken a few steps when she heard a noise. That's all she could identify it as. A sound. She didn't know what it was or where it had come from but it spooked her. Silly really.

She took two more steps and heard it again. There was someone else in the house.

'Elspeth? *Elspeth?*'

328

Was it up or down? She stood and listened even though a part of her was tempted to head for the front door and get out. A big old house like this could get scary really quickly if you believed in ghosts like Liz did. No way Elspeth would have let her be in this long without speaking to her. She'd have been along to harp on about the dusting, for one thing.

There it was again. It was like the last swirl of water going down a drain. Had Elspeth left the bath running or was there a leak? It was upstairs, she was sure of that much now. *Hell*, she'd better have a look.

She trod slowly, quietly back up the stairs, listening but hearing nothing. The bathroom was off to the left and she warily edged the door wide and stepped inside with one hand on the frame, ready to close it again. There was no one inside. The bath taps weren't running but she turned them off tighter just to be sure, then did the same with the sink.

Back in the hallway, she stood still. Hoping to hear something, and yet not. Was that a noise from the big bedroom, Elspeth's room? *Shit.*

She pushed the door with the tips of her fingers and it eased slowly away from her. A cat, that's what it probably was. A cat that had sneaked in. Or maybe a bird that had got in through the chimney.

'Hello?'

Reluctantly, she inched inside. Ready to turn and run or to laugh at herself for being so stupid. There was no noise, no need to stay, best just to go. She was fully inside the door before she saw anything.

When she did, she stopped still, not knowing what to do, not sure she could believe her eyes. There was a scream stuck somewhere between her throat and her stomach but it couldn't escape. She stumbled back a bit, her back slamming into the door and closing it behind her, shutting her in with the body on the bed.

She'd never seen so much blood. For one irrational moment, she wondered how the hell she'd get it out of the duvet.

It hit her, though. Elspeth, poor old Elspeth, was staring at the ceiling or the stars or heaven or whatever she believed in. She was in her nightie, it looked like it might have been the pink one but oh God it was so difficult to tell.

She was soaked in it. White as a ghost. Skin like milk. Lips pale as powder. Face battered.

Liz put a hand to her mouth, thinking she was going to vomit. She was terrified too, fearing the noise meant there was still someone else in the house.

She had to call the police. Except she couldn't move. The phone was by the bed, by Elspeth's head. She couldn't go there. Her own phone, her mobile, God she couldn't think. She leaned back against the door and scrambled to get the phone out of her pocket. Her hands shook as she punched in 999.

Police, please, Ambulance too. She told the woman the address and told her what it was. A murder. A big hole in her chest. So much blood. And there might be someone else still in the house. Hurry. *Please.*

330

The woman told her not to leave the room. The police were on their way.

Even from the door, Liz could see stab wounds, lots of them. Someone had ripped the woman to shreds. She found the courage to take a few nervous steps forward but could barely breathe. As she got closer, she saw the mess the old lady's face was in and felt her breakfast rush to her throat.

Liz nearly soiled herself when the noise came again.

It was coming from Elspeth. What the hell was it? She went closer still, lowering her head despite all her senses telling her not to. She had to wait for what seemed like forever. *There.* A gurgle. Like water struggling to swirl down a drain.

She backed away, more frightened than before, picking up her phone again and calling them back. They *really* had to hurry. *Please!*

Taking her hand, she tried to find a pulse but didn't really know what she was doing. Elspeth felt so cold.

'Jesus Christ, Mrs Broome. Who did this to you?'

CHAPTER 49

Carlaverock Road was already a crime scene by the time Narey got there. She had to park at the corner of the street and weave her way through a gaggle of nosy neighbours and past uniforms on guard outside the Broome house and another inside the front door.

The ambulance was still outside, rear doors wide open, waiting to accept its passenger then make a quick getaway. Narey knew that meant the paramedics were treating her where she lay or else they'd have been in the Queen Elizabeth by now. At least she'd get a chance to see it as it was.

She took the stairs two at a time, hearing chaos above her, orders being shouted. Rico Giannandrea was standing at the bedroom door, deep in conversation with a uniformed constable before sending him downstairs with instructions to get the neighbours further back from the property.

'She alive, Rico?'

'Last I looked, yes. It's touch and go though. She's lost a hell of a lot of blood and they've already had to use the defibrillator to keep her going. They're trying to make sure she's strong enough to move but they say there's no guarantee she'll make it out of here.'

'Thanks for calling me, Rico. I appreciate it.'

'It's your case, boss. We all want you to get this guy.'

'We don't know it was him. Unless you've got more than you've told me.'

Giannandrea allowed himself a smile. 'Nothing other than guesswork and you're right, shouldn't get ahead of myself. Baxter says she's lain there for a few hours. He estimates around twenty-five entry wounds plus severe trauma to the face.'

'Christ.'

'He reckons the attacker used a long-bladed knife and there's one missing from a holder in the kitchen that fits the description.'

'Where's Broome?'

'I've sent a car to his offices to pick him up and bring him here. I haven't heard back from them yet so he might be on his way.'

'Good. I want to see his face. First though, I want to see his mother.'

The bedroom was a buzz of controlled chaos. Paramedics hovered over the bed, working quickly, while another readied a stretcher. There was an oxygen mask over Mrs Broome's face and a tube in her mouth but Narey could still see the damage that had been inflicted there.

She moved closer, drawing a disapproving look from a squat, dark-haired male paramedic who was standing over the old woman. Her clothes had been cut open so they could treat her, stemming what was left of the blood flow. The wounds to her chest and abdomen were deep, visceral and frenzied, unmissable even soaked in rusty red.

There were defensive wounds to her hands and cuts to her shoulders. There were severe contusions to her head, dark purple bruises and her nose had been broken, one cheek too. The facial damage harked back to Lainey Henderson, to Jennifer Buchanan and to Leah Watt.

It was an annihilation. This was done by someone who didn't know when to stop. This had been done in a fury. This had been personal.

Narey's eyes strayed beyond the obvious wounds, seeing the white of the woman's thighs in contrast to her bloodied trunk and wondering about other atrocities.

Her thoughts were disturbed by a gurgling noise as Broome's mother protested, causing the paramedic to adjust the tubing into her mouth and offer reassurance. It struck Narey that it was the first sign she'd seen or heard that the victim was indeed alive. Barely alive, though, and who knew for how long. There were a hundred questions she was desperate to ask her but they all boiled down to just one.

Please let it have been him, she thought. *Please let it be him.*

'Okay, let's move her.' The paramedics were done, as confident as they could be that she could and should be moved. 'Everyone out of the way, please. Everyone.' The repetition was for Narey's sake.

'Is she going to make it?'

The paramedic just shrugged and pushed past. They didn't have time to chat, no matter who she was.

Narey stood at the top of the stairs, watching Elspeth Broome being manoeuvred carefully down the stairs and to the waiting ambulance. She took a breath then sought out first Baxter and then Giannandrea.

Two Soups was stomping unhappily around the ground floor. The necessities of keeping the woman alive had meant the paramedics taking priority over his SOCOs and the subsequent trampling all over his crime scene. His job was so much easier when the victim wasn't still breathing.

There were no signs of a forced entry to the house, he told her. No windows broken, no lock forced. It seems whoever did it had been let into the house or had a key.

Giannandrea was on the phone as she approached and he held up a finger to signal to her to wait. His brows were knotted, jaw set. Something had changed.

'And what time was that? Shit. Get a hold of his mobile number from them. And leave someone at the house until I tell you otherwise.'

There was a further reply on the other end of the phone, frustrating Narey's desperation to discover what was going on.

'What is it, Rico?'

'The two uniforms I sent to Broome's office have come up empty-handed. He wasn't in the office and staff said he hadn't been in today although he should have been. He had some important meeting scheduled for ten o'clock. When he didn't show, they eventually called him at home and on his mobile but got no answer. They emailed and texted him but no reply.'

'Have they checked his house?'

'Our boys have just been there. It's locked up and no one's home. His car isn't there either. He's disappeared.'

'So, do we know when he was last seen or spoken to?'

'His assistant says she spoke to him last night. He was at home then, seemed to be nothing out of the usual. Broome had said he was having an early night and would be in the office early this morning but didn't show.'

'That it?'

'One of his neighbours thinks they saw him leave in his car about eight this morning. More than enough time to have got to his office.'

'Or to here.'

'And up early enough that he might have read the newspapers before he left or at least seen the headlines online.'

'You think he saw Tony's article and then came straight over to see his mother, demanding to know why she'd said those things?'

He lifted his shoulders. 'We know the guy's got a temper. Might have been enough to set him off.'

'It was the first thing I thought when you called to say she'd been attacked. Why couldn't I have married an accountant or a plumber, Rico?'

'Two reasons. One, you don't know how to make life easy for yourself. And two, you don't want to.'

'Do you never get fed up always being right? Anyway, I need you to go get a DC to the hospital, Kerri Wells would be good. Make sure she tells me as soon as Mrs Broome is well enough to talk. If she ever is. And make sure that the examiner checks Mrs Broome out for any indications of forced sexual activity. Bruising, vaginal tearing, that sort of thing.'

'Oh Jesus ...'

'We just need to check.'

She left the house to a salvo of photography and her name being called. The press was there en masse, smelling a new twist to the story that had already fed them so well. She searched their ranks, looking for one face behind the battery of cameras and one body amid the flurry of notebooks and digital recorders.

There he was. Back left, his lens trained on her like she was a stranger.

She pushed on past the uniformed constables, ready to barge her way through the media throng to her car. The calls were relentless.

'*Inspector, can you confirm that the victim is Elspeth Broome?*'

'*Inspector Narey. Over here.*'

'*Inspector, can you tell us if this is a murder enquiry?*'

'*Inspector, can you give us a statement, please?*'

She would normally go straight by them, ignoring their pleas and leave them out there in the cold. This time she didn't.

'Okay, I'll take a few questions. However, I cannot

confirm any identities until the next of kin have been notified.'

It took them by surprise and there was a momentary holding of breath before they exploded into voice again, each of them fighting to be heard. She made a show of looking around as if deciding whose question to take, but she'd already decided.

She pointed at him, a dozen pair of eyes following her finger, seeing Winter in the firing line.

He hesitated, aware he was venturing into a minefield and was in danger of being blown up in full view of his colleagues and rivals.

'Inspector, can you confirm that the householder is Elspeth Broome and that you're treating this as attempted murder?'

It was her turn to pause, but only to let him sweat.

'I can tell you that the assault on a seventy-two-year-old woman is being treated as suspicious, yes. As to whether it will be murder or attempted murder, that's in the hands of her doctors.'

Other questions were called, urgent voices pleading to be heard. She pointed at him again. Heads swivelled, faces twisted. No one was happy at this but some sensed a show about to start.

'Can you confirm that the householder is the victim?'

Her eyes burned into his. 'I said I wasn't going to identify the victim, so you'll have to draw your own conclusions. Next question.'

She knew the look on his face. Hurt. Guilt. Wanting

to be told it wasn't his fault. She wasn't going to let him off that hook, not today. He was going to have to ask.

'Inspector, do you have any evidence as to the motive for this attack?'

She let it hang there, twisting in the wind.

'No I don't, Mr Winter. *Do you?*'

CHAPTER 50

The three of them ate a silent dinner. Winter, Narey and Danny. Appetites and conversation suppressed by what had happened or what was about to. They pushed food around their plates and stared at it, worry being multiplied by worry.

Narey hadn't forgiven him but had already moved on in her mind to how to deal with it. In the meantime, she was continuing to let him suffer.

When dinner was done, Danny fed the plates into the dishwasher and announced he was going out. He didn't say why.

'Where are you off to, Dan?'

'I'm going out for a beer. Don't wait up.'

His evasiveness stirred Narey's curiosity. 'Where are you going?'

'A place called the Rum Shack.'

'On Pollokshaws Road?'

'Yes. You know it?'

'Oh, I know where it is. It's right next door to the hair-dressers where Leah Watt worked when she was attacked.

So why would you be going to the south side for a beer in a bar that really doesn't sound like your kind of place?'

Danny looked from her to Winter, his surprise obvious. 'I didn't know Leah worked next to it. That's not why I'm going.'

'So why? Seems a hell of a coincidence.'

He shrugged. 'I don't know if it's a coincidence or not. I'll know more once I've been.'

'You still haven't said why.'

Danny huffed, knowing she wouldn't let it go until he told them. 'I'm troll hunting. I've got a lead on one of the dicks that have been hassling you through Twitter. I'm going to check it out, see if I can get to him.'

'The guy is there?' Winter was suddenly very interested. 'I'm going with you.'

'No, you're not, son. You'll go steaming in there and risk blowing everything. You stay here.'

'Danny . . .'

'Let me handle it.'

'Danny's right,' Narey stepped in. 'Leave him to it. He's been working this and you're likely to go in with all guns blazing. It's not what's needed. And neither's sending in cops, before you suggest it. The guy would just walk out and we'd never know who he was.'

'How about I stay outside? As back up. I come in if you need me.'

Danny laughed. 'Tony, I'm not looking to battle anyone. Chances are this is a spotty teenager weighing about ten stone. I think I can look after myself.'

*

Narey had been right. The Rum Shack wouldn't have been Danny's normal choice of pub. It had a theme, it had a cocktails board, it served curried goat. All he wanted was a few taps with beer, a good gantry of whisky and a barman who knew when to leave you alone.

This would never be his kind of place. It was trying too hard.

One wall was papered in a blue map of the Caribbean, a palm tree propping up one corner. Assuming the tree wasn't made of plastic, it would have lasted two minutes if some bam opened a window. The laminated floor was light-coloured and shiny, the stools at the bar in worn shades of yellow or red.

There were odd groups of singles and couples, most of them less than half Danny's age. He was too old for the joint but no one seemed to notice or care. That was probably the rum.

He glanced around, seeing what everyone else was drinking, keen not to stand out any more than he had to. When a barman approached, he ordered a bottle of beer even though he was pretty sure he'd hate it. A sip confirmed his fears but he held it to him as cover.

A few lone wolves stalked the bar, some drunk, some getting there at a rate. There were couples and groups, loud ones and quiet ones, filled with rum and mischief. All of them were dressed normally, a nasty little shit of a troll hiding in plain sight somewhere among them.

Danny tried to tune in to conversations, an old trick

from his days on the job, being able to separate one or two voices from the bedlam while looking the other way. He caught words in passing but nothing that worked for him.

Bottle in hand, he wandered into another room, the floor darker and worn, the tables all wearing an empty rum bottle with a candle wedged in it. On the wall, framed posters announced reggae musicians he hadn't heard of, while a stage area at the back was dominated by a large, wooden pulpit.

There were ten people in the second room. Three young women, who'd presumably flown straight in from Havana given how much their clothing was at war with the Glasgow weather, giggled over blue drinks at one table. Four young guys were knocking back rum and beer, their eyes flirting back and forth with the sunbed Cubans. Three middle-aged men in suits, office types who'd forgotten where home was, were arguing over something none of them could remember.

He stood long enough to weigh each of the men up but not so long as to invite the question as to what the fuck he was doing. None of them ticked many boxes for Tormentor. His money was still on his target being on his own. He went back to the front bar where the singles lingered, where people wandered in and out.

He sipped his beer at the bar, seeking out faces in reflections, listening to what he could. He *knew* Tormentor was in here. All he had to do was find him and all he could do was wait.

It was twenty minutes later when he became aware of

another body next to him, another thirsty soul pressing against the bar.

'Red Stripe, my man. Thank you kindly.'

Danny didn't look round. God, he wanted to, but he didn't. He wanted to turn and grab and swing. Instead he sucked on the bottle, breathed deep and waited as long as he could. At length, he moved round on the stool and looked beyond the tall guy next to him in the suit and open-necked shirt, gulping on a beer. Looked beyond him till the guy stopped noticing.

He was in his late thirties, hair receding, indents at his nose and ears where spectacles normally rested. There was a beer buzz in his eyes and a glow to his cheeks.

Danny turned to the bar again, paying no obvious attention. He waited. And waited some more. When he finally saw the movement out the corner of his left eye, he made his move, turning at the same time the guy did, his elbow smashing into the glass, causing some of it to leap and spill.

'Fuck. Sorry, mate. Sorry. My fault.'

'S'awrite. Don't worry about it. Accident, my man. Accident.'

'No, no. My fault. Let me get you another one.'

'Well, I'm no going to say no. You're a gentleman.'

Danny shouted up another pint of Red Stripe for his man and a rum for himself. He had another look at the guy and took a chance.

'Shame about the beer on the floor. Still, bound to be a woman round here who can clean it up.'

The man snorted and raised his new glass. 'Too right, my man. Get the wench in here and get the floor cleaned. I'll drink to that.'

The barman caught their sexism and shook his head at the pair of them. As he wandered to the other end of the bar, Danny gestured towards him for his new friend's benefit.

'Fucking snowflake. I bet his bird carries his balls around in her handbag.'

More snorts and another pint glass salute. The man leaned in confidentially. 'Guys like him are the problem. Let women walk all over them. The bitches take advantage and it's guys like us have to pay the price. I'm Davie, by the way.'

'How are you doing, Davie Bytheway. I'm Danny Neilson.'

'Davie Meiklejohn. Good to meet a fellow soldier.'

'In the war against women?'

Meiklejohn took a swig of beer and nodded furiously. 'Aye, and we're losing. Guys your age, no offence, they had it right. It worked for us and it worked for them. Everyone knew what their place was, everyone knew what they had to do. One went out to work, the other stayed at home, brought up the kids and had dinner on the table. Them? They had it easy but didn't know it. Now they're all whining about how hard it is in the workplace and kids are running riot cos they're not being brought up right. Fucking ridiculous, my man. World's gone to pot.'

Danny leaned his head in towards the fucker. 'You

are right, pal. You are totally right. But no one's doing anything about it. They're just letting the women away with it all. Nobody's even as much as telling them they're wrong.'

Meiklejohn gave a sly grin and tapped the side of his nose. 'Some of us are doing something about it. Can't say too much but we're not all sitting on our arses letting them do what they like. The war's being fought, my man. The war's being fought.'

'Well, I'll drink to that. Fight the good fight.'

Danny worked the guy, drained him of information without Meiklejohn being aware he was giving it up. He was thirty-nine, a financial advisor, divorced for five years after being married for eight, paying through the nose for it after the bitch took him to the cleaners, two kids that he never saw. He lived in a flat on Allison Street, would have been somewhere much better if it hadn't been for the bitch, of course. He didn't hate women, not most of them anyway, he just wanted men to get treated equally. Wasn't too much to ask.

He was an odious prick.

It was rolling towards midnight and Meiklejohn drained a glass of rum, wiping the last of it from his lips. He put an arm on Danny's shoulder and patted it, solidifying their status as part of a band of brothers.

'I'm off,' he announced.

Danny swallowed the last of his beer and bounced the glass off the counter. 'Me too. Hang on, I'll follow you out.'

The pair of them staggered onto Pollokshaws Road,

shifting right towards Allison Street just fifty yards away on the corner. Before then, though, they had to pass Barbreck Road, which was little more than a lane. As they swayed past its entrance, Danny lurched right, his shoulder barging into Meiklejohn's and knocking the other man towards the lane while making a muttered apology. Meiklejohn was carried on the wind, laughing for a bit then confused. He was alarmed but all too late.

They were further from the lights of the main road as Danny grabbed the man's wrist and twisted his arm behind his back, making him yelp as he nudged it towards breaking point. He raced him towards the wall and forced his face hard against it, his shoulder socket screaming in pain.

'What the fuck're you doing?'

Danny shoved a big hand against the guy's mouth, forcing it against the wall and forcing it quiet. 'Anything I want to. How does it feel to be helpless?'

All he got in reply was a submissive grunt.

'I know who you are,' Danny told him. 'I know who you are and what you've been doing. And I'm going to make you pay for it.'

Meiklejohn shook his head in protest but Danny simply twisted his arm another couple of degrees. 'Don't argue. Be a good boy and just answer whatever I ask. Okay?'

This time there was no argument.

'You're Tormentor, right?'

His eyes opened wide but he nodded. Danny couldn't

help but pull the guy from the wall and slam him against it again.

'First thing is, did you deliver that rat to Rachel Narey's doorstep?'

'No. I swear I didn't.'

'But you know who did?'

He nodded again.

'Okay, good. Now, the police are going to want to talk to you. It could go very bad for you or it could be easier. If you tell me all that I want to know then I can make it go easy. Tell me why you made those tweets and for your own fucking good, tell me without using the word bitch.'

'I thought you understood. It's the fight—'

'You might believe that pish but I don't. You're just a nasty little shit and so are your impotent pals. I want their names and I want to know where they are. Don't bother telling me you don't know.'

Meiklejohn hesitated just long enough to encourage Danny to apply more pressure to his arm.

'Okay! Who do you want?'

'BigWeegie. ItsaMansWorld. BlueSnake.'

'Weegie is Ryan Cochrane. Lives in Dennistoun. Jason Burns is BlueSnake. Comes from Bishopbriggs.'

'I'll need full addresses.'

'I can get them.'

'You will. And who is ItsaMansWorld?'

Meiklejohn hesitated then screamed when the twist came. 'I can't ...' Danny convinced him that he could.

'Broome!' he shouted. 'MansWorld is William Broome.'

Meiklejohn made hard contact with the wall again, just to take the edge off Danny's anger.

'Tell me. Everything.'

'We thought MansWorld was just one of us. Me and Jason and Ryan. And he was, he is, but he's also Broome. We didn't know at first. It came out later. We were tweeting Broome all the time, he had a voice, could speak to the mainstream media for us. When we found out he was Mansworld, we just ... just wanted to follow him all the more. He's a soldier. One of us.'

'He's a fucking rapist.'

'No, no. That woman lied. The court said so.'

Danny sighed and fought the urge to hit him. 'No, it didn't. Who put her name on Twitter? Who made Leah Watt's name public?'

'Broome told us it. Only seemed fair. He'd been named so why not her? We just made sure everyone knew it. It spread like wildfire.'

Danny crashed a fist into the man's stomach, causing him to double up and breath to rush out of him.

'Because there's laws, that's why not. And you've broken them. Who put the rat on Narey's doorstep?'

'Ryan. It was Broome's idea.'

'And you followed her, photographed her?'

Meiklejohn nodded, at least having the grace to look ashamed.

'Broome's idea?' He nodded again. 'What about the fake Twitter account in her name?

The man tried to look away but Danny grabbed his jaw and pulled his head back round. 'Who set it up?'

CRAIG ROBERTSON

'Me.'

Danny drew his fist back but stopped it just short of Meiklejohn's face. Instead he grabbed his arm and hauled him nearly off his feet.

'Where are we going now?' the man whined.

'We're going to your flat. Some nice policemen are going to turn up and you're going to let them look in your computer.'

CHAPTER 51

There was a constable posted outside Elspeth Broome's room at the Queen Elizabeth University Hospital. There had been someone on guard duty since she'd been admitted, in case her son tried to come back to finish the job.

Inside, Narey was greeted by a wall of white, the sterile functionality of an intensive care unit. Tubes and wires connected the woman to the world, breathing for her and feeding her. The word was she was no longer in immediate danger, but far from out of the woods. Critical but stable, the surgeon said.

Elspeth's face was a riot of colours and lumps. Dark purples and blues, a mess of distortion. Yet the real damage was out of sight. Punctured lung, broken ribs, huge blood loss and intestinal damage. All vital signs were terribly weak.

She was skin and bone. Liver spots and knotted veins. Her wrists were thin, her fingers bony. Her thin peel hung loose from her carcass, discoloured through time and too big for the body that had shrunk within its patinated casing. Narey thought if she waited ten minutes longer, there would be visibly even less of the woman. Or there would be none of her at all.

When Elspeth Broome's eyes slid open, Narey had to stop herself from taking a step back in surprise.

There was a wet focus, a blurry awakening. She could see the woman's eyes contract in confusion, trying to work out where she was and who was standing in front of her. The light was dim but she was still in there, still hanging on.

Narey stepped closer and put a hand gently on the woman's arm, feeling it limp and sticky to the touch.

'Mrs Broome. Do you know where you are?'

The woman looked back at her, eyes rimmed red and sunken, skin creased by the feet of a hundred crows. The stare back was blank but there was little chance of telling if that was through choice or circumstance.

'Mrs Broome, I'm Detective Inspector Rachel Narey of Police Scotland. When you're well enough, I'd like to ask you some questions.'

She turned her head away as best she could. No more than an inch or two to her right, a flop toward the pillow, but the message was clear enough.

Narey moved till she was in her eye line again.

'Do you understand, Mrs Broome? Do you know who did this to you?'

The old woman stared back, her eyes wet and sad. The nod was so faint it was almost missed.

'And will you tell us who it was?'

The shake of her head was firmer, more certain.

'Okay, Mrs Broome. I'd like you to think about it. Because I'll be back and I will want to talk to you.'

The woman's eyes slid shut and the room slipped into silence but for the beep of the machine keeping her alive.

CHAPTER 52

The address the woman calling herself Jennifer Buchanan had given was on a corner of Paisley Road West near Lorne Street. Two floors of red stone flats propped up by an ice cream parlour, a hair salon and a halal food store. Winter waited until after six in the evening, when lights were on behind the lace curtains and vertical blinds.

Once inside the close, he went door to door, beginning at the bottom and working his way up. No one knew or remembered Jennifer. On the top floor was the flat Jennifer had given as hers. He knocked and heard someone approach the door, stopping to squint through the peephole. Winter did his best to look unthreatening. After some thought, the door opened on a chain.

A man in his late thirties peeked out from behind it, his face hiding in the darkness of the hall. Winter could see he wore a few days' growth on his chin and a white vest despite the freezing temperatures outside.

'Yeah?'

'Hey, how you doing?'

'Who's asking?'

'My name's Tony Winter. I'm a journalist.'

He saw the man's eyes widen at the mention of journalist. Did he have something to hide? Most people did.

'Nothing to worry about,' he assured the guy. 'It's not you I'm looking for Mr . . .' he made a show of looking at the nameplate on the door. 'Mr Ormond. I'm just trying to find someone who might have lived here.'

'What's this to do with?'

'I'm looking for a woman named Jennifer Buchanan. Is the name familiar at all?'

Ormond shook his head. 'Never heard of her.'

'Fair enough. Mind taking a look at a photograph of her? Just in case you've maybe seen her about.'

The eyes blinked at him from the gloom. 'Suppose.'

Winter handed over one of the prints of Jennifer that Lainey had identified. Standing slim and petite at a bus stop, dark auburn hair and a leather handbag strapped over her shoulder.

Ormond took the photograph from him and took a half step back from the door to look at it. Seconds later, he handed it back.

'Never seen her. Sorry.'

Winter nodded. 'No worries. It was worth a try. She gave this as her address but we think she just made it up. How long have you lived here?'

The man hesitated. 'Five or six years.'

'That all?'

'Yeah. Six at the most.'

'Well, even if she had lived in these flats, it was before

your time. Listen, thanks for your help. Sorry to have bothered you.'

'S'okay.'

Winter spun on his heels and the man shut the door behind him, the chain chinking against the wood as it was taken off. He stood on the doorstep and counted to ten then turned back and knocked again.

Moments later, the door opened again, Ormond standing there impatiently.

'What now?'

Winter stuck his foot into the gap so the door couldn't be closed. Ormond was alarmed and confused.

'What do you want? I told you I didn't know anything.'

'Well, yes, but you lied to me.'

'I didn't!'

Winter smiled. 'Oh, but you did. First of all, you said you'd lived here for six years – I've already checked the electoral roll going back to 2008 and lo and fucking behold Thomas Ormond was living here then.'

His face dropped. 'I made a mistake. Couldn't remember.'

'Sure. Also, when I gave you the photo, you moved back into the hall where it was darker rather towards the door where there was more light. No one does that unless they don't want to see what they're looking at. Unless they maybe already know who the picture is going to be of.'

The man shot wary looks across the landing, on the lookout for eavesdropping neighbours.

'What do you want?'

'To ask you the same questions I did before but to get honest answers.' He put his hand against the door frame. 'And to come in.'

Ormond was sullen but had nowhere else to go. 'You can have five minutes but you're wasting your time.'

He turned and led Winter into a room right off the hall. There was a freezing wind blowing in from an open window onto Paisley Road West. Ormond shivered in his vest.

'So, I'm going to ask you again, do you know Jennifer Buchanan?'

'No.'

'Do you know the woman in the photo I showed you?'

'No.'

'Liar. I'm a bit of a poker player, Tommy. You have to get to know when someone's telling the truth and when they're not. You gave me a different tell when you answered those two questions.'

'Fuck you.'

Winter smiled. 'That's an unhelpful attitude. All I want is to know who the woman in the photo is. It's important. Consider it your civic duty. I bet you can help if you put your mind to it.'

'Why should I?'

'It's a fair question,' he conceded. 'Well, for one thing I have a lot of pals that are cops and one phone call would have your front door knocked down properly and when they find the cannabis plants in that room back there, you'd be in the shit up to your neck.'

Ormond's eyes nearly touched his ears they opened that wide.

'What you talking about?'

He sighed. 'You've got a window open when it's baltic out there. You're wearing a vest despite the fucking cold. It's not rocket science.'

'I just like fresh air.'

Winter laughed. 'Aye? And you keep those blocks of Ono on the shelf there because you like the fragrance of fresh linen? Bollocks. It's an odour neutraliser, so that your neighbours don't smell the weed you're growing in the heat in that other room.'

Ormond threw his head back in anguish. 'Fucksake. Bastard.'

'Aye and don't you forget it. So, who is she?'

'This is no fair. I'm just growing a bit of ganja. I don't want to do this.'

'Tommy, I don't give a fuck about your ganja. But the cops will. And I don't want to make you do this but I'm going to. Who is she?'

He screwed his eyes up, maybe keeping tears back, swearing three times under his breath.

'She's my sister.'

'Her name Ormond too?'

'I don't want to talk about this.'

'Come on, Tommy. You're over halfway there. What's your sister's name?'

'I can't help you find her.'

'What's her name? Her surname is Ormond, right?'

The man was beaten now, having ratted out his own

flesh and blood. 'No. She was married when she was young. Still took that arsehole's name even though she got divorced. His surname was Murdoch. It's Vonnie Murdoch you're looking for. Veronica.'

'I'm not out to hurt her, Tommy. I'm trying to help someone. Your sister too.'

He laughed, something Winter wasn't getting. 'Aye? Well, good luck with that.'

Winter persevered. 'Do you remember someone else coming here looking for her? Nearly ten years ago. A woman named Lainey Henderson?'

Ormond screwed his face up, tired of this. 'Ah remember her. Don't mind the name.'

'Why did you lie to her?'

'Why'd you think? It sounded like bad news and my sis had had enough of that. She was going through a bad time. Really struggling. I was just looking out for her.'

'That's fair. And you can look out for her again now by telling me where she is.'

Tommy Ormond sighed and dragged his hand through his thinning hair, tears trickling down his cheek.

'I can't! Just leave me alone, please.'

'I will. As soon as you tell me where I can find Vonnie.'

'Cardonald Cemetery.'

'*What?*'

'Vonnie killed herself.'

The tears were flowing now and Winter felt like a bastard.

'She took a hot bath and some pills. Was found four days later. You're nine years too late, pal.'

'Oh shit. I'm sorry, Tommy. I didn't know. When did it happen?'

'April 2008. She hadn't been happy for a while. I knew that but didn't know what it was. I should have helped her but . . .'

Winter wasn't going to make the man's pain any greater by telling him why his sister killed herself. It wouldn't do anyone any good for him to have to live with that too.

'Look, I'm sorry I put you through this. Don't worry about the weed. I won't be telling anyone.'

'Why are you looking for Vonnie? After all these years.'

He had to think fast. 'She was a witness to something. A murder.'

'Vonnie was? How . . . I don't get this. Why are you back now?'

'There's been an appeal. I'm looking for the original witnesses. I guess your sister never wanted to be found because she gave a false name. I'll let them know she can't be found. Sorry, Tommy. About all of this.'

Ormond was lost in thought. 'Someone tried to frighten her. Scare her off. I remember now. Must have been whoever she'd seen. Whatever she was a witness to.'

'How do you know this?'

'I stayed over at her place a few times when she was really down. Slept on the couch. I got woken one night, well after midnight, when the phone went. I heard Vonnie saying yes, yes, she'd forget it. She was saying that it never happened. It shook me because I could tell how scared she was. I asked her about it but she wouldn't say, told me it was nothing. I knew it wasn't, though.'

'But you've no idea who it was that called her?'

'No.'

'You're probably right. Someone trying to make her not testify.' Winter got up to go, offering a handshake which Ormond shrunk away from.

'Fair enough. Don't blame you. Let me ask you one last thing, though. Where did Vonnie live? It wasn't here, so where was it?'

'What does it matter?'

'It could be important.'

'Okay, okay. She lived in a flat on Cartvale Road in Battlefield.'

'Which floor?'

'Fucksake. Ground floor. Why?'

'I just need to know. Look, I'm sorry about all this. And about your sister.'

Winter stopped outside the close, aware of Tommy Ormond's eyes on him from the flat above. He breathed deep before letting a lungful of sigh escape like smoke into the frosty night.

Jennifer Buchanan, lost and found. Vonnie Murdoch, lost forever.

He'd check out Ormond's story, just in case, but he

had no doubt there would be a death certificate to back it up. He knew the man wasn't lying.

He strode off in search of his car, tread heavier than before, not looking back, knowing there was no point. He'd already learned that when you search for someone, you have to be prepared for what you find. You can't change it. At the end of the day, missing people only came in two sizes. Alive or dead.

CHAPTER 53

Getting parked at the Queen Elizabeth, known as the Death Star by locals owing to its fourteen floors and star shape, could be a nightmare. Narey had heard the scare stories about nurses turning up three hours early for their shift and sleeping in their cars to make sure they could park. After circling the multi-storey twice before she finally found a bay, she was prepared to believe them.

Her head was spinning after Tony's call about the woman they'd thought of as Jennifer. She'd not had the chance to tell Lainey yet and wasn't looking forward to doing so. There was also Danny's detective work to get her head round, him finding the bastards responsible for the fake Twitter page and the calls in the middle of the night. From what Danny told her, they might give enough to prosecute Broome, but she needed him to be done for much more than that.

She weaved her way through crowds of patients, visitors and staff, and headed for Elspeth Broome's ward. She didn't recognise the young constable posted at the door but he clearly knew who she was, jumping from his chair and standing to attention like a rookie as she turned into the corridor.

She nodded at him. 'All quiet?'

'Yes, ma'am. There was a nurse in to see her about ten minutes ago. And she managed some food an hour before that.'

'Okay, good. Are you going to let me in or are you going to ask to see my ID?'

He stammered, unsure of the right answer. She tried not to sigh too loudly.

'What's your name?

'PC Hartley, ma'am.'

'Okay, PC Hartley, you're going to ask for ID, aren't you? Because you wouldn't just let anyone walk in there, even if you think you recognise them.'

'Yes, ma'am. May I ...'

She held her warrant card up for inspection and waited for him to nod nervously and let her past.

The old woman was lying with her eyes closed and her frail arms crossed over her chest. One eye opened warily at the sound of the door closing. When she saw who her visitor was, her eyes scrunched in annoyance.

'How are you, Mrs Broome?'

The loose flesh around the woman's mouth tightened into a scowl. A weak voice stole through barely parted lips. 'I'm okay.'

'Have you had more time to think about what I said the last time I was here? About telling me who did this to you?'

364

Her head lifted an inch or so from the pillow. 'Lots of time,' she croaked. 'Nothing else *but* time.'

'And do you want to tell me who did it?'

Elspeth's eyes closed over again and she mouthed a silent no.

Narey went closer, right up to the bedside, allowing her to keep her voice low but still be heard.

'I don't understand, Elspeth. You say you know who did this but you won't tell me who it was. That really doesn't make any sense. Who are you protecting?'

The woman's head swayed from side to side, little defiant movements that brooked no disagreement. Narey still tried to push past them.

'I'm trying to help you, Elspeth. All I need is his name. I just need to hear you say it.'

Voices slid under the door of the ward. Raised, arguing voices.

Narey stepped reluctantly back from the bed, a final glance at the elderly patient before pushing through the doors into the corridor.

William Broome was in the constable's face, cheeks flushed, finger jabbing.

'She's *my* mother. I'll see her if I want. You've no right to keep me out.'

'My instructions are that you're not allowed—'

'It's okay, constable,' she interrupted him. 'I'm here. Let Mr Broome past. He's quite right. It's his mother, after all.'

'Yes, ma'am.'

Broome took a step back, clearly surprised but trying

not to show it. Straightening his collar and taking a breath.

'I want to see her on my own.'

'No chance.'

'She's my—'

'With me or not at all.'

'Okay. *Okay*.'

He brushed past her, Narey taking his heel, keen not to miss the reaction from the mother seeing the son.

She'd heard the voices though, surely, a chance to ready herself, steady herself. They'd soon see.

The old woman's eyes fluttered and opened. Narey saw them widen. She thought she saw fear.

Broome stepped across her path, blocking her view, closing in on the bed and kissing his mother, his body shielding her. His head near hers, his mouth by her ear.

Narey pushed round to the other side of them just as Broome straightened up and took a small step back.

'How are you, Mum? I got here as soon as I heard. They say you're going to be okay.'

Elspeth made a noise that Narey couldn't interpret. Something between a groan and a whimper, maybe just a cry for help. Maybe a mother's call to her son.

'Who did this to you, Mum? *Who did this?*'

'You . . .' she choked and started again, scraping out words. 'You don't have to worry. I'll be okay.'

Broome's head swung slowly round towards Narey.

'Hear that, Inspector? She's going to be okay. It's a miracle, don't you think?'

The smugness of his words scratched at her like broken glass.

'I've never believed in miracles, Mr Broome. I've always thought the hand of man was more likely to be to blame than the hand of God.'

He grinned, making her skin crawl. 'Miracles are good things, Inspector. No one is to blame for them.'

'I don't believe in accidents, either. Where have you been, Mr Broome? You said you got here as soon as you heard but your mother has been in hospital for days.'

'I've been away. On business and out of phone mast range. Texts got through this morning and I came straight here.'

'I'll need to check that.'

'I thought you would.'

Narey turned to the old woman.

'Are you sure you don't want to tell me who did this to you, Elspeth? You will be safe.'

Broome motioned to speak but Narey silenced him with a look. *Let her speak.*

Elspeth aged ten years as Narey looked at her. She went from old to ancient as she shrunk back in her skin, peering between her eyelids as she switched her gaze between cop and child. Covered by a single white sheet, she looked more like a corpse than a recovering patient.

There was a tremble to her lip, the effort of trying to speak and the worry of what might come out. Tears formed in her eyes, making them bleary and red.

She stared at her son through slits, the two of them communicating in their own way, messages passing back and forth. Narey felt outside it, helpless and unable to translate.

A bony finger beckoned Narey closer. Close enough she could hear the beat of her heart and the wheeze in her chest.

'My son wouldn't hurt me. He loves me. He's his mammy's boy.'

Broome stood taller, the sneak of a smirk on his face.

'Is there anything else, Inspector? My mother needs to rest.'

'I'll need the name and address of the place you say you stayed at. And the names of people who can say you were there.'

'Of course.'

The way he said it, she knew she'd be wasting her time but would go through with it anyway. She had to go, had to get away from him, from her, from them. She pushed the door open, seeing the constable get to his feet.

'PC Hartley. In here, please. I need you to supervise Mr Broome's visit with his mother. Take notes of anything that's said between them and call in a nurse to assist and supervise.'

It was more show than anything else. She knew nothing would be said that would incriminate Broome. All the important things had been said already. She pushed through the door, letting it swing shut behind her. She didn't want to turn around but she did and paid the inevitable price.

He was looking back at her, the smile widening.

CHAPTER 54

She climbed the stairs to the first floor of the flats on the corner of Marlborough Avenue in Broomhill, pressed the bell and waited. Moments later, a silhouette appeared like a ghost in the frosted door. Lainey Henderson stood still, frozen like the glass and hiding in plain sight.

Did she think the frosting made her invisible or was she just hoping Narey would go away? After a few beats more, she relented and opened the door.

'Morning, Lainey. If it's not a good time, I can call back later.'

'Late night last night, that's all. You're here now though. You better come in.'

She turned and padded through the hallway to the living room, leaving Narey to follow her. The room was dominated by two large bookcases and a huge sofa smothered in multicoloured throws and cushions. Shawls and scarves were pinned to the walls, fighting for space with plants and candles and buddhas. Whatever the opposite of minimalist was, this was it.

Lainey lit a cigarette and tilted her head back to take the first draw deep.

'What can I do for you, Inspector?'

'I wanted to talk about Leah.'

'We've done that. There's nothing more I can tell you.'

'Or will tell me?'

Lainey shrugged unapologetically. 'We've been through that.'

'Lainey, I need more information to work with. It's important and I need to know everything Leah told you.'

'*Important?* You're actually telling me it's important like I don't know that?' Lainey jabbed her cigarette towards Narey accusingly. 'You think you're the only one that's worrying about her? I read the newspapers. I watch the TV. I'm terrified about what has happened to her. You should be arresting Broome. Trying to force that bastard to talk rather than me.'

'Lainey . . .'

'No, I think you should go. I've not got time for this.'

Narey didn't budge.

'Lainey, I get the whole client privilege thing. But if Leah's been murdered or kidnapped or whatever then your duty of care extends to helping find her killer.'

'You're fucking lecturing me. And I can't deal with that kind of "if". I can't guess. Guessing is your job. I have to deal with the reality and just look after Leah.'

'Then help me do the same. I need to know what she was thinking. If I can understand that then I'll be in a better position to know what she might have done, where she might have gone.'

'Or what might have happened to her.'

'Of course. But the same thing is true. I need to know how much danger she might have put herself in. Just how far she would have gone to put things right. Do you think she would have gone to challenge Broome?'

'I don't know.'

'Can we just drop this, Lainey. You *do* know. If you don't, no one does. Your whole job was to talk to Leah about what she was thinking and why she was thinking it. You talked to her about how she felt about Broome and about the collapse of the court case.'

'But I can't tell you ... I mean no, I haven't talked to her about the case.'

'Not at all or not since it ended?'

'For fucksake, you're just trying to confuse me.'

'Yes, and it seems to be working. Not that you'd have to worry unless you were lying. You *have* counselled her since she was in court, haven't you? She was here last week, three days after the trial collapsed. I know she was, so drop the pretence.'

Lainey stabbed her cigarette into the ashtray and drew another from the packet.

'Okay, she was here. I didn't want to talk to you about the session, about what she'd told me. So, it seemed easier just to say it hadn't taken place than have you give me all this grief over it. I was just protecting my client.'

'No, what you were doing was obstructing a police

investigation. You lied to an officer in the execution of their duties and perverted the course of justice. You obstructed a potential murder investigation.'

Lainey lit the new cigarette and Narey saw the tremble in her hands.

'Leah's friend Shaz said that her last words to her were that she wasn't taking this shit any more. What do you think she meant by that, Lainey?'

She sucked on the cigarette, buying herself time.

'Leah had been pushed against a wall and had nowhere else to go, nothing else to do but push back. She felt everything and everyone had let her down. Those she'd trusted and put her faith in couldn't be relied upon. She probably thought she had nothing left to lose. People don't make the best choices when they're thinking like that.'

'So, you think she would have gone to challenge Broome?'

'Maybe. She was angry. She had no one left she could rely on other than herself.'

'And you.'

Lainey said nothing.

'Did she tell you or suggest to you that she was going to confront him?'

'No. And I'd have tried to talk her out of it if she had. I know how dangerous that man is.'

'Yes, he is. What do you think she hoped to achieve by going there? Did she really think he would confess and tell the world he'd raped her? That doesn't sound like Broome.'

Lainey was on her feet, agitated and smoking furiously.

'Is that really what's important here? Are you really blaming Leah for putting herself in that position rather than the bastard who's hurt her? That's like blaming the rape victim for wearing a short skirt or being drunk rather than the rapist.'

Narey bit her tongue one more time. 'This isn't about blaming Leah. It's about understanding her actions. Again, what do you think she was trying to do?'

Lainey's anger boiled over.

'I'd think it was obvious that she was trying to do what you failed to. To bring a rapist to account for *his* actions.'

'Not a murderer?'

'What?'

'You said rapist rather than rapist and murderer. You don't think Broome killed Leah?'

'I ... I didn't say that. I don't know but ...'

'You do know though, don't you? You know exactly what happened to Leah.'

'I don't know what you're talking about but you need to get out of here. This is harassment.'

Narey laughed. 'Do you know how much trouble you are in, Lainey? Do you have any idea? I don't think Leah would want you to get arrested for lying to the police, for obstructing an active investigation.'

There was a noise from somewhere behind Lainey. It came from the adjoining room.

'No! Look, I can't take any more of this right now.

373

I'll tell you anything I can but you need to go and give me peace to think about it.'

Narey stood up. 'I think it's too late for that. Leah knows that even if you don't. Isn't that right?'

The inner door to the room swung open and Leah Watt walked through it.

'She's right, Lainey. It's too late to lie to her.'

CHAPTER 55

Leah looked drained. She was pale and her eyes were propped up by dark rings. The clothes she was wearing clung to her like she'd outgrown them and they clearly weren't her own. On the plus side, she was alive.

She was scared too, that much was obvious, her body half-turned away from Narey as if ready to run. She could barely look her in the eye.

'When my daughter, Alanna, does something stupid and hurts herself, maybe climbing on something she shouldn't and falling off, I have to hug her first to make sure she's okay. Only then can I give her a telling off.'

Leah curled a lip. 'You're not my mother.'

'I'd still like to hug you.'

'Does it have to come with a lecture?'

'Definitely.'

The younger woman huffed then gave in. The air escaped from her and she seemed to shrink three sizes. When her eyes reopened, they were wet and red. Narey took two steps and enveloped her.

Leah howled into Narey's chest, letting go days, months, of fear and frustration. Narey wrapped her tighter in her arms and barely managed to fight off tears of her own. She held her like that until Leah cried herself dry.

When she let her go, it was gradual. Lots of mother-hen checks before finally releasing her. They sat together on the couch, Lainey staring at them.

'So, tell me about it. What were you thinking?'

The shrug was like that of a five-year-old. Knowing but unknowing. Hoping it would all just go away.

'Okay, let's try it another way. Talk me through what you did after you left your parents' house. Where did you go?'

'Into town. I got the bus in and got off at Buchanan Street. I walked up near to where your police station is. Near the passport office. I wandered around for a bit then back into the city centre.'

'You had a plan?'

'No. Yes. I suppose so. I knew what I was going to do.'

'You weren't going to take this shit any more.'

Leah's eyes opened wide. 'You spoke to Shaz? *Shit*. Is she okay?'

'She thinks you've been murdered. How do you think she is?'

Fresh tears formed. 'I didn't think. I just had to ... When the idea came to me, I wasn't thinking about anyone else. Just him. And me.'

'Where did you go next?'

She managed to look ashamed. The five-year-old who wanted to lie but didn't know how.

'To Broome's offices at the Templeton Building.'

'How did you find your way there?'

Leah started and stopped. Her brain working out that Narey knew the answer to the question or else she wouldn't have asked it.

'I used Google Maps. Followed it from the city centre.'

'Even though you knew exactly how to get there.'

'Yes. But how did you know that?'

'Shaz told me the two of you used to go to the Barrowlands for gigs. So even if you didn't know how to get to Templeton's, you wouldn't have had to use your phone for directions until after the ballroom. You were using it because you knew it could and would be traced.'

Leah just nodded sullenly.

'I knew this before I took a team to search Templeton's but it suited me to go there anyway to noise him up. I figured you wanted to make sure everyone knew where you'd gone.'

'Not everyone. *You*. I wanted *you* to know I'd gone to his office. I wanted you to follow me. To ... investigate.'

Narey wasn't a fan of being played. 'You wanted me to arrest Broome for murder. So, you faked it. The blood, the torn clothing.'

A guilty nod, eyes down. After a deep breath, she rolled back the sleeve of the borrowed sweatshirt to reveal a bandage wrapped tightly around her wrist.

'I cut it. Let it spray. It took longer to stop it than I'd thought. I was prepared but it still gushed. I nearly passed out but I didn't.'

'Christ, Leah. You could have killed yourself.'

'So? I felt dead anyway. What kind of life was I going to have with him doing that to me and getting away with it? More than getting away, lording it on television. Calling me names, saying it was all my fault. All my fault and yours. I thought if you could arrest him, put him away, it would work out for you, too.'

Narey wanted to hug her but also to slap some sense into her.

'And you were going to hide all your life? Let your mum and dad think you were dead? And Shaz and your other friends? How did you think you could keep it going?'

'I never . . . I just . . .'

'Leah had been through an incredibly traumatic—'

'Whoa!' Narey cut Lainey off mid flow, 'I want to hear this from Leah, not you. We'll get to you in a minute. Don't worry about that.'

Leah switched between them, conflicted and confused.

'I hadn't thought it through but I didn't care. I still don't. I feel bad if people are worried but he needed to be stopped. That's all I was thinking about. What he did to me . . . I couldn't have him doing it to anyone else. How did you know that I was here? With Lainey.'

'I didn't. Not for sure. But Lainey lied to me, told me she hadn't seen you when I knew you'd been at the café and that meant you'd most likely been to see her. I studied CCTV at Templeton's and saw a car stopping briefly near the building. It looked familiar and when I ran a check, I found Lainey owned a make and model that matched. It wasn't enough in itself but it made me wonder. I came in here suspicious but the more Lainey talked, the surer I was that you were here.'

'I was just looking after her!' Lainey reacted furiously. 'She had to be somewhere safe. When she told me what she'd done, I tried to convince her to go to you. But when I realised she wouldn't be persuaded, I took her in. And I don't regret it. No matter what happens to me.'

'It's not her fault,' Leah was desperate. 'I made her. Didn't leave her with any choice. It's all down to me. Please, Rachel. Don't arrest her, please! Just me. It was all me.'

Narey could only shake her head at the pair of them.

'I'm not sure which of you is the more fucking stupid. Actually, I do. Leah has an excuse, a huge excuse. But *you*, you should have known better. You're the grown-up here.'

'I said I don't regret it and I don't. I saw it as my job to protect her. And I still do.'

'Give me fucking strength.'

'What are you going to do, Rachel?' Leah's voice was pleading.

She stared at them both. Made them sweat. Made them work for it.

'I'm going to do nothing. For now, at least. I want you to stay here.'

'*What?*'

'I want you to stay here, get some rest and some sleep. It's the safest place for you. Just because Broome didn't harm you when you went to his office, doesn't mean he won't.'

Lainey was not getting this at all.

'You want us to keep on pretending? To let people think Leah has been killed?'

'Oh, I'm not happy about this, Lainey. Far from it. What Leah did was stupid and dangerous. She could easily have been killed. But . . . stupid or not, it has done a job. The case against Broome was all but over until her little stunt.'

'So, it's—'

'It's an utter fuck up, that's what it is. Don't take any credit for this. That's not how it works. You're putting my job at risk. You're putting the chance of nicking Broome at risk. But the damage is done and you show-ing your face now is just going to make it worse. You stay put as long as you can, give me a chance to make this right. Once it's done, if it's done, then I'll figure out a way for you to reappear without us all going to jail.'

They were open-mouthed.

'Do you get all that?'

They nodded.

She sighed hard. 'I'm glad someone does.'

CHAPTER 56

It had taken three attempts but Narey had finally persuaded Elspeth Broome to agree to listen to someone she wanted to bring into the hospital room to talk to her. It was a grudging acceptance and shared by a dark-haired nursed who hovered by Elspeth's bed like a guard dog.

Narey didn't wait for anyone to change their minds. She opened the door to the room and gave the signal to come in. The sound of heels on linoleum quickly followed.

Suzie O'Brien, red hair tied behind her, took up a seat in front of Elspeth Broome's bed and told her story. How she was out with friends, how she lost the night and her memory. How she knew she'd had sex even though she had no recollection of it, even though there's no way she could have given consent.

Elspeth looked shocked, confused too.

'I'm sorry. That must have been terrible for you. But I don't understand why you're telling me this.'

Suzie looked to Narey, who nodded at her to continue.

'Well, as I think you know, a collection of photographs was found in your son's house. Photographs of women, taken without their knowledge or permission. My photograph was among that collection. In fact, there were two of them, taken on different days. Going by some of the things in those photos, I think they were taken just a few weeks before I was drugged. Before I was raped.'

Elspeth didn't want to hear it. The word smelled and her nose wrinkled.

'I don't know what you're talking about. I think you should leave now. I really think you should go.'

The nurse, Anne according to her name badge, got to her feet, but Narey saved her the trouble of saying anything.

'Okay. If that's what you want. Anyway, Suzie has told you what happened to her. You've heard it. She's going to go now.'

Elspeth looked the other way as Suzie left. Only turning her head back once the door had closed again.

'That woman didn't see anything. Didn't even know anything had happened. She might just have had too much to drink and woke up somewhere she shouldn't have been.'

Narey didn't respond. She just let Elspeth talk it through.

'I mean, I'm sorry for her. She's obviously upset. She's been through a lot, I can see that. But nothing at all might have happened to her. And it's got nothing to do with my son.'

Narey expected no less. Suzie was always going to

be a hard sell. She hadn't convinced Elspeth, just as she probably wouldn't have persuaded a judge or a jury. It was why she'd been sent in first.

'Okay, Mrs Broome. I understand that. I really do. But please keep in mind what Suzie said, even if you can't accept it. There's someone else I'd like you to meet.'

The woman sighed and rolled her eyes in protest. The nurse spoke for her.

'Inspector, do I need to remind you that Mrs Broome is extremely frail. I don't want her upset or tired unnecessarily.'

'Oh, it's necessary. I wouldn't be doing this otherwise. I won't make this take any longer than it needs to.'

The nurse clearly wasn't happy but conceded defeat. 'Okay, but I'm staying and if I think you're putting her condition at risk, I'm calling a halt to it.'

Narey led Khalida Dhariwal into the room. The lawyer was immaculately dressed in a sharp, black business suit and open-necked white blouse, her dark hair pulled back but hanging loose in a ponytail. She projected an air of confidence and professionalism, someone to be believed and listened to.

She took up a seat close to Elspeth's bed. Close enough to be intimate, not so close as to be threatening. She then made sure to ask after the woman's health, warm and caring.

'Thank you for agreeing to see me, Mrs Broome. This isn't easy, for either of us, but I do think it's very important and I appreciate your time in such trying circumstances. I want to tell you what happened to me. It's not something I am happy to talk about but I will. I want you to hear it.'

Elspeth didn't want to hear it, but was won over by the visitor's honesty and openness. Simple politeness prevented her from sending Khalida away.

'Okay. If you must. I'm listening.'

'Thank you, Mrs Broome. I really do appreciate it.'

The lawyer took a deep breath and began.

'It was nine years ago, two years after I'd graduated in law from Glasgow University. I was with a firm in the city, a good starter job and I was loving it. I had a boyfriend, a car that just about got me from A to B, and good friends. I ran, I sang in a choir, I visited my parents at least once a week. Life was pretty great, Mrs Broome. I was healthy and happy and going places.

'It was a Thursday night. I'd stayed at home to study even though friends had been urging me to go out. After I put the books away, I spoke with my boyfriend on the telephone for about ten minutes, I poured myself a glass of wine and I watched the Graham Norton show on BBC2. I can even remember who his guests were that night. Ricky Gervais, Thandie Newton and Anastacia.

'I went to bed not long after midnight. I distinctly remember thinking how I was glad I'd stayed at home, how I'd feel all the better for it the next morning and how I was getting too old for all-night partying. Too old at twenty-five. How foolish we are when we're too young to know.

'It was exactly 2.04 when I was wakened by a noise

in the flat. I sleep light. I remember sitting up, knowing that the noise was wrong, that even though I'd heard it in my sleep, I knew it was something that shouldn't have been there. I listened and heard more noise, I was scared but I was also ready to do something about it.

'I was young, fit and stupid. I had a baseball bat in the corner of my room and I knew the law. If it was just lying there then I could pick it up on the way past and use it to defend myself. Glasgow has a very high ratio of baseball bats to baseballs.

'I was halfway to the bedroom door when it opened. I got stuck between moving to attack or flee and defend. So, when he came into the room, I was standing there in T-shirt and shorts, legs planted and a bat ready to swing.

'He was dressed all in black. Black boots, black jeans, a black jacket. And a black balaclava. All I could see were his eyes. They were blue. Startlingly light blue. He was tall and slim, wiry. Strong. I estimated him to be six feet two.'

Khalida paused to let that sink in, to let Elspeth draw breath and consider it all.

'He rushed me and I swung at him. He ducked it easily and moved to the side. I swung again and caught him on the arm but he charged into me, crowding me so I couldn't use the bat. He forced me back on the bed and his weight pinned me down. He just held me there, letting me thrash and use up energy. He called me a slag. Said I'd pay for hurting his arm.

'He licked my face. Licked from my chin to my

temple. Maybe that doesn't sound much given everything else but it disgusted me.

'He smelled of sweat. Sweat and some musky after-shave. I could feel his breath on my ear. It was as if he thought I'd like it. I didn't, I really didn't. I tried to throw an elbow back into him but he punched me in the neck and then the throat, calling me a slag over and over. I was choking but he put something on my mouth, a cloth doused in what I think was chloroform. I fought it but he kept his hand clamped on my mouth till I went under.'

Mrs Broome was following every word. Khalida kept her voice calm, didn't break down or waver. She used all her training to stay composed enough to simply tell what happened.

'When I came round and saw the clock, it was 5.28. I remember putting my hand to my face because it hurt and when I brought it back into view, it was bloody. It took minutes to remember what had happened earlier. When I did, I was scared, terrified. I had to creep into the next room and the next to make sure he was gone.

'When I looked in a mirror, I saw my nose was probably broken, my face had been punched. I knew I'd been raped. Probably more than once.

'Do you know what the temptation was, Mrs Broome? To go back under the covers of my bed, curl up into a ball and go to sleep. To stay there till I healed enough that no one could see what had happened to me. Maybe to pretend, even to myself, that nothing had happened.

'But I picked up the phone, dialled 999 and told the police I'd been raped. I need you to know how difficult that was. I need you to know how difficult it was to tell my parents. How difficult it was to tell my boyfriend. Then, a few years later, to tell the man who was to become my husband. My boyfriend at the time? He dumped me when I needed him most because he couldn't cope with it. He thought it had happened to him.'

Tears began to form in Elspeth Broome's eyes. Khalida leaned forward and place a hand gently on the old woman's arm. But she wasn't finished.

'My wounds healed pretty quickly. I think I was luckier than most because he didn't have to punch me into unconsciousness. What didn't heal was trust. That took a long time. It took forever for the fear to go away and it probably still hasn't. Noises in the night spook me. Men approaching suddenly, men who look at me because they're attracted to me, sometimes just men who have the height and build of the man who raped me. Dozens of times, I've seen tall men with light blue eyes and wondered, was it him? That's so unfair on them and on me.

'I'm strong, Mrs Broome. Strong and smart with good family and friends and someone who loves me. I hate to think what that rape would have done to someone without those things because I know how hard it's been for me.' Khalida paused and held Elspeth's gaze. 'Mrs Broome, my photograph was found in your son's photo collection.'

*

Elspeth let her head sink back onto her pillow as she looked at the ceiling and blinked back tears. When her eyes closed, it was with a sigh of relief that it was over. Except it wasn't.

Narey's voice came from across the room. 'I'm sorry Mrs Broome, but we're not finished. There are others.'

The dark-haired nurse looked at Narey, concern clear on her face, but this time she made no objection.

'I'll give you a few minutes, Mrs Broome. I know this isn't easy. It's not easy for anyone.'

She left the ward and made her way to a waiting area round the first corner. Khalida was already there, a comforting arm round a young woman who was clutching a soft toy and fidgeting very nervously.

'Are you ready for this?'

The woman closed her eyes and blew out breath. 'No.'

'Come on, let's do it.'

She reluctantly got to her feet, took a final hug and a whisper of good luck from Khalida, before following Narey into the room.

By the bed, she stood behind Narey, practically hiding. She saw the old woman, battered and half-dead, and was immediately assaulted by flashbacks of her own. She took half a step back but then steeled herself and took a pace forward, then another. Narey smiled at her and nodded in approval.

'Mrs Broome, this is Leah Watt.'

CHAPTER 57

Leah cried. So too did Elspeth Broome. Their tears were the same yet different.

One laid out every painful moment of the night when the other's son destroyed her life. The other had to listen and endure.

Narey knew what it took for Leah to do it and she was proud of her. Still angry at her, still fearful for her, but in the moment, nothing greater than pride that she'd found enough in herself to talk to Broome's mother and try to help put an end to this.

Leah was nearly at the end of the first part of her story. The end of the beginning.

'I woke covered in my own blood. Nearly passed out when I saw my face. But I'd seen *his* face, that much I was sure of. I don't think he knew, though. I surfaced somewhere in the middle of it and saw him. Then saw another punch.

'It was five weeks later, living at my mum and dad's, when I saw his face in the newspaper. Completely by chance. William Broome. Your son. I ran to the bathroom and threw up. I went to the police and started things that couldn't be stopped.'

Elspeth couldn't look her in the eye. She listened, hung on every word but with her stare fixed on the ceiling.

'You were in court. I remember seeing you there and wondering what kind of woman would produce a son like that.'

That stung. Elspeth jumped as if electrocuted but said nothing.

'I went there to see your son. To face him. To see him before I'd have to give evidence against him. It was all supposed to be simple but it didn't work out that way. It felt like everything was going wrong. The photographs he'd taken, all those women, they were taken away, taken out of evidence. I was so scared. It was like I had no control of anything. Then your son spoke to me.

'It was very quick. Just a few words in the middle of all the chaos that broke out. But it was enough. He told me my parents' address. Told me he'd already come to me once and he'd come to me again. That was all he said but I saw the look in his eyes as he said it. You've maybe seen it too. It was terrifying.'

Elspeth looked like she was trying to burn a hole in the white ceiling above.

'That look on his face. I saw him, what he's really like. His eyes were like an animal's. I've never seen anyone else with that look. It was like he could kill and not care. I saw it when he wore the balaclava, when he raped me. And I saw it in court.

'I ran, Mrs Broome. I don't mind admitting I ran and I hid. I know what people thought. What you probably thought. That I was a liar, that I'd made it all up. Well, I didn't. I only lied when I said I didn't recognise him and I only did that because I was scared your son would kill me.

'I'm not running any more though. I'm done with that. This has to stop, Mrs Broome. In the name of God, it has to stop.'

Anna Collins came in. Helen Scanlon too, all the way from New Zealand after multiple emails. DC Kerri Wells was there too, offering logistical and emotional support. Witnesses paraded in the court of one woman's opinion. The procession was slow and traumatic for all involved. Narey could see the attendant nurse was on edge, battered by the information she was trying to process and torn between that and her patient. When she finally stood and said that it had to stop, it suited Narey fine. It left the impression the line was long.

'You're right, Mrs Broome has heard enough, I'm sure.'

The old woman didn't reply. Her eyes were firmly closed. Narey moved nearer.

'There are other women out there like these. All raped, all beaten. All by your son. We don't know how many but we are trying to find them. We don't want there to be any more. We need to bring an end to this. Will you help us?'

Elspeth tried to speak but broke down. The nurse got to her feet and gave her water, shooting warning glances at Narey, who ignored them. The patient managed to raise a hand just enough to shoo the nurse aside and wheeze out a reply.

'Inspector, it's a mother's job to protect her child. To do anything, everything, to keep them safe. That job never ends, no matter how old they get or how old you get. It's something you have to do. You say you've got a child, Inspector, so you'll know. You'd do anything for them.'

'But Mrs Broome, surely—'

'I'm not finished.'

Narey heard the unsaid words. The shift in the tone. She shut up and listened.

'It's also a mother's job to bring her child up. To teach them the right thing and to teach them the wrong thing. A mother can shape her child, make them some of the person they turn out to be. I know what I'd think of another mother whose son did these things. So, I know what I have to think of myself.'

Elspeth broke off to gulp air and compose herself. 'I didn't do my job. I ignored things, told myself they weren't what they looked like. Right from when he was young, there were things explained away as accidents or just a flash of temper. Sometimes people got hurt, sometimes animals did. I always thought it couldn't be William's fault, just couldn't be because he wasn't like that. Well, he was. He *is* like that.'

Narey had to resist the temptation to respond, to push it. Her pulse was racing and the defining questions were fighting to leap from her. She had to let Elspeth say it.

'He's my son. I love him, Inspector. You've got to understand that.'

'I do.'

'It's my fault. Some of it. Maybe all of it. But I'm sure he did those things. The things these women have said. I know what he's like. I know now.'

The question couldn't be held back any longer.

'Mrs Broome, do you know now because of what happened to you? Did your son do this to you?'

The old woman spoke with her eyes closed and tears streaming from them.

'Every time he punched me, he called me "slag".'

Narey and Wells looked at each other, daring to hope.

'He punched and called me a slag. Punched and called me a slag. Same as with the women you brought in here. My own son.'

It was close. Narey could feel it. Enough that it scared her. She took a deep breath and asked. 'Mrs Broome, will you—'

'Yes. God forgive me but yes, I will. I'm not doing this for you, Inspector. I'm not even doing it for those women, even though my heart bleeds for them. I'm doing it for my son. I'm doing this for William's own good.'

I don't care why, Narey thought. *I only care that you do it. Don't tease me. Say it. End it.*

'I will press charges. I will name him. I will go to court and I will identify William as the person who did this to me. The rest of it is up to you.'

CHAPTER 58

Broome and his lawyer walked into the interview room with the air of tourists who'd just seen one castle too many. He'd been here before and wasn't much impressed the first time.

He had to know this was different, though. Not least because there had been no cosy arrangement, no deals on what could and couldn't be asked, no provision for him and Constance to leave when the going got tough.

This time, he'd been detained for interview.

He and his lawyer sat at one side of the table, Narey and Wells on the other. Formalities were taken care of, the tape started and the interview begun.

'We have a statement from one of your mother's neighbours, Mr Martin Naysmith. He saw you enter the house at around 8.30. He didn't see you leave but another of the neighbours did. Mrs Pauline Stewart was taking her son to Newlands Park at approximately 9.15 and saw you drive off. She described your mood as "agitated".'

There it was. The edginess. The air of doubt that Narey wanted to see. It was in his eyes.

Constance, on the other hand, was still collected. '*Agitated?* We're all agitated in the mornings, Inspector. Stresses of work, of getting there on time, of dealing with elderly parents, of being harassed by the police. There are no end of perfectly valid reasons for anyone to be *agitated.* You know as well as I do that will carry no weight, even if this were unlikely enough to get to court.'

Narey looked at her papers as she murmured a non-committal response, not seeming to care what the lawyer had to say on the matter.

'The time you were at your mother's house is entirely consistent with the time she was attacked, as suggested by her injuries.'

Constance jumped in again. 'As I'm sure is an hour earlier or an hour later. That's a very imprecise science, Inspector, and in evidential terms an unreliable one.'

She didn't lift her head, didn't look at or respond to the lawyer. She thumbed the papers some more.

'The person who attacked Mrs Broome would have been covered in blood. The spatter would have been extensive and unavoidable. A person in that position might have thought it expedient to hide from public view. Just as you did, Mr Broome.'

'My client had already explained his absence even though there was no compulsion on him to do so.'

'When Mr Naysmith saw you arrive, you were wearing a jacket but no coat. When Mrs Stewart saw you leave, you were wearing a coat. Perhaps the sort of thing someone would do if they had to cover their clothing.'

'Really, Inspector. This is getting more and more ridiculous. If you don't have anything more substantial than what you've offered then I fail to see how you can justify detaining my client any longer.'

Narey levelled Constance then Broome in turn with a measured stare. She saw Constance blink and his client swallow hard. They knew that if she had an ace, then it was to be played now.

She slid a sheaf of paper across the desk to the lawyer. He and Broome watched it skim to their side of the table as if it was an approaching army.

Constance began reading the top copy but swiftly flipped to the end, seeking confirmation of a name and a signature. A frown creased his forehead as he read it. He turned to Broome and authenticated it with a curt nod.

Broome snatched it from his hand, disbelieving, scanning it to his own dissatisfaction.

'That slag. That fucking *slag*.'

The irony of his words were lost on him as he scraped back his chair and got to his feet, his arms waving aggressively. Narey didn't flinch.

'Sit down please, Mr Broome.'

'My own fucking mother. She's insane. Certifiable. That will never stand up in court.'

'I said *sit down*, Mr Broome.'

Constance urged Broome to do as she said but he

continued to stand and rant. Narey gestured to the constable by the door and he manoeuvred Broome forcefully back into his chair, inevitably making the man even angrier.

'Your client did not seem to read that statement fully, Mr Constance. I think it might be helpful to all of us if I read it aloud for the benefit of the tape.'

She paused just long enough to ensure she was meeting no resistance.

'Statement by Elspeth Broome of Carlaverock Road, Newlands, Glasgow. I was at home in bed on the morning of 28 November 2017 when my son William Broome entered the house. He has his own apartment but I still consider my house to be his home. He has his own key and is free to come and go as he pleases.

'I heard the door slam shut and William's voice, shouting. He was clearly unhappy but I couldn't make out what he was saying. I could hear him rushing up the stairs and I was wondering what the problem was. He'd been under a significant amount of stress so I expected it was connected to that.

'He burst into my room, pushing the door back against the wall. It frightened me.

'He was shouting. Shouting about the article in the newspaper. Saying that I'd embarrassed him, that I'd made him out to be a mummy's boy. That was the phrase he kept repeating. I told him that I didn't think there was anything wrong with that. He *was* his mummy's boy and he should be proud of that because I was proud of it.

'That was when he first hit me. He punched me in the face. William had never struck me before. In the past, he has been angry but never violent.

'He was immediately regretful and apologised but was saying that it was my own fault for making him do it. He said I'd forced him to punch me by saying the things I did.

'I should have kept quiet. I shouldn't have antagonised him further but everything I said was wrong. I said I forgave him. I said I forgave him because he was my son, my baby boy. He screamed at me, I wasn't even sure what he was saying he was so enraged. He swept things off my dresser, I could hear them smashing. I kept saying it was okay, it was all okay, but that just made him worse.

'He ran at me and started punching me. Lots of punches one after the other. Then it was one punch at a time. Calling me "slag" then punching. Repeating that over and over. After a while it stopped and I realised he wasn't there. I hoped he'd gone but in a few minutes, he returned. I couldn't see too well but enough to know he had a knife in his hand.

'He stood over me and said I had to tell him it was all my own fault. That I'd made him hit me. That he'd had to do it. I should have said that but I said he didn't need to feel bad. That I forgave him.

'He stabbed me. He stabbed me several times. He stabbed me until I passed out.

'When I regained consciousness, our cleaner, Elizabeth Johnstone, was in my room. She called the police and an ambulance. I did not see my son William again until he visited me in hospital three days later. He made no reference to assaulting me and seemed to be pretending it hadn't happened.

'I confirm that this is a true and accurate statement of the attack upon my person by my son William Broome and that I have made it of my own free will.'

Broome's body language was shouting loud and clear. He was slumped in his chair, shoulders turned inwards, arms crossed over his chest. His mouth hung open and slack.

It was time to finish him off.

'Mr Broome, you will be arrested for the attempted murder of your mother. You—'

'I didn't mean to kill her! I didn't! I just ... just ... she ...'

'Mr Broome, as your lawyer will doubtless tell you, your intentions are not the issue here. Mr Constance?'

The lawyer didn't get the chance to reply. Broome was on his feet again, eyes wide and wild, his mouth jabbering more with intent than with intelligible words, tears streaming down his cheeks.

He had to slow himself, spit out each word to make them heard.

'I *did not* try to kill her. She's my mother. I wouldn't. I just had to stop her talking. I had to.'

'So, you punched her and stabbed her.'

'She *made* me. She wouldn't shut up.'

'So, you *had* to stab her.'

'Yes!'

Constance looked as if he'd been sick in his own mouth.

'I'd like the opportunity to speak to my client alone, please, Inspector.'

'I thought you might.'

The pair returned with Broome's composure seemingly recovered. His expression was tight, eyes harder, anger controlled.

It was surface deep though, Narey knew that, and was confident she could puncture it when needed.

'My client would like to make a statement,' Constance announced.

'Well, we'd be delighted to hear it.' She was aware she sounded like she was enjoying it too much but didn't give a damn. 'I remind you that you are under caution.'

Broome swallowed, fixed his eyes straight ahead. 'I struck my mother. An act which I regret very much. I did so under great stress and provocation. I lost control and accept that I stabbed her but have no recollection of doing so. I believe I was temporarily incapable of understanding or being aware of my actions.'

She resisted a sigh. 'Mr Broome, you are admitting to the attempted murder of your mother, is that correct?'

Constance jumped in. 'It was an act of assault to severe injury. With diminished responsibility.'

'It was attempted murder. And he was fully aware of what he was doing.'

'We'd challenge that.'

'You'll need to.'

She could see Constance was itching to come back but he had precious few cards to play. He was trying to carve out a deal with a plastic spoon. She had to make him dig into concrete with it.

'As you and your client are aware, this is not the only matter of interest to us.'

She saw their postures groan and loved it.

'Mr Broome, I want to talk to you about the collection of photographs found in your flat.'

'Those have been ruled inadmissible and have been returned to my client. You know that.'

Narey let that hang there for a bit. Let them think they had a little something.

'They've been ruled out in the case of Leah Watt, yes. I want to talk to you about Julie Petrie.'

Constance didn't know. *Fuck*. He didn't know that was coming. He sure as hell knew who Julie Petrie was but didn't know of the connection. She saw the look of surprise on his face. Surprise and shock and irritation.

He was certain to ask for another break to speak to his client again but she wasn't going to give him time to regroup. She was on the charge.

'Mr Broome, there were three photographs of Julie Petrie in your collection. Can you confirm that for me, please?'

'I did not kill that woman.'

'I'm asking you if she featured among your photographs. Did she?'

'I didn't kill her.'

'Was she among your photographs?'

Broome and Constance shouted over each other.

'Inspector, my client has never acknowledged that those photographs were—'

'She was among them but I did not fucking kill her. I did *not* fucking kill her.'

Narey heard it. The desperate ring of truth. Sure, it was muffled among the anger and rage and hate but she was sure she'd heard it. She'd pretend otherwise though.

'Bullshit.'

'I swear I didn't. I did not kill the Petrie woman. I did *not*.'

'You've lied every step of the way. You don't know any other way to be. You're a liar, Mr Broome.'

His hands were knotting. Frustration. Veins rising in his neck.

'You have to believe me.'

She laughed. 'Why the hell should I? You lied about attacking your mother. You lied about raping Leah Watt. Why should I believe you now?'

Constance saw the trap but saw it a beat too late. '*Inspector . . .*'

'Because I didn't *do* this!'

'You did the others but expect me to accept you didn't do this?'

'Yes! I didn't kill that woman. I swear it. I won't be fitted up for something I didn't do.'

She laughed in his face. 'Fitted up? You've been watching too much television. Your mother is going to court and she's going to testify that you beat her to within an inch of her life. You've just admitted raping Leah Watt. Do you really think a jury is going to take your word that you didn't murder Julie Petrie?'

'I didn't kill her. Her husband did! Iain Petrie. He murdered her and buried her in those woods.'

Narey felt a familiar tightening in her gut. She had to force herself to take her time, slow play it.

'Yes, of course he did. That's a bit convenient for you, isn't it?'

Broome's face flushed, blood rushing, boiling, to the surface.

'I can prove it.'

Here it is.

'How?'

'I photographed him doing it.'

CHAPTER 59

'I photographed Julie Petrie.'

'Why?'

'She had an interesting look. I was attracted to her. There's no law against that.'

'There's a law against stalking.'

'That law defines stalking as causing harassment to another person. Julie Petrie didn't know I photographed her, therefore she could not be harassed. She was not placed in a position of fear, upset or annoyance.'

Narey had long since cultivated a professional detachment. It was a way of protecting herself and the people she interviewed. It meant leaving her personal prejudices at the door along with anger and emotion. This man tested that detachment more than most.

'How often did you photograph Julie Petrie?'

Broome shrugged as if it wasn't important or that he couldn't care enough to remember.

'Four or five maybe.'

'How did you first see her? Was it just by chance?'

'It was a Saturday and I was walking down Buchanan Street and she was walking up. She caught my eye. The way attractive women do. I noticed her and liked what I saw.'

'So, you photographed her?'

'Not immediately, no. I turned and followed her into the Buchanan Galleries. Went up the escalator after her. It was like a game, to see where she went, who she was. A *legal* game.'

He waited for a response to that but didn't get one.

'I managed to walk ahead of her. She was browsing in windows so I could walk past but be sure of where she was going. I sat on a bench and had my phone out as she approached. It would have appeared as if I was checking email or whatever. But I photographed her. She had no idea I'd done it. No harassment. She was in a public place with no expectation of privacy. I was entitled to photograph her.'

'And how did you manage to find her to photograph her again?'

He preened, pleased with himself and how clever he was. She wanted to ram his teeth down his throat. Out of the corner of her eye, she saw Kerri Wells sit up and wondered if the DC might actually punch him. She also wondered if she'd try to stop her.

'It's quite easy. People are creatures of habit. Same places, same times. In her case, the same bus in from Cambuslang. She came into Glasgow every Saturday. I liked her. She was one of my favourite models.'

'*Model?* Models choose to be photographed. They

get paid for it. Julie Petrie was not a model. None of these women were.'

Broome smiled patronisingly. She clearly didn't get it.

'They're models to me. Living, breathing models. Women of the city. They *are* Glasgow. I'm an observer, a chronicler of the city. Like Oscar Marzaroli.'

'Bullshit! Marzaroli was an artist. You're a fucking rapist.' Wells had exploded.

'It's not so different. Marzaroli photographed the slums and the people that lived in them but he didn't ask them to pose. He just photographed them. Same as me.'

'Yeah, like Fred West is the same as Mary Poppins.'

Narey saw his reaction to Wells and knew it for what it was. Hate and anger and barely suppressed violence. She couldn't allow it to get in the way.

'It's completely different,' she told him. 'And you know it. Tell us what happened next with Julie Petrie.'

Broome switched back to her, tearing his glare from Wells. 'I got to know her.'

'You spoke to her?'

'No. I got to know where she went, what she did, where she lived.'

'Why?'

'Like I said, it was a game. It was what I did with my models. I needed to know more about them to get the full picture. To make my photographs complete.'

She had to bite hard to resist calling him on it until she got what she needed.

'And sometimes you followed them to find out where they lived?'

He shrugged again. 'Sometimes.'

'And did you do that with Julie Petrie?'

'Yes.'

The shameless, unapologetic gall of it was making her skin crawl. Wells was itching too.

'You went to her house in Cambuslang?'

'I just said so.'

Broome's resurgent confidence was bothering her now. She glanced at Constance and he wore a look that said, 'what kept you?'

'We want to deal, Inspector. You wouldn't expect us to give you something for nothing, now, would you?'

'He's not in a position to deal,' Wells butted in. 'He's admitted to attempted murder and to rape. He's only in a position to bend over and go to jail.'

'No.' Constance's tone was condescending. 'My client has admitted to assault to severe injury on Mrs Broome. He'd be prepared to admit the same with Leah Watt.'

'Why would we be interested in accepting that?' Wells persisted, her voice louder, her eyes straying to Narey.

'Because my client can close a murder case for you. Because he can help you bring closure to a horrendous crime and ensure justice prevails.'

'*Justice?*' Wells was apoplectic. 'You're a fucking parasite. What the hell do you care about justice?'

Constance stared at her coldly. 'Detective Inspector Narey may take a different view from you, DC Wells. A more pragmatic view.'

All eyes were on her now. Broome. Constance. Wells. All wanting something different from her. What did *she* want?

'If Mr Broome has proof of the murder of Julie Petrie then I'd want to see it. It would need to be conclusive. Nothing less would do. I'm not in a position to cut a deal, you know that's down to the PF, but I'd be sure to let him know Broome has been extremely helpful. As long as that's the case.'

'That's reasonable,' said Constance.

'I don't fucking believe this,' said Wells.

'Oh, it's conclusive,' said Broome.

CHAPTER 60

He took them back to Carlaverock Road.

Back to his childhood home, back to where he'd battered and stabbed his mother.

Narey and a far-from-happy Kerri Wells, Constance, two constables and a camera-wielding SOCO made the trip with him.

Curtains twitched at the sight of police cars returning to the street, a far from familiar sight in this leafy part of the south side. Narey, keen to avoid a circus, hustled everyone inside as quickly as possible.

They followed Broome upstairs, but instead of turning right into the bedroom where they'd been on their previous visit to the house, they went left. The instant impression was that the room felt like a shrine, like it had been maintained the way it was when the thirty-something teenager left it.

A life-size, fibreglass Star Wars stormtrooper stood guard in one corner, a large plasma TV screen in another and an Xbox in between. The bed was draped in black silk sheets and covers as if it had slid out of an eighties porn movie.

Broome opened a built-in wardrobe, talking on the record as he rummaged inside.

'I'd followed Julie Petrie to her home three times. Not that I knew her name until I saw her photograph in the papers. She was my favourite back then. She had a classic quality to her that I liked. But there was a sadness to her too. I knew she wasn't happy with her husband. You could just tell.'

Narey and Wells shared glances. The constables furrowed brows at the man's lack of awareness and at his strangeness. None of them said anything.

'Once you know where someone lives then it becomes easy to know everything about them. I followed her from there to the school she worked in. After that, I knew when she'd be finishing every day from Monday to Friday. One Tuesday in December 2009, I waited outside the school for her and followed her home. Because I could. Because she was mine.'

Broome stepped out of the closet with a box that had once contained a laptop, sitting on the bed and putting it at his side.

'She was taking her normal route when suddenly she signalled and pulled over. As I went past, I saw she was on the phone and knew she'd stopped because someone had called her. I drove on a bit then I pulled in too and waited. Two minutes later, she drove off again and I followed. She didn't go home.'

He opened the old laptop box, sliding a hand inside

to produce a black leather diary with a lock on it. Every pair of eyes in the room drifted to it.

'She drove onto a country road and pulled in to a layby. I was a fair way back but saw there was another car already there, a black Mondeo. I recognised it. She got out and got into the passenger seat of the Mondeo. I could maybe have given it up at that point and gone home but I was curious. It felt weird.'

Broome got up and went to the rear of the bed, crouching to reach behind one of its wooden legs. They heard the quiet rasp of tape being peeled and when he stood, he had a small silver key in his hand.

'They drove south on quiet roads. It was easy to stay well back and follow because there was nowhere else for them to go and no one to get in between us. A bit after Strathaven, near a wee place called Caldermill, they turned right. I saw them make the turn and had to stop or else I'd have been too close. There was a big wood and the single-track road was skirting it.'

He slid the silver key into the lock and sprung it. The diary opened and his fingers stole between its leaves.

'I let them go well ahead. By the time I got round to the far side of the wood, the Mondeo was parked up near a wind farm. I passed the car and kept driving for a few hundred yards then found somewhere to stop. I cut back across the fields as quickly but as quietly as I could. At first, I thought I'd lost them but I followed a trail and then heard a noise, something metallic. Then it happened again and then again. They were in the woods and getting deeper.'

He held four photo prints in his hands, their backs to an expectant crowd.

'I sneaked up on them. Except it was only him that was there. He'd no idea I was there. No idea I was watching and photographing him.'

He turned the prints like a magician doing a card trick.

Iain Petrie, spade in hand, standing over a hole in the ground. Petrie bundling a body into it. Petrie shovelling dirt into the hole. Petrie staring down at the grave that held his wife.

'The hole had already been dug. There was no way he'd had time to do it from parking the car until I got there. All he'd had time to do was bash her brains in with the spade. He'd had it all planned.'

'You could have called the police, even anonymously.'

'I thought about it. I was mad at him. Really, really angry. I'd liked her. She'd been my favourite and he'd taken her away. But I wasn't going to take the risk of phoning the police. I had too much to lose. I thought about sending the photographs to the police or a newspaper but I didn't. I didn't really care what he'd done, only that she'd been mine and he'd stopped that.'

'So, you took one of your prints of her and cut the face from it?'

He seemed surprised, but nodded. 'She wasn't mine any more.'

'She was never *yours*,' Wells had had enough. 'You don't *own* people. Especially not people you don't know. Is that why you thought you could rape them? Because you thought they were yours?'

He just looked at her, uncaring and unapologetic.

His lawyer stepped in to prevent any more admissions on Broome's part.

'Inspector, you can have the photographs and my client's sworn testimony along with our goodwill and civic duty.'

She knew the last remark was intended to wind Wells up even further.

'You have your deal, Mr Constance. Don't push your luck.'

Wells burst into a fit of barely disguised expletives, forcing Narey to take her by the elbow and guide her into a corner of the room.

'Kerri, I'm doing this. It's a murder case and this puts the guilty party away. It has to be done.'

'So, murder trumps rape?'

'You know that's not what I'm saying. He'll get done for the attempted murder of his mother and he'll do more on top for assaulting Leah.'

'But not for *raping* her.'

'I'm doing what I have to do, Kerri. Trust me, if I could put him away for raping Leah then I would.'

'He'll get eighteen months maximum and will serve less than half of that. And you know it. I can't be a part of this.'

Wells all but spat at her feet. She turned and slammed the door closed behind her as she stormed out.

CHAPTER 61

Broome put his signature to his statement, somehow managing to be both resentful yet smug.

His lawyer oversaw his admission to the charges, taking a final look over the papers, mentally dotting i's and crossing t's. He placed his pen on the last page and glanced up, expressionless.

'I believe that concludes our business for today, Inspector Narey.'

She waited until both men had half-risen from their chairs.

'Not quite, Mr Constance.'

They caught her tone and she enjoyed seeing their expressions change. As they settled reluctantly back into their seats, she made a point of shuffling the papers in front of her. Sure that she had their attention, she began to speak.

'I have here a statement from Tony Winter, a journalist with the *Scottish Standard* newspaper.' She left just enough of a pause for them to swim in, maybe to drown.

'In the interests of transparency, I should also state

that Mr Winter is my husband. However, his statement is made in a purely professional capacity.'

'What is this, Inspector?' Constance was shaken. 'Bring Your Husband to Work Day?'

She ignored him.

'My name is Tony Winter and I've been undertaking investigative work on behalf of my newspaper, tracing women in a collection of photographs that came into my possession. Photographs that were owned by, and taken by, William Broome.'

'This is outrageous,' Constance blustered. 'Those photographs . . .'

She pressed on regardless, holding up sheets of paper inside a clear plastic bag. 'I have statements from four women whose images featured amongst that collection. These women are Anna Collins, Khalida Dhariwal, Suzie O'Brien and Helen Scanlon. Each testify that they were raped by William Broome.'

Narey let that hang there, holding the papers high, making Broome and Constance stare at them, making them ask to see them.

'If I may, Inspector.'

Broome's eyes were crazed, forehead veins popping. 'Those slags. Those fucking *slags*.'

Constance warned him off. 'Not a word, please, Mr Broome. Not a word.'

With blackened brows, he studied the four statements, mouth pursed tight. He didn't lift his head until he'd read all four. He exhaled hard as if he'd been holding his breath the whole time.

416

'None of these women have made an identification of my client. None of them say they have seen the face of their attacker.'

Narey shut him down. 'That's because their *attacker* wore a balaclava. The *rapist* who attacked all four of them, and others, was a coward and covered his face during these atrocities. There was a pattern to his attacks, consistent in these cases and in the attack on Leah Watt which your client has already confessed to. These women will attest to that and to the height and build of the rapist, and to the words he used and how and when he used them. You will be aware of the Moorov Doctrine, Mr Constance. Evidence of cases so similar in nature that they can be used as actual corroboration and often used in rapes and sexual assaults where there is only the victim's word, but many victims. Where the MO is so similar and unique that they corroborate the fact that the same person may have carried them out. That's what these women will do. They will also testify that their photographs are among Mr Broome's conceited and odious collection.'

Constance reddened. Maybe embarrassment, maybe anger.

'Those photographs were ruled inadmissible and you were ordered to return them to my client. If these women were traced using the—'

'The victims were not traced by the police. We did not use those photographs in any way nor were we complicit in them being in the possession of Mr Winter or the *Standard*. However, you can rest assured we will be petitioning the court to have them returned back into evidence and I have no doubt that will happen.

'No, Mr Constance, the victims made their statements after the result of a journalistic investigation which was aided by information contained in a file compiled about a serial rapist. You are that serial rapist, Mr Broome.'

Constance cut off any response from his client. 'Don't say anything. Let me handle this. Inspector, the provenance of these statements will come under the strongest scrutiny, believe me. But regardless of how they were obtained, they still amount to circumstantial evidence with *no* identification of my client.'

Narey smiled at him, a simple act that caused Constance's heart to tighten.

'Helen Scanlon fought back against her attacker. She scratched at him. When she was examined by the police, there was skin under her fingernails.'

The colour drained from the lawyer's face. Broome looked ready to explode.

'The police found no DNA match to those skin cells at the time because you had never been arrested. But that has now changed. The chance of the DNA being a match to anyone other than Helen's rapist is sky-high. A billion to one maybe. It will match your DNA, Mr Broome. We all know that.'

Broome tore at his hair, fingers digging at his scalp as the heel of his hands rubbed against his face.

'It's up to you,' she told him. 'Confess, don't confess, I'm not sure I mind much either way. You will be

THE PHOTOGRAPHER

convicted whatever you do. Your lawyer knows that, even if you don't. Personally, I'd enjoy seeing this played out in court, the world seeing you for what you are, seeing what a despicable, cowardly excuse for a human being you are. The downside to that would be these women would have to testify and, although every one of them is prepared to do so, I'd rather spare them that. You pleading guilty would achieve that and would be reflected in your sentence.'

Constance confirmed what she'd said with a curt nod to his client.

Broome screwed his eyes shut tight and stretched his mouth wide into a silent scream. It went on for an age before his body slumped.

'You fucking slag. Happy now, are you? Real pleased with yourself, I bet. Fine, okay, have it your way. I'll tell you everything. *You fucking slag.*'

And he did.

CHAPTER 62

He started with the how rather than the why.

He followed *his* women, got to know their routines, what they did, where they lived. If it turned out that they were married or had boyfriends then he'd usually back off. Partly because they'd disappointed him by taking partners but more because of the risk. Those separated from the herd were the most pleasing to him and the most vulnerable prey.

Anna Collins, Khalida Dhariwal, Suzie O'Brien and Helen Scanlon all lived in ground floor properties. So too had Leah Watt, Lainey Henderson and Vonnie Murdoch. Broome conceded that was his method and often the deciding factor as to whether he took his obsessions further.

'They didn't care enough about their security. They should have. But because they didn't, I knew I could go in and see them when I wanted.

'Getting in was usually pretty straightforward. Windows left unlocked, doors that could be forced or Yale locks that were easy to slip open with pieces of plastic you can buy online. If I had to, I could break a window and be in in seconds. Bungalows, ground-floor flats, they were easy. They'd have been as well leaving the front door open.'

He was both boasting and being cold-bloodedly practical. Narey had to push on past it.

'Why did you start talking photographs?'

She had to ask it four times before he began to answer her. He deflected and diverted, he roared and declared it none of her business, that she wouldn't, couldn't, understand. She played dumb, asking him to explain in a way she might get. He finally relented and summed it up in three words.

'To keep them.'

He wasn't trying to shock her, not attempting to dramatise it. It was a simple statement of fact. And that was the most shocking thing about it.

'You need to tell me more than that.'

He smirked and groaned, making it obvious he'd been right about her not understanding.

'I'd see women that I liked. It could have been their face or the way they walked, it might have been their hair or their figure or the way they looked at me. If they had something about them that grabbed my attention then I'd want them. I'd want to keep them. If I photographed them, I'd be able to take them home with me, look at them when I wanted. They'd be mine.'

'They are people. Not objects. They're not *things* to be owned or kept.'

Broome *knew* she wouldn't understand. His face said so.

'Everything is a thing. Everyone is a thing. You, me, her, him. All things. This idea that people are different from dogs or cars or clothes is ridiculous. They can all be owned, all collected or thrown away. In this world, you're either an owner or you're owned. I prefer to be an owner. They were owned because that's the way they were. Public property. I photographed them and claimed them, I took them home with me and made them mine.'

'And you hunted them down and raped them.'

He shrugged. 'Some of them. The ones that wanted it. Asked for it.'

'*None* of them asked for it. That's why you had to force yourself on them, beat them. Did you really believe they wanted you?'

He didn't look at her, seemingly couldn't. 'They would have done if they'd got to know me. But they were too good for that. Just slags. The world is full of them. Strutting around, showing what they've got, hanging it out there to tease you but then not giving you the time of day. They asked for everything they got.'

'So, you couldn't handle the rejection? Your fragile little-boy ego just couldn't take it?'

'No!' The shout didn't make it sound any more convincing. 'I did it because I wanted to. I was in control, not them. The decisions were mine.'

She settled for just looking at him for a while. His words not worth her wasting any in return.

'Are there others?'

'What?'

'Have you raped and beaten women other than Anna Collins, Khalida Dhariwal, Susie O'Brien, Helen Scanlon, Leah Watt and Vonnie Murdoch? It's a very simple question.'

She saw all sorts on his face. Defiance. Fear. Pleading. 'No.'

'No other women?'

'No!'

'You're a liar. I *know* of other women. And I have no doubt there's others that I don't know of. Yet.'

'Well, you'll have to find them then.'

'Oh, I will. I'll get your photographs back, every single one of them. And I'll have all the time and resources I need to track down every woman that is in them. If you've hurt any of them, I'll find out. Believe that. Do everyone a favour and tell me now.'

Broome looked from Constance to her and back again. The lawyer gave him nothing, this was his choice to make. She felt him swing towards her then away, any conscience that he had battling with ego and cowardice and practicalities.

'Like I said, you'll have to find them. Is that it?'

No. No it fucking isn't.

'No, there's something else I want you to know. The file that was used to trace your victims, the file that will put you in prison for many, many years, was compiled by a lady named Lainey Henderson. Is that name familiar to you?'

Broome shook his head sullenly.

'I thought not. In 2004, Ms Henderson lived in a ground-floor flat in Craigpark Drive in Dennistoun. Does that address sound familiar?'

Broome said nothing.

'Someone broke into Ms Henderson's flat, beat her up and raped her. Do you remember *that*?'

'Fuck you.'

'Lainey Henderson remembers it. She's remembered it every day since. She was not going to let it go and she was going to stop it happening to anyone else. She didn't quite manage that, but she's stopped it now.'

CHAPTER 63

Narey left the interview room, a sigh escaping through parted lips and a wave of exhaustion beginning to wash over her. It was only tickling at her toes but she knew it would drown her before the day was out.

Sitting opposite and looking up expectantly were Winter and Wells. She eased their anxieties with a single nod. It was over.

Winter stood and slipped an arm around her waist, hugging her to him for as long as their surroundings allowed.

'I'll see you at home,' he told her as he let her go. 'I'm off to see our daughter. Danny's got her at the park.'

She squeezed his hand. 'Kiss her for me. I'll do it myself soon.'

As he left, Kerri Wells got to her feet, awkward and nervous in a way Narey had never seen before, gnawing at her own lip.

'He's confessed?'

'Yes. To four rapes. Are you planning to shout at me again, Kerri? I'm hoping not.'

'Boss, I need to ... I didn't know what you were doing. I'm sorry. Really sorry. I just lost it. I couldn't believe you'd let him off with pleading on the attack on his mother and Leah Watt's rape. I should have known better.'

Narey led her further down the corridor by the shoulder, finding the first empty room and guiding her inside, closing the door behind them.

'Yes, Kerri. You should have known better. I understand why you lost your temper in there but that doesn't excuse it. You need to get a better handle on it. Don't lose the passion, that's part of what makes you the cop you are, but control it better. Okay?'

'Yes, ma'am.'

'Listen, the attack on his mother might have got knocked down to assault anyway. And as for Leah, I was happy not having to put her through the trauma of going to court to testify again. She'd also done something that wouldn't exactly have made her the perfect witness. They were easy trades when I knew what cards I still had to play.'

'Why didn't you tell me?'

'How would you have reacted when I did the deal with Broome and his lawyer if you'd known?'

Wells grimaced. 'Not the way that I did. Not the way you wanted me to. Okay, I get that. But it left me angry enough that I was insubordinate. A borderline disciplinary matter.'

'I moved the border, so don't worry about that. Maybe I should have told you and saved your blood pressure from taking the hit. But, as you said, I got the reaction I expected and Broome and Constance saw it.'

'It was worth it. You were right.'

'I'm glad you agree.'

'Sorry. Again. Can I go now?'

'No, hang on. You know, the victims in Lainey Henderson's file probably wouldn't have been traced without the help she got over the years from a female PC. She took some risks, whoever she was, but it paid off. I wish I had the chance to thank her.'

'Right. Well, sorry, but I don't know what you're talking about, boss.'

'Yeah, that's what I thought. Same thing goes for whoever sent Broome's photographs to Tony. Very risky, but Broome would probably have walked without it.'

'Yes, I'm glad someone did that. Anyway, I better get on.'

'Of course. But Kerri, if you ever want to talk about anything, anything at all, then I'm here.'

Wells hesitated, questions and answers dying on her lips.

'I won't, but thanks anyway.'

CHAPTER 64

The pale granite slab in front of them was topped with snow turned to frost, looking like a heavy grey coat with a dusting of winter on its shoulders. It stood not far from the trees, giving them some respite from the northerly wind that scudded across the cemetery lawn at Cardonald and reddened their cheeks.

Only one of the three women had ever met Vonnie Murdoch but they all felt like they had.

It was why they were there. A brief and silent vigil, a hello and a goodbye, an apology of sorts and a hope they'd made some of it right.

Narey, Lainey and Leah were uneasy sharing their space with each other, swamped with enough mixed emotions not to have room for anyone else's. They were dressed up in barbed positives – redemption, revenge and relief – but regret was still under their feet.

They shuffled from foot to foot, sidestepping the frost and their own shame at being happy it had ended as it did. It was called survivor guilt but knowing that didn't make it magically disappear.

As the aftermath of Broome's admissions played out, all the pieces fell as they should. That didn't bring anyone back, didn't turn back time or heal any wounds, but it made the unbearable somehow less so.

Iain Petrie had confessed to murdering his wife and burying her in the woods. His self-righteous anger and denial had lasted only as long as it took him to be shown Broome's photographs.

Addison and Narey had watched the lie crumble on his face, seeing him go from indignant to broken in an instant. A man who'd told his story so often and for so long that he almost believed it himself, until confronted with the brutal truth of hard evidence.

For eight years, he'd resented others who'd suspected that same truth. He'd squirmed on the gossiping tongues of neighbours and relatives, of strangers who'd known him only as the man who'd probably killed his wife. When the chance came to get out from under the pitchforks of suspicion, he'd grabbed at it.

He thought fate had delivered him a way out, the perfect fall guy in the shape of Broome. Petrie sent the coordinates of the woods near Caldermill to Winter and let him do the work from there. He believed it was time for Julie to rise from her shallow grave and for the man who'd photographed her to take the blame for her murder. It wasn't just convenient in Petrie's mind, it was right. Broome had violated her rights, violated his too, stalked his wife like a rapist and deserved everything he had coming to him.

CRAIG ROBERTSON

The only problem for Petrie was that none of it worked out the way he'd planned.

Tony had got his front page. Three of them in fact. Big, ripe, juicy exclusives that were picked up by television and the nationals. First Petrie's arrest, then Broome's, followed finally by a follow-up when other women came forward to name Broome as their attacker.

Archie Cameron was so pleased with Winter's work that he nearly told him. Together, they wrung as much ink from each story as the contempt of court laws would allow. Broome's army of internet trolls slowly deserted him as the sheer scale and savagery of his assaults were laid bare.

Danny's troll hunting paid off. Davie Meiklejohn, Ryan Cochrane and Jason Burns all got jail sentences. There were hundreds, probably thousands more who deserved the same fate but three of them were a start. The damage couldn't be undone, either to Rachel or to Leah, but a message was sent to those who cowered and crowed behind their laptops that they could be found and dragged out into the light.

'Do you believe in evil?'

It was Lainey who broke the silence that held court above Vonnie Murdoch's grave. Her question caught Leah by surprise, her eyes widening that Lainey could even ask.

'Yes! Don't you? If Broome isn't evil then I don't know what it means. Don't you think we were both victims of evil?'

430

Lainey drew a cigarette from the packet that she slipped from somewhere inside her coat. She cupped her hands around her mouth, protecting the flame of her lighter from the wind, then drawing deep on it before answering.

'What he did was wicked, no doubt about that. What he did to me, you, Vonnie and all the others. Is he evil though? I'm not sure I'd let him off that easily. The idea that he was born bad gives him an out, like he couldn't help his nature. Born that way? I don't think so.'

She knelt by the headstone, cigarette in her mouth, and traced a finger around the shape of Vonnie's name.

'William Broome chose to be a rapist. He chose to photograph women he was attracted to, then attack and rape them. If there really is a hell then I want him to rot in it for eternity but I'm not letting him off with an excuse. He is what he is because he wanted to be.'

Leah looked wary, almost frightened by the ferocity in Lainey's voice. 'What do you think, Rachel?'

Narey was reading the lines on Vonnie's headstone and didn't shift her gaze from them.

'I don't think it matters,' she answered at last. 'Evil, not evil, it's all a bit biblical and I'm not in the philosophy business. All that matters is what they do, not why. I'll let someone else worry about whether it makes them evil or whether evil exists. If they break the law, it's my job to catch them, not analyse them.'

Both women looked at her, not entirely convinced she meant it and both thinking she agreed with them.

Lainey and Leah went right as they came out of the cemetery gates, Narey turned left. They'd shared hugs and promises to keep in touch, then went their separate ways.

Narey slid into the passenger seat of the slush-streaked silver Volvo and fell back against the warm leather seat, some of the tension melting at the touch.

'Was that tough?'

She nodded, eyes closed, initially content to let the sigh speak for her.

'Yeah. You could say that. I'd never met Vonnie, never worked her case. But it felt like I did.'

Winter nodded, understanding but not quite agreeing. 'You say you didn't work her case but you cracked it. You put the guy away.'

'Years too late for Vonnie, though.'

He wasn't letting her away with that. 'Too late for her to know but not too late.' He turned to cast a glance at the seat behind them. 'You made sure no one else had to go through what they did.'

'Not just me. Lainey and Leah too. And you.'

She shifted round to see the blonde bundle asleep in the car seat behind. As Narey looked, Alanna stirred, eyes fluttering and focusing until she saw her mother in front of her.

The look on her face adjusted itself from confused to delighted. She began smiling and squealing, her hands clapping together in excitement.

'I think she might be pleased to see you,' Winter smiled.

'Well, the feeling's mutual. It was all for her. Every moment of it. Let's go home.'

ACKNOWLEDGEMENTS

The nature of the crimes in this book meant I had to rely even more heavily than usual on the knowledge, advice and support of others. Some are named here, others are not.

I owe thanks to rape crisis worker Helen Lambertin, whose insight and expertise helped convince me I could tackle such a sensitive subject. As a male author, I am grateful for the safety net of feedback from two brilliant female crime writers, Eva Dolan and my wife, Alexandra Sokoloff.

As ever, I am indebted to the fantastic team at Simon & Schuster, particularly my wonderful editor Jo Dickinson, and to Mark Stanton, the best agent a man could share a Guinness with.

Craig Robertson

Murderabilia

The first commuter train of the morning slowly rumbles away from platform seven of Queen St station. And then, as the train emerges from a tunnel, the screaming starts. Hanging from the bridge ahead of them is a body. Placed neatly on the ground below him are the victim's clothes.

Why?

Detective Inspector Rachel Narey is assigned the case and then just as quickly taken off it again. **Tony Winter**, now a journalist, must pursue the case for her. The line of questioning centres around the victim's clothes – why leave them in full view? And what did the killer not leave, and where might it appear again?

Everyone has a hobby. Some people collect death. To find this evil, **Narey** must go on to the dark web, and into immense danger ...

Available in print and eBook

Craig Robertson

In Place of Death

**A tense and gripping crime novel set in
the dark underbelly of Glasgow ...**

A young man enters the culverted remains of an
ancient Glasgow stream, looking for thrills. Deep
below the city, it is decaying and claustrophobic
and gets more so with every step. As the ceiling
lowers to no more than a couple of feet above
the ground, the man finds his path blocked by
another person. Someone with his throat cut.

As **DS Rachel Narey** leads the official
investigation, photographer **Tony Winter**
follows a lead of his own, through the shadowy
world of urbexers, people who pursue a
dangerous and illegal hobby, a world that
Winter knows more about than he lets on.

And it soon becomes clear that the
murderer has killed before, and has no
qualms about doing so again.

Available in print and eBook

Craig Robertson
The Last Refuge

John Callum is fleeing his past, but
has run straight into danger.

When **John Callum** arrives on the wild and desolate
Faroe Islands, he vows to sever all ties with his
previous life. He desperately wants to make a
new start, and is surprised by how quickly he is
welcomed into the close-knit community. But still,
the terrifying, debilitating nightmares just won't stop.

Then the solitude is shattered by an almost
unheard of crime on the islands: murder. A
specialist team of detectives arrives from Denmark
to help the local police, who seem completely
ill-equipped for an investigation of this scale. But
as tensions rise, and the community closes rank
to protect its own, John has to watch his back.

But far more disquieting than that, John's nightmares
have taken an even more disturbing turn, and he
can't be certain about the one thing he needs to
know above all else. Whether he is the killer ...

Available in print and eBook

Craig Robertson

Witness the Dead

Red Silk is back ...

Scotland 1972. Glasgow is haunted by a murderer
nicknamed Red Silk – a feared serial killer who
selects his victims in the city's nightclubs. The case
remains unsolved but Archibald Atto, later imprisoned
for other murders, is thought to be Red Silk.

In modern-day Glasgow, **DS Rachel Narey** is called to
a gruesome crime scene at the city's Necropolis. The
body of a young woman lies stretched out over a tomb.
Her body bears a three-letter message from her killer.

Now retired, former detective Danny Neilson spots a
link between the new murder and those he investigated
in 1972 – details that no copycat killer could have
known about. But Atto is still behind bars. Must Danny
face up to his fears that they never caught their man?
Determined finally to crack the case, Danny, along
with his nephew, police photographer **Tony Winter**,
pays Atto a visit. But they soon discover that they are
going to need the combined efforts of police forces
past and present to bring a twisted killer to justice.

Available in print and eBook

Craig Robertson
Cold Grave

A murder investigation frozen in time is beginning to melt.

November 1993. Scotland is in the grip of an ice-cold winter and the Lake of Menteith is frozen over. A young man and woman walk across the ice to the historic island of Inchmahome which lies in the middle of the lake. Only the man returns.

In the spring, as staff prepare the abbey ruins for summer visitors, they discover the body of a girl, her skull violently crushed.

Present day. Retired detective Alan Narey is still haunted by the unsolved crime. Desperate to relieve her ailing father's conscience, **DS Rachel Narey** risks her job and reputation by returning to the Lake of Menteith and unofficially reopening the cold case.

With the help of police photographer **Tony Winter**, Rachel prepares a dangerous gambit to uncover the killer's identity – little knowing who that truly is. Despite the freezing temperatures the ice cold case begins to thaw, and with it a tide of secrets long frozen in time are suddenly and shockingly unleashed.

Available in print and eBook

Craig Robertson
Snapshot

A series of high-profile shootings by a
lone sniper leaves Glasgow terrorised and
police photographer **Tony Winter** – a man
with a tragic hidden past – mystified.

Who is behind the executions of some of
the most notorious drug lords in the city?
As more shootings occur – including those
of police officers – the authorities realise
they have a vigilante on their hands.

Meanwhile, Tony investigates a link between
the victims and a schoolboy who has been
badly beaten. Seemingly unconnected, they
share a strange link. As Tony delves deeper, his
quest for the truth and his search for the killer
lead him down dark and dangerous paths.

Available in print and eBook

Craig Robertson

Random

Glasgow is being terrorised by a serial killer
the media have nicknamed The Cutter. The
murders have left the police baffled.

There seems to be neither rhyme nor reason
behind the killings; no kind of pattern or
motive; an entirely different method of murder
each time, and nothing that connects the
victims except for the fact that the little fingers
of their right hands have been severed.

If **DS Rachel Narey** could only work out the
key to the seemingly random murders, how and
why the killer selects his victims, she would
be well on her way to catching him. But as the
police, the press and a threatening figure from
Glasgow's underworld begin to close in on
The Cutter, his carefully-laid plans threaten
to unravel – with horrifying consequences.

Available in print and eBook